December 2011

Dear Friends,

I had to drive my husband Wayne's car recently, and after adjusting the mirrors, seat and steering wheel, I turned on the radio. It was set to an "oldies" station playing songs from the 1960s and '70s. I remembered those songs and soon found myself singing at the top of my lungs to a Beatles hit that came out while I was in high school. It was a nostalgic moment. I remembered that I'd just broken up with my boyfriend at the time and cried as though it was the end of the world. Ah, those were the days (and I'm saying that with irony as well as affection!).

Learning to Love, the volume you're holding, consists of two books, *Sugar and Spice* and *Love by Degree,* written early in my career when I was still—yes—learning to write. So you could consider them my "oldies but goodies" as the DJs on those popular stations like to say. Both are romances that I (and my Harlequin and MIRA editor) have reread and refreshed. We've done our best to unobtrusively update them so that you won't be pulled out of the story by some long-dated reference or some allusion that's no longer relevant.

I found I enjoyed reading them and hope you do, too.

Hearing from my readers is always a pleasure. You can reach me via regular mail at P.O. Box 1458, Port Orchard, WA 98366 or by logging on to my website, DebbieMacomber.com, and leaving a message on my guest page.

Thank you for your ongoing support of my books— and all the best wishes for 2012!

Debbie Macomber

DEBBIE MACOMBER

Learning to LOVE

MIRA®

ISBN-13: 978-0-7783-1298-7

Recycling programs for this product may not exist in your area.

LEARNING TO LOVE

Copyright © 2011 by MIRA Books

The publisher acknowledges the copyright holder of the individual works as follows:

SUGAR AND SPICE
Copyright © 1987 by Debbie Macomber

LOVE BY DEGREE
Copyright © 1987 by Debbie Macomber

For questions and comments about the quality of this book please contact us at Customer_eCare@Harlequin.ca.

www.Harlequin.com

Printed in U.S.A.

Also by Debbie Macomber

Blossom Street Books
The Shop on Blossom Street
A Good Yarn
Susannah's Garden
Back on Blossom Street
Twenty Wishes
Summer on Blossom Street
Hannah's List
The Knitting Diaries
 "The Twenty-First Wish"
A Turn in the Road

Cedar Cove Books
16 Lighthouse Road
204 Rosewood Lane
311 Pelican Court
44 Cranberry Point
50 Harbor Street
6 Rainier Drive
74 Seaside Avenue
8 Sandpiper Way
92 Pacific Boulevard
1022 Evergreen Place
A Cedar Cove Christmas
 (*5-B Poppy Lane* and
 Christmas in Cedar Cove)
1105 Yakima Street
1225 Christmas Tree Lane

The Manning Family
The Manning Sisters
The Manning Brides
The Manning Grooms

Christmas Books
A Gift to Last
On a Snowy Night
Home for the Holidays
Glad Tidings
Christmas Wishes
Small Town Christmas
Trading Christmas
*There's Something About
 Christmas*
Christmas Letters
Where Angels Go
The Perfect Christmas
Angels at Christmas
 (*Those Christmas Angels*
 and *Where Angels Go*)
Call Me Mrs. Miracle

Dakota Series
Dakota Born
Dakota Home
Always Dakota

Heart of Texas Series

VOLUME 1
(*Lonesome Cowboy* and *Texas Two-Step*)
VOLUME 2
(*Caroline's Child* and *Dr. Texas*)
VOLUME 3
(*Nell's Cowboy* and *Lone Star Baby*)
Promise, Texas
Return to Promise

Midnight Sons
VOLUME 1
(*Brides for Brothers* and *The Marriage Risk*)
VOLUME 2
(*Daddy's Little Helper* and *Because of the Baby*)
VOLUME 3
(*Falling for Him, Ending in Marriage* and
Midnight Sons and Daughters)

This Matter of Marriage
Montana
Thursdays at Eight
Between Friends
Changing Habits
Married in Seattle
 (*First Comes Marriage* and
 Wanted: Perfect Partner)
Right Next Door
 (*Father's Day* and *The Courtship of
 Carol Sommars*)
Wyoming Brides
 (*Denim and Diamonds* and
 The Wyoming Kid)
Fairy Tale Weddings
 (*Cindy and the Prince* and
 Some Kind of Wonderful)
The Man You'll Marry
 (*The First Man You Meet* and
 The Man You'll Marry)
Orchard Valley Grooms
 (*Valerie* and *Stephanie*)
Orchard Valley Brides
 (*Norah* and *Lone Star Lovin'*)
The Sooner the Better
An Engagement in Seattle
 (*Groom Wanted* and *Bride Wanted*)
Out of the Rain
 (*Marriage Wanted* and *Laughter in the Rain*)

Debbie Macomber's Cedar Cove Cookbook
Debbie Macomber's Christmas Cookbook

CONTENTS

SUGAR AND SPICE   9

LOVE BY DEGREE   185

SUGAR AND SPICE

To the girls of Saint Joseph Academy—Class of 1966

One

"You're going, aren't you?" Gloria Bailey asked for the third time.

And for the third time Jayne Gilbert stalled, taking a small bite of her egg-salad sandwich. She always ate egg salad on Tuesdays. "I don't know."

The invitation to her class reunion lay in the bottom of Jayne's purse, taunting her with memories she'd just as soon forget. The day was much too glorious to think about anything unpleasant. It was now mid-May, and the weather was finally warm enough to sit outside as they had lunch at a small café near the downtown Portland library.

"You'll regret it if you don't go," Gloria continued with a knowing look.

"You don't understand," Jayne said, pushing her glasses onto the bridge of her nose. She set aside the whole-wheat sandwich. "I was probably the only girl to graduate from St. Mary's in a state of grace."

Gloria tried unsuccessfully to swallow a chuckle.

"My whole senior year I had to listen while my class-mates told marvelous stories about their backseat adventures," she said wryly. "I never had any adventures like that."

"And ten years later you still have no tales to tell?"

She nodded. "What's worse, all those years have slipped by, and I've turned out exactly as my classmates predicted. I'm a librarian and living alone—*alone* being the operative word."

Jayne even looked the same. The frames of her glasses were more fashionable now, but her hair was the same shade of brown—the color of cedar chips, just a tad too dark to be termed mousy. She'd kept it the same length, too, although she preferred it clasped at the base of her neck these days. She no longer wore the school's uniform of red blazer jacket and navy pleated skirt, but she wore another one, of sorts. The straight black skirt or tailored pants, white silk blouse and business jacket were her daily attire.

Her romantic dreams had remained dreams, and the love in her heart was showered generously upon the children who visited her regularly in the library. Jayne was the head of the children's department, while Gloria was a reference librarian. Both of them enjoyed their jobs.

"That's easy to fix," Gloria returned with a confidence Jayne lacked. "Go to the reunion looking different. Go dressed to the teeth, and bring along a gorgeous male who'll make you the envy of every girl in your class."

"I can't be something I'm not." Jayne didn't bother to mention the man. If she hadn't found a suitable male in ten years, what made Gloria think she could come up with one in two months?

"For one night you can be anything you want."

"It's *not* that easy," Jayne felt obliged to argue.

Until yesterday, before she'd sorted through her mail, she'd been content with her matter-of-fact existence. She liked her apartment and was proud of her accomplishments, however minor. Her life was uncomplicated, and frankly, she liked it that way.

But the last thing Jayne wanted was to go back and prove to her classmates that they'd been right. The thought was too humiliating. When she was a teenager, they'd taunted her as the girl most likely to succeed—behind the pages of a book. All her life, Jayne had been teased about her love for reading. Books were everything to her. She was the only child of doting parents who'd given up the hope of ever having children. Although her parents had been thrilled at her late arrival, Jayne often wondered if they'd actually known what to do with her. Both were English professors at a Seattle college and it seemed natural to introduce her to their beloved world of literature at an early age. So Jayne had spent her childhood reading the classics when other girls were watching TV, playing outside and going to birthday parties. It wasn't until she reached her teens that she realized how much of a misfit she'd become. Oh, she had friends, lots of friends… Unfortunately the majority of them lived between the covers of well-loved books.

"You need a man like the one across the street," Gloria said.

"What man?" Jayne squinted.

"The one in the raincoat."

"Him?" The tall man resembled the mystery guy who lived in her apartment building. Jayne thought of him that way because he seemed to work the oddest hours. Twice she'd seen him in the apartment parking lot making some kind of transaction with another man. At the time she'd wondered if he was a drug dealer. She'd immediately discounted the idea as the result of an overactive imagination.

"*Look* at him, Jayne. He's a perfect male specimen. He's got that lean hardness women adore, and he walks as if he owns the street. A lot of women would go for him."

Watching the man her friend had pointed out, Jayne was even more convinced he was her neighbor. They'd met a few times in the elevator, but they'd just exchanged nods; they'd never spoken. He lived on the same floor, three apartments down from hers. Jayne had been living near him for months and never really noticed the blatantly masculine features Gloria was describing.

"His jaw has that chiseled quality that drives women wild," Gloria was saying.

"I suppose," Jayne concluded, losing interest. She forced her attention back to her lunch. There was something about that man she didn't trust.

"Well, you aren't going to find someone to take to your class reunion by sitting around your apartment," Gloria muttered.

"I haven't decided if I'm going yet." But deep down,

Jayne wanted to attend. No doubt it was some deep-seated masochistic tendency she had yet to analyze.

"You should go. I think you'd be surprised to see how everyone's changed."

That was the problem; Jayne *hadn't* changed. She still loved her books, and her life was even more organized now than it had been when she was in high school. Ten years after her graduation, she'd still be the object of their ridicule. "I don't know what I'm going to do," she announced, hoping to put an end to the discussion.

Hours later, at her apartment, Jayne sat holding a cup of green tea while she fantasized walking into the class reunion with a tall, strikingly handsome man. He would gaze into her eyes and bathe her in the warm glow of his love. And the girls of St. Mary's would sigh with envy.

The problem was where to find such a man. Not any man, but that special one who'd turn women's heads and make their hearts pound wildly.

Stretching out her legs and crossing her bare feet at the ankle, Jayne released a steady breath and conjured up her image of the perfect male. She'd read so many romances in her life, from the great classics to contemporary titles, that the vision of the ideal man—nothing like the one Gloria found so fascinating—appeared instantly in her mind. He would be tall, with thick, curly black hair and eyes of piercing blue. A man with sensitivity, desires and goals. Someone who'd accept her as she was…who'd think she was a special person. She wanted a man who could look past her imperfections and discover the woman inside.

A troubled frown creased her brow. She knew that for too many years, she'd buried herself in books, living her life vicariously through the escapades of others. The time had come to abandon her sedentary life and form a plan of action. Gloria was right—she wasn't going to find a man like that while sitting in her apartment. Drastic needs demanded drastic measures.

Rising to her feet Jayne took off her glasses and pulled the clasp from her hair. The curls cascaded over her shoulder, and she shook her head, freeing them. Plowing her fingers through her hair, she vowed to change. Or at least to try. Yes, she felt content with her life, but she had to admit there was something—or rather *someone*—missing.

Not until Jayne had left her apartment and was inside the elevator did it occur to her that she hadn't the slightest idea of where to meet men. Mentally she eliminated the spots she knew they congregated—places like taverns, pool halls and sports arenas. Her hero wasn't any of those types. A singles bar? Did people even use that term anymore? She'd never gone to one, but it sounded like just the place for a woman on a man-finding mission. Gloria would approve.

Jayne walked out of her building and ten minutes later, she sat in the corner of a cocktail lounge several blocks away. It had the rather obscure name of Soft Sam's. An embarrassed flush heated her face as she wondered what had possessed her to enter this place. Each time an eligible-looking man sauntered her way, she slid farther down into her chair, until she was so low her eyes were practically level with the table. The men in this bar were not the ones of which dreams were made. Thank goodness the room was as dark as a theater, with candles flickering atop the small round tables. The pulsing music, surly bartender and raised voices made her uncomfortable. Repeatedly she berated herself for doing anything as naive as coming here. Her parents would be aghast if they knew their sweet little girl was sitting in what they'd probably call a den of iniquity.

Forcing herself to straighten, Jayne's fingers coiled around her icy drink, and the chill extended halfway up her arm. According to what everyone said, the internet and a bar were the best ways to meet men. She was wary of resorting to online dating services, but she might have to consider it. And as for the bars… What her friends hadn't told her was the *type* of man who frequented such places. A glance around her confirmed that this was not where she belonged. Still, her goal was important. When she returned to Seattle, she was going to hold her head up high. There would be an incredible man on her arm, and she'd be the envy of every girl in her high school class. But if she had to lower her standards to this level, she'd rather not go back at all.

Her shoulders sagged with defeat. She'd been a fool to listen to Gloria. In her enthusiasm, Jayne had gone about this all wrong. A bar wasn't the place to begin her search; she should've realized that. *Books* would tell her what she needed to know. They'd never failed her yet, and she was astonished now that she could've forgotten something so basic.

Jayne squinted as she studied the men lined up at the polished bar. Even without her glasses, she could see that there wasn't a single man she'd consider taking to her reunion. The various women all seemed overdressed and desperate. The atmosphere in the bar was artificial, the surface gaiety forced and frenetic.

Coming here tonight had been a mistake. She felt embarrassed about letting down her hair and hiding her glasses in her purse—acting like someone she wasn't. The best thing to do now was to stand up and walk out of this place before someone actually approached her. But if it had taken courage to walk in, Jayne discovered that it took nearly as much to leave.

Unexpectedly the door of the lounge opened, dispersing a shaft of late-afternoon sunlight into the dim interior. Jayne pursed her lips, determined to escape. Turning to look at the latest arrival, she couldn't help staring. The situation was going from bad to intolerable. This man, whose imposing height was framed by the doorway, was the very one Gloria had been so excited about this afternoon. He quickly surveyed the room, and Jayne recognized him; he was definitely her neighbor. The few times they'd met in the elevator, Jayne had sensed his disapproval. She didn't know what she'd done to offend him, but he seemed singularly unimpressed by her, and Jayne had no idea why. On second thought, Jayne told herself, he'd probably never given her a moment's notice. In fact, he'd probably paid as much attention to her as she had to him—almost none.

His large physique intimidated her, and the sharp glance he gave her was just short of unfriendly. He was more intriguing than good-looking. Though she knew that some women, like Gloria, found him attractive, his blunt features were far too rugged to classify as handsome. His hair was black and thick, and he was well over six feet tall. He walked with a hint of aggression in every stride. Jayne doubted he'd back down from a confrontation. She didn't know anything about him— not even his name—but she would've thought this was the last place he'd look for a date. But then, anyone who glanced at her would assume she didn't belong here, either. And she didn't.

Standing up, Jayne squared her shoulders and pushed back her chair while she studied the pattern on the carpet. Without raising her eyes, she fastened her raincoat and tucked her purse strap over her shoulder. The sooner she got out of this regrettable place, the better. She'd prefer to make her escape without attracting his attention, although with her hair down and without her glasses, it was unlikely that he'd recognize her.

Unfortunately her action caught his eye and he paused just inside the bar, watching her. Jayne hated the superior glare that burned straight through her. Blazing color moved up her neck and into her pale cheeks, but she refused to give him the satisfaction of lowering her gaze.

Jayne walked decisively toward the exit, which he was partially blocking. Something danced briefly in his dark blue eyes and she swallowed nervously. Slowly he stepped aside, but not enough to allow her to pass. The hard set of his mouth drew her attention. Her determined eyes met his. Brows as richly dark as his ebony hair rose slightly, and she saw a glimmer of arrogant amusement on his face.

"Well, well. If it isn't Miss Prim and Proper."

Jayne knew her expression must be horrified—he *had* recognized her—but she gritted her teeth, unwilling to acknowledge him. "If you'll excuse me, please."

"Of course," he murmured. He grinned as he gave her the necessary room. Jayne felt like running, her heart pounding as if she already had.

Humiliated, she hurried past him and stopped outside to hold her hand over her heart. As fast as her fingers would cooperate, she took her glasses from her purse. What on earth would he think of her being in a place like this? She didn't look like her normal self, but that hadn't fooled this sharp-eyed man. If he said something to her when they met again, she'd have an excuse planned.

She brushed the hair from her face and trekked down the sidewalk. He wouldn't say anything, she told herself. To imagine he'd even give her a second's thought would be overreacting. The only words he'd ever said to her had been that one taunting remark in the bar. It was unlikely that he'd strike up a conversation with her now. Especially since he so obviously found her laughable…

The following day at lunch, Jayne ordered Wednesday's roast-beef sandwich while Gloria chatted happily. "I've got the books on my desk."

"I only hope no one saw you take them."

"Not a soul," her friend said. "They look promising, particularly the one called *Eight Easy Steps to Meeting a Man.*"

"If you want, I'll pass it to you when I'm finished," Jayne offered.

"I just might take you up on that," Gloria surprised her by saying. Divorced for several years, she dated even less than Jayne did. "Don't act so shocked. I've been feeling the maternal urge lately. It would be nice to find a man and start a family."

The roast beef felt like a lead weight in the pit of Jayne's stomach. "Yes, it would," she agreed with a sigh. The worst thing about the lack of a husband was not having children. She always enjoyed them, and as the children's librarian she spent her days with other people's kids.

"I take it you've reconsidered my idea," Gloria continued.

"It might be worth a try." Jayne was much too embarrassed by her misadventure at the bar to say anything to her friend about it.

"You know, if that *was* your neighbor yesterday, you don't need to look too hard."

As far as Jayne was concerned, she never wanted to see *him* again.

"I suppose," she mumbled. "But I'd like to find a man with more…culture."

"Up to you," Gloria said, shaking her head.

The same afternoon, her arms loaded with borrowed books on meeting men, Jayne stepped onto the elevator—and came face-to-face with her neighbor. Her first instinct was to turn around and dash out again. His eyes darkened with challenge as they met hers, and she refused to give him the satisfaction of letting him know how much he unnerved her. With all the dignity she could muster, Jayne moved to the rear of the elevator, feeling unreasonably angry with Gloria.

His eyes flickered over her flushed face. Reaction more than need prompted her to push up her glasses, and she struggled to disguise her nervousness with deep breaths.

"Ninth floor, right?" he murmured.

"Yes." Her voice came out sounding like a frog with laryngitis. She'd been so flustered she hadn't even punched in her floor number. Hugging the books to her chest, she kept her eyes on the orange light that indicated the numbers above the elevator door.

"I have to admit it was a surprise seeing you last night," he said smoothly, clearly enjoying her discomfort.

Hot color flashed from her face like a neon light. "I beg your pardon?" If she could have gotten away with it, she would have given him a frown of utter bewilderment, as if to say she had no idea what he was talking about. But Jayne had never been a good liar. Her eye would twitch and her upper lip quiver. Fooling her parents had been impossible; she wouldn't dream of trying to deceive this way-too-perceptive man.

"I didn't know prim and proper little girls went into bars like that."

Clearing her throat, she sent him a look of practiced

disdain usually reserved for teenagers she caught necking in the upstairs portion of the library. "Let me assure you, I am not the type of woman who frequents such places." She wished she didn't sound quite so stilted, and for the twentieth time in as many hours, she lamented her foolishness. Her back and shoulders ached with the effort to stand there rigidly. If he knew anything about body language, he'd get her message.

"You're telling me," he said and chuckled softly. Mischief glimmered in his eyes, and with an effort Jayne looked away.

"You must have mistaken me for someone else," she told him sternly, disgusted with herself for lying. Immediately her right eye started to twitch, and her grip on the books tightened. The elevator had never made its ascent more slowly. She finally relaxed when it came to a grinding halt on her floor. The minute the door opened she rushed out. In her haste, her shoe snagged on the thick carpet and propelled her forward. With a cry of alarm she went staggering into the wide hallway, the books flying from her arms. The wall opposite the elevator halted her progress when she was catapulted into it, catching herself with open palms.

"Are you okay?" A gentle hand touched her shoulder. She turned and gave a convulsive jerk of her head as humiliation robbed her of speech. The dark eyes that had been probing hers were now filled with concern.

"I—I'm fine," she managed, wiping a shaking hand over her eyes, hoping to wake and find that this entire episode was a nightmare.

"Let me help you with your books."

"No!" she cried breathlessly and scrambled to gather up her collection. The last thing she wanted was his pity. He'd made his feelings known. He didn't think much of her, but he was entitled to his opinion—and his fun. "I'm fine. Just leave. Please. That's all I want." She was only getting what she deserved for behaving so irrationally and going into that stupid bar in the first place. Now she'd made everything worse. Never had she felt more embarrassed, and it was all her own fault.

Her hands shook as she fumbled with the clasp of her purse and took out her apartment key. She didn't turn around, but she could feel his eyes on her. Her whole body was trembling by the time she entered the apartment. She shut the door and leaned against it, closing her eyes.

Several minutes passed before she was able to remove her coat and pile the books on her kitchen table. She hung her coat in the hall closet, went into her bedroom and set her purse on the dresser. Organization gave guidance and balance to Jayne's life, and there was never a time she'd needed it more.

The teapot was filled and heating on the stove. Trying to put the unfortunate encounter in the elevator out of her mind, she looked through the books she'd brought home. *Finding a Man in Thirty Days or Less* was the first book in the stack. That one sounded helpful. She glanced at the next one, *How to Get a Man Interested in You.* These self-help books would provide all the advice she needed, Jayne mused. And if they worked for her, she'd pass them on to Gloria later. As always, Jayne would find the answer in books. The next title made her smile. *How to Convince a Man to Fall in Love with You Forever.* Nice thought, but all she really cared about right now was the one night of her class reunion.

She heard knocking and lifted her head abruptly, then slowly moved to the door, her legs weighted by reluctance. She was acquainted with only a few people in Portland. There was no one, other than Gloria, whom she'd call a good friend.

"Who is it?" she asked.

"Riley Chambers."

"Who?"

"Your neighbor."

Groaning inwardly, Jayne closed her eyes, dreading the thought of seeing him again for any reason. Hesitantly she turned the lock. "I'm perfectly fine," she said, opening the door.

"I thought you might be looking for this." He leaned against the doorjamb, leafing indolently through the pages of a hardcover book.

Jayne's breath jammed in her throat as she struggled not to grab it from his hands. Noting the title, *How to Pick Up a Man,* she felt her face redden.

Brilliant little flecks of light showed in his eyes, which glinted with humor. "Listen, Ms. Gilbert, if you're so interested in finding yourself a man, I'd advise you to stay away from bars like Soft Sam's. They're not good places for little girls like you."

She frowned. "How do you know my name? Oh—the building directory."

He nodded.

"Well, *Mr. Chambers,* if you've come to make fun of me…"

"I haven't." The expression in his eyes hardened. "I don't want to ever see you there again."

"You have no business telling me where I can and cannot go." Her hands knotted at her sides in outrage. He was right, of course, but she had no intention of letting him know that. She jerked the book from his hand and when he stepped away, she slammed the door.

Two

Riley dropped his arms and grinned at the door that had closed in his face. So prim little Ms. Gilbert had a fiery temper. She might act like a shy country mouse, but his opinion of her went up several notches. With that well-tamed hair and those glasses, she hadn't left much of an impression the few times he'd seen her in the elevator. Her air of blind trust and hopeful expectation made her look as though she'd stepped out of the pages of a Victorian novel. She'd better watch out, or she'd be wolves' prey. He'd wanted to tell her to open her eyes and look around her. She was too vulnerable for this day and age. This was the twenty-first century, not some romantic daydream.

It'd surprised him to see her in Soft Sam's. Admittedly, she'd been a fish out of water. She was absolutely correct; it was none of his business where she went, but he felt oddly protective of her.

Ms. J. Gilbert—he didn't even know her first name—was as untouched and naive as they come. All sugar and spice and everything nice. Rubbing a hand over the back of his neck, Riley sighed impatiently. He didn't have time to think about a woman—any woman. But a smile formed as he recalled the fire that had flared in her eyes when she'd grabbed that book from his hands. She had spunk. Briefly he wondered what other treasures were waiting to be discovered in her. Riley gave himself a mental shake. Years of following his instincts told him that women like this could be trouble for men like him. Besides, his days were filled with enough conflict. He didn't need a woman distracting him from the problems at hand. Maybe when this business with Priestly was over, he'd have the time— No! The best thing he could do was forget Ms. Sugar and Spice.

If she was in the market for a husband—which she obviously was—there were better men. She was far too wide-eyed and innocent for him. In the end he'd only hurt her. She deserved someone who hadn't become cynical, who wasn't hardened by life.

Jayne stared out at the rain that rolled down the side of the grimy bus window. A low gray fog hovered over the street. After five years in Portland, she was accustomed to gloomy springs. The paper lay folded in her lap; the headlines were the same day after day, although the names and places changed. War, death, disease and destruction. She saw that a prominent state official had been questioned by the FBI about ties to the underworld. Jayne wondered if Senator Priestly was one of the officials who'd visited the library recently. She'd been impressed with the group on the tour; there had been a number of men Gloria would have approved of. But then, that could mean neither Gloria nor Jayne was a good judge of character.

Riley Chambers was a perfect example of their poor judgment. He might not have been impressed with her, but from the first she'd thought he was…intriguing. A man of mystery. Despite the fact that they'd barely glanced at each other whenever they'd met in the elevator, she *might* have been interested in getting to know him. Her current opinion was decidedly different. He had a lot of nerve telling her not to go back to Soft Sam's! If it was such a terrible place, what was he doing there? The next time she saw him, she'd make a point of asking him exactly that.

Agitated, she pulled the cord to indicate that she wanted to get off at the next stop. She tucked the newspaper under her arm and hurried to the rear of the bus.

Avoiding a puddle, she leapt from the bottom step to the sidewalk and paused to open her umbrella. Riley Chambers didn't deserve another minute of her consideration. He'd made his views of her obvious. He'd called her a little girl. She had a good mind to inform him that at five-seven she could hardly be described as *little.* Even now his taunting comment rankled. Jayne had the feeling that he'd said it just to get a reaction out of her. Well, he'd succeeded, and that should please him.

Gloria was waiting for her when Jayne arrived at the library.

"Well, what did the books say?" her friend asked as soon as Jayne had put her bag inside her desk.

"Plenty. Did you know one of the best places to meet

men is in the supermarket? Can you see me sauntering up to someone in the frozen-food section and suggesting we have children together?"

Gloria's laughter floated around the room. "That may be worth a try. What other place did they suggest?"

"The art gallery."

"That's perfect for you!"

Jayne sighed and tucked a stray curl into her tightly coiled chignon. "I suppose."

"You've got to show more enthusiasm than this, m'dear." Opening the paper on Jayne's desk, Gloria ran down a list of current city events.

"The Portland Art Gallery is showing work by one of your favorite artists—Delacroix. I bet you were planning on attending, anyway. Now all you need to do is keep your eyes peeled for any handsome, eligible men."

"I don't know, Gloria. I can't even catch a cold, let alone a man. Especially a handsome one."

"You can do it."

"Now you sound like a cheerleader," Jayne moaned, not sure she wanted any of this.

"You need me," Gloria insisted. "Look upon me as your own personal cheering section. All I ask is that you think of God, country and your best friend as you stroll through that gallery."

"What?"

"Well, if this works for you, then I may give it a try."

Jayne had her doubts. Over the past several years, she'd visited a variety of galleries and had yet to see a single attractive man. However, she hadn't actually been on the lookout.

"Well?" Gloria stared at her with her hands positioned challengingly on her hips. "Are you or are you not going to the Delacroix show?"

"Gloria…" Jayne said, hedging.

"Jayne!"

"Fine, I'll go."

"When?"

"Tomorrow afternoon."

Although she might have agreed to Gloria's suggestion, Jayne wasn't sure she was doing the right thing. All day she fretted about the coming art show. By five she was a nervous wreck. Feeling that she needed the confidence a new outfit would give her, Jayne decided to go shopping after work. This was no easy decision. She equated clothes-shopping with trauma. Nothing ever seemed to fit well, and she dreaded standing in front of those three-way mirrors that revealed every imperfection.

At the end of the day, Jayne walked down the library steps, balking at the thought of this expedition. Sheer force of will led her into The Galleria, the downtown shopping center, where she found a navy wool dress with side pockets and long sleeves. The dress didn't do much for her, but it was the first one that fit without looking like a burlap bag flung over her head. Feeling somewhat relieved, she paid the saleslady and headed for the escalator that would take her to the transit mall. On her way out Jayne noticed a young woman draped on the arm of a much older man. She batted her long lashes and paused at an expensive jeweler's window display.

"Last month's emerald is so, so lonely," Jayne heard the woman's soft voice purr.

"We can't have that, can we, darling," the older man murmured as he steered the blonde inside the store.

The episode left a bad taste in Jayne's mouth, and she wondered if the woman had met her sugar daddy in Safeway. It was beyond her imagination that men would be attracted to women so shallow. If this was the type of behavior men sought, Jayne simply couldn't do it.

Saturday afternoon, wearing her new dress, Jayne strolled bravely through the Portland Art Gallery. Wandering around, she saw a man standing against a wall; he seemed to be more interested in the patrons than the art. Gathering her nerve and her resolve, she stood in front of a Delacroix painting, *Horse Frightened by a Storm,* the most famous of the paintings on loan from the Seattle Art Museum. Jayne had long been an admirer of Delacroix's work and knew it well. He was, in her opinion, the greatest of the Romantic painters.

Again she studied the man, sizing him up without, she hoped, being too obvious. He was attractive, although it was difficult to tell for sure without her glasses. From what she could see, he looked approachable. Her hands felt clammy, and she resisted the urge to wipe them dry on the sides of her dress. Clearly she didn't know much about luring a man. But neither was she totally ignorant. She *had* dated before and had even felt the faint stirrings of desire. But her relationships usually died a natural death from lack of nourishment. Sad as it seemed, Jayne preferred her books.

She moved across the marble floor toward the man. Coming closer, she confirmed that he was attractive in a slender, refined way—not like Riley Chambers. Just the thought of *that* arrogant man brought a flash of hot color to her cheeks.

Trying to ignore the tension that knotted her stomach, Jayne mentally reviewed the books she'd read. Each had repeatedly stated that she couldn't wait for the man to take the initiative. One book had gone so far as to list ways of starting a conversation with a prospective love interest. Fumbling her purse clasp, Jayne pulled out the list of ideas she'd jotted down. She could ask for change for the parking meter, but she didn't own a car and lying would make her eye twitch. She discarded that plan. Next on the list was pretending not to notice the targeted male and accidentally-on-purpose walking straight into him. Too clichéd, Jayne decided. She wanted to be more original. The book had suggested asking him what time it was. Okay, she could try that.

Dropping the list in her purse, she took three strides toward the blonde man and did an abrupt about-face. She was wearing a watch! How could she ask the time when there was a watch on her wrist? She'd look like an idiot!

Jayne's heart felt as though it was pounding right out of her chest. Who would've supposed that anything this simple could be so difficult? Sighing, she remembered the look Gloria had given her as she hustled her out the door of the library. If she didn't make her move, Gloria would never let her live it down.

Eyes closed, she took slow, even breaths until calm reason returned. This whole idea was ludicrous. Dressing up and loitering around an art gallery hoping to meet men was so contrary to her painfully shy personality that she could hardly believe she was doing it. The girls of St. Mary's wouldn't be impressed by such desperate measures. Who did Jayne think she was going to fool? She'd turned out exactly as they'd predicted, and there was nothing she could do to change that.

"Excuse me." A male voice interrupted her thoughts. "Do you happen to have the time?"

Jayne's eyes flew open. "The time," she repeated.

The man Jayne had noticed came to stand beside her. Instantly her eyes went to her wrist. He must have read the same book!

"I'm afraid I forgot to replace the battery in my watch," he said with a sheepish smile, dispelling that notion.

"It's nearly three," she stammered, holding out her arm so he could examine her watch.

"I saw you were looking at the Delacroix painting of the horse."

"Yes," Jayne murmured. It'd worked! It had really worked. She smiled up at him brightly, remembering the adoring look on the young woman's face as she'd stared into the eyes of her sugar daddy.

"By the way, my name's Mark Bauer."

"Jayne Gilbert," she said and offered him her hand. Recalling "darling's" reactions, Jayne lowered her lashes alluringly so that they brushed the arch of her cheek.

"He's my favorite artist—Eugene Delacroix." Mark gestured at the painting with one hand.

Ferdinand Victor Eugene Delacroix, Jayne added mentally.

"When Delacroix died in 1863 he left behind a legacy of eight hundred oil paintings," Mark lectured.

And twice as many watercolors, Jayne said—but only to herself. "Is that a fact?" she simpered.

Warming to his subject, Mark continued by explaining the familiar painting, pointing out the colors chosen by the artist to establish mood. He went on to describe how particular lines in the work expressed certain feelings. Jayne batted her lashes at Mark and pretended to be impressed by his knowledge. She wished she had her glasses on so she could see more clearly what he looked like. From a distance he'd appeared attractive enough; close up he was a little blurry.

By the time Jayne was on the bus for the return trip to her apartment, she was thoroughly disgusted with herself. She wasn't any better than that syrupy blonde clinging to the arm of her generous benefactor. She was sure she knew much more about art than Mark did and yet she'd played dumb. He'd apparently done a quick search on Google to collect some basic facts, then spun them into the art history lecture she'd just heard. And she'd pretended to be awed….

Something was definitely wrong with her. She'd always been such a sensible woman. It astonished her that Mark hadn't seen through her act. She wasn't convinced she even liked the man. He spoke for half an hour on a subject he obviously knew very little about while Jayne continued to play dumb and batted her lashes every ten seconds. She supposed he was hoping to impress her, but, in fact, had accomplished just the opposite. The whole production had been pointless—for both of them. He'd asked for her phone number, but she figured she'd never hear from him again.

A walk in the park helped her clear away the confusion that clouded her perspective. She'd thought she'd known what she wanted. Suddenly she was unsure. Knights riding around on white horses, looking for women to escort to class reunions, seemed to be few and far between these days. But then, she didn't know much about knights and even less about men. Quite possibly, each and every one of them would turn out to be like Riley Chambers. The thought caused a shiver of apprehension to race over her skin and she realized for the first time that a slow drizzling rain had begun to fall. Of course, she'd left her umbrella at home. And of course there were no cabs in sight.

Burying her hands deep in her pockets, she quickened her pace. She was three blocks from her building when the clouds burst open in sheets of rain that pelted the sidewalk relentlessly. Jayne was drenched within seconds. Rivulets of water ran down the back of her neck until her hair fell in limp strands. When she stepped into the lobby, her glasses fogged, and her new dress was plastered to her. She felt the overwhelming desire to sneeze. This had been the most miserable day of her life. Not only had she behaved like an idiot over the first man to fall in with her schemes, but she'd been foolish enough to get caught in a downpour. The only thing worse would be to run into Riley Chambers.

No sooner had the thought formed than the man materialized.

Jayne groaned inwardly and stepped into the open elevator, praying he'd take another. The way her luck was going, Jayne should have known better.

Riley followed her inside and stared blatantly at the half-drowned country mouse, a small puddle of water forming at her feet. He couldn't resist a tiny smile as he studied her. Ms. J. Gilbert was badly in need of someone to watch over her. He hadn't seen her in the past couple of days, and it hadn't taken long to realize she was avoiding him. That was fine. She brought out his protective instincts with those wide, innocent eyes, which was something he couldn't really afford. She disturbed him, and innumerable times in the past two days thoughts of her had flitted through his head. Casually he'd tossed them aside, chalking up his curiosity to concern that she might go back to Soft Sam's.

Jayne turned her head away. "Go ahead and laugh," she told him as they began their slow ascent. "I know you're dying to make fun of me."

Riley scowled briefly. Suddenly she reminded him of a cat backed into a corner, its fur bristling and claws unsheathed. Riley had no desire to antagonize her. Instead, he felt the urge to comfort her—and that astonished him. "Are you still angry because I saw the title of your book?" he asked.

"Furious." She slipped her steamed glasses to the end of her nose so she could see him above the frames.

"I didn't mean to make fun of you." She looked vulnerable, and he ignored the impulse to ask her first name. He didn't see her as a Jessica or a Jennifer. Possibly a Jacqueline.

"Why not make fun of me?" she flared. "Everyone else has…all my life. People have always thought I'm some kind of weirdo. I like books. I like to read." He saw tears in her eyes, and she twisted around so he couldn't look at her.

The instant the elevator doors parted, she escaped, her shoulders back, her head held high, and glided down the hall to her apartment.

Riley went to his own door, walking slowly. He withdrew the keys from his pocket with a frown, then wearily turned the lock and stepped into his dark apartment. A flick of the wall switch flooded the room with cheerless light. He threw his raincoat over the back of a chair and went into the kitchen to put a frozen dinner in the microwave.

Once again the little mouse, as he still thought of her, had fired to life, turning on him. Even cold and miserable, she'd walked out of the elevator with her chin raised. Her back was ramrod straight, and she moved with as much dignity as any princess. He smiled as he recalled the way her wet dress had clung to her, revealing full breasts, round hips and a trim waist. She had long legs, nicely shaped. He couldn't imagine why she chose to hide behind those generic business suits. The dress she wore today was the first he could remember seeing her in. The dark navy color wasn't right for her. With that chestnut hair and those large honey-brown eyes she should wear lighter shades. At least she'd had her hair down, which was a definite improvement. Although it had been wet and clinging, he just knew it was soft. Silky. He wanted to lift it in his fingers and—

Slumping into a chair, Riley shook his head. He didn't like the things Ms. J. Gilbert brought to the surface in him. It had been a lot of years since he'd given a woman this much thought. What he felt was pity, he assured himself. She was lonely. For that matter, so was he.

The microwave made its annoying sound, and he removed the tray, wondering what the country mouse was having for her dinner.

Holding a tissue to her nose, Jayne sneezed loudly. Her eyes itched, and her throat felt scratchy. A glance at her watch told her it would be another three long hours before she could go home and soak in a hot tub. Thankfully Gloria had offered to handle storytime today. While the preschoolers huddled around her friend, Jayne sat at her desk and cut out brightly colored letters for the June bulletin board. Her class reunion was only seven weeks away. Like the ominous approach of a thunderstorm, defeat settled over her. She wouldn't go. It was as simple as that.

"Could you tell me where you keep the biographies?"

She raised her eyes, and they met a familiar blue gaze. Riley Chambers... She clutched the scissors so hard that her thumb ached. "Pardon?" Stunned, she couldn't remember what he'd asked.

"The biographies."

In an effort to stall for time, she put the scissors down. Riley Chambers was on her turf now. "They're directly to your left."

"Could you show me where they are?"

"Yes, of course, but you look like a man who knows his way around."

"Not in this library," he mumbled.

She stood, pausing to push the glasses up onto her nose, then led him to the section he'd requested. "The area to the right is the children's fiction department for ages three to six. If you like, we'll stop here so you can browse."

Riley ignored that. He'd had one heck of a time finding out where she worked. Their apartment manager had to have the most closed mouth of anyone he'd ever known. Generally speaking, he approved of that, but with a lie about undefined but urgent "legal matters," he'd managed to get his answer. "The name Jayne suits you," he said. He'd seen the nameplate on her desk.

"As long as you aren't Tarzan."

"I don't live in a jungle."

"But you obviously speak the language." A smile tugged at the corner of her mouth.

After delivering Riley to the section he'd requested, Jayne watched as he took down several volumes and flipped through the pages. She studied him with helpless fascination. Riley Chambers was a cynical man who looked at the world through wary eyes. Nonetheless, she had a glimmer—more than a glimmer—of his sensuality. Horrified at her thoughts, Jayne quickly returned to her desk. She resumed her task, doing her best to pretend he wasn't anywhere around.

"I'd like to check these out," Riley said, setting two thick volumes on the corner of her desk.

"Do you have a library card?"

"Yeah. It's tricky borrowing books without one."

"You don't need me for that." Jayne didn't know why he'd come. He probably wanted to throw her off guard. That wasn't going to work. Not in the library.

"I assumed that as a public employee you'd be willing to help me."

"Books are checked out at the front desk."

"I want you to do it."

"Why?"

"Why not?"

"I'm the children's librarian."

"That doesn't surprise me. You look like someone who'd prefer the world of make-believe and happy ever after."

"Is that so wrong?" she replied, her temper flaring.

"Just as long as you don't expect to find your heroes in a sleazy bar."

Color heated Jayne's already flushed face, and she glanced around, wondering if Gloria had heard him. Gloria raised her head long enough to wink encouragingly. "Why are you here?" Jayne whispered.

"You confuse me," he admitted after a minute. "Or maybe *disturb* would be a better word."

"Why?"

"I don't know. Probably because you look like an accident waiting to happen."

"I don't need a fairy godfather." Not when Gloria insisted on waving a magic wand over her head every morning.

"I know what you're after," he whispered back. "I saw the book, remember?"

Jayne bit her lip. Riley was playing with her, amusing himself at her expense. "I'm not looking for a husband. I…only need a man for one night."

"So that's it." The corner of his mouth edged up.

"No!" she cried at his knowing look. Her cry attracted the attention of the entire room. The library went silent as heads turned toward them. Embarrassed half to death, Jayne lowered her chin and pleaded, "Would you please just go away?"

Riley abandoned his books and stalked outside, berating himself with every step. Talk about stupid! What kind of game did he think he was playing? Earlier that afternoon the workload had gotten to him, and when he couldn't tolerate it anymore, he'd leaned back in his chair and closed his eyes. A picture of the alluring Jayne Gilbert, all sugar and spice, had immediately entered his mind. He didn't know why she fascinated him so much. Maybe it was because of her innocence, her gentle beauty and the goodness he sensed in her.

After a day like this one, he needed some of that innocence. It'd taken him the better part of an hour to get the information about her job out of the building manager. Discovering she was a librarian hadn't come as any surprise. It fit his image of her. But showing up here hadn't been one of his more brilliant ideas. He hadn't meant to browbeat Jayne and he'd been amused by her witty comebacks. She'd held her own.

Feeling angry and frustrated with himself, Riley went back to the office. He'd apologize to her later. Ms. Gilbert deserved that much.

By the time all the paperwork had been cleared from his desk, it was close to eight. He rubbed a hand over his face, feeling more tired than he'd been in years. He was getting too old for this work. Grabbing his jacket from the back of his chair, Riley tossed his empty paper cup into the garbage can. He hadn't had anything but coffee since early afternoon. The way things were going in this madhouse, it was a miracle he didn't have an ulcer.

Once he'd parked in the apartment lot and headed across the street to the building, thoughts of Jayne flooded his mind. He sighed, unable to disperse them.

The elevator stopped on the ninth floor. He stood for a full minute outside her door before deciding it would be better to get this apology over with. He knocked once, loudly.

Jayne was miserable. Her throat felt like fire every time she swallowed. Her head ached, and the last thing she wanted was company. Housecoat cinched tight around her waist, she unlocked the door.

"You again?" she whispered, hardly caring. "What's the matter, didn't you have enough fun earlier?"

Riley disregarded her comment. "You look awful."

"Thanks."

"Are you sick?"

"No," she answered hoarsely and coughed. "I enjoy looking like this."

Without an invitation, Riley walked into her apartment and demanded, "Have you seen a doctor?"

Jayne stood by the door, holding it open and staring pointedly into the empty hallway. "Make yourself at home," she said with heavy sarcasm. As it was, she'd spent a good part of the afternoon explaining Riley's visit to Gloria. Somehow her friend refused to believe it was a coincidence that he'd come into the library. According to Gloria, Riley was definitely interested in Jayne. That suggestion only made her laugh.

"You might have a fever. Have you taken your temperature?"

"I was about to do that." The man appeared oblivious to her lack of welcome. She closed the door and turned around, leaning against it.

"Sit down," he said.

"Are you always this bossy?"

"Always."

Too weak to argue, Jayne did as he said.

"Where's your thermometer?"

She pointed to the kitchen counter and tucked her bare feet underneath her. "Why do you keep pestering me?"

He didn't respond, seemingly intent on reading the thermometer. Impatiently he shook it.

"Open your mouth," he ordered, and when she complied, he gently inserted it under her tongue.

Curious, Jayne followed his progress as he paced the carpet in front of her, checking his watch every fifteen seconds. He picked up a book from the coffee table, read the title and arched his brows. Replacing the book, he resumed his pacing.

"I came because I wanted to apologize for this afternoon. I had no business, uh, pestering you."

"Then why did you?" she mumbled, holding the thermometer in her mouth as she spoke.

"I don't know." His hand sliced the air. "Probably for the reason I mentioned earlier. You...disturb me."

"Why?" she asked again.

"If I knew the answer to that, I wouldn't be here."

"Then go away."

"I thought misery loved company."

"Not this misery."

"Too bad." Carefully he withdrew the thermometer and examined it.

"Well? What does it say? Will I live?"

"A little over ninety-nine. Got any aspirin?"

Jayne shook her head. "I'm never sick."

He studied her skeptically, and Jayne waited for a harangue that never came.

"I'll be back." He left her door slightly ajar, and Jayne felt too miserable to get up and lock him out.

Riley returned a couple of minutes later, his arms loaded with a variety of objects: soup can, a box of tissues, bottle of aspirin, frozen lemonade and the paper.

"Are you moving in?" she asked irritably. The other day she'd assumed that she couldn't meet a man in her own living room. Riley was proving her wrong.

He scowled and stalked wordlessly into her tiny

kitchen. What an odd man he was, Jayne thought. He obviously felt *something* for her if he was going to all this trouble, and yet he didn't seem to want her company.

After a moment Jayne decided to investigate. Struggling to her feet, she paused in the middle of the room to sneeze and blow her nose.

Riley stuck his head around the corner. "Sit," he ordered, giving her a ferocious glare.

Jayne glared back at him. "What are you doing in my kitchen?"

"Making dinner. Don't be ungrateful."

"I'm not hungry," she said, advancing a step. Riley would never be able to figure out her organizational methods. He'd look in her cupboards and claim that even her groceries were filed under the Dewey decimal system.

"Is it feed a cold and starve a fever or the other way around?" Riley asked next.

He made quite a sight with his white shirtsleeves rolled halfway up his arms and an apron tied high around his waist. The top two buttons of his shirt were opened to reveal dark curling hair. Jayne couldn't help smiling.

"Now what's so funny?" His own smile was lazy.

"You."

"What?" He glanced down at his flowered apron. "What's the matter, haven't you ever seen a man working in the kitchen?"

"Not in mine."

"Then it's time you did." He turned away from her

and took a saucepan from the top of the stove, then opened and closed her cupboard doors until he located glasses and bowls. "You should smile more often," he said casually as he worked, pouring equal amounts of soup into the wide bowls.

"I've got a cold. My head hurts, my throat feels raw, and there's a crazy man in my kitchen, ordering me around. Give me a day or two, and I'll find the humor in all of this." She didn't add that she had seven weeks to come up with a man who'd make heads turn when he walked into a room.

"Sit."

"Again? See what I mean?" she complained, but she did as he asked, pulling out the high-backed oak chair.

Riley brought her a bowl of hot soup, a steaming mug and two aspirin. Jerking the apron from around his waist, he took the chair across from her.

"What is it?" she asked, staring at the steaming bowl.

"Chicken noodle soup." He pointed to the bowl, then the mug. "And hot lemonade."

"Couldn't you be more original than that?"

"Not on short notice."

"Are you eating here, too?"

"What's the matter? Do you expect the help to eat in the kitchen?"

Jayne smiled again. "Why are you doing this?"

Riley shrugged. "Because I owe you. I didn't mean to make fun of you earlier."

"When?" To her way of thinking, he'd done it more than once.

"This afternoon. I shouldn't have come in and given you a hard time. I want to apologize."

"If you're in the mood to make amends, you might mention the other night, as well."

"No." He scowled briefly, letting his eyes drop to her lips. "You brought that on yourself."

Jayne set her spoon aside. "I don't know if I like you. I've never met anyone who confuses me the way you do."

"Then that makes two of us. Listen, I've lived most of my life without women, and I don't want a prim little country mouse messing things up at this late date." The words were harsher than he'd intended, but Jayne was stronger than her soft, vulnerable manner had led him to believe. She had an inner strength he was only beginning to recognize.

Jayne bristled, her hand gripping the spoon tightly. "I didn't invite you here." She'd have a heck of a time explaining this to Gloria if her friend ever found out.

"I'm aware of that."

The phone rang, jerking Jayne's attention across the room.

"Do you want me to answer it?" Riley asked.

"No," she answered, rising from her chair. "I will." She reached the phone on the fourth ring and grabbed it. "Hello," she said, slightly out of breath.

"Jayne, it's Mark Bauer. Do you remember me? We met at the art gallery last Saturday."

Three

"Hello, Mark, of course I remember you." Jayne leaned against the chair, trying to ignore Riley, who was standing behind her.

"You don't sound the same," Mark continued.

"I've got a cold." That had to be the understatement of the year.

"Not a bad one, I hope."

"Oh, no, I'll be fine in a day or two." Muffled sounds coming from behind Jayne made her tense. Riley was either pacing or fooling around in her kitchen. She wondered if he'd discovered how organized she was. Even her soup cans were stored in alphabetical order.

"Do you think you'd be well enough to go to a movie with me Friday night?" Mark asked.

Jayne was stunned. After behaving in such a ridiculous way, she hadn't expected to hear from Mark again. Least of all to have him ask her out. "I'd like that, thank you."

"Shall we say seven, then?"

"Seven will be fine."

Jayne replaced the receiver and stared at the phone, dumbfounded. A prickly feeling attacked the base of her neck and slithered down her spine. The dumb act had worked once, but she doubted she could maintain it for any length of time. Keeping it up for the seven weeks until her class reunion would be impossible. And once they were in Seattle, she couldn't suddenly tell him: *Surprise! It was all an act. I'm really brilliant.* "I shouldn't have agreed to go." Jayne was shocked to realize she'd spoken aloud.

"Why not?"

Feeling a bit sick to her stomach, Jayne turned to face Riley, who was standing beside the kitchen table. One large hand rested over the back of the polished oak chair. Their eyes met. "I...don't know exactly what he looks like," she admitted honestly, but that wasn't the reason for her hesitancy. Someone like Riley would have instantly seen through her act. Unfortunately—or fortunately—Mark wasn't Riley.

"What do you mean?"

"When we met, I wasn't wearing my glasses." Jayne vowed that if Riley so much as snickered, she'd ask him to leave.

"If wearing glasses bothers you, why don't you get contacts?" he asked matter-of-factly, reaching for his spoon. That night at Soft Sam's she hadn't worn her glasses, he remembered and stiffened.

"I've tried but I can't. My eye doctor recommended a book on how to use them, but..."

"It didn't help you?"

Jayne lowered her hands to her lap. "Sadly, no."

"Where did you meet this Mark guy?" He struggled to keep his voice calm and disinterested. He'd been trained not to reveal interest or emotion. It should come easy, but with Jayne, for some reason, it didn't.

"At the art gallery last Saturday." She caught a sneeze with her napkin just in time. "One of those books said that was a good place to meet men."

Relaxing, Riley tried his first spoonful of lukewarm chicken noodle soup. He might not be an inventive chef, but this meager meal would take the edge off his hunger. The fact that Jayne was sitting across from him with her quiet wit and seductive eyes made even soup more appealing.

They ate in silence, but it was a companionable one as if they were at ease with each other for the first time. Jayne wasn't hungry, but she managed to finish her soup. Riley insisted on doing the dishes, and she didn't argue too strenuously. There were only a couple of bowls and a saucepan that he rinsed and tucked in the dishwasher.

"Is there anything else I can do for you?" Riley asked, standing by the door.

Jayne smiled shyly and shook her head. "No, you've been very kind. Thank you." He was an attractive man, and she didn't know why he was paying her so much attention. His concern was so unexpected that she didn't know how to categorize it. They were neighbors, and it would be good to have a friend in the apartment complex. Riley was probably thinking the same thing, Jayne mused. Their relationship was mutually beneficial.

"I'll see you later," he said.

"Later," she agreed.

The next morning, Jayne woke feeling a hundred percent better. The ache in her throat was gone, as was the stiffness in her arms and legs. Declaring herself cured, she dressed for work, humming as she moved around the bedroom. For several days she'd been dreading the approach of summer and her class reunion, but this morning things looked brighter. Mark had asked her out, and she was determined to keep his interest in her alive. That shouldn't be difficult with Gloria's coaching.

Although the day was predicted to be pleasantly warm, Jayne reached for her jacket on the way out the door. She half looked for Riley as she waited for the elevator, but she'd only seen him a few times in the mornings. Their paths didn't cross often. She would like to have told him how much better she felt and thank him again for his help.

Standing at the bus stop, she noticed that the clouds were breaking up. The air smelled fresh and springlike. Jayne had to remember that this was June, yet it felt more like April or early May. School would be out soon, and her section of the library would be busier than usual.

When a sleek black car pulled up by the curb, Jayne instinctively stepped back, then experienced a flush of pleasure when she recognized the driver.

Riley leaned across the front seat and opened the

side door. "It might not be a good idea for you to stand out in the cold. I'll give you a ride downtown."

"I feel great this morning," she told him. "Thanks for the offer," she felt obliged to say, "but the bus will be here any minute."

Riley's grip tightened on the door handle. "I'll give you a ride if you want. The choice is yours." He said it without looking at her.

Jayne still didn't understand why he was so concerned about her health, but now wasn't the time to question his solicitude. She slid into the front seat, closed the door and fastened her seat belt. "You're going to spoil me, Mr. Chambers."

"I don't work far from you," he said, checking the side mirror before merging with the snarled traffic.

That explained why she and Gloria had seen him at lunchtime. Jayne studied him as he maneuvered the car. He might have offered her a ride, but he certainly didn't seem happy about it. His lips were pursed, and his forehead creased in a frown. Although traffic was heavy and sluggish, that didn't seem to be the reason for his impatience. She assumed it had something to do with her.

Jayne folded her hands in her lap, regretting that she'd accepted his invitation. She couldn't understand why he'd offer her a ride when her presence was clearly upsetting to him.

"You're quiet this morning," Riley commented, glancing her way.

"I was afraid to say anything." Jayne focused her

gaze on her laced fingers. "You looked like you'd bite my head off if I did."

"When has that ever stopped you?"

"Today."

Riley's frown grew, if anything, fiercer. "What made you think I was angry?"

"You look like you ate rattlesnakes for breakfast," she replied.

"I do? Now?"

A quick movement—what Jayne termed an "almost smile"—touched his mouth.

"Your face was all scrunched up," she said, "and your expression was terribly intense. I was wondering why you're giving me a ride when it's clear you don't want me in the car with you."

"Not want you in the car?" he repeated. "That's not it at all. I was just thinking about a problem…at the office."

"Then your thoughts must be deep and dark."

"They have been lately." His face softened as he averted his eyes from the traffic to briefly look at her. "Don't worry, I've never been one to do anything unless it's exactly what I want."

Pleased by his response, Jayne relaxed and smiled. Riley was different from anyone she'd known before. Yet in certain ways they were alike. He was at ease with her quiet manner. In the past Jayne had felt it necessary to make small talk with men. Doing that had been contrary to her nature; finding things to talk about was always difficult, even with Gloria. Mark would expect it, and she'd make the effort for his benefit.

Riley stopped at a red light, and Jayne watched as his fingers loosened their grip on the steering wheel. He turned to her. "You're looking better this morning."

"Like I said, I feel wonderful. It was probably the soup."

"Undoubtedly," Riley agreed with a crooked grin.

"Thank you again," she said shyly, astonished by how much a smile could alter a man's appearance. The glow in his blue eyes warmed Jayne as effectively as a ray of sunlight. "You mentioned an office. What do you do?"

The hesitation was so slight that Jayne thought she must have imagined it.

"I'm an inspector."

"For the city?" Somehow his words didn't ring entirely true, but Jayne attributed that notion to reading too many thrillers and suspense novels.

"Yeah, for the city. I'll let you off at the next corner." Not waiting for her response, he switched lanes and stopped at the curb.

"I'm in your debt again," she murmured. Her hand closed over the door handle. "Thank you."

"Have a good day, Miss Prim and Proper."

Jayne flashed angry eyes at him. When she clenched her hands and stalked away, Riley grinned. Jayne Gilbert was easy to bait. Her reaction to teasing suggested she was an only child. That would also account for her quiet, independent nature. He appreciated that quality in her. Without realizing it, Riley smiled, his troubled thoughts vanishing in the face of a simple display of emotion. Who would've guessed a shy librarian could have that effect on him?

Jayne was watching the evening news two days later while a casserole baked in the oven, when Riley's image flitted into her restless mind. The news story relayed the unsavory details of a prostitution ring that had recently been broken. The blonde woman on the screen looked vaguely familiar, and Jayne wondered if she'd seen her that night in Soft Sam's, the night she met Riley. But she hadn't been wearing her glasses, and it was difficult to tell.

Jayne didn't know what made her think of Riley. She hadn't seen him for a few days. In fact, she'd been half looking for him. At first he'd made his views of her plain. Now she wasn't sure what he thought of her. Not that she expected to bowl him over with her natural beauty and charm. She didn't expect that from any man. She liked Riley, enjoyed his company, and that was rare. The fact was, Jayne didn't know what to make of her relationship with him. Perhaps it was premature to even call it a relationship. Friends—she hoped so. But nothing more. Riley wasn't the type of man she pictured walking into her class reunion. No, she'd reserve Mark for her classmates' inspection. Riley was too…rough-edged. Mark seemed smoother. More sociable.

Shaking her head, Jayne felt guilty that her thoughts about Riley—and Mark, for that matter—could be so self-serving. After all, Riley had gone out of his way for her.

On impulse, she pulled the steaming casserole from

the oven and divided it into two equal portions. With giant oven mitts protecting her hands, she carried the steaming dish down the hallway to Riley's apartment. She knocked at the door, balancing the casserole in one hand, and waited impatiently for him to answer.

The door was jerked open in an angry motion, but his frown disappeared as soon as he saw her. "Jayne?"

"Hi." Now that she was there, she felt like an idiot, but she'd been behaving a lot like one lately. "The library got a new cookbook this week. I read through it and decided to try this recipe."

"And you're looking for a guinea pig?"

"No." The comment offended her. "I wanted to thank you for fixing me dinner the other night and for the ride to work."

"It isn't necessary to repay me."

Jayne sighed. "I know that. But I wanted to do this. Now are you going to let me in, or do I have to stand here while we argue?"

"I don't know—you look kind of appealing like that."

"I didn't think men found 'prim and proper' appealing." She loved turning his own words back on him.

Riley grinned, and his whole face relaxed with the movement. The dark blue eyes sparkled, and Jayne was reminded that he could be devastatingly attractive when he wanted to be.

"Prim and proper women can be fascinating," he said softly.

Jayne sucked in her breath. "Don't play with me, Riley. I'm not good at games. The only reason I'm here is to thank you."

"I should be thanking you—this smells delicious." He stepped aside, and Jayne brought the dish to his kitchen. Riley's apartment was similar to her own, although Riley possessed none of her sense of orderliness. His raincoat had been carelessly tossed over the back of a living room chair, and three days worth of newspapers littered the carpet.

"It's chicken tamale pie," she told him, feeling awkward without the dish in her hands.

"Will you join me?"

Jayne was convinced the invitation wasn't sincere until she remembered his claim that he never said or did anything without meaning it.

"No, my dinner is waiting for me. I just wanted—"

"—to thank me," he finished for her.

"No," she said mischievously. "I came to prove that prim and proper girls have talents you might not expect."

"Given half a chance, I'd say they'd take over the world."

"According to what I remember from Sunday school class, we're supposed to inherit it." She gave him a comical glance. "Or is that the meek and mild?"

"Never meek, Ms. Gilbert." Chuckling, Riley closed the door after her and sighed thoughtfully. He wasn't so sure Jayne was going to control the world as he'd teased, but he was genuinely concerned that he could be falling for her. And then, without much trouble, she'd end up ruling his heart and his life.

He swept a hand across his face, trying to wipe out the memory of her standing in his apartment. Instead, he realized how *right* it had felt to be with her, even if it was only for those few minutes. This woman was entering his life when he was least prepared to deal with it. He was in his thirties and cynical about the world. She was *much* too innocent for him, yet he found himself attracted to her. She touched a vulnerable part of him that Riley hadn't known existed, a softness he thought had vanished long ago.

For both their sakes, it would be best to avoid her.

Several times before her date with Mark, Jayne studied her dating advice books. With Gloria choosing her outfit, Jayne dressed casually, or what was casual for her—a plaid skirt and light sweater. She used lots of mascara and left her hair down. It fell in gentle waves to her shoulders and shone from repeated brushing. Rereading *How to Get a Man Interested in You* while she waited, Jayne mentally reviewed the discussion topics Gloria had given her and recalled her friend's tips on how to keep a conversation going. She hoped Mark would do most of the talking and all that would be required of her was to smile and bat her eyelashes. Granted, that felt a bit false, but she was starting to believe that social interactions, especially male-female ones, often were.

Mark arrived precisely when he said he would. Their evening together went surprisingly well. And fortunately she was farsighted so she had no trouble seeing the screen, even without her glasses. The movie was a comedy with slapstick humor.

After the movie, Mark suggested a cup of coffee.

Jayne agreed, and her hand slid automatically inside her pocket to the list of conversation ideas. But she didn't need them. Mark was a nice man with a huge ego. He spoke in astonishing detail about his position as an office manager. She didn't know why he felt the need to impress her with his importance, but as the books suggested, she fawned over every word, exhausting though that was.

In return she told him she worked for the city, but not in what capacity. Librarians were stereotyped. It didn't matter that she fit that stereotype perfectly. Later, as they went back to her apartment, Jayne thought wryly that Gloria needn't have worried about making up a list of topics to discuss. As she'd originally hoped, Mark had done most of the talking. She should've been relieved, even pleased, but she wasn't. With Mark she felt like...like an accessory.

Outside her apartment door, clenching her keys, Jayne looked up at him. "I had a lovely time. Thank you, Mark."

He placed his hand on the wall behind her and lowered his head. Jayne felt a second of apprehension. She wasn't sure she wanted him to kiss her. Nonetheless, she closed her eyes as his mouth settled over hers for a gentle kiss. Pleasant, but not earth-shattering. "Can I see you again?" he asked, his breath fanning her temple.

"Ah...sure."

"How about dinner Wednesday night? Do you like to dance?"

"Love to," she told him, wondering how quickly a book and CD could teach her. She had about as much rhythm as a piece of lint. The class reunion was bound to have some kind of dancing, and she'd need to learn sooner or later, anyway. She'd check out an instruction book and CD on Monday. Her motto should be *By the Book,* she decided with a satisfied grin.

Monday afternoon, when she was walking home from the bus stop, she heard Riley call her from the parking lot across the street.

"Hello," Jayne called and waved back, feeling unreasonably pleased at seeing him again. He carried his raincoat over his arm, and she wondered if he ever wore the silly thing. She'd only seen it on him once or twice, yet he had it with him constantly.

Checking both sides of the street before jogging across, Riley joined her in front of the apartment building and smiled roguishly when he noted the CDs poking out of her bag. "Don't tell me the books on manhunting didn't help and you're advancing to audio?"

Jayne studied the sidewalk between her shoes. "No, Mark asked me to go dancing, and…I'm not very good at it."

"Two left feet aren't uncommon." Riley resisted the urge to fit his hand under her chin and lift her gaze to his. He wanted to pull her hair free of that confining clasp and run his fingers through it. The thought irritated him. He didn't want to feel these things. This woman was like a red light flashing *trouble.* She didn't hide her desire to get married, or at least find a man, while Riley had no intention of settling down. Yet he was like a moth fluttering dangerously close to that very same light. The light warning there was trouble ahead…

"I went to a few dances in high school, but that was years ago," Jayne said. "Ten, to be exact, and I don't remember much. I don't think just shuffling my feet around will work this time."

"Do you want any help?" The offer slid from his mouth before he could censor it. Silently he cursed himself.

"Help?" Jayne repeated, surprised. "You'd do that?"

He nodded. Yes, he'd do that, just so she'd marry this Mark guy and get out of his life. He sighed. Who was he trying to kid? He'd do it so he could stop wondering how she'd feel in his arms.

"It *would* be easier with a partner," Jayne murmured. She saw Riley's eyebrows drawn together in a dark glower as if he already regretted making the offer. "If you're sure."

"I'll be at your place in an hour."

"Let me cook dinner, then…as a means of thanking you," she added hurriedly.

This cozy scene was going to be difficult enough as it was. "Another time," he said, putting her off gently.

Calling himself every kind of fool, Riley knocked on Jayne's apartment door precisely one hour later. He'd never felt more mixed up in his life. His arms ached for the warm feel of this woman, and yet at the same time he dreaded what that sensation would do to him.

Jayne opened the door, and Riley mumbled something under his breath as he stalked past. She couldn't understand what he was saying. She'd changed out of her "uniform" and into linen pants the color of summer wheat and a soft cashmere sweater. The instruction book that came with the CD was open on the coffee table.

"You ready?" Riley's voice had a definite edge to it.

"Yes, of course," she said too quickly, turning on the CD player. "The first part is a guide to waltzing. The book says…" Feeling ridiculous, Jayne placed her hands on her hips and boldly met his scowl. "Listen, Riley, I appreciate the offer, but you don't have to do this."

"I thought you wanted to learn how to dance."

"I do, but with a willing partner. From the looks you're giving me, one would assume you're furious about the whole idea."

Indecision showed in every weather-beaten feature of his face. "I don't want you to get the wrong impression, Jayne. I'm rotten husband material."

She valued his honesty. He wasn't interested in her, not romantically. They hadn't even gone out on a date. He didn't think of her in those terms, yet he'd made an effort to seek her out, talk to her, be with her. If he wanted to be just friends, it was fine with her. In fact, wasn't friendship what *she* preferred, too? "I think I realized that from the first time I saw you in the elevator. You'd make some poor girl a terrible husband, Riley Chambers. What I don't understand is why you've appointed yourself my fairy godfather."

A slow smile crept into his eyes. "If you turned into a pumpkin at midnight, that might be the best thing all the way around."

"You don't know your fairy tales very well, Mr. Chambers. The coach turned back into a pumpkin. Not Cinderella."

The sweet sounds of a Viennese waltz swirled around them. An instructor's voice rang out. "Gentlemen. Place one hand on the lady's waist…"

Riley bowed elegantly. "Shall we?"

Pretending to fan her face, Jayne batted her lashes and gave him a demure look. "Why, Rhett, you have the most charmin' manner."

Loosely Riley took Jayne in his arms. She followed his lead, and he could tell by the concentration on her face that this was difficult for her. "*One,* two, three. *One,* two, three," the instructor's voice chanted.

"Pretend you're enjoying yourself," he told her, "otherwise Mark's going to think you're in pain."

Jayne laughed involuntarily. She *was* trying too hard. "Don't be so anxious for me to step on your toes."

"I'm not!" Riley positioned his hands so the need to touch her was at a minimum. He adjusted his fingers at her shoulder and then at her hip, all to no avail. Each time his hands shifted, he became aware of the warmth that lay just beneath his fingertips. He tried desperately not to notice.

Swallowing, he concentrated on moving to the music and held his breath. Fairy godfather indeed! He should be arrested for the thoughts that were racing at breakneck speed through his head. This entire situation was ridiculous. Riley had held women far more intimately than he was embracing Jayne, and yet he was acting like a teenage boy on his first date. Briefly he wondered if she had any suspicion of what she was doing to him. He doubted it; knowing Jayne, she'd have to read about it first. Or maybe she had. Maybe this whole thing was an experiment, just like her visit to Soft Sam's. Gritting his teeth, Riley did his utmost to ignore the feel and the flowery scent of the woman in his arms—to ignore the texture of her soft skin, the way her body moved in perfect rhythm with his.

Jayne nodded happily to the music. *One,* two, three... This was going so much better than she'd imagined. Riley was obviously a good dancer, moving confidently with a grace she wouldn't have expected in a man his size. She felt a warmth where he positioned his hands at her waist, and forced her body to relax.

"How am I doing?" she asked after a while.

"Fine," he muttered. He was more convinced than ever that Jayne had no idea what she was doing to him. He had to endure this torture, so he'd do it with a smile. "When you go out with Mark, do you plan to leave your hair up?" He inched back to put some distance between them.

"Probably not."

"Then maybe you should let it down now. You know, to...uh, practice." He couldn't believe he was suggesting this, well aware that he was only making things worse.

"Okay." She reached up and took off the clasp; the dark length fell free.

"What about your glasses?" he asked next, resisting the urge to lift a strand of hair and feel its texture.

"Mark has never seen me in glasses."

"Then take them off."

"All right." She laid her glasses beside the hair clasp on the end table. A fuzzy, blurred Riley smiled down at her.

"No squinting."

"I can't see you close up."

"You won't see Mark, either, so it shouldn't make any difference."

"True," she agreed. But it *did* make a difference. She didn't need her glasses or anything else to know it was Riley's arms around her. When she slid into his embrace once again, it felt completely natural. His hold on her tightened ever so slightly, and when he pressed his jaw against the side of her neck, Jayne's eyes slowly closed. They danced, and she observed that they fit together perfectly.

Riley drew her closer, and Jayne's mind whirled with a confused mixture of emotions. She shouldn't be feeling this. Not with Riley. But she didn't want to question it, not now....

"This feels good," she whispered, fighting the impulse to trace the rugged line of his jaw. He smelled wonderful, a blend of spicy aftershave and—what? Himself, she decided.

Riley smoothed her hair, letting his hand glide down the silky length from the crown of her head to her shoulder. Reluctantly he stopped when the last notes of the waltz faded away.

"Yes, it does feel good," Riley said, his voice husky. *Too good,* his mind added.

He dropped his arms, and Jayne thrilled at his hesitancy when he stepped back. "I don't think you'll have any problems with the waltz."

"I shouldn't have," she said. "Anyway, with Mark all I need to do is look at him with adoring eyes and bat my lashes, and he's happy."

Riley didn't like the idea of Jayne flirting with another man. He knew that didn't make sense, since he was helping her prepare for a date with this Mark guy. "That won't satisfy a man for long," he muttered.

"It'll satisfy Mark," she countered. "I'm not exactly a flirt, you know. I'm not even sure how most women do it."

"It seems to me you're doing a good job learning."

"What do you mean?"

"Just now—dancing. You were practically throwing yourself at me."

"I was not!"

"You sure were."

Jayne was too humiliated to argue. She vaulted across the room and removed the CD. Her hands shook as she returned it to the plastic case. "That was an awful thing to say."

"It's about time you woke up and realized what men are like."

"I've already told you I don't need a fairy godfather."

"You need *someone* to tell you the score."

Jayne glared at him angrily. "And I suppose you're the one to enlighten me."

"Yup. Someone has to. You can't go flaunting yourself the way you just did with me."

"Flaunting?" Jayne almost choked on the word.

"That's right—flaunting." Riley hated himself for the things he was saying. He was both furious and unreasonable—a bad combination.

"*You* were the one who offered to show me how to dance. I…I even told you—"

"You can't tease a man, Jayne," he interrupted, coming to grips with his emotions. "Not me, not Mark, not any man."

"And how many times do I have to tell you I'm not a tease? Honestly, look at me!"

"That's the problem. I *am* looking."

"And?" she whispered, shocked at the tightness of his voice.

"And…" He hesitated. "All I can think about is doing this." He reached for her, taking her in his arms and covering her mouth with his.

Jayne was too stunned to react. The kiss had the sweetest, most tantalizing effect, momentarily causing her to forget the angry censure in his voice.

Regaining her composure—or pretending to—she broke away. "What made you do that?"

The look he was giving her told Jayne he wasn't pleased about that kiss. "I don't know. It was a mistake."

"I…yes." And yet Jayne didn't want to think of it that way.

"You go out with Mark, and we'll leave it at that."

"But—"

"Just go out with him, Jayne."

She dropped her gaze to the carpet. "All right."

Four

After she'd buzzed Gloria in, Jayne jerked open the apartment door. "What took you so long? Mark's due any minute."

Flustered, Gloria shook her head. "If you weren't so afraid to wear your glasses, you'd see exactly what he looks like."

Being the good friend she was, Gloria had volunteered to be there when Mark arrived so she could tell Jayne if he'd be an acceptable date for the high school reunion. Mark's image remained a bit fuzzy in her mind, but as the day of her reunion drew closer, Jayne discovered how badly she wanted to go. But she'd decided early on not to attend without a handsome man at her side. The problem was that Mark was her only likely prospect. And she didn't even know if he'd be interested!

"You look fantastic," Gloria commented, stepping back to examine Jayne's outfit. "Are you sure you can dance in that?"

Jayne had wondered the same thing. The silk blouse

was new, pale blue with a pleated front. The black skirt was standard straight fare, part of her everyday uniform. She'd spent what seemed like hours on her hair, but to no avail. It was too straight and thick to manage. In the end, she'd tied it at the base of her neck with a chiffon scarf that was a shade deeper than her blouse.

"I shouldn't have any trouble dancing." But then she hadn't graduated beyond the waltzing stage. Riley had left soon after their kissing fiasco, and she hadn't seen him since. Every time Jayne thought about what had happened, she grew angry…not with Riley, but with herself. She hadn't meant to flirt with him, but she wasn't so naive that she didn't know what was happening. Pride had demanded that she pretend otherwise. But she regretted the kiss. It had been so wonderful that four days later the warm taste of his mouth still lingered on hers. Nor could she erase the sensation of being held in his arms.

"You're sure I look okay?" Jayne raised questioning eyes to her friend. As it was, she had to drum up enthusiasm for this date.

"You look fine."

"Before, it was fantastic."

"Fantastic, then."

Straightening the chiffon scarf at her neck, Jayne closed her eyes. She had a bad feeling about tonight. If she was honest, she'd admit she'd rather be going with Riley. She felt comfortable with him. Except, of course, for that kiss. And it'd been…not comfortable but exciting. Memorable. However, Riley hadn't spoken to her in days. She wasn't entirely sure he even liked her; the signals she'd received from him were conflicting. It was almost as though he didn't want to be attracted to her but couldn't resist.

The buzzer went, and she cast a frantic glance in Gloria's direction and quickly tucked her glasses inside her purse.

"Calm down," Gloria said. "You're going to have a wonderful time."

"Tell me why I don't believe that," Jayne mumbled on her way to the door.

Riley Chambers pressed the button on his remote control to change channels. He'd seen fifteen-second segments of no fewer than ten shows. Nothing held his interest, and there was no point trying to distract himself. Jayne was on his mind again. Only she didn't flit in and out of his thoughts the way she had before. Tonight she was a constant presence, taunting him. Television wasn't going to help; neither was reading or the internet or any other diversion he could invent.

Standing, Riley paced to the window to stare at the rain-soaked street. He buried his hands in his pockets. So she was going out with this Mark character. Dinner and dancing. He shouldn't care. But he did. The idea of another man with his arms around Jayne disturbed him. It more than disturbed him, it made him completely crazy.

She'd felt so good in his arms. Far better than she had any right to. Days later, he still couldn't banish the feel, the taste, the smell of her from his mind. Avoiding her hadn't worked. Nothing had. She lived three doors down from him, yet she might as well have packed her bags and moved into his apartment. She was there every minute of every night and he didn't like it. What he really wanted to do was exorcise her from his life. Cast those honey-brown eyes from his memory and go about his business the way he was paid to do. *No.* He turned. What he really wanted to do was find out what Mark was like.

Before he could analyze this insanity, he grabbed his raincoat and stormed out the door.

"Hello, Mark." Jayne greeted him with a warm smile. "I'd like to introduce my friend Gloria."

"Hello, Gloria." Mark stepped forward to shake Gloria's hand, then held it far longer than necessary. His eyes caressed her face until Jayne noticed the pink color in her friend's cheeks.

"It's nice meeting you." Gloria pulled her hand free. "But I have to be going."

"No," Jayne objected. "Really, Gloria, stay."

Gloria threw her a look that could have boiled water. "No. You and Mark are going out. Remember?" The last word was issued through clenched teeth.

"The more the merrier, I always say." Mark was staring at Gloria with obvious interest, or what Jayne assumed was interest. She couldn't really tell without her glasses.

"No, I have to go," Gloria insisted.

"That's a shame," Mark said.

There was another knock at the door, and three faces glared at it.

"I'll get that," Jayne said, excusing herself. The few steps across the floor had never seemed so far. It could only be a neighbor, yet she wasn't expecting anyone. Least of all Riley.

"Riley." She breathed his name in a rush of excitement.

His gaze flew past her to Mark and Gloria. "I stopped by—" he paused, suddenly realizing he had to come up with a plausible excuse for his unexpected arrival "—to get the recipe for the casserole you made the other night. It was delicious," he said.

"Of course. Come in, please." Jayne stepped aside, trying to disguise her reaction, and Riley strolled past her.

"Riley Chambers, this is Mark Bauer and Gloria Bailey." Somehow she made it through the introductions without revealing her pleasure at Riley's unexpected visit.

"Pleased to meet you," Mark said stiffly, and the two men shook hands.

"Gloria." Riley nodded in the direction of Jayne's friend.

"Riley lives down the hall from me," Jayne felt obliged to add. "Gloria and I work together," she explained.

Riley nodded.

"I'll get you that recipe," Jayne told him.

"I'll help," Gloria said hurriedly, following her into

the kitchen. "What's going on?" Gloria whispered the minute they were out of sight.

"I don't know."

"You don't really think he cares about that stupid recipe, do you?"

Jayne thought back to all the times she'd been with Riley. He bewildered her. He'd come to the library intent on harassing her, then had looked after her when she was ill. Most surprising had been his willingness to teach her to dance—which had turned into a scene that wouldn't soon be forgotten by either of them. "With Riley, I never know."

"He's here to check out Mark."

Jayne's eyes widened with doubt. "I have trouble believing that."

"Trust me, kiddo, the guy's interested."

"Two men at the same time? The girls of St. Mary's would keel over if they knew." Two men interested in her was a slight exaggeration. The minute Mark had met Gloria he couldn't stop looking at her.

"What are you going to do?" Gloria wanted to know.

"What do you mean?"

"From the look of things, Riley isn't leaving."

Jayne bit her bottom lip. "What should I do, invite him along?"

"Invite us both."

"But what will Mark think?"

"It won't matter. The way Riley's giving him the evil eye, Mark's not likely to risk life and limb by asking you out again."

"Oh, I can't believe this."

"Where's that cookbook?" Gloria whispered, glancing into the living room.

There wasn't any point in looking. "I returned it last week."

"Then tell him that, for heaven's sake!"

Back in the living room, Jayne found the two men sitting on the sofa, staring at each other like angry bears. It was as if one had invaded the other's territory.

Riley stood. Slowly Mark followed suit.

"I'm sorry, Riley, but I returned that book to the library. I'll see if I can pick it up for you, if you'd like."

"Please."

Gloria stepped forward, linking her hands together. "Jayne and I were just thinking that since the four of us are all here maybe we could go out together."

Jayne nodded. "Right," she said boldly. "We were."

"Not dancing." Riley categorically dismissed that.

"There's a new movie at the Lloyd Center," Gloria suggested.

"A movie would be fun." Jayne nodded, looking at Mark. After all, he was supposed to be her date. "We could always eat later."

"That sounds fine," Mark agreed with little enthusiasm.

For that matter, eagerness for this impromptu double date was remarkably absent. The silence in Mark's car as they drove to the shopping complex grated on Jayne's fragile nerves. But she knew better than to even attempt a conversation.

At the theater Mark and Riley bought the popcorn while the two women found seats. The place was

crowded and they ended up far closer to the front than
Jayne liked.

"This isn't working," she whispered.

"You're telling me. The temperature in that car was
below freezing."

"I know. What should I do?" Jayne could hear the
desperate appeal in her own voice.

"Nothing. Things will take care of themselves."
Gloria sounded far more confident than Jayne felt.

The two men returned, and to her delighted surprise,
Riley claimed the seat beside her. Mark took the one
next to Gloria. The women glanced at each other and
shared a sigh of relief. Apparently Mark and Riley had
settled things in the theater lobby.

For his part, Riley wasn't pleased. His instincts told
him Jayne was going to be hurt by this guy. He'd seen
the looks Mark was giving Gloria. Three minutes in
the lobby, and the two men had come to an agreement.
Riley would sit with Jayne, Mark with Gloria. If Jayne
was out to find herself a decent man, he thought grimly,
Mark Bauer wasn't the one. She should look elsewhere.

The theater darkened, and after the previews the
credits started to roll. Jayne squinted, then pulled her
glasses out of her purse. It was ridiculous to pretend
any longer. She doubted Mark had even noticed.

Before they'd entered the theater, Jayne hadn't paid
much attention to the movie they were about to see. She
soon realized it was going to be filled with blood and
gore. She swallowed uncomfortably.

"What's wrong?" Riley whispered and grinned when
he noticed she'd put her glasses back on.

"Nothing." She couldn't think of a way to tell him that any form of violence greatly upset her. She detested movies like this where men treated life cheaply, and grotesque horror was all part of an intriguing plot.

At the first gory scene, Jayne clutched the armrests until her fingers ached and closed her eyes, praying no one was aware of her odd behavior.

"Jayne?"

Riley's voice was so low she wasn't even sure she'd heard him. Opening her eyes, she turned to look at him. "Are you all right?" he asked solicitously.

With a weak smile, she nodded. A blast of gunfire rang from the screen, and she winced and shook her head.

"Do you want to leave?"

"No."

Watching her, Riley wasn't surprised that she was troubled by violence. It fit with what he knew of her— all part of the innocence he'd come to like so much, the goodness he'd come to count on. He didn't want to fall for her, but he knew the signs.

His interest in the movie waned. Her hand still clenched the armrest in a death grip, and with a gentleness he hardly knew he possessed, Riley pried her fingers loose and tucked her hand in his, offering her comfort. She turned to him with a look of such gratitude that it took years of hard-won self-control not to lean forward and kiss her. He didn't like this feeling. Now wasn't the time to get involved with a woman, especially *this* woman. It was too dangerous. For him and possibly for her.

Thursday morning, Gloria was waiting for Jayne on the front steps of the library.

"Morning," Jayne muttered, feeling defeated. She'd been standing at the bus stop when Riley drove past. He hadn't even looked in her direction, and she'd felt as though a little part of her had died at the disappointment. "How did everything go with Mark?" Jayne's original date had taken Gloria home.

"Fine…I guess."

"Did he ask you out?"

"Yeah, but I'm not interested." Gloria wrapped her arms around her waist and shook her head. "I finally figured out what's wrong. Mark reminds me too much of my ex."

"Mark's off my list, as well."

"I would think so. Riley would probably skin him alive if he showed up at your door again."

"I don't understand Riley," Jayne murmured. "He barely even said good-night when he dropped me off. He wouldn't even look at me." And men claimed they didn't understand women! For all her intelligence, all the reading she'd done, Jayne was at a loss to explain Riley's strange behavior. She had thought they'd shared something special during that horrible movie, and then the minute they got outside, he treated her as though she had some contagious disease.

"Who would you rather go to the reunion with? Riley or Mark?"

Jayne didn't need to mull that over. "Riley."

"Then you need to change tactics."

"Oh, Gloria, I don't know. You make this sound like some kind of game."

"Do you want to attend the reunion or not?"

"I do, but…"

"So, form your plan and choose your weapons."

Jayne might not have needed to ponder which man interested her most, but tactics were something else. She liked Riley, and she sensed that her feelings for him could grow a lot more intense. But the opposite side of the coin was the reality that if she chose to pursue a relationship with this man, she could be hurt.

That evening, still undecided about what to do, Jayne was surprised to receive a call from Mark, asking her out again. Apparently the man didn't scare off as easily as Gloria and Riley seemed to think. Or it could be that Mark had noticed Riley's lack of interest following the movie. It didn't matter; she politely declined.

When she didn't see Riley the following day, either, Jayne was convinced he was avoiding her again. Only this time she was armed with ammunition and reinforcement from Gloria.

That evening, Jayne made another casserole from the Mexican cookbook—which she'd taken out again—and delivered it to Riley's door.

Surprise etched fine lines around his eyes when Riley answered her knock.

"Hello." Jayne forced a bright smile.

He frowned, obviously not pleased to see her.

"I brought you dinner." It had all sounded so simple

when she'd discussed her plans with Gloria earlier in the day. Now her stomach felt as though a weight had settled there, and her resolve was weakening more every minute. "It's another casserole from the same cookbook you asked about the other night."

His hand remained on the door. "You didn't need to do that."

"I wanted to." Her smile was about to crumple. "You mentioned it the night Mark was by…. You do remember, don't you?" He still hadn't asked her into his apartment. She wasn't any good at this flirting business. Chagrined, she dropped her gaze to the floor. "I can see you're busy, so I'll just leave this with you."

Reluctantly he stepped aside.

Rarely had Jayne been more miserable. Things weren't supposed to happen like this. According to Gloria, Riley would appreciate her efforts and gratefully ask her to join him.

She moved into his kitchen and saw the box from a frozen microwave dinner sitting on the counter.

After setting the casserole on the stove she removed her oven mitts. "Don't worry about returning the baking dish." She didn't want him thinking she was looking for more excuses to see him. She had been, but that didn't matter anymore. Embarrassed and ill at ease, she gave him a weak smile. "Enjoy your dinner."

"Jayne." His hand on her shoulder stopped her, and when she raised her eyes to his, he pulled away, thrusting his fingers into his hair. "I wish you hadn't done this."

"I know," she said and swallowed miserably. "I won't

again. I…I don't know what I did to make you so upset with me, but your message is coming through loud and clear."

"Jayne, listen. I saw those books you're reading. I'm not the man for you. I told you already—I'd make a terrible husband." He took a step toward her.

"Husband!" she spat. "I'm not looking for a husband."

"Then what *do* you want?" He knew his voice was raised, he couldn't help it. Jayne did that to him. He saw the tears in her eyes and watched as she tried to blink them away. "Then why are you reading those ridiculous books?" he asked.

With her fists clenched, Jayne met his glare. "I have my reasons."

"No doubt." The proud tilt of her chin tore at his heart. He didn't know what Jayne thought she was doing, but if she was serious about a relationship with him, the timing couldn't be worse. The dangers of this undercover assignment were many and real. He had enough to worry about without having his head messed up by a woman. But Jayne wasn't an ordinary woman. He'd known it the first time she'd flared back at him. She was genuine and sweet and, yes, naive. She was also smart and he sensed the passion beneath her demure exterior.

"What you think of me is irrelevant," she said, flexing her hands at her sides. "If you must know, all I really want is to attend my high school reunion. And I'm going even if I have to hire a man to go with me." Her voice rose with every word. "And furthermore, I'm going to learn to dance, and if you won't help me, fine. I'll find someone else who will."

"So *that's* what this is all about? And the casserole is in exchange for dancing lessons?" No way was he addressing the issue of a hired companion. But at least she hadn't mentioned Mark Bauer.

"Yes."

"Fine." He walked across the room and flipped on the radio. Soft music filled the apartment. "Come on, let's dance, if that's all you want."

The invitation held as much welcome as cold charity. Jayne's first response was to throw his offer back in his face, but she managed to swallow her pride. After all, finding a way into his arms was exactly the reason she'd come here tonight.

When she walked into his embrace, he held her stiffly. His tense muscles kept her away from him, so there was only minimal contact.

"You didn't hold me like this the other day," she protested.

Gritting his teeth, Riley brought her closer into his arms. Eyes shut, he breathed in the scent of her hair. She reminded him of springtime, fresh and eager and so unbelievably trusting that it frightened him.

His hands sought her hair. Silky, glorious, just as he'd known it would be. He removed the clasp and let it fall to the floor. His fingers tangled with her hair as a tenderness for the woman enveloped him.

The music changed to an upbeat song with a bubbly rhythm, but their steps remained unchanged. Dancing was only an excuse to hold each other, and they both knew it.

Riley wrapped his arms around her. Their feet barely shifted as the pretense lost its purpose.

Jayne's arms were tight around his neck. She didn't dare move for fear her actions would break this magical spell. There was something strong and powerful about Riley that she couldn't resist. Her mouth found his neck, and her warm breath left a film of moisture against his skin. Lightly she kissed him there.

Riley stiffened, his whole body tensing at her seemingly playful kiss. "Jayne," he breathed. "What are you trying to do to me?"

"The same thing you're doing to me," she answered. Her own voice was weak. "I've never felt like this before…."

The only response he seemed capable of was a groan.

"Riley, kiss me," she said urgently. "Please kiss me."

He angled her head to one side and slanted his mouth over hers with a desperate hunger that burned in him like a raging fire.

He kissed her again with an intensity that drove him beyond his will. His mouth sought hers until they were both weak and trembling.

"Jayne," he whispered harshly, "tell me to leave you alone. Tell me to stop."

"But I like it."

"Don't say that."

"But, Riley, it feels so good. *You* feel so good."

"Jayne," he pleaded, wanting her to stop him. Instead she arched into him, her mouth on his.

"I want to kiss you forever," she whispered.

"Don't tell me that," he said, fighting with everything that was in him and losing the battle with every breath he took.

Instinctively she moved against him, and Riley thought he'd die with the pleasure and pain. He lowered his hands to her waist. "No more of that. Understand?"

"I don't think I do. I never dreamed anything could feel this wonderful."

Riley didn't even hear her as he pressed his mouth to her cheek, her ear, her hair, anyplace but her lips.

"Jayne," he said a moment later. "We have to stop." He pressed his cheek to hers. His eyes were closed, and his breathing was labored as he struggled within himself.

Jayne moved so that her mouth found his, tasting, licking and kissing him until Riley feared she'd drive him mad.

"No more," he said harshly, breaking the contact. He held her away at arm's length, clasping her shoulder. "What's the matter with you?"

Jayne blinked.

"You're acting like a child with a new toy you've just discovered."

"But it feels so good." How flimsy that sounded, even to her.

"And just where did you think this kissing and touching would end?"

"I thought…" She didn't know what she thought.

Riley looked down into Jayne's bewildered face and cursed the anger in his voice. "Listen, maybe you'd better find someone else for these lessons you're so keen to learn."

Jayne swallowed down the hurt. She didn't consider Riley her teacher. She'd believed they were exploring those exquisite sensations together. Her face felt hot with shame.

"Maybe I should!" she cried. "I'm sure Mark would be willing."

"Oh, no, you don't. Not with Mark."

"Who then? It isn't like I've got hordes of admirers lined up, dying to go out with me." Dramatically, she flung out her arm.

"That's not my problem." He attempted a show of indifference. "Find whoever you want. Just stay away from me."

"Don't worry." After this humiliation, she had no intention of ever seeing him again.

She couldn't get out of his apartment fast enough. Once inside her own, she felt tears of hurt and anger burning for release. They rolled down her face, despite all her efforts to hold them back.

Sinking into the soft cushion of her sofa, she buried her face in her hands. She was a twenty-seven-year-old virgin, hurrying to catch up with life, and it had backfired. She'd behaved like an irresponsible idiot just as Riley had claimed.

A loud knock sounded on the apartment door.

Aghast, she stared at it. There wasn't anyone in the world she wanted to see right now.

"Jayne!" Riley shouted. "Open up. I know you're in there."

She was too shocked to move. Riley was the last person she expected to come to her now.

Riley gave a disgusted sigh. "The choice is yours. Either open that door, or I'll kick it down."

His threat was convincing enough to prompt her to unlatch the lock and open the door.

Riley stood in front of her and handed her the oven mitts. "You forgot these."

Wordlessly she took them.

The guilt he felt at the sight of her red eyes knotted his stomach. "I think we'd better talk."

Like a robot, she moved aside. Riley stalked past her and into the apartment. "You want to attend that reunion? Fine. I'll take you."

"Why?"

"Haven't you ever heard that expression about not looking a gift horse in the mouth?"

"But why?"

"Because!" he shouted.

"That's not a reason."

"Well, it'll have to do."

Five

The glorious June sunshine splashed over the street, silhouetting the Burnside Bridge that towered above Riverside Park. The Saturday market was in full swing, and noisy crowds wandered down the busy street. Some gathered to watch a banjo player while others strolled past, their arms heavy with a variety of newly discovered treasures.

Jayne nibbled on a cinnamon-covered "elephant ear" pastry as she strolled from one booth to the next. Riley was at her side, carrying the shopping bag that grew increasingly heavy with every stop.

"I can't believe you've lived in Portland all these months and you didn't know about the Saturday market," she remarked.

"You do most of your shopping here?"

"Just the produce." Jayne offered him a bite of her elephant ear. "They're good, aren't they?"

Chewing, Riley nodded. "Delicious."

Finishing it off, Jayne brushed the sugar from her

fingers and dumped the napkin in the garbage. Riley took her hand and smiled. "Where to next?"

"The fish market. I want to try a new salmon recipe." They strolled down the wide street to the vendor who displayed fresh fish laid out on a bed of crushed ice.

"I didn't know it was legal to catch salmon this small," Riley commented as the vendor wrapped up Jayne's choice.

"That's a rainbow trout," she said and laughed.

"I thought you said you were buying salmon."

"I changed my mind. The trout looked too good to resist."

"At the moment, so do you."

His lazy voice reached through the noisy crowd to touch her heart. Tears filled her eyes, and she quickly looked away, not wanting him to see the effect his words had on her.

The stout vendor handed Riley the fish, and he tucked it in the brown shopping bag. Before his attention returned to her, Jayne brushed the tears from her cheek.

"Jayne." Concern was evident in his tone. "What's wrong?"

She smiled up at him through her happiness. "No one's ever said things like that to me."

"Like what?" His brow compressed.

"That I'm irresistible."

"My sweet little librarian," he said, placing an arm around her shoulders, drawing her close to his side. "You tie me up in knots a sailor couldn't undo."

"Oh, Riley, do I really?" She felt excruciatingly pleased. "I owe you so much."

Despite his efforts not to, Riley frowned. He was grateful that Jayne didn't seem to notice. He wondered how this virtuous librarian, whom he'd once thought of as a prim and proper young woman, could inspire such desire in him. Over the years, he'd been with a number of women. None of them compared to her. None of them had meant to him what she did. At night, unable to sleep, he often lay awake imagining Jayne. This woman tugged, like a swift undercurrent, at his senses. Jayne in bed, soft and mussed, her hair spilling over the pillow. The image of her was so strong that it was a constant battle not to make it real. The intensity of his feelings for her shocked him even now, weeks after having accepted her into his life. This wasn't the time to be caught up with a woman. Losing sight of his assignment could be dangerous. It could cost him his life. But if he hadn't acted when he did, he could have lost *her,* and that thought was intolerable. As soon as this job was over, he was getting out. The time had come to think about settling down. Jayne had done that to him, and he realized for the first time how much he wanted the very lifestyle he'd previously shunned.

Therein lay the problem. Being with her had placed a burden on him. She made him ache with need; at the same time, he experienced the overpowering urge to protect her. This was a dilemma—because there was no one to protect her from him but his own conscience. The weight of that responsibility fell heavily on his shoulders.

"You're very quiet," Jayne commented when they reached the parked car. "Is something wrong?"

"No." He smiled down on her and was instantly drawn into those warm brown eyes.

"I'm glad you came with me."

Riley had to admit he looked for excuses to be with her. Carrying her bags was one, offering her a ride was another. Simple things to do, but they brought him pleasure out of all proportion to the effort they entailed.

They drove back to the apartment building in companionable silence. After parking in his assigned spot, Riley carried her purchases into the building.

"Will you come in?" she asked outside her door.

"Only for a minute."

Setting the shopping bags on the kitchen counter, Riley watched the subtle grace with which she moved around her small kitchen. "I'll have a surprise for you later," she announced.

"Dinner?"

"No. Not that." Every time Riley kissed her, he ended up pulling the clasp from her hair. Her surprise was an appointment with the hairdresser to restyle her hair so that when Riley held her again, he could do whatever he liked with it. "You'll have to come by this evening and see."

"I'll do that."

"Riley?" She turned to him and leaned against the counter, hands behind her back.

He looked at her intent face. "Hmm?"

"May I kiss you?"

"Now?" He swallowed; she didn't make keeping his hands off her easy.

"Please."

"Jayne, listen…"

"Okay." She moved to his side and slipped her arms over his chest to link her fingers behind his neck. Her soft body conformed to the hardness of his.

Riley groaned, finding it nearly impossible to maintain his resolve. He was convinced that she had no idea of the powerful effect she had on him.

"Do you like this?" She pressed her lips to his, and Riley felt his legs weaken. He was grateful for the support of the kitchen counter.

"Yes," he groaned.

She began to kiss him again, straining upward on her toes, but Riley quickly took charge. He kissed her with the hunger that ate at his insides.

Jayne moved restlessly against him, but he broke away.

"No," he said abruptly, his chest heaving. "That's enough."

Jayne hung her head as the heat of embarrassment colored her cheeks. "I'm sorry, Riley."

"Think next time, will you? I'm not some high school kid for you to experiment with. I told you that before." He hated to see the hurt he was inflicting on her, but she didn't seem to understand the stress she was putting him under.

Jayne took a step backward.

He plowed his fingers through his hair. "I'll talk to you later. Okay?"

"Sure."

The door closed, and Jayne winced. Oh, dear, she was doing everything wrong. Riley wanted to cool things down just when she wanted to really heat them up for the first time in her life. Several men had kissed her over the years, but she'd never responded to any of them the way she did to Riley. He didn't merely light a spark; Riley Chambers ignited a bonfire within her. Jayne was as surprised as anyone. She'd thought she was too refined, too shy, trapped with too many hang-ups to experience the very physical desires Riley evoked in her. He'd taught her differently, and now she was riding a roller coaster, speeding downhill ahead of him. If it wasn't so ironic, she'd laugh.

Listening to the radio, Jayne finished putting away the morning's purchases. She changed clothes for her hair appointment and left the apartment soon after one. The beauty salon was a good mile away, but the day was gloriously warm, and she decided to walk instead of taking the bus. She wanted time to think.

As she strolled along, it seemed as if the whole world was alive. She saw and heard things that had passed her notice only weeks before. Birdsong filled the air, as did the laughter of children in the park.

Jayne cut a path through the lush green boulevard, pausing to watch several children swooping high on the park swings. She recognized a little girl from the library's story hour and waved as she continued down the meandering walkway.

Looking both ways before crossing the street, Jayne's gaze fell on Soft Sam's. She gave an involuntary shudder as she remembered the desperation of that first visit.

She'd been so naive, thinking that because the place was in her neighborhood it would fulfill her requirements. Now she couldn't believe she'd even gone inside. She could just imagine what Riley had thought when he first saw her there. He'd warned her about the bar several times since, but he needn't have bothered. People went into Soft Sam's with one thing on their minds, and it wasn't companionship.

Jayne started across the street, and as she stepped off the curb, Riley came into view. He was standing in the doorway of Soft Sam's. She raised her arm, then paused, not knowing if she should call out to him or not. Before she could decide, a tall blonde woman joined him, slipping an arm through his and smiling boldly up at him. Her face was familiar, and it took Jayne several troubled seconds to realize the woman was the same one she'd seen on the evening news.

The hand she'd raised fell lifelessly to her side. Jayne felt as though someone had kicked her in the stomach. The numbing sensation of shock and disbelief moved up her arms and legs, paralyzing her for a moment.

A car horn blared, and she saw that she was standing in the middle of the street. Hurriedly she moved to the other side. Pausing to still her frantically beating heart, she rested her trembling hand on a fire hydrant for support.

Hadn't she just admitted the reason men and women went to a place like Soft Sam's? Riley was there now, and it wasn't his first visit. He could even be a regular customer. And from the looks that…that woman was giving him, they knew each other well.

The pain that went through her was white-hot, and her eyelids fluttered downward.

"Are you all right, miss?"

Jayne opened her eyes to find a police officer studying her, his face concerned.

"I'm fine. I...just felt dizzy for a minute."

The young man smiled knowingly. "You might want to check with a doctor."

"I will. Thank you, officer."

He touched the tip of his hat with his index finger. "No problem. You sure you'll be okay?"

"I'm sure."

With a determination that surprised even her, Jayne squared her shoulders and walked in the direction of the beauty salon. She'd read about men like Riley. If there was a blessing to be found in this, it was learning early on that there was another side to him. One that sought cheap thrills.

Her hand was on the glass door of the salon when she hesitated. She wasn't having her hair done for Riley, she told herself; she was doing it for the reunion. She wanted to go back looking different, didn't she? *None* of this was for Riley. None of it. It was for her.

Three hours later the reflection that greeted her in the salon mirror was hardly recognizable. Instead of thick, straight hair, soft, bouncy curls framed her face. Jayne stared back at her reflection and blinked. She looked almost pretty.

"What a difference," the hairdresser was saying.

"Yes," Jayne agreed. She paid the stylist and left a

hefty tip. Anyone who could create the transformation this young woman had deserved a reward.

Jayne took the bus home. She sat staring out the side window, absorbed in what she'd witnessed earlier. For days she'd been planning this small surprise for Riley. Now she didn't care if she ever saw him again.

But perhaps that was a bit rash. If she was going to break things off, she'd wait until after the reunion. She knew she should be grateful to learn this about him, only she wasn't. The experience of undiluted love had been pure bliss.

Back inside her apartment, Jayne felt the need to talk to someone. She wouldn't mention what she'd seen. For that matter, she doubted she could put words to the emotions that simmered in her heart. She needed human contact so she wouldn't go crazy sitting here alone, thinking. She reached for the phone and called Gloria.

"Jayne, I'm so glad to hear from you," Gloria's voice boomed over the wire.

"Oh. Did something exciting happen?"

"I cannot believe my luck."

"You won the lottery!" It took effort to force some energy into her flat voice.

"Remember when you returned those how-to books about meeting men to the library?"

Of course she did. When Riley had said he'd attend the reunion with her, she hadn't seen any reason to keep them.

"Well, guess who checked them out?"

"Who?" The answer was obvious.

"Me. And, Jayne, guess what? They work! I met this fantastic man in the Albertsons store today."

"At the grocery store?"

"Sure," Gloria said. "Remember how that one book says the supermarket on Saturdays is a great place to meet men? I met Lance in the frozen-food section."

"Congratulations."

"We're going to dinner tonight."

"That's great."

"I have a feeling about this man. He's everything I want. We even like the same things. Looking through our grocery carts, we discovered that we have identical tastes."

"I hate to rain on your parade," Jayne said, smiling for the first time. "But there's more to a compatible relationship than both of you liking broccoli."

"It's not only broccoli, but fish sticks and frozen orange juice. We even bought the same brand of microwave dinners."

The thought of cardboard meals reminded Jayne of Riley's haphazard eating patterns. She did her best to dispel all thoughts of him, with little success.

"I didn't mean to jabber on. You must've called for a reason."

"I just wanted to tell you about my hair."

"Oh, goodness, I was so excited about meeting Lance that I forgot. What does Riley think?"

"He hasn't seen it yet."

"All right, how do *you* feel about it?"

"It's…different."

"I knew it would be," Gloria said with a laugh.

"Listen, I've got to go. I'll talk to you Monday, and you can tell me all about your hot date." On second thought, it had been a mistake to phone Gloria. Jayne's mind was in turmoil, and she wondered if she'd made any sense at all.

"Okay, see you then."

After a few words of farewell, Jayne hung up.

Riley—she assumed it was him—knocked on her door at about seven. Jayne had known he'd come by, but she didn't have the nerve to confront him with what she'd seen. There wasn't anything she could say. The hurt was still too fresh and too poignant.

Careful not to make any noise, she sat reading a new mystery novel. She could immerse herself in fiction and forget for a time.

After three loud knocks he'd left, and she'd breathed easier.

Sunday morning she went out early and returned late. She couldn't avoid him forever, but she needed to put distance between them until she'd dealt with her emotions. When they did meet, she didn't want what she'd learned to taint her reactions.

Early Monday afternoon Riley tossed an empty paper cup in the metal garbage can beside his desk. Jayne was avoiding him. He didn't blame her; he'd hurt her feelings by abruptly putting an end to their kissing. Someday, God willing, there wouldn't be any reason to stop. For now, he had to be in control and for more than the obvious reasons.

The report on his desk made him frown. He didn't

like the sound of this. For that matter, he didn't like anything to do with Max Priestly. The man was a slimeball; Riley always felt as though he needed a shower after being around him. How anyone like Priestly had been elected to public office was beyond Riley.

Standing, he reached for his coat. He'd dealt with enough mud this weekend. He needed a break. Only he wasn't going to get it. He missed Jayne, missed her fresh, sweet scent and the way he felt about himself when he was with her. She brought out the best in him. For the first time in recent memory, he was being noble. Twice now he could have taken what she was so freely offering, and he hadn't. She didn't know or even appreciate his self-control, but in time she would. And he could wait.

A glance at his watch confirmed that he could probably catch her at the library. He'd take her to lunch and ease her embarrassment. There was always the possibility that Priestly would see them together, but it was a relatively small risk and one worth taking. Pulling on his raincoat, he walked out of the office.

His steps echoed on the floor of the main library as Riley made his way to the children's department. He stopped when he found Jayne. At first he didn't recognize her. She looked fabulous. A beauty. She was holding up a picture book to the children gathered around her on the floor.

One small boy raised his hand and said something Riley couldn't hear. Jayne reacted by laughing softly and shaking her head. Leaning forward, she spoke to the group of intent young faces.

Just watching her with those children made Riley's heart constrict. He loved this woman with a depth that astonished him. *Loved her.* The acknowledgment felt right and true. Jayne closed the book, and the kids got up and surged closer, all chattering happily. Seeing her with these children created such intense desire in Riley that for a minute he couldn't breathe. Jayne was everything he could ever want. And a lot more than he deserved.

Gloria moved to Jayne's side and whispered in her ear. Instantly Jayne's gaze darted in Riley's direction. For a moment her eyes held a stricken look but that was quickly disguised. She stood, put the picture book down and said goodbye to the children, then walked over to him.

"Hello, Riley." Her voice held a note of hesitancy.

"Can I take you to lunch?"

She opened her mouth to tell him she'd already made other plans, when Gloria intervened. "Go ahead," Gloria urged. "You haven't had lunch yet. And if you're a few minutes late, I'll cover for you."

There was nothing left for Jayne to do but agree.

Riley's gaze held hers. He wasn't sure he understood the message he found there. Jayne looked almost as though she was afraid of him, but he couldn't imagine why. "I like your hair."

Self-consciously she lifted her hand to the soft curls. "Thank you."

"Where would you like to eat?"

"Anywhere."

Her lack of enthusiasm was obvious. "Jayne, is something wrong?"

Her stricken eyes clashed with his. "No...how could there be?" Immediately her right eye began to twitch.

Riley argued with himself and decided not to pursue whatever was troubling her. Given time, she'd tell him, anyway.

"There's a little restaurant on Fourth. A hole in the wall, but the food's excellent."

"That'll be fine," she said formally.

She knew that his hand at her elbow was meant to guide her. Today it was a stimulation she didn't want or need. It wasn't fair that the only man she'd ever really fallen for preferred women who frequented a sleazy bar—and worse. Remembering the type of people at Soft Sam's, Jayne knew she could never be as worldly and sophisticated as they were. There was no point in even pretending. She wasn't that good an actress.

"You're quiet today." Riley led the way outside to his parked car and in a few minutes pulled into the busy afternoon traffic.

She managed a smile. "I sent in my money for the reunion this morning. It's less than a month away now."

"I'm looking forward to it." Riley studied her, growing more confused by the minute. Whatever was bothering her was more serious than he'd first believed. He forced himself not to pressure her to talk.

"So am I."

"I missed seeing you Saturday evening. You said you had a surprise for me." He found a parking space and pulled into it. "The restaurant's over there. I hope you like Creole cooking."

"That sounds fine."

He noted that she'd avoided responding to his first statement. "I recommend the shrimp-stuffed eggplant."

"That's what I'll order then." It would be a miracle if she could choke down any lunch.

They were seated almost immediately and handed menus. The selection wasn't large, but judging by the spicy smells wafting from the kitchen, Jayne guessed that the food would be as good as Riley claimed.

"I tried to call you Sunday," he told her, setting his menu aside. "I didn't leave a message."

"I rented a car and drove to Seaside for the day."

Riley knitted his brow. She'd left the apartment to get away from him. He would have sworn that was the reason. "You should've said something. I would have taken you."

Jayne lowered her eyes. "I didn't want to trouble you."

"It wouldn't have been any trouble. The trip could have been interesting. I've heard a lot about the Oregon coastline, but haven't had the chance to see it yet."

"It's lovely."

The waitress came, and they placed their order.

Jayne twisted the paper napkin in her lap, staring down at it, not looking at him.

"What did you do in Seaside all day?"

"Walked. And thought." She hadn't meant to admit that.

"And what were you thinking about?"

"You." No point in lying. Her eye would twitch, and he'd know, anyway.

"What did you decide?"

"That I wasn't going to let you hurt me," she whispered fervently.

He'd hurt her in the past and had discovered that any pain she suffered mirrored his own at having done something to upset her. "I would never purposely hurt you, Jayne."

He already had. Her napkin was shredded in half. "I'm different from other women you know, Riley. But being…inexperienced shouldn't be a fault."

"I consider your lack of experience a virtue." He didn't know where all this was leading, but they were on the right path.

A virtue! Jayne almost laughed. He'd gone from her arms to those of that…other woman without so much as a hint of conscience.

Their lunch arrived, and Jayne stared at the large pink shrimp that filled the crispy fried eggplant. She had no appetite.

"Why'd you change your hair?"

Jayne picked up her fork, refusing to meet his probing gaze. "For the reunion."

"Is that the only reason?"

"Should there be another one?"

"You said you had a surprise for me," he coaxed.

"Not exactly *for* you."

"I see." He didn't, but it shouldn't matter.

Tasting a shrimp, Jayne marveled at the wonderful flavors. "This is good."

"I thought you'd enjoy it."

They ate in silence for several minutes. Riley's appetite was quickly satisfied. He'd finished his meal before Jayne was one-third done. He saw the way she toyed with the shrimp, eating only a couple before laying her fork on the plate and pushing it aside.

"I guess I'm not very hungry," she murmured.

Riley crumpled his paper napkin. "Why is it so important for you to go to that reunion?" he asked bluntly.

Jayne had asked herself the same question over and over. Her hand went around the water glass. The condensation on the outside wet her hand, and she wiped her fingers dry on a fresh napkin.

"I'm not sure," she finally said. "I'd like to see everyone again. It's been a long time."

"You've kept in contact with them?"

"A few. Mainly a girl named Judy Thomas. She was the closest friend I had there."

"What about the boys?" They were the ones who worried Riley. Once her male classmates realized what an unspoiled beauty she'd turned out to be, they might give him a run for his money. He wouldn't relinquish this woman easily. He'd waited a lifetime for her.

"There weren't any. I attended a private girls' school."

Riley smiled at the unexpected relief that went through him. "That must have been tough."

"Not really. I attended a women's college, as well."

"So that's where you got your case of repressed relationship development." He tried to make a joke of it but saw quickly that his humor had fallen flat. Riley was baffled at the ready tears that sprang to her eyes.

"Jayne, I didn't mean that the way it sounded." His hand reached for hers.

Jayne jerked her fingers away. "Did you enjoy her, Riley?"

The question was asked in such a small, broken voice that his face tightened with alarm. "Who?"

"The blonde from Soft Sam's."

Six

Regret went through Riley like a hot knife. Little wonder Jayne had been avoiding him. But how could he ever explain this to her? "You saw me?"

"I saw both of you," Jayne whispered. Her soft, pain-filled gaze held his, begging him to tell her it wasn't true. That she was mistaken, and it was only someone who resembled him.

Riley considered lying to her. She might have believed him, but Riley couldn't and wouldn't do it. "I wasn't with her for the reason you think."

Jayne closed her eyes for a moment. "What other reason could there be? I may be inexperienced, but I'm not stupid."

"We're friends." That was a huge exaggeration, but it wouldn't be wise to tell her any more than that for her own safety. Priestly had introduced him to the blonde, and later Riley had used his influence to get her off prostitution charges. By doing so, he'd gotten all the information she could feed him. He couldn't expect

Jayne to understand any of this. For that matter, telling her the truth could put her in danger, and he refused to risk that.

"From the look of it, I'd say you were *very* good friends." To her humiliation, Jayne's voice cracked, but she continued speaking in a hoarse whisper. "How could you go to…her after the wonderful morning we shared? That's what hurts the most, knowing that you—"

"Jayne, I swear on everything I hold dear that I didn't touch her." His deep voice had a fervency she'd never heard from him.

Jayne desperately wanted to believe Riley, but she didn't know if she dared. He had the potential to hurt her more than anyone. Trusting him now could prove to be a terrible mistake later. "Then why were you with her?"

"I told you. She's a friend." His gaze didn't waver under the scrutiny of hers.

Jayne lowered her eyes to the lunch she'd barely tasted. "What does she have that I don't?"

"Jayne…"

"You went from my arms to hers with hardly a breath in between. Tell me. I want to know. What attracted you to this particular *friend* on this particular Saturday?"

Riley hedged. "The arrangements to meet had already been made. I would've met with her even if I hadn't been with you that morning."

"I see."

"I'm sure you don't, and quite honestly, I wouldn't blame you if you didn't believe me. But I'm asking you to trust me." He paused to study her tight features and silently cursed himself for the timing of this relationship. If he was going to fall in love, why did it have to be *now?* He felt torn. There was so much to live for with Jayne in his life. He had to get out of this business, and the quicker the better. For his sake as well as hers.

"I want to trust you." Indecision played across her face.

"Can you believe that I didn't touch her?" he asked.

In response, her eyes delved into his. "I believe you," she murmured. She had to trust Riley or go crazy picturing him in the arms of another woman. The image would destroy her.

"There's only one woman who interests me."

"Oh?"

"One exceptionally lovely woman with honey-brown eyes and a heart so full of love she can't help giving it away." He remembered finding her with the children in the library and again felt such overwhelming desire for her that he ached with it. As he watched her, he could picture her with their child. Until recently, Riley hadn't given much thought to a family. Because of his job, he lived hard, often encountering danger, even when he least expected it. No, that wasn't true; he *always* expected it. He'd seen other men, men with families, attempt to balance their two worlds, and the results could be disastrous. In an effort to avoid that, Riley had pushed any hope of a permanent relationship from his mind, and succeeded. Until he met Jayne.

"Come on," he said, standing. "Let's get out of here." He pulled his wallet from his back pocket and tossed a few bills on the table before waving to someone in the back kitchen. Then he led her outside.

When Jayne moved toward his car, Riley stopped her and directed her to a dark alley.

"I know this isn't the right time or place," he whispered, pressing her against the building's brick wall. His hands were on both sides of her face. "But I need this."

He kissed her hungrily, and Jayne responded the same way.

She couldn't get enough of him. She could feel his kiss in every part of her. Sensations tingled along her nerves. The doubts that had weighed on her mind dissolved and with them the pain of the past two days. Lifting her arms, she slid them around his middle and arched toward him.

"Oh, my sweet Jayne." His voice was raspy and filled with emotion. "Trust me, for just a little longer."

"Forever," she whispered in return. "Forever and ever."

Riley closed his eyes. With his current case he was going to demand a lot more of her trust. He wanted to protect her and himself and walk away from this part of his life and start anew. His prayer was that they could hold on to this moment for all time, but he already knew that was impossible.

When Jayne got back to the library, she was ten minutes late. Her lips were devoid of lipstick and her hair was mussed.

"Sorry I'm late," she said, taking her seat and avoiding Gloria's probing gaze.

"Where'd you go?"

"I...don't recall the name of the restaurant, but they serve Creole food. It's on Fourth."

"They must've been busy."

"Why?" Jayne's eyes flew to her friend.

"Because you're late."

"As a matter of fact, we were lucky to find a table." Her right eye gave one convulsive jerk, and she quickly changed the subject. "Have you heard from Lance?"

"I already told you we're going out again tonight."

"So you did," Jayne mumbled, having momentarily forgotten.

"He's wonderful."

"I'm really happy for you." Who would have believed that after months of searching, Gloria would finally meet someone in the frozen-food section of Albertsons?

"Don't be in too much of a hurry to congratulate me," Gloria said. "It's too soon to tell if he's a keeper. So far, I like him quite a bit, and we seem to have several common interests—besides groceries. But then that's not always good, either."

"Why not?" The more time Jayne spent with Riley, the more she discovered that they enjoyed many of the same things. They were alike and yet completely different.

"Boring."

Jayne blinked. "I beg your pardon?"

Gloria took a chair beside her and crossed her legs.

"Sometimes people are so much alike that they end up boring each other to death."

"That won't be a problem with Riley and me. In fact, I was thinking that although we're alike in some ways, we're quite different in others." Smiling, she looked at Gloria. "I like him, you know. I may even love him."

Gloria smiled back. "I know."

"I'm trying a new recipe for spaghetti sauce, if you'd like to come over for dinner," Jayne told Riley on Friday morning. He gave her a ride downtown most days now and phoned whenever he couldn't. His working hours often extended beyond hers, so she still took the bus home in the evenings. But things had worked out well. Since she arrived home first, she started preparing supper, taking pleasure in creating meals because it gave her an excuse to invite Riley over.

"I'll bring the wine."

"Okay." She smiled up at him with little of her former shyness.

"Jayne—" he paused, taking her hand "—you don't have to lure me to your place with wonderful meals."

Her eyes dropped. She hadn't thought her methods were quite that transparent. "I enjoy cooking," she said lamely.

"I just don't want you going to all this trouble for me. I want to be with you, whether you feed me or not. It's you I'm attracted to. Not your cooking. Well, not *just* your cooking."

"I like being with you, too."

Since their lunch on Monday, they'd spent every available minute in each other's company. Often they didn't do anything more exciting than watch television. One night they'd sat together, each engrossed in a good book, and shared a bottle of excellent white wine. That whole evening they hadn't spoken more than a dozen times. But Jayne had never felt closer to another human being.

Riley kissed her and touched her often. It wasn't uncommon for him to sneak up behind her when she was standing at the stove or rinsing dishes. But he never let their kissing get out of control. Jayne wasn't half as eager to restrain their lovemaking as Riley seemed to be.

That evening Jayne had the sauce simmering on the stove and was ready to add the dry spaghetti to the boiling water when Riley called.

"I'm going to be late," he said gruffly.

"That's fine. I can hold dinner."

"I don't think you should." His voice tightened. "In fact, maybe you'd better eat without me."

"I don't want to." She'd been having her meals alone almost every night of her adult life, and suddenly the thought held no appeal.

"This can't be helped, Jayne."

The city worked its inspectors harder than necessary, in Jayne's opinion. "I understand." She didn't really, but asking a flurry of questions wouldn't help. As it was, his responses were clipped and impatient.

He sighed into the phone, and Jayne thought she

heard a car honk in the background. "I'll talk to you in the morning," he said.

"Sure, the morning will be fine. I'll save some dinner for you, and you can have it for lunch. Spaghetti's always better the next day."

"Great," he said. She heard a loud shout. "I've got to go," he said hurriedly.

"See you tomorrow."

"Right, tomorrow," Riley said with an earnestness that caused a cold chill to race up Jayne's spine. She held on to the phone longer than necessary, her fingers tightening around the receiver. As she hung up, a feeling of dread settled in the pit of her stomach. Riley hadn't been calling her from his office. The sounds in the background were street noises. And he was with someone. A male. Something was wrong. She could feel it. Something was very, very wrong.

Jayne didn't sleep well that night, tossing and turning while her short conversation with Riley played back in her mind. She went over every detail. He'd sounded impatient, angry. His voice was hard and flat, reminding her of the first few times she'd talked to him.

When she finally did drift off to sleep, her dreams were troubled. Visions of Riley with that woman from Soft Sam's drifted into her mind until she woke with an abrupt start. The dream had been so real that goose bumps broke out on her arms, and she hugged her blankets closer.

The following morning, Saturday, Riley was at her door early. Jayne had barely dressed and had just finished her breakfast.

"Morning." She smiled, not quite meeting his gaze.

"Morning." He leaned forward and brushed his mouth over hers. "I'm sorry about last night." He gently pressed his hands against the sides of her neck, forcing her to meet his eyes.

"That's okay. I understand. There are times I need to work late, as well." All her fears seemed trivial now. He was a city inspector, so naturally he didn't spend all his time in an office or on his own. She'd overacted. Her niggling worries about why he'd canceled melted away under the warmth of his gaze.

He broke away from her and walked to the other side of her living room. "This next week is going to be busy, so maybe we shouldn't make any dinner plans."

Jayne rubbed her hands together. "If that's what you want."

"It isn't."

He said it with such honesty that Jayne could find no reason to doubt him.

After a cup of coffee, they left for Riverside Park. Together they did the shopping for the week, making several stops. When they returned to the apartment building, their arms were filled with packages.

"I want to stop off at the manager's," Riley announced as they stepped into the elevator.

"I'll go on up to my place and put these things away." She didn't want the ice cream to melt while Riley paid his rent.

"I'll be up shortly."

The elevator doors closed, and Jayne watched the light that indicated the floor numbers. She smiled at

Riley, recalling similar rides in times past and how she'd dreaded being caught alone with him. Now she savored the moment.

Riley smiled back. Their morning had been marvelous, he thought. It seemed natural to have Jayne at his side, and he'd enjoyed going shopping together like a long-married couple. He experienced a surge of tenderness that was so powerful it was akin to pain. He'd been waiting for this woman for years. He was deeply grateful to have her in his life, especially after the unsavory people he'd been dealing with these past few years. He loved her wry wit. Her sense of humor was subtle and quick. Thinking about it now made him chuckle lightly.

"Is something funny?" She raised wide inquisitive eyes to him.

"No, just thinking about you."

"I'm so glad I amuse you." She shifted her shopping bag from one hand to the other.

"Here." Deliberately he took her bag and set it on the elevator floor. Before she could realize what he was doing, he turned her in his embrace and slid his arms around her waist. "You're the most beautiful woman I've ever met, Jayne Gilbert."

"Oh, Riley." She lowered her gaze, not knowing how to respond. No man had ever said anything so wonderful to her. From someone else it would have sounded like a well-worn line, but she could see the sincerity in his eyes. That told her *he* believed it, even if she couldn't.

"Do you doubt me?"

She answered him with a short nod. "I've seen myself in plenty of mirrors. I know what I look like."

"An angel. Pure, good, innocent." With each word, he drew closer to her. Sweeping her hair aside, he brushed her neck with his mouth. She tilted her head, and the brown curls fell to one side. When his lips moved up her jawline, Jayne felt her legs grow weak. She leaned against the back of the elevator for support. Finally his mouth found hers in a long, slow kiss that left her weak and clinging to him.

The elevator stopped then, and Riley released her for a few seconds, closing the door again.

"Riley, that was our floor," she objected.

"I know." His eyes blazed into hers, and he leaned forward and kissed her again.

Jayne clung to him, awed that this man could be attracted to her. "I can't believe this," she murmured, and tears clogged her throat.

"What? That we're kissing in an elevator?"

"No," she breathed. "That you're holding me like this. I know it's silly, but I'm afraid of waking up and discovering that this is all a dream. It's too good to be true."

"You'd have a hard time convincing me that this isn't real. You feel too right in my arms."

"You do, too."

Her heart swelled with love. Riley hadn't said he loved her, but he didn't need to. With every action he took and every word he spoke, he was constantly showing her his feelings. For that matter, she hadn't told him how she felt, either. It was unnecessary.

Reluctantly he let her go and pushed the button that would open the elevator doors. "I'll be back in a couple of minutes." He grinned. "I need to go all the way down again."

"I'll start the spaghetti."

"Okay." He caressed her cheek. "I'll see you soon."

She stepped out of the elevator and instantly caught sight of a tall man. She didn't recognize him as anyone from her building and certainly not from the ninth floor. Judging by his age, as well as the leather he wore, he could have been a member of some gang. Jayne swallowed uncomfortably and glanced back at Riley. The elevator doors were closing, and she doubted he saw her panicked look.

Squaring her shoulders, Jayne secured her small purse under her arm and moved the shopping bag to her left hand. Remembering a book she'd read about self-defense, she paused to remove her keys from her purse and held the one for her apartment between her index and middle fingers. If this creep tried to attack she'd be ready. Watching him, Jayne walked to her apartment, which was in the middle of the long corridor. Her breath felt tight in her lungs. With every step she took, the young man advanced toward her.

His eyes were dark, his pupils wide. Fear coated the inside of her mouth. Whoever this was appeared to be high on some sort of drug. All the headlines she'd read about drug-crazed criminals flashed through her mind. Getting into her apartment no longer seemed the safest alternative. What if he forced his way in?

Jayne whirled around and hurried back to the elevator, urgently pushing the button.

"You aren't going to run away, are you?" The man's words were slurred.

In a panic, Jayne pushed the button again. Nothing.

He was so close now that all he had to do was reach out and touch her. Lifting one hand, he pulled her hair and laughed when she winced at the slight pain.

"What do you want?" she demanded, backing away.

"Give me your money."

Jayne had no intention of arguing with him and held out her purse. "I don't have much." Almost all the cash she carried with her had been spent on groceries, and she hadn't brought any credit cards. Or her cell phone…

He grabbed her purse and started pawing through it. When he discovered the truth of her statement, he'd be furious, and there was no telling what he'd do next. If she was going to escape, her chance was now.

Raising the bag of groceries, she shoved it into his chest with all her strength and took off running. The stairwell was at the other end of the corridor, and she sprinted toward it. Fear and adrenaline pumped through her, but she wasn't fast enough to beat the young man. He got to the door before she did and blocked her only exit.

Jayne came to an abrupt halt and, with her hands at her sides, moved slowly backward.

She heard the elevator door opening behind her and swung around. Riley stepped out. Jayne's relief was so great she felt like weeping. "Riley!" she called out.

Instantly her attacker straightened.

Riley saw the fear sketched so vividly on her face and felt an overwhelming instinct to protect. Wordlessly he moved toward her pursuer.

The man took one step toward Riley. "Give me your money."

Riley didn't say a word.

In her gratitude at seeing Riley, Jayne hadn't stopped to notice the lack of fear in him. With her back against the wall, her legs gave out, and she slumped helplessly against it.

Riley's face was as hard as granite and so intense that Jayne's breath caught in her lungs. The man who'd kissed her and held her in the elevator wasn't the same man who stood in the hallway now. This Riley was a stranger.

"Hey, buddy, it was just a joke," the young man said, reaching for the doorknob.

Jayne had never seen a man as fierce as Riley was at that moment. She hardly recognized him. Deadly fury blazed from his eyes, and Jayne felt cold shivers racing over her arms.

From there, everything seemed to happen in slow motion. Riley advanced on the young man and knocked him to the ground with one powerful punch.

The man let out a yelp of pain. Riley raised his fist to hit him again. Hand connected with jaw in a sickening thud.

Jayne screamed. "Riley! No more. No more."

As if he'd forgotten she was there, Riley turned back to her. Taking this unexpected opportunity to escape, the man propelled himself through the stairwell door and was gone.

Jayne forced back a tiny sobbing breath and stumbled to his side. She threw her arms around him as tears rained from her eyes. "Oh, Riley," she cried weakly.

Riley's body was rigid against hers for several minutes until the tension eased from his limbs and he wrapped his arms around her. "Did he hurt you?"

"No," she sobbed. "No. He was after my money, but I didn't have much."

His arms went around her with crushing force, driving the air from her lungs.

"If he'd hurt you—"

"He didn't, he didn't." No more words could make it past the constriction in her throat. Jayne realized it wasn't fear that had prompted this sudden paralysis, but the knowledge that Riley was capable of such violence. She didn't want to know what he might've done if she hadn't stopped him.

His hold gradually relaxed. "Tell me what happened," he said, leading her toward her apartment door.

"He wanted my money."

"You didn't do anything stupid like argue with him, did you?"

"No…I read in this self-defense book that—"

"You and your books."

She could almost laugh, but not quite. "I'm so grateful you got here when you did." She was thinking of her own safety, but also of the would-be mugger and what Riley would have done to him had he actually hurt her.

"I've never seen anyone fight like that," she murmured, stooping to pick up her purse and the groceries that littered the hallway.

"It's something I learned when I was in the military." Riley strove to make light of what he'd done. The last thing he wanted to do now was to fabricate stories to appease Jayne's curiosity.

He bent down to gather up some of the spilled groceries. Her hands trembled as she deposited one item after another in her bag.

"Are you sure you're all right?" Doubt echoed in his husky voice.

"Yes. I was more scared than anything."

"I don't blame you."

Her returning smile was wooden. "I surprised myself by how quickly I could move."

Getting to his feet, Riley brought the bag with him. "Let's get these things put away. I'll bet the ice cream is starting to melt."

Rushing ahead of him to unlock the apartment door, Jayne had the freezer open by the time he arrived in her kitchen. He handed the carton of vanilla ice cream to her; she shoved it inside and closed the door.

"Do you think we should call the police?" she asked, still shaking.

"No. He won't be back."

"How do you know?" His confidence was unnerving.

"I just do. But if it'll make you feel better, go ahead and call them."

"I might." She watched for his reaction, but he gave none. Maybe it was her imagination, but she had the distinct feeling that Riley didn't want her to contact the authorities.

Riley paced the floor. "Jayne, listen, I've got something to tell you."

"Yes?" She raised expectant eyes to him.

"I'm going away for a while."

"Away?"

"On vacation. A fishing trip. I'm leaving tonight."

Seven

"A fishing trip?" Jayne asked incredulously. Riley didn't know the difference between a salmon and a trout. "Isn't this rather sudden?"

"Not really. The timing looked good, so we decided to go now, instead of waiting until later in the summer." Riley opened the refrigerator and took out the bowl of spaghetti sauce, setting it on the counter.

Jayne moved to the cupboard and got a saucepan. She worked for the city, too, and knew from experience that vacation times were often planned a year in advance. One didn't simply decide "the timing looked good" and head off on vacation. "How long will you be gone?"

His eyes softened. "Don't worry. I'll be back in time for your reunion."

Jayne was apprehensive, but it wasn't over her high school reunion. This so-called vacation of Riley's had a fishy odor that had nothing to do with trout. Busy at the sink, she kept her back to him, swallowing down her doubts. "You must have had this planned for quite a while."

"Not really. It was a spur-of-the-moment decision." He didn't elaborate, and she didn't ask. Quizzing him about the particulars would only put a strain on these last few hours together.

She *should* ask him about these spur-of-the-moment vacation plans and how he'd arranged it with the city. From what he'd told her, Riley was a city inspector. But Jayne had doubts about that; she couldn't help it. Although he seemed to keep regular hours, he often needed to meet someone at night. She'd watched him several times from her living room window, seeing him in the parking lot below. She'd never questioned him about his late hours, though, afraid of what she'd discover if she pursued the subject.

She bit her bottom lip, angry with herself for being so complacent.

"You've got that look on your face," Riley said when she set the pan of water on the stove to boil.

"What look?"

"The one that tells me you disapprove."

"How could I possibly object to you taking a well-deserved vacation? You've been working long hours. You need a break. Right?"

"Right."

But he didn't sound as though he was excited about this trip. And from little things he'd let drop, Jayne suspected he didn't even know what a fishing pole looked like. He certainly didn't know anything about fish!

Standing behind her, Riley slipped his arms around her waist and pressed his mouth to the side of her neck. "A watched pot never boils," he murmured. "Jayne, listen—I shouldn't be gone any more than ten days. Two weeks at the most."

"Two weeks!" The reunion was in three. Turning, she hugged him with all the pent-up love in her heart. "I'll miss you," she whispered.

"I'll miss you, too." Tenderly, he kissed her temple, then tilted her head so that his mouth could claim hers.

Jayne marveled that he could be so loving and gentle only minutes after punching out a mugger. The whole incident had frightened her. There were depths to this man that she had yet to glimpse, dangerous depths. But perhaps it was better not to see that side of his nature. An icy sensation ran down her arms, and she shivered.

"You're cold."

"No," she said. "Afraid."

"Why?" He tightened his hold. "What do you have to fear?"

"I don't know."

"That mugger won't be back."

"I know." After what Riley had done to him, Jayne was confident the man wouldn't dare return.

Forcing down her apprehension, she smiled and raised her fingers to his thick dark hair, then arched up and kissed his mouth. She was being unnecessarily silly, she told herself. Riley was going on a fishing trip. He'd return before her reunion, and everything would be wonderful again.

Reluctantly breaking away from him, she sighed. "I'll get lunch started. You probably have a hundred things you need to do this afternoon."

"What things?"

"What about getting all your gear together?" She added the dry noodles to the rapidly boiling water, wanting to believe with all her heart that Riley was doing exactly as he'd said.

"The other guy is bringing everything."

"But surely you've got stuff you need to do."

"Perhaps, but I decided I'd rather spend the day with you."

"When are you leaving?" One of her uncles was an avid sportsman, and from what Jayne remembered, he was emphatic that early morning was the best time for fishing.

"Tonight."

"Where will you be? Are you camping?"

He shrugged. "I don't know. I've left all the arrangements to my friend."

That sounded highly questionable, and her manufactured confidence quickly crumpled. Under the weight of her uncertainty, Jayne bowed her head.

"Honey." He tucked a finger beneath her chin, and her eyes lifted to his. "I'll be back in no time."

Despite her fears, Jayne laughed. "I sincerely doubt that." He hadn't even gone, and she already felt an empty void in her life.

"I know how important your reunion is to you."

Riley was more important to her than a hundred high school reunions. A thought went crashing through her mind with such searing impact that for a moment she was stunned. She wondered if she'd finally figured out why Riley paid her so much attention. "You seem awfully worried about my reunion."

"Only because I know how much you want to go."

With trembling hands she brought down two dinner plates from the cupboard. "I don't need your charity or your pity, Riley Chambers."

"What are you talking about?" His jaw sagged open in astonished disbelief.

Jayne's brown eyes burned with the fiery light of outrage. "It just dawned on me that…that all this attention you've been giving me lately could be attributed to precisely those reasons."

"Charity?" he demanded. "Pity? You don't honestly believe that!"

"I don't know what to think anymore. Why else would someone as…as worldly as you have anything to do with someone as plain and ordinary as me?"

Riley stared at her in shock. Jayne, plain and ordinary! Vivacious and outgoing she wasn't. But Jayne was special—more than any woman he'd ever known. He opened his mouth to speak, closed it and stalked across the room. What had gotten into her? He'd never known Jayne to be illogical. From her reaction, he could tell she wasn't falling for this fishing story of his. Telling her had been difficult enough. He hadn't wanted to do it, but there was no other option. He couldn't tell her the real reason for this unexpected "vacation," but he was lying to her for her own protection. The fewer people who were in on it, the better.

Jayne carried the plates to the table, feeling angry, hurt and confused; most of all, she was suspicious. How easily she'd been swayed by his charm and his kisses. She'd been a pushover for a man of Riley's experience.

From the beginning she'd known that he wasn't everything he appeared to be. But she'd preferred to overlook the obvious. Riley was up to no good. She told herself she had a right to know what he was doing, and yet in the same breath, she had no desire to venture into the unknown mysteries he'd been hiding from her.

"Jayne, please look at me," he said quietly. "You can't accuse me of something as ridiculous as pitying you, then walk away."

"I didn't walk away...I'm setting the table." She turned to face him, her expression defiant.

"Charity, Jayne? Pity? I think you need to explain yourself."

"What's there to explain? I've always been a joke to people like you. Except that for a woman who's supposed to be smart, I've been incredibly stupid."

Riley was at a complete loss. His past dealings with women had been brief. In his line of work, it had been preferable to avoid any emotional ties. Now he discovered that he didn't know how to reassure Jayne, the first woman who'd touched his heart. He couldn't be entirely honest, but perhaps a bit of logic wouldn't be amiss....

"Even if you're right and everything I feel for you is of a charitable nature," he began, "what's my motive?"

"I don't know. But then I wouldn't, would I?"

He took a step toward her and paused. He couldn't rush her, although every instinct urged him to take her in his arms and comfort her. "That's not what's really bothering you, is it?"

Tears clouded her eyes as she shook her head. "No."

He reached for her, but Jayne avoided him. "Honey…" he murmured.

She blanched and pointed a shaking finger in his direction. "Don't call me *honey*. I'm not important to you."

"I love you, Jayne." He didn't know any other way to tell her. The flowery words she deserved and probably expected just weren't in him. He could only hope she trusted him—and that she'd give him time.

Jayne's reaction was to place her hand over her mouth and shake her head from side to side.

"Well?" he said impatiently. "Don't you have anything to say?"

Jayne stared at him, her eyes wet. "You *love* me?"

"It can't have been any big secret. You must've known, for heaven's sake."

"Riley…"

"No, it's your turn to listen. I've gone about this all wrong. Women like moonlight, roses, the whole deal." He paced the kitchen and ran a hand through his hair. "I'm no good at this. With you, I wanted to do everything right, and already I can see it's backfiring."

"Riley, I love you, too."

"Women need romance. I realize that and I feel like a jerk because you're entitled to all of it. Unfortunately, I don't know the right words to tell you about everything inside me."

"Riley." She said his name again, her voice gaining volume. "Did you hear what I said?"

"I know you love me," he muttered almost angrily. "You aren't exactly one to disguise your feelings."

She crossed her arms over her chest with an exasperated sigh. "Well, excuse me."

"I'm not good enough for you," he continued, barely acknowledging her response. "Someone as honorable and kind as you deserves a man who's a heck of a lot better than me. I've lived hard these past few years and I've done more than one thing I regret."

Jayne started to respond but wasn't given the opportunity.

"There hasn't been room in my life for a woman. But I can't wait any longer. I didn't realize how much I need you. I want to change, but that's going to take time and patience."

"I'm patient," Jayne told him shyly, her anger forgotten under the sweet balm of his words. "Gloria says I'm the most patient person she's ever known. In fact, my father gets angry with me because he feels I'm too meek...not that meekness and patience are the same thing, you understand. It's just that—"

"Are you going to chatter all day, or are you going to come over here and let me kiss you?" His eyes took on a fierce possessive light.

"Oh, Riley, I love you so much." She walked into his waiting arms, surrendering everything—her heart, her soul, her life. And her doubts.

They kissed, lightly at first, testing their freshly revealed emotions. Then their lips stayed together, gradually parting as their mouths moved, slanting, tasting, probing.

Jayne whimpered. She couldn't help herself. There was so much more she longed to discover....

His kisses deepened until he raised his head and whispered hoarsely. "Jayne. Oh, my sweet, sweet, Jayne."

"I love you," she said again and kissed him softly.

Riley tunneled his fingers through her hair and buried his face in the slope of her neck. But he didn't push her away as he had in the past. Nor did he bring her closer. His breath was rushed as he struggled with indecision.

"Riley…"

"Shhh, don't move. Okay?"

"Okay," she agreed, loving him more and more.

Gradually the tension eased from him, and he relaxed. But his hold didn't loosen, and he held her for what seemed like hours rather than minutes.

They spent the rest of the day together. After lunch they walked in the park, holding hands, making excuses to touch each other. Riley brought along a chessboard and set it up on the picnic table, and they played a long involved game. When Jayne won the match, Riley applauded her skill and reset the board. He won the second game. They decided against a third.

At dinnertime they ate Chinese food at a small hole-in-the-wall restaurant and brought the leftovers home.

Standing just inside her apartment door, Jayne asked, "Do you want to come in for coffee?"

"I've got to pack and get ready."

She nodded. "I understand. Thank you for today."

"No, thank *you*." He laid his hand against her cheek, and when he spoke, his voice was warm and filled with emotion. "You'll take care of yourself while I'm gone, won't you?"

"Of course I will." She couldn't resist smiling. "I've been doing a fairly good job of that for several years now."

"I don't feel right leaving you." He studied her. He wished this case was over so he could give her all the things she had a right to ask for.

"You're coming back."

The words stung his conscience. There was always the possibility that he wouldn't. The risks and dangers of his job had been a stimulant before he'd fallen in love with Jayne. Now he experienced the first real taste of dread.

Fear shot through Jayne at the expression on Riley's face. She saw the way his eyes narrowed, the way his mouth tightened. "You *are* coming back, aren't you?" She repeated her question, louder and stronger this time.

"I'll be back." His voice vibrated with emotion. "I love you, Jayne. I'm coming back to you, don't worry."

Not worry! One glimpse at the intense look in his eyes, and she was terrified. From the way Riley was behaving, one would assume that he was going off on a suicide mission.

Riley smiled and brought his hand to her face. He touched her cheek, then her forehead, easing the frown between her brows. "I'll be back. I promise you that."

"I'll be waiting."

"I won't be able to contact you."

She nodded.

The story about his fishing trip was forgotten. Jayne

didn't know where he was headed or why. For now, she didn't want to know. He said he was coming back, and that was all that mattered.

"Goodbye, my love," he said with a final kiss.

"Goodbye, Riley."

He turned and walked out the door, and Jayne was left with an aching void of uncertainty.

The library was busy on Monday morning. Jayne was sitting at the information desk in the children's department when the chief librarian approached, carrying a huge bouquet of red roses in a lovely ceramic vase.

"How beautiful," Jayne said, looking up.

"They just arrived for you." Her boss placed them on the desk.

"For me?" No one had ever sent her flowers at work.

Gloria walked across the room and joined her. "Who are they from?" she asked, then answered her own question. "It must be Riley."

"Must be." Jayne unpinned the small card and pulled it from the envelope.

"What's it say?" Gloria wanted to know.

"Just that he'll be home by the time these wilt."

"He must have sent them from out of town."

Jayne frowned. "Right." Except that the card was scrawled in Riley's own unmistakable handwriting. He could have ordered them before he went, or…or maybe he hadn't left Portland yet.

She squelched the doubts and possibilities that raced through her mind. She loved Riley and he loved her, and that was all that mattered. Not where he was or what he was doing. Or even whether he was fishing.

Without him, the days passed slowly. Jayne was astonished that a man she'd known and loved for such a short time could so effectively fill her life. Now her days lacked purpose. She went to work, came home and plopped down in front of the television. During the first week that he was gone, Jayne ate more microwave dinners than she'd eaten the whole previous month. It was simpler that way.

"You look like you could do with some cheering up," Gloria commented Friday afternoon.

"I could," Jayne murmured.

"How about if we go shopping tomorrow for a dress to wear to your reunion? I know just the place."

Jayne would need something special for the reunion, but she didn't feel like shopping. Still, it had to be done sooner or later. "All right," she found herself agreeing.

"And in exchange for my expert advice, you can take me to the Creole restaurant where you and Riley had lunch."

"Sure. If I can remember where it is. We only went there once." That day had been so miserable for Jayne that she hadn't paid much attention to the place or the food.

"You said it was on Fourth."

"Right." She remembered now, and she also recalled why she'd been so miserable. That was when she'd seen Riley with the blonde.

Gloria showed up at her apartment early Saturday morning. Jayne had no enthusiasm for this shopping expedition.

Gloria got a carton of orange juice from the refrigerator and poured herself a glass. "I checked out this new boutique, and it's expensive, but worth it."

"Gloria." Jayne sighed. The longer Riley was away, the more unsure she felt about the reunion. "I've probably got something adequate in my closet."

"You don't." Gloria opened the fridge again and peeked inside. "I'm starved. Have you had breakfast yet?"

Jayne hadn't. "I'm not hungry, but help yourself."

"Thanks." Pulling out a loaf of bread, Gloria stuck a piece in the toaster. "When you walk in the grand ballroom of the Seattle Westin, I want every eye to be on you."

"I'll see what I can do to arrange a spotlight," Jayne said.

"I mean it. You're going to be a hit."

"Right." In twenty-seven years, she hadn't made an impression on anything except her mattress.

"Hey, where's your confidence? You can't back down now. You've got the man, kiddo. It's all downhill from here."

"I suppose," Jayne said.

"I thought you should get something in red."

"Red?" Jayne echoed with a small laugh. "I was thinking more along the lines of brown or beige."

"Nope." The toast popped up, and Gloria buttered it. "You want to stand out in the crowd, not blend in."

"Blending in is what I do."

"Nope." Gloria shook her head. "For one night, m'dear, you're going to be a knockout."

"Gloria." Jayne hesitated. "I don't know."

"Trust me. I've gotten you this far."

"But…"

"Trust me."

Two hours later, Jayne was pleased that she'd had faith in her friend's judgment. After seeing the inside of more stores than she'd visited in a year, she found the perfect dress. Or rather, Gloria did—and not in the new boutique she'd been so excited about, either. This was a classic women's wear shop Jayne would never have ventured into on her own. The dress was a lavender color, and Gloria insisted Jayne try it on. At first, Jayne had scoffed; in two hours, she'd dressed and undressed at least twenty times. She was about to throw up her arms and surrender—nothing fit right, or if it did fit, the color was wrong. Even Gloria showed signs of frustration.

Everything about this full-length gown was perfect. Jayne stood in front of the three-way mirror and blinked in disbelief.

"You look stunning," Gloria breathed in awe.

Jayne couldn't stop staring at herself. This one gown made up for every prom she'd ever missed. The off-the-shoulder style and close-fitting bodice accentuated her full breasts and tiny waist to exquisite advantage. The full side-shirred skirt and double lace ruffle danced about her feet. She couldn't have hoped to find a dress more beautiful.

"Do we dare look at the price?" Gloria murmured, searching for the tag.

"It's lovely, but can I afford it?" Jayne hesitated, expecting to discover some reason she couldn't have this perfect gown.

"You can't afford not to buy it," Gloria stated emphatically. "This is *the* dress for you. Besides, it's a lot more reasonable than I figured." She read the price to her, and Jayne couldn't believe it was so low; she'd assumed it would be twice as much.

"You're buying it, aren't you?" The look Gloria gave her said that if Jayne didn't, she'd never speak to her again.

"Naturally I'm buying it," Jayne responded with a wide grin. Excitement flowed through her, and she felt like singing and dancing. Riley would love how she looked in this dress. Everything was working out so well. She'd shock her former classmates. They'd take one look at her in that gown with Riley at her side, and their jaws would fall open with utter astonishment. And yet…that didn't matter the way it once did.

"Now are you going to feed me?" Gloria fluttered her long lashes dramatically as though to say she was about to faint from hunger.

"Do you still want to try that place Riley took me to?"

"Only if we can get there quickly."

Smiling at her friend's humor, Jayne paid for the dress and made arrangements to have it delivered to her apartment later in the day.

She and Gloria chatted easily as they walked out to the street. Gloria drove, and with Jayne acting as navigator, they made their way down the freeway and across the Willamette River to the heart of downtown.

"There it is," Jayne announced as Gloria pulled onto Fourth Avenue. "To your left, about halfway down the block."

"Great." Gloria backed into a parking space. A flash of black attracted Jayne's attention. She glanced into the alley beside the restaurant and saw a sports car similar to Riley's. She immediately decided it wasn't his. There was no reason he'd be here—was there?

"I don't mind telling you I'm starved," Gloria said as she turned off the ignition.

"What's with you lately? I've never known you to show such an interest in food."

"Yes, well, you see…" Gloria paused to clear her throat. "I tend to eat when something's bothering me."

"What's bothering you?" Jayne instantly felt guilty. She'd been so involved with her own problems that she hadn't noticed her friend's.

"Well…"

"Is it Lance?" It had to be. Gloria hadn't talked about him all week, although the week before she'd been bubbling over about her newfound soul mate. "He's not turning out to be everything you thought?"

"I wish." Gloria reached for her purse and stepped out of the car door.

"What do you wish?"

"That he wasn't so wonderful. Jayne, I'm scared. Look at me." She held out her hand and purposely shook it. "I'm shaking all over."

"But if you like him so much, what's wrong?"

They crossed the street together and entered the restaurant, taking the first available booth. "I've been married once," Gloria told her unnecessarily. "And when that didn't work out, I was sure I'd never recover. I know it sounds melodramatic to anyone who hasn't been through a divorce, but it's true."

Gloria was right; Jayne probably couldn't fully understand, but she thought about Riley and how devastated she'd be if they ever stopped loving each other.

"Now I'm falling for another man and, Jayne, I'm so tied up in knots I can't think straight. Being with you today is an excuse not to be with Lance. Every time we're together, the attraction grows stronger and stronger. We're already talking about marriage."

"I guess it works that way sometimes," Jayne murmured, thinking she'd marry Riley in a minute. Gloria had met Lance only a couple of weeks after Jayne had started seeing Riley.

"We both want a family and we believe strongly in the same things."

"Are you going to marry him?"

Gloria shrugged. "Not yet. It's too serious a decision to make so quickly. Remember the old saying? Marry in haste and repent at leisure."

"And…"

"And I haven't told Lance. I know him, or at least I think I know him. He's just like a man."

"I should hope so." Jayne chuckled.

"Once he decides on something, he wants it *now*. I have this horrible feeling that I'm going to tell him I want to wait, and he's going to argue with me and wear me down. He may even tell me to take a hike. There aren't many men around as good as Lance. I could be walking away from the last opportunity I have to meet a decent man."

"If he loves you, he'll agree. And if he's too impatient, you'll have your answer, won't you?"

"No, because knowing me, I'll want him even more."

The waitress came with glasses of water and a menu. They ordered, ate lunch and chatted over several cups of coffee and cheesecake.

Glancing at her watch, Gloria said, "Listen, I've got to get back. Lance is picking me up in an hour."

Drinking the last of her coffee, Jayne stood. "Then let's get going."

Outside the restaurant, Jayne idly checked the alley for the black car as she crossed the street. It was still there. She could have sworn it was Riley's. But it couldn't be. Could it?

Eight

There had to be a thousand black sports cars in Oregon like the one Riley drove, Jayne told herself repeatedly over the next twenty-four hours. Probably more than a thousand. She was being absurd in even wondering if Riley's car was the one in the alley beside the Creole restaurant. He was fishing with friends. Right?

Wrong, said a little voice in the back of her mind. He'd lied about that; Jayne was sure of it. He'd never introduced her to any of his friends. He was new in Portland, having lived in the city for only a few months. He'd admitted there were things in his life he regretted. He'd said he wanted to change and that he wasn't good enough for her.

All weekend, Jayne's thoughts vacillated. Even if he'd lied about the fishing trip, it didn't automatically mean he was doing anything illegal, although those mysterious meetings in the parking lot weren't encouraging. And if he was doing something underhanded, she didn't want to know about it. Ignorance truly was bliss. If she inadvertently found anything out… She simply preferred not to know because then she might be required to act on it.

Monday morning on the bus ride into town, Jayne sat looking out the window, the newspaper resting in her lap. She hadn't heard anything from Riley, but then she hadn't expected to.

She glanced at the headlines. The state senator whom she'd met several months earlier had been arrested and released on a large bail. Apparently Senator Max Priestly, who'd lobbied heavily for legalized gambling in Oregon, had ties to the Mafia. She skimmed the article, not particularly interested in the details. His court date had already been set. Jayne felt a grimace of distaste at the thought that a public official would willingly sell out the welfare of his state.

Setting aside the front-page section, she turned to the advice column. Maybe reading about someone else's troubles would lighten her own. It didn't.

At lunchtime Jayne decided not to fight her uncertainty any longer. She'd take a cab to the Creole restaurant and satisfy her curiosity. The black sports car would be gone, and she'd be reassured, calling herself a fool for being so suspicious.

Only she wasn't reassured. Even when she discovered that the car was nowhere to be seen, she didn't relax. Instead she instructed the driver to take her to Soft Sam's.

The minute she climbed out of the taxi, Jayne saw the familiar black car parked on a nearby side street.

Her heart pounded against her ribs as dread crept up her spine. Absently she handed the driver his fare.

Just because the car was there didn't mean anything, she told herself calmly. It might not even be his.

But Jayne took one glance at the interior, with Riley's raincoat slung over the seat, and realized it *was* his car.

Stomach churning, Jayne ran her hand over the back fender, confused and unsure. From the beginning of this so-called fishing trip, she'd suspected Riley was lying. She didn't know what he was hiding from her or why—she just knew he was.

Her appetite gone, Jayne backed away from the car and returned to the library without eating lunch.

That evening when she arrived at her apartment, Jayne turned on the TV to drown out her fears. The first time she'd ever seen Riley, she'd thought he looked like…well, like a criminal. Some underworld gang member. He wore that silly raincoat as if he were carrying something he wanted to conceal—like a gun.

Slumping onto the sofa, Jayne buried her face in her hands. *Could* he be hiding a weapon? The very idea was ridiculous. Of course he wasn't! She'd know if he carried a gun. He'd held her enough for her to have felt it.

The local news blared from the TV. The evening broadcast featured the arrest of Senator Max Priestly, who'd been caught in a sting operation. This was the same story she'd read in the morning paper.

Jayne stared at the screen and at the outrage that showed on Priestly's face. He shouted that he'd been framed and he'd prove his innocence in court. The commentator came back to say that the state's case had been damaged by the mysterious disappearance of vital evidence.

Deciding she'd had enough unsavory news, Jayne stood and turned off the TV.

In bed that night, she kept changing positions. Nothing felt comfortable. She couldn't vanquish her niggling doubts, couldn't relax. When she did drift into a light sleep, her dreams were filled with Riley and Senator Max Priestly. Waking in a cold sweat, Jayne lay staring at the dark ceiling, wondering why her mind had connected the two men.

Pounding her pillow, she rolled onto her side and forced her eyes to close. A burning sensation went through her, and her eyes opened with sudden alarm. She'd connected the two men because she'd seen Riley *with* Max Priestly. She hadn't met the state senator at the library, as she'd assumed. She'd seen him with Riley. But when? Weeks ago, she recalled, before she'd started dating Riley. Where? Closing her eyes again, she tried to drag up the details of the meeting. It must have been at the apartment. Yes, he was the man in the parking lot. She'd seen Priestly hand Riley a briefcase. At the time, Jayne remembered that Senator Priestly had looked vaguely familiar. Later, she'd associated him with the group of state legislators that had toured the library. But Max Priestly hadn't been one of them.

And Riley wasn't on any fishing trip. If he was somehow linked with this man—and he appeared to be— then he probably knew that Priestly had been arrested. Riley could very well have spent this "vacation" of his awaiting Priestly's bail hearing. No wonder he hadn't been able to give her the exact date of his return.

The first thing Jayne did the next morning was to rip through the paper, eagerly searching for more information. She didn't need to look far. Again Max Priestly dominated the front page. An interview with his secretary reported that the important missing evidence was telephone logs and copies of letters Max had dictated to her. They'd simply disappeared from her computer. When questioned about how long they'd been missing, the secretary claimed that their absence had been discovered only recently. After that, Jayne stopped reading.

The morning passed in a fog of regret. Jayne didn't know what her coworkers must think of her. She felt like a robot, programmed to act and do certain assignments without thought or question, and that was what she'd done.

When Gloria started talking about her relationship with Lance during their coffee break, Jayne didn't hear a word. She nodded and smiled at the appropriate times and prayed her friend wouldn't notice.

"Isn't it terrible, all this stuff that's coming out about Senator Priestly?"

Jayne's coffee sloshed over the rim of her cup. "Yes," she mumbled, avoiding Gloria's eyes.

"The news this morning said he has connections to the underworld. Apparently he was hoping to promote prostitution rings along with legalized gambling."

"Prostitution," Jayne echoed, vividly recalling the bleached blonde on Riley's arm that afternoon. She'd refused to believe he had anything to do with the woman, even though she knew what the woman was. Somehow she'd even managed to overcome the pain of seeing Riley with her. Now she realized that Soft Sam's was more than simply a bar. Riley had repeatedly warned her to stay away from it. She hadn't needed his caution; Jayne had felt so out of place during her one visit that she wouldn't have returned under any circumstances.

After her coffee break with Gloria, Jayne's day went from bad to worse. Nothing seemed to go right for the rest of the afternoon.

That evening, stepping off the bus, she saw Riley's car parked in his spot across the street. He was back. A chill went through her. She wouldn't tell him what she knew but prayed that he loved her enough to be honest with her.

She hadn't been inside the apartment for more than five minutes when Riley was at her door. Jayne froze at the sound of his knock. Squaring her shoulders, she forced a smile on her lips.

"Welcome back," she said, pulling open the door.

Riley took one look at her pale features and walked into the apartment. For nearly two weeks, he'd tried to put Jayne out of his mind and concentrate on his assignment. A mistake could have been disastrous, even deadly. Yet he hadn't been able to forget her. She'd been with him every minute. All he'd needed to do was close his eyes and she'd be there. Her image, her memory, comforted him and brought him joy. *So this was love.* He'd avoided it for years, but now he realized the way he felt was beyond description.

"I've missed you," he whispered, reaching for her.

Willingly Jayne went into his arms. She couldn't doubt the sincerity in his low voice.

"Oh, Riley." His name became an aching sigh as she wound her arms around his neck and buried her face in his chest.

Her tense muscles immediately communicated to Riley that something was wrong. "Honey," he breathed into her hair. "What is it?" His hand curved around the side of her neck, his fingers tangling with her soft curls. He raised her head the fraction of an inch needed for her lips to meet his descending mouth. He'd dreamed of kissing her for days....

Jayne moaned softly. She loved this man. It didn't matter what he'd done or who he knew. Riley had said he wanted to change. Jayne's love would be the bridge that would link him to a clean, honest life. Together they'd work to undo any wrong Riley had been involved in before he met her. She'd help him. She'd do nothing, absolutely nothing, to destroy this blissful happiness they shared.

Their gentle exploratory kiss grew more intense. Riley lifted his head.

"Oh, my love," he moaned raggedly into the hollow of her throat. "I've missed you so much."

"I missed you, too," she whispered in return.

He buried his hands deep in her hair and didn't breathe. Then he mumbled something she couldn't hear and reluctantly broke the contact.

For days he'd dreamed about the feel of her in his arms, yet his imagination fell short of reality. Her lips were warm and swollen from his kisses, and he could hardly believe that this shy, gentle woman could raise such havoc with his senses. "Has anything interesting happened around here?" he asked, trying to distract himself.

"Not really." She shook her head, glancing down so her twitching eye wouldn't be so noticeable. "What about you?" She approached the subject cautiously. "Did you catch lots of fish?"

"Only one."

"Did you bring it back? I can fry up a great trout."

Riley hated lying to her and pursed his lips. He swore that after this case he never would again. "I gave it to…a friend."

"I didn't think you had many friends in Portland." Her voice quavered slightly.

"I have plenty of friends." He raked his hand through his hair as he stalked to the other side of the room. He'd broken the cardinal rule in this business; the line between his professional life and his personal one had been crossed. He'd seen it happen to others and swore it wouldn't happen to him. But it was too late. He'd fallen for Jayne with his eyes wide open and wouldn't change a thing. "So, nothing new came up while I was away?"

Sheer nerve was the only thing that prevented Jayne from collapsing into a blubbering mass of tears. She wanted to shout at him not to lie to her—that she *knew*. Maybe not everything, but enough to doubt him, and it was killing her. She loved him, but she expected honesty. Their love would never last without it.

"While you were gone, I bought a dress for the reunion."

His eyes softened. "Can I see it?"

"I'd like to keep it a surprise."

Unable to help himself, he leaned forward and pressed a lingering kiss to her lips. "That's fine, but you aren't going to surprise me with how beautiful you are. I've known that from the beginning."

Despite her efforts to the contrary, Jayne blushed. "You won't have any problem attending the reunion, will you?" If Riley was mixed up with Senator Priestly, then he probably wouldn't be able to leave the state.

Riley gave her an odd look. "No, why should I?"

"I don't know."

His eyebrows arched. "There's no problem, Jayne, and if there was, I'd do anything possible to deal with it." He wouldn't disappoint her. Not for the world. They were going to walk into that reunion together, and he was going to show her the time of her life.

The phone rang, and Jayne shrugged. "It's probably Gloria," she said as she hurried into the kitchen to answer it.

"I'm going down to collect my mail," Riley told her. "I'll be back in a minute."

"Okay."

Jayne was off the phone by the time Riley returned. He started to sort through a variety of envelopes, automatically tossing the majority of them. "What did Gloria have to say?" he asked with a preoccupied frown.

Jayne poured water into the coffeepot. "It...wasn't Gloria."

"Oh?" He raised his eyes to meet hers. "Who was it?"

"Mark Bauer." She had no reason to feel guilty about Mark's call, but she did, incredibly so.

"Mark Bauer," Riley repeated, lowering his mail to the counter. "Has he made a habit of calling you since I've been gone?"

"No," she said. "Of course not."

Riley responded with a snort. He'd recognized Mark's type immediately. The guy wasn't all bad, just seeking a little companionship. The problem with Mark was that he had the mistaken notion that he was a lady-killer. He kept the lines of communication open with a dozen different women so that if one fell through there was always another. Only this time Mark had picked the wrong woman. Riley wasn't about to let that second-rate would-be player anywhere near Jayne.

"It's true, Riley," Jayne protested. Mark hadn't contacted her in weeks.

"What did he want?"

"He suggested a movie next Saturday."

"And?"

"And I told him I wasn't interested."

"Good." Reassured, Riley resumed sorting through ten days' worth of junk mail.

"But…I'd go out with him if I wanted. It just so happens that I didn't feel like a movie, that's all." If he could lie to her so blithely, she could do the same. Jayne wouldn't have gone out with Mark again, but she didn't need to admit that to Riley.

Swiftly, she retreated into the living room, grabbing the remote and flicking on the TV, hoping to catch the evening news. If the early broadcast gave more details about the Max Priestly case, she could judge Riley's reaction to it.

Riley stiffened as he watched Jayne walk away, her spine straight and defiant. So she'd go out with other men if the mood struck her? Fine. "Go ahead," he announced.

Jayne turned around. "What do you mean?"

"You want to go out with other men, then do so with my blessing." Anger quivered in his voice. He didn't know what game Jayne was playing, but he wanted no part of it.

"I don't need your blessing."

"You're right. You don't." His teeth hurt from clenching them so tightly. "Listen, we're both tired. Let's call it a night. I'll talk to you in the morning."

"Fine." Primly, she crossed her arms and refused to meet his gaze.

But when the door closed, Jayne's confidence dissolved. Their meeting hadn't worked out the way she'd wanted. Instead of confronting Riley with what she'd learned, Jayne had tried to test his love.

After ten minutes of wearing a path in her carpet, Jayne decided that she was doomed to another sleepless night unless they settled this. She'd go to him and tell him she'd seen his car parked at Soft Sam's when he was supposedly fishing with friends. She'd also tell him she remembered seeing him and Senator Priestly in the apartment parking lot. Once she confronted Riley with the truth, he'd open up to her. And they were desperately in need of some honesty.

Standing outside his door, Jayne felt like a fool. Riley

didn't answer her first tentative knock. She tried again, more loudly.

"Just a minute," she heard him shout.

Angrily Riley threw open the front door. His quickly donned bathrobe clung to his wet body. Droplets of water dripped from his wet hair.

"Jayne," he breathed, surprised to see her. "I was in the shower."

She stepped into the apartment, nervously clasping her hands. "Riley, I'm sorry about what I said earlier."

His smile brightened his dark face. "I know, love."

Awkwardly she began pacing. "We need to talk." They couldn't skirt the truth anymore. It had to come out, and it had to be now.

"Give me a minute to dress." He paused long enough to kiss her before disappearing into the bedroom.

Feeling a little out of place, Jayne moved into the living room. "Would you mind if I turned on the television?" she called out. The evening newscast could help her lead into the facts she'd unwittingly discovered.

"Sure, go ahead" came Riley's reply. "Remote's on top of the TV."

As she walked across the room, Jayne caught sight of a reddish leather briefcase sticking out from under the TV. She froze. This was the case she'd seen Senator Priestly hand over to Riley that afternoon so long ago. At least it appeared to be. She hadn't seen many of this color and this particular design.

Trembling, Jayne sank to her knees on the carpet and pulled out the briefcase. Her heart felt as though it was about to explode as she pressed open the two spring locks. The sound of the clasp opening seemed to reverberate around the room. For a panicked second she waited for Riley to rush in and demand to know what she was doing.

When nothing happened, Jayne pushed her glasses higher on her nose and carefully raised the lid. The briefcase was empty except for one file folder and one computer flash drive. Her heart pounding, Jayne opened the file. What she saw caused her breath to jam in her throat. She lifted the sheet that was a telephone log—Senator Priestly's calls. Sorting through the other papers, Jayne discovered copies of the incriminating letters that were said to be missing. Riley had in his possession the evidence necessary to convict Priestly. The very evidence that the police needed.

Feeling numb with shock and disbelief, Jayne quietly closed the case and returned it to its position under the TV.

She was sitting with her hands folded in her lap while Riley hummed cheerfully in the background. She couldn't confront Riley with what she'd found. At least not yet. Nor could she let him know what else she'd learned. If she was going to fall in love, why, oh why, did it have to be with a money-hungry felon?

Hurriedly Riley dressed, pleased that Jayne had come to him. He didn't understand why she'd started acting so silly. It was obvious that they were in love, and two people in love don't talk about dating others. His hands froze on his buttons. Maybe Jayne had seen him with Mimi again. No, he thought and expelled his breath. Jayne wouldn't have been able to hide it this well. He'd known almost instantly that there was something drastically wrong the first time she'd been upset. Something was bothering Jayne now, but it couldn't be anything as major as seeing him with that woman.

Walking into the living room, Riley paused. Jayne's spine was ramrod straight, and tears streamed down her ashen face.

"Jayne," he whispered. "What is it?"

She came to him then, linking her arms around him. "I love you, Riley."

"I know, and I love you, too."

She sobbed once and buried her face in his shoulder.

"Honey, has someone hurt you?" he asked urgently.

She shook her head. "No." Breaking free, she wiped her cheeks. "I'm sorry. I'm being ridiculous. I...don't know what came over me." Immediately her right eye started twitching, and she stared down at the floor. "I just wanted to tell you I regret what happened earlier," she said in a low voice.

"I understand." But he didn't. Riley had never seen Jayne like this. "Are you hungry? Would you like to go out for dinner?" Showing himself in a public restaurant wouldn't be the smartest move, but they could find an out-of-the-way place.

"No," she said quickly, too quickly. "I'm not hungry. In fact, I've got this terrible headache. I should probably make it an early night."

Riley was skeptical. "If you want."

She backed away from him, inching toward the door. "Good night, Riley."

"Night, love. I'll see you in the morning."

Turning, she scurried across the room and out the door like a frightened mouse. More confused than ever, Riley rubbed his jaw. From the way Jayne was behaving, he could almost believe she knew something. But that was impossible. He'd gone to extreme measures to keep her out of this thing with Priestly.

Back inside her apartment, Jayne discovered that she couldn't stop shaking. The Riley Chambers she'd fallen in love with didn't seem to be the same man who'd returned from the fishing trip. Riley might believe he loved her, but secretly Jayne wondered how deep his love would be if he was aware of how much she knew.

Ignorance had been bliss, but her eyes were open now, and she had to take some kind of action. But *what* kind?

She'd refused to believe what the evidence told her about Riley; now she had to accept it. She didn't have any choice. No matter what the consequences, she had to act.

A sob escaped as she thought about that stupid class reunion, which had gotten her into this predicament in the first place. At this point, going back to St. Mary's was the last thing she wanted to do.

Tears squeezed past her tightly closed eyes, and Jayne gave up the effort to restrain them. She let them fall, needing the release they gave her. No one had ever told her that loving someone could be so painful. In all the books she'd read over the years, love had been a precious gift, something beyond price. Instead she'd found it to be painful, intense and ever so confusing.

Jayne didn't bother to go to bed. She sat in the darkened room, staring blankly at the walls, feeling wretched. More than wretched. The bitter disappointment cut through her. She didn't know what would happen to Riley once she talked to the police. If he hadn't already been arrested, they'd probably come for him after that.

Once again she entertained the idea of confronting him with what she'd discovered and asking him to do the honorable thing. And again she realized the impossibility of that request. Riley had lied to her several times. She couldn't trust him. And yet, she still loved him....

As the sky lightened with early morning, Jayne noticed that the clouds were heavy and gray. It seemed like an omen, a premonition of what was to come.

Knowing what she had to do, Jayne waited until she guessed Riley was awake before phoning him.

"I won't be going to work today," she told him, unable to keep the anguish out of her voice.

Riley hesitated. It sounded as if Jayne was ready to burst into tears. "Jayne," he said, unsure of how much to pressure her right now, "honey, tell me what's wrong."

"I've...still got this horrible headache," she said on a rush of emotion. "I'm fine, really. Don't worry about me. And, Riley, I want you to know something important."

"What is it?" Momentarily he tensed.

"I care about you. I'll probably never love anyone more than I love you."

"Jayne..."

"I've got to call the library and tell them I won't be in."

"I'll talk to you this evening."

"Okay," she said hoarsely.

Ten minutes later, she heard him leave. She waited another fifteen and made two brief phone calls. One to Gloria at the library and another to a local cab company, requesting a taxi.

The cab arrived in a few minutes, and Jayne walked out of the lobby and into the car.

"Where to, miss?" the balding driver asked.

She reached for a fresh tissue. She hadn't put on her glasses because she kept having to take them off to mop up the tears. "The downtown police station," she whispered, hardly recognizing her own voice. "And hurry, please."

Nine

Lieutenant Hal Powers brought Jayne a cup of coffee and sat down at the table across from her. She supposed this little room was normally used for the interrogation of suspects. This morning she felt like a criminal herself, reporting the man she loved to the police.

"Now, Ms. Gilbert, would you like to start again?"

"I'm sorry," she murmured, brushing away the tears. "I told myself I wouldn't get emotional, and then I end up like this."

Lieutenant Powers gave her an encouraging smile. Jayne had liked him immediately. He was a sensitive man, and she hadn't expected that. From various mysteries she'd read, Jayne had assumed that the police often became cynical and callous. Lieutenant Powers displayed neither of those characteristics.

She gripped the foam cup with both hands and stared into it blindly. "I live in the Marlia Apartments, and I…have this neighbor. I suspect he may be involved in something that could get him into a great deal of trouble."

"What has your neighbor been doing?" the lieutenant asked gently.

"I think highly of this neighbor, and I…I don't want to say anything until I know what would happen to him."

Lieutenant Powers frowned. "That depends on what he's done."

Jayne took another sip of coffee in an effort to stall for time and clear her thoughts. "To be honest, I can't say for sure that…my neighbor's done anything unlawful. But he's holding something that he shouldn't. Something of value."

"Does it belong to him?"

Jayne's eyes fell to the smooth tabletop. "Not exactly."

"Do you know who it does belong to?"

With dismay in her heart, she nodded.

"Who?"

Jayne was silent. There'd never been a darker moment in her life.

"Ms. Gilbert?"

"What I found," she said as tears once again crept down the side of her face, "belongs to Senator Max Priestly."

The lieutenant straightened. "Do you know how your neighbor got this—whatever it is?"

"It's a briefcase with telephone logs and incriminating letters." Now that she'd finally spilled it out, she didn't feel any better. In fact, she felt worse.

"How did your neighbor get this briefcase?"

"I saw the senator give it to Ril—my neighbor." She

hurried on to add, "He, my neighbor, doesn't realize that I saw the exchange or that I know what's inside."

"How *do* you know?"

Jayne's gaze locked with his. "I looked."

"I see." The lieutenant rose and walked to the other side of the room. "Ms. Gilbert—"

"Could you tell me what will happen to him?"

One side of his mouth lifted in a half smile. "I'm not sure...." He appeared preoccupied as he moved toward the door. "Could you excuse me for a minute?"

"Of course."

Lieutenant Powers left the room, and Jayne covered her face with both hands. This was so much worse than she'd imagined. Her deepest fear was that the police would insist she lead them to Riley. She felt enough like an informer. A betrayer... If only she'd been able to talk to Riley, confront him—but that would've been impossible. Loving him the way she did, she would've been eager to believe anything he told her. Jayne couldn't trust herself around Riley. So she'd done the unthinkable. She'd gone to the police to turn in the only man she'd ever loved.

The door opened, and Lieutenant Powers returned. "I think you two have something you need to discuss."

Jayne suddenly noticed that the lieutenant wasn't alone. Behind him stood Riley.

Jayne's mouth sagged open in utter disbelief.

"I'll wait for you outside," Powers added.

"Thanks, Hal," Riley said as the lieutenant walked out the door.

"Oh, Riley!" Jayne leapt to her feet. "I'm so sorry I had to do this!" she cried through her tears.

"Jayne…"

"No." She held up her hand to stop him. "Please, don't say anything. Just listen. I told you this morning that I love you, and I meant that with all my heart. We're going to get through this together. I promise you that I'll be by your side no matter how long you're in prison. I'll come and visit you and write every day until…until you're free again. You can turn your life around if you want. I believe in you." She spoke with all the fervency of her love.

Riley's mouth narrowed into a hard line.

"You told me once that you wanted to change," Jayne reminded him. "Let me help you. I want to do everything I can."

"Jayne—"

Her hand gripped his. "Riley, I beg you, please, please tell them everything."

He pulled his hand free. "Jayne, honestly, would you stop being so melodramatic!"

Melodramatic? She blinked, unsure that she'd heard him correctly. "What do you mean?"

"There's no need for you to write me in prison."

"But…"

"Jayne, I'm with the FBI. I've been working undercover for six months." Witnessing her distress, Riley cursed himself for not having told her sooner. He also realized that he *couldn't* have told her. Doing so could have put the entire operation in jeopardy. Breaking cover went against everything that had been ingrained in him from the time he was a rookie. But seeing the anguish Jayne had suffered was enough to persuade him that he had to explain.

"Honey, I couldn't tell you."

Stunned, Jayne managed to nod.

"I would've put you in danger if I had."

She continued staring at him. Riley, her Riley, worked for the FBI. She waited for the surge of relief to fill her. None came.

"Why do you have the evidence needed to convict Senator Priestly?" Her voice sounded frail and quavering.

"I'm working undercover, Jayne. I can't really say any more than that."

She didn't understand what being undercover had to do with anything. Then it dawned on her. "You're trying to catch someone else?"

Riley nodded.

"Doesn't that put you in a dangerous position?"

He shrugged nonchalantly. "It could."

Hal Powers stuck his head inside the door. "You two got everything straightened out yet?"

"Not quite," Riley answered for them.

"You want a refill on that coffee?" Powers asked Jayne.

She looked down at the half-full cup. "No, thanks."

"What about you, Riley?"

Riley shook his head, but Jayne noticed the look of respect and admiration the other man gave him.

"This isn't the first time you've done something like this, is it?" she asked.

"She doesn't know about Boston?" Hal stepped into the room, his voice enthusiastic. He paused to glance at Riley. "You've got yourself a famous neighbor, Ms. Gilbert. We even heard about that case out here. Folks call it the second French Connection."

Riley didn't look pleased to have the lieutenant reveal quite so much about his past.

"If you're working undercover, what are you doing here, in the police station?"

"He came to talk to you," Powers inserted.

Riley tossed him an angry glare. "I said I wasn't interested in coffee," he stated flatly.

Powers didn't have to be told twice. "Sure. If you need me, give me a call."

"Right." Riley crossed the room and closed the door behind the other man.

Given a moment's respite Jayne blew her nose and stuffed the tissue inside her purse. Her hand shook as she secured the clasp. She'd made a complete fool of herself.

"How did you know about the briefcase?" Riley asked, turning back to her.

"You were careless, Riley," she said in a small voice. "The corner was poking out from under your TV."

Riley didn't bother to correct her. The briefcase was exactly where it was supposed to be.

"What made you check the contents?" Jayne wasn't the meddling type. She must have suspected something to have taken it upon herself to peek inside that briefcase.

"I saw Max Priestly give it to you weeks ago…before

I knew you. It was late one Saturday afternoon, in the parking lot."

Riley frowned. "Since you seem to have figured out that much, you're probably aware that my fishing trip—"

She gave a tiny half sob, half laugh. "I know. You don't need to explain."

Riley doubted she really knew, but he wasn't at liberty to elaborate. "I didn't want to lie to you. When this is over, I'll never do it again."

Jayne stood up. All she wanted to do now was escape. "I was obtuse. If I hadn't been so melodramatic, as you put it, I would have guessed sooner."

"You did the right thing. I know how difficult coming here must have been."

Jayne didn't deny it. She was sure there'd never be anything more physically or mentally draining—except telling Riley goodbye. Her hand tightened around the strap of her purse as she prepared to leave. "I…"

"Let's get out of here." Riley took her hand and raised it to his lips. "I'm sorry for having put you through this."

She quickly shook her head. "I put myself through it."

"We're done in here," Riley told Lieutenant Powers on the way out the door. He slipped his arm around Jayne's waist. "Where do you want me to drop you off?"

"But…you don't want to be seen coming out of here, do you?"

"Having you with me would make an explanation easier if the wrong person happens to see me. Do you want to go home?"

"Yes, please. I didn't sleep well last night."

Again Riley felt the bitterness of regret. Unwittingly he'd involved Jayne in this situation and put her through emotional distress. Once he was through with the Priestly case, he planned to accept a management position in law enforcement and work at a desk. He'd had enough risk and subterfuge. More than enough. He wanted Jayne as his wife, and he wanted children. He pictured a son and daughter and felt an emotion so strong that it seemed as though his heart had constricted. Jayne was everything honest and good, and he desperately needed her in his life.

The ride back to the apartment building was completed in silence. Although she'd been awake all the night, Jayne didn't think she'd be able to sleep now. Her mind had shifted into double time, spinning furiously as she sorted through the facts she'd recently learned.

When Riley parked the car and walked her into the building, Jayne was mildly surprised. She hadn't expected him to be so solicitous. Besides, she'd prefer to be alone, for the next few hours anyway.

She paused outside her apartment door, not wanting him to come in. "I'm fine. You don't have to stay."

She didn't look fine. In fact, he couldn't remember ever seeing her this pale. "Do you need an aspirin?" he asked, following her inside.

"No." Jayne couldn't believe that he hadn't noticed her lack of welcome. Too much had happened, and she needed time alone to find her place in the scheme of things—if she had a place. Everything was different now. Nothing about her relationship with Riley would remain the same.

"There's aspirin in my apartment if you need some."

"I'm fine," she said again. "Really."

He helped her out of her jacket and glanced at the heap of discarded tissues on the coffee table. The evidence that Jayne had spent a sleepless night crying lay before him. "Honey, why didn't you say something when you found the briefcase?"

She shrugged, not answering.

"You must've been frantic." He picked up the wadded tissues and dumped them in the kitchen garbage. The fact that Jayne had left a mess in her neatly organized apartment told him how great her distress had been. Riley wanted to kick himself for having put her through this.

"I was a little worried," was all she'd admit.

"I can't understand why you wouldn't confront me with what you knew." He'd raised his voice, but his irritation was directed more at himself than at Jayne. Riley didn't know what his response would have been had she come to him, but at least he could have prevented this night of anxious tears.

"I couldn't!" she cried angrily. She pulled another tissue from the box.

Riley frowned tiredly. "Why not?"

"It's obvious that you don't know anything about love," she said sharply. "When you love someone, it's so easy to believe the excuses he or she gives you— because you want to trust that person so badly. You've lied to me repeatedly, Riley…. You've had to. I understand that now. But…but—" She paused to inhale a deep breath. "I couldn't tell you *before* I knew that. I couldn't have counted on you telling me the truth, and worse, I couldn't have trusted my own response."

"Oh, my love." Riley wrapped her in his arms, fully appreciating her dilemma for the first time.

The pressure of his hands molded her against him, and her hands slipped around his neck. Her pulse thundered in her ears when he raised her chin and then she felt the warmth of his mouth on hers. His kiss melted away the frost that had enclosed her heart.

When the kiss was over, Jayne reeled slightly. His hands steadied her. "I've got to get back," he said.

She took a step away from him, breaking all physical contact, trying to put distance between them. It was far too easy to fall into his arms and accept the comfort of his kiss. "I understand. Don't worry about me, Riley. I'll go to bed and probably sleep all day." At least she hoped she would, but something told her differently.

"I'll call you this afternoon."

"Okay," she told him and walked him to the door. He kissed her again briefly and was gone.

Standing in the hallway, Riley felt like ramming his fist through the wall. He would've given anything to have avoided this. She looked so small and lost, her face drained, her expression shocked. He'd thought Priestly and his accomplice would've made their move by now. He'd been waiting days for this thing to be over. Jayne's reunion was this coming weekend; he'd make sure all the loose ends were tied up by then.

Putting on her glasses, Jayne wandered over to the

living room window and watched from nine floors above as Riley, carrying the briefcase, approached his car. He got in and pulled out of the lot and onto the street. Still standing at the window, Jayne saw another car pull out almost immediately after and follow him. Her heart jumped into her throat when she realized that he was being tailed.

Craning her neck, she saw the blue sedan behind him turn at the same intersection. Nervously she rubbed her palms together, wondering what she should do. She had no way of contacting Riley. The only phone number she had was for his apartment, not his cell.

Running into the kitchen, she called the police and asked for Lieutenant Powers, saying it was an emergency.

"Powers here," she heard a moment later.

"Lieutenant," Jayne said, fighting down her panic. "This is Jayne Gilbert. Riley dropped me off at my apartment, and I saw someone follow him."

"Listen, Ms. Gilbert, I wouldn't worry. Riley's been working undercover a lot of years. He can take care of himself."

"But…"

"I doubt anyone would tail Riley Chambers without him knowing about it."

"But he's concerned about me. He may not be paying attention the way he should. Could you please contact him and let him know?" She raised her voice, trying to impress the urgency of her request on him.

"Ms. Gilbert, I don't think—"

"Riley's life could be in danger!"

She could hear the lieutenant's sigh of resignation. "If it'll reassure you, then I'll contact him."

"Thank you." But Jayne wasn't completely mollified; she was also worried about how Riley would react. He wouldn't appreciate her warning. He might even be insulted. As Powers had claimed, Riley had been around a long time. He knew how to take care of himself.

Sagging onto the sofa, Jayne found that her knees were trembling. She couldn't help imagining Riley caught in a trap from which he couldn't escape. Forcefully she dispelled the images from her mind. This wasn't Riley's first case, she reminded herself, and it probably wouldn't be his last. That knowledge wasn't comforting. Not in the least. Loving Riley Chambers wasn't going to work. Could he really change the way he lived? He'd tasted adventure, lived with excitement; a house with a white picket fence would be so mundane to someone like him.

Jayne woke hours later, shocked that she'd managed to sleep. She rubbed a hand along the back of her neck to ease the crick she'd gotten from sleeping with her head propped against the sofa arm. Brilliant sunlight splashed in through her open drapes, and a glance at her watch said it was after five. She suddenly realized that Riley hadn't called. She wouldn't have slept through the ringing of the phone.

Pushing the hair away from her face, she swallowed down the fear that threatened to overtake her. Fleetingly she wondered if Powers had warned him about the blue sedan. She doubted it. It was obvious from their conver-

sation that the lieutenant thought she was overreacting.
Maybe she was.

In an effort to calm her fears, Jayne looked out her
window. His parking space was empty, she noted sadly,
and then felt a surge of relief when his car made a left-
hand turn a block away. She also took consolation from
the knowledge that there wasn't a blue car anywhere
near Riley's.

But her relief quickly died when Jayne noticed a blue
sedan parked on the side street. It might not have been
the same one, but the resemblance was close enough to
alarm her. Jayne was undecided—should she do anything?—until she saw a man climb out of the car. He
paused and looked both ways before crossing the street
to head in Riley's direction.

Jayne's heart flew into her throat when she watched
him step behind a parked car, apparently to wait. It occurred to her that he could be planning to ambush Riley.
Instantly she knew she was right. Jayne could sense it,
could feel the threat. She had to get to Riley and warn
him.

Without another thought, she raced out of her apartment and down the hall. For once, the elevator appeared
immediately. By the time the wide doors opened into
the lobby, Jayne was frantic.

She ran outside and came to an abrupt halt. She
couldn't run up to Riley. She might be putting him in
even greater danger if she intervened now. The thing
to do was remain calm and see what the man planned
to do—if anything.

Walking into the lot, Jayne saw Riley standing beside

his car with the briefcase. He wasn't moving. The other man faced him and had his back to her. Approaching the pair at an angle, Jayne caught a flash of metal. The man had a gun trained on Riley.

Tension momentarily froze her, but she knew what she had to do. She broke into a run.

Riley saw her move, and terror burned through him. A scream rose in his throat as he called out, "Jayne... no!"

Ten

Jayne saw the way Riley's face had become drawn and white as she'd started to run. She didn't know much about martial arts, but after the incident with the mugger, she'd read a wonderfully simple book filled with illustrations. When she'd finished the book, Jayne had felt fairly confident that she could defend herself, if need be. Seeing a gun pointed at Riley's heart was all the incentive she needed to apply the lessons she'd learned.

Unfortunately her skill wasn't quite up to what she'd hoped it would be, and her aim fell far below his chest, possibly because she wasn't wearing her glasses. But where her foot struck caused enough pain to double the man over and send him slumping to the pavement. The gun went flying.

Riley recovered it. His face was pinched and drawn. "For crying out loud, Jayne. I don't believe you." He rubbed a hand over his face. "You idiot! Couldn't you see he had a gun?"

Feeling undeniably proud of herself, Jayne smiled shyly. "Of course I saw the gun."

"Did it ever occur to you that you might've been shot?" he shouted.

She shrugged. "To be honest, I didn't really think of that. I just…acted."

The man she'd felled remained on the ground, moaning. From seemingly nowhere, a uniformed officer appeared and forced him to stand before handcuffing his wrists.

Riley paced back and forth, and for the first time Jayne noticed how furious he was. The self-satisfied grin faded from her face. The least Riley could do was show a little appreciation. "I saved your life, for heaven's sake."

"Saved it?" He shook his head, momentarily closing his eyes. "You nearly cost us both our lives."

"But…"

"Do you think I'm stupid? I knew that Simpson—Priestly's campaign manager and accomplice—was in the parking lot. We were surrounded by three teams of plainclothes detectives. In addition, a squad car was parked on the other side of the building."

"Oh," Jayne replied in a small voice.

"You scared me half to death." He groaned. "And you're the one who hides her eyes during movies." He raked his fingers through his hair. "How do you think I'd feel if something happened to you?" Some of the harsh anger drained from his voice.

"I did what I thought I had to," Jayne returned, feeling faintly indignant.

Riley shook his head again. "I don't think my system could take another one of your acts of heroism. Where did you learn to leap through the air like that?"

"In a book…"

"You mean to tell me you learned that crippling move from something you read?"

"The illustrations were excellent, but I have to admit I was off a bit. I was actually aiming for his chest."

Riley just rolled his eyes.

"Under the circumstances," she said, trying to maintain her dignity, "I thought I did rather well."

Briefly his gaze met hers, and a reluctant grin lifted his mouth. "You did fine, but promise me you'll never, *ever* interfere again."

"I promise." Now that everything was over, reaction set in, and Jayne began to tremble. She'd seen Riley in terrible danger and responded without a thought for her own welfare. Riley was as incredulous as the policemen who milled around, shaking their heads in wonder at this woman who'd downed an armed man.

"Are you all right?" he asked, draping an arm around her shoulders and pulling her close. He savored the warmth of her body next to his.

"I'm fine." She wasn't, but she couldn't very well break down now.

"I've got to go downtown and debrief, write my report. But I'll be back in a couple of hours. Will you be all right until I return?"

"Of course."

Riley hesitated. Jayne was putting on a brave front, but he could tell that she was frightened now that she'd realized what could have happened. He didn't want to leave her, but it was unavoidable.

"I'll walk you to your apartment," he said, wanting to reassure her that everything was under control.

"I'm fine," she insisted in a shaky voice. "You're needed at the station."

"Jayne," he said, then paused.

"Go on," she urged. "I'll be waiting here. I'm not going anyplace."

He dropped a quick kiss on her mouth. "I love you, Jayne." And he did love her—so much that he doubted he could have survived if anything had happened to her.

As he left, Jayne went back to her apartment, telling herself Riley was safe, and that was what mattered most.

An hour later, Jayne reached her decision. It wasn't so difficult, really. She'd known it would come to this sooner or later, and she'd prefer it to be sooner. Again, as she had in the parking lot, she was only doing what she had to.

By the time Riley appeared, she was composed and confident. She opened her door and stepped aside as he entered her apartment. He bent to kiss her, and she let him, savoring the moment.

"We need to talk." She spoke first, not giving him a chance to say anything.

"You're telling me," Riley said with a grin. "I still can't get over you." If he lived for another century, Riley doubted he would forget those few seconds when Jayne had come running toward Simpson. And she'd done it to protect *him*—Riley Chambers. Naturally, she'd been unaware that he wasn't in any danger. All the way back from the jail, Riley was lost in the memory of those brief moments. He'd found himself an exceptional woman. And he wasn't going to lose her. He'd already started looking at diamond rings. On the night of her reunion he was going to ask her to marry him.

"Riley, about the reunion."

"What about it?"

"I've asked Mark to take me."

"What?"

"I want you to know I appreciate the fact that you were willing to attend it with me, but—"

"Jayne, you're not thinking straight," Riley countered, still not believing what she'd said.

She forced out a light laugh. "Actually, I've been giving it some thought over the past few days. This wasn't a sudden decision. When I went to the police this morning, I knew there was every likelihood that you wouldn't be able to go to Seattle with me."

Riley frowned. "So you asked Mark?"

"Yes." Her right eye remained still. Riley had taught her several things, and one of those was how to lie. The smoothness with which she told him this one was shocking. What a sad commentary on their relationship, Jayne mused unhappily. She'd love Riley forever, and years from now, when the hurt went away, she'd be able to look back on their weeks together and be glad she'd known and loved him—however briefly.

Riley clenched his fists. "Something's not right here. You're lying."

"I'm not the expert in that department. You are."

She stalked into the kitchen. "Here," she said, handing him the telephone receiver. "If you don't believe me, call Mark."

Riley stared at the phone in utter astonishment. "Jayne...don't do this." His gut instinct told him she was lying.

"How was I supposed to know you weren't some crook? I couldn't take that chance. So...I asked Mark."

"Then unask him."

"I won't do that."

"Why not?" Riley was becoming angrier with every breath.

"Because I'm not sure you're the type of man I'd want to go with—the type of man I want to be with." The pain of what she was doing was so powerful that Jayne reached out to hold on to the kitchen counter. "I'm sorry, Riley, I am. I've known for some time that things weren't working out."

"Not sorry enough." Abruptly he swiveled around. "I'd suggest you have fun, but I doubt you will with Mark Bauer."

"I'm sure I'll have a perfectly good time," she lied, but the effort to hold back her tears made the words unintelligible.

"Jayne, darling, let me look at you." Dorothy Gilbert held her daughter by the shoulders and shook her gray head. Jayne's parents had met her at the train station. "You look fabulous."

Jayne smiled absently. The train had arrived on time. She was afraid to fly, but she beamed proudly at the thought of the one shining moment in her life when she'd ignored her fear and attacked a gunman. Such ironies were common with her.

"The new hairstyle suits you."

"Thank you, Mom." But the happiness she felt at seeing her parents didn't compensate for the emptiness inside her after that last confrontation with Riley. From her mother's arm, Jayne moved forward to receive her father's gruff embrace.

"Good to see you, sweetie," Howard Gilbert said.

"Thank you, Daddy."

Slowly they walked toward the terminal where Jayne was to collect her luggage.

"That Thomas girl arrived this morning from California. You might want to call her at her parents' house," Dorothy told Jayne as she put an arm around her waist. "She's already called to ask about you."

"I...I'd like to talk to her."

"She's married and has two daughters."

"How nice." Jayne wasn't married. Nor did she have children. She was the prim and proper woman Riley had accused her of being. It was what she'd been destined to be from the time she'd graduated from high school. She had been a fool to believe otherwise. Angry with herself for the self-pitying thoughts, Jayne smiled brightly at her mother.

"Judy said the reception at the Westin starts about eight."

"They mailed me a program, Mom." Jayne had decided she'd attend the reunion alone. Her dream had been to arrive with Riley at her side, but that was out of the question. So, as she'd done most of her life, Jayne would pretend. She'd walk into the reception with her head held high and imagine everyone turning toward her and sighing with envy.

She hadn't seen Riley. Not once since that fateful afternoon. For all she knew he could have moved out of the building. She was grateful he'd accepted her lies, making it unnecessary to fabricate others. She'd purposely hurt him to be kind. She wasn't the right woman for him, and his life was too different from hers.

She'd read about the charges against Priestly and Simpson. The articles and news reports gave an abbreviated version of Riley's part in all this, mentioning only that an FBI agent had worked with police departments statewide to destroy Priestly's organization.

Her father collected her suitcase, and then the three of them walked to the car parked across from the King Street Station.

"I have a lovely new dress," Jayne said.

"I'm so pleased you're attending this reunion, Jayne. I'd been worried you might not want to go." She stared intently at Jayne.

"I wouldn't miss it, Mom."

"Those girls never appreciated you," her father commented, placing Jayne's suitcase in the trunk of the car.

"Nonsense, Dad, I had some good friends."

"She did, Howard."

They chatted companionably on the drive toward Jayne's childhood home on Queen Anne Hill.

Once she got home, Jayne phoned her high school

friend, Judy Thomas, and they chatted for nearly an hour.

"It's so good to talk to you again," Judy said. "I can hardly wait to see you."

"Me, too."

"I think I'd better get off the phone. Dad's giving me disapproving looks just like he did ten years ago."

"I guess we'll always be teenagers to our parents."

"Unfortunately." Judy giggled.

Jayne smiled when her mother stuck her head around the corner. "Don't you think you should start to get ready?"

Jayne contained a smile. Judy was right. They would always be teenagers to their parents. "Okay, Mom, I'll be off in a minute."

"See what I mean?" Judy said.

"Oh, yes. Listen, I'll see you tonight."

"See you then."

Jayne spent most of the next hour preparing for the reunion. Her mother raved about how the dress looked on Jayne. Gazing at her mirrored reflection, Jayne's astonishment was renewed. The dress was the most beautiful one she'd ever owned.

Adding the final touches to her makeup, Jayne heard her mother and father whispering in the background.

"We'd like to get some pictures of you and your young man," her father said when Jayne stepped out of her bedroom.

"Pardon me, Dad?"

"Pictures," he repeated, taking his camera from the case. "Go stand by the fireplace."

"All right." She went into the living room and stopped cold. Before her stood Riley. Tall, polished, impeccable and so incredibly good-looking in his tuxedo that she felt as though all the oxygen had escaped her lungs.

"Riley…what are you doing here?"

"Taking you to the reunion."

"But how did you know—"

"I believe your father wants to take a few pictures." Gently he took her lifeless hand in his and tucked it into his elbow.

Smiling, Dorothy and Howard Gilbert moved into the living room.

"Oh—Mom and Dad, this is Riley Chambers."

Riley came forward and shook hands with her parents. "Glad to see you again, Howard. And good to meet you, Dorothy."

Gruffly, her father motioned for the couple to stand in front of the fireplace while he took a series of photos.

"I believe these young people need a few minutes alone."

"Daddy—"

"You need to talk to your fiancé," Howard said, taking his wife by the arm and leading her into the kitchen.

Jayne didn't move and barely breathed, and she couldn't seem to speak.

"Having her father announce it isn't the most romantic way to tell the woman you love that you want to marry her," Riley said once her parents had left.

"Oh, Riley, please don't."

"Don't what? Love you? That would be impossible."

"No," she whispered miserably, hanging her head. "Don't ask me."

"But I am. Maybe it was presumptuous of me, but I bought a ring." He pulled out a jeweler's box from his inside pocket. "I don't know why you lied about inviting Mark. I don't even care. I love you, and we're going to have a marvelous life together."

"Riley." She swallowed a sob. "No, I won't marry you."

He put the jeweler's box on the mantel behind him and stared at her, his look incredulous. "Why?"

"Because I'm me. I'll never be anything other than a children's librarian. That's all I've ever wanted to be. You live life in the fast lane, while I crawl along at a snail's pace—if you'll forgive the clichés."

"But, Jayne, I'm sick of that life…"

"For how long? A year? Maybe two?"

"Jayne, I've already accepted a job—a desk job—with the Portland police. My undercover days are over."

"Riley, are you sure that's what you want?"

"I've never been more sure of anything." His eyes held a determination that few would challenge. "I've waited half my life for you, Jayne Gilbert, and I'm not taking no for an answer."

The blunt words took Jayne aback. Her lips tightened as she shook her head.

"Do you love me so little?" he asked in a voice that was so soft she could hardly hear it.

"You know I love you!" she cried.

"Then why are you fighting me?"

"I'm…afraid, Riley."

He took a step toward her, extending his hand. "Then put your hand in mine. No man could ever love you more than I do. I'm ready for everything you have to give me. I've been ready for a lot of years."

Jayne couldn't fight him anymore. Tentatively, she raised her hand and placed it in his.

"I believe we have a reunion to attend."

"It isn't necessary. You know that, don't you? All I've ever needed is you." She blinked back tears. "Now, don't make me cry. It took me ages to get this makeup right."

"You're beautiful."

She laughed and reached up to kiss him. "Thank you, but I have trouble believing that."

"After tonight, you won't. I'll be the envy of every man there."

"Then it's true," Jayne said with a trembling smile. "Love is blind."

Riley turned to retrieve the jeweler's box and offered it to her. Smiling tremulously, she let him slide the engagement ring on her finger.

"What would you say to a fall wedding?"

Before Jayne could respond, Howard and Dorothy reappeared, and Dorothy protested, "Oh, no, that's nowhere near enough time!"

"It's fine, Dorothy," Howard said. "The only thing that matters to me is whether our daughter's marrying the right man. And I'm convinced she couldn't find anyone better than Riley." He winked at his wife. "I know you, of all people, can pull off a wedding in four months."

Dorothy gave a resigned sigh. "Have fun, you two," she murmured.

"We will, Mom."

On the way down the sidewalk to Riley's parked car, Jayne gave him an odd look. "When did you talk to my father?"

"A couple of days ago when I asked his permission for his daughter's hand."

"Riley, you didn't!"

He raised his eyebrows. "I did. I told you before that I was going to do everything right with you. We're going to be married as soon as possible—in a church before God and witnesses. We're going to be very happy, Jayne."

A brilliant smile curved her lips. "I think we will, too," she said.

A half-hour later, Riley pulled into the curved driveway of the downtown Westin where the reunion was being held. He eased to a stop, and an attendant opened Jayne's door and helped her out.

They walked through the hotel lobby and took the elevator to the Grand Ballroom.

"Ready?" Riley asked as they approached.

Her breath felt tight in her lungs. "I think so."

One step into the room, and Jayne felt every eye on her. The room went silent as she turned and smiled into the warmth and love that radiated from Riley's gaze.

Whispers rose. And the girls of St. Mary's sighed.

* * * * *

LOVE BY DEGREE

To all my friends at the Vero Beach Book Center—
Chad, Cynthia, Sheila, Debbie, Jamie and Rose Marie.
Thank you for all you do to support my books.

One

The melodious sounds of a love ballad drifted through the huge three-storey house in Seattle's Capitol Hill. Ellen Cunningham hummed along as she rubbed her wet curls with a thick towel. These late-afternoon hours before her housemates returned were the only time she had the place to herself, so she'd taken advantage of the peaceful interlude to wash her hair. Privacy was at a premium with three men in the house, and she couldn't always count on the upstairs bathroom being available later in the evening.

Twisting the fire-engine-red towel around her head, turban style, Ellen walked barefoot across the hallway toward her bedroom to retrieve her blouse. Halfway there, she heard the faint ding of the oven timer, signalling that her apple pie was ready to come out.

She altered her course and bounded down the wide stairway. Her classes that day had gone exceptionally well. She couldn't remember ever being happier, even though she still missed Yakima, the small apple-growing community in central Washington, where she'd been raised. But she was adjusting well to life in the big city. She'd waited impatiently for the right time—and enough money—to complete her education, and she'd been gratified by the way everything had fallen into place during the past summer. Her older sister had married, and her "baby" brother had entered the military. For a while, Ellen was worried that her widowed mother might suffer from empty nest syndrome, so she'd decided to delay her education another year. But her worries had been groundless, as it turned out. James Simonson, a widower friend of her mother's, had started dropping by the house often enough for Ellen to recognize a romance brewing between them. The time had finally come for Ellen to make the break, and she did it without guilt or self-reproach.

Clutching a pot holder in one hand, she opened the oven door and lifted out the steaming pie. The fragrance of spicy apples spread through the kitchen, mingling with the savory aroma of the stew that simmered on top of the stove. Carefully, Ellen set the pie on a wire rack. Her housemates appreciated her culinary efforts and she enjoyed doing little things to please them. As the oldest, Ellen fit easily into this household of young men; in fact, she felt that the arrangement was ideal. In exchange for cooking, a little mothering on the side and a share of the cleaning, Ellen paid only a nominal rent.

The unexpected sound of the back door opening made her swivel around.

"What's going on?" Standing in the doorway was a

man with the most piercing green eyes Ellen had ever seen. She noticed immediately that the rest of his features were strongly defined and perfectly balanced. His cheekbones were high and wide, yet his face was lean and appealing. He frowned, and his mouth twisted in an unspoken question.

In one clenched hand he held a small leather suitcase, which he slowly lowered to the kitchen floor. "Who are you?" He spoke sharply, but it wasn't anger or disdain that edged his voice; it was genuine bewilderment.

Ellen was too shocked to move. When she'd whirled around, the towel had slipped from her head and covered one eye, blocking her vision. But even a one-eyed view of this stranger was enough to intimidate her. She had to admit that his impeccable business suit didn't look very threatening—but then she glanced at his glowering face again.

With as much poise as possible, she raised a hand to straighten the turban and realized that she was standing in the kitchen wearing washed-out jeans and a white bra. Grabbing the towel from her head, she clasped it to her chest for protection. "Who are *you?*" she snapped back.

She must have made a laughable sight, holding a red bath towel in front of her like a matador before a charging bull. This man reminded her of a bull. He was tall, muscular and solidly built. And she somehow knew that when he moved, it would be with effortless power and sudden speed. Not exactly the type of man she'd want to meet in a dark alley. Or a deserted house, for that matter. Already Ellen could see the headlines: Small-Town Girl Assaulted in Capitol Hill Kitchen.

"What are you doing here?" she asked in her sternest voice.

"This is my home!" The words vibrated against the walls like claps of thunder.

"Your home?" Ellen choked out. "But…I live here."

"Not anymore, you don't."

"Who are you?" she demanded a second time.

"Reed Morgan."

Ellen relaxed. "Derek's brother?"

"Half-brother."

No wonder they didn't look anything alike. Derek was a lanky, easy-going nineteen-year-old, with dark hair and equally dark eyes. Ellen would certainly never have expected Derek to have a brother—even a half-brother—like this.

"I—I didn't know you were coming," she hedged, feeling utterly foolish.

"Apparently." He cocked one eyebrow ever so slightly as he stared at her bare shoulders. He shoved his bag out of the doorway, then sighed deeply and ran his hands through his hair. Ellen couldn't help making the irrelevant observation that it was a dark auburn, thick and lustrous with health.

He looked tired and irritable, and he obviously wasn't in the best frame of mind for any explanation as to why she was running around his kitchen half-naked. "Would you like a cup of coffee?" she offered congenially, hoping to ease the shock of her presence.

"What I'd like is for you to put some clothes on."

"Yes, of course." Forcing a smile, Ellen turned abruptly and left the kitchen, feeling humiliated that she could stand there discussing coffee with a stranger when she was practically naked. Running up the stairs, she entered her room and removed her shirt from the end of the bed. Her fingers were trembling as she fastened the buttons.

Her thoughts spun in confusion. If this house was indeed Reed Morgan's, then he had every right to ask her to leave. She sincerely hoped he'd made some mistake. Or that she'd misunderstood. It would be difficult to find another place to share this far into the school term. And her meager savings would be quickly wiped out if she had to live somewhere on her own. Ellen's brow wrinkled with worry as she dragged a brush through her short, bouncy curls, still slightly damp. Being forced to move wouldn't be a tragedy, but definitely a problem, and she was understandably apprehensive. The role of housemother came naturally to Ellen. The boys could hardly boil water without her. She'd only recently broken them in to using the vacuum cleaner and the washing machine without her assistance.

When she returned to the kitchen, she found Reed leaning against the counter, holding a mug of coffee.

"How long has this cozy set-up with you and Derek been going on?"

"About two months now," she answered, pouring herself a cup of coffee. Although she rarely drank it she felt she needed something to occupy her hands. "But it's not what you're implying. Derek and I are nothing more than friends."

"I'll just bet."

Ellen could deal with almost anything except sarcasm. Gritting her teeth until her jaws ached, she replied in an even, controlled voice. "I'm not going to stand here and argue with you. Derek advertised for a housemate and I answered the ad. I came to live here with him and the others and—"

"The *others?*" Reed choked on his mouthful of coffee. "You mean there's more of you around?"

Expelling her breath slowly, Ellen met his scowl. "There's Derek, Pat and—"

"Is Pat male or female?" The sheer strength of his personality seemed to fill the kitchen. But Ellen refused to be intimidated.

"Pat is a male friend who attends classes at the university with Derek and me."

"So you're all students?"

"Yes."

"All freshmen?"

"Yes."

He eyed her curiously. "Aren't you a bit old for that?"

"I'm twenty-five." She wasn't about to explain her circumstances to this man.

The sound of the front door opening and closing drew their attention to the opposite end of the house. Carrying an armload of books, Derek Morgan sauntered into the kitchen and stopped cold when he caught sight of his older brother.

"Hi, Reed." Uncertain eyes flew to Ellen as if seeking reassurance. A worried look pinched the boyishly

Send For
2 FREE BOOKS
Today!

I accept your offer!

Please send me two free
Romance novels and two
mystery gifts (gifts worth about
$10). I understand that these
books are completely free—
even the shipping and handling
will be paid—and I am under no
obligation to purchase anything,
ever, as explained on the back of
this card.

194/394 MDL FH92

Please Print

FIRST NAME

LAST NAME

ADDRESS

APT.#   CITY

STATE/PROV.   ZIP/POSTAL CODE

Visit us online at
www.ReaderService.com

handsome face. Slowly, he placed his books on the counter.

"Derek."

"I see you've met Ellen." Derek's welcoming smile was decidedly forced.

"We more or less stumbled into each other." Derek's stiff shoulders relaxed as Reed straightened and set the mug aside.

"I didn't expect you back so soon."

Momentarily, Reed's gaze slid to Ellen. "That much is obvious. Do you want to tell me what's going on here, little brother?"

"It's not as bad is it looks."

"Right now it doesn't look particularly good."

"I can explain everything."

"I hope so."

Nervously swinging her arms, Ellen stepped forward. "If you two will excuse me, I'll be up in my room." The last thing she wanted was to find herself stuck between the two brothers while they settled their differences.

"No, don't go," Derek said quickly. His dark eyes pleaded with her to stay.

Almost involuntarily Ellen glanced at Reed for guidance.

"By all means, stay." But his expression wasn't encouraging.

A growing sense of resentment made her arch her back and thrust out her chin defiantly. Who was this... this *man* to burst into their tranquil lives and raise havoc? The four of them lived congenially together, all doing their parts in the smooth running of the household.

"Are you charging rent?" Reed asked.

Briefly Derek's eyes met Ellen's. "It makes sense, doesn't it? This big old house has practically as many bedrooms as a dorm. I didn't think it would hurt." He swallowed. "I mean, with you being in the Middle East and all. The house was...so empty."

"How much are you paying?" Reed directed the question at Ellen. That sarcastic look was back and Ellen hesitated.

"How much?" Reed repeated.

Ellen knew from the way Derek's eyes widened that they were entering into dangerous territory.

"It's different with Ellen," Derek hurried to explain. "She does all the shopping and the cooking, so the rest of us—"

"Are you sure that's all she provides?" Reed interrupted harshly.

Ellen's gaze didn't waver. "I pay thirty dollars a week, but believe me, I earn my keep." The second the words slipped out, Ellen wanted to take them back.

"I'm sure you do."

Ellen was too furious and outraged to speak. How dared he barge into this house and immediately assume the worst? All right, she'd been walking around half-naked, but she hadn't exactly been expecting company.

Angrily Derek stepped forward. "It's not like that, Reed."

"I discovered her prancing around the kitchen in her bra. What else am I supposed to think?"

Derek groaned and cast an accusing look at Ellen. "I just ran down to get the pie out of the oven," she said in her own defence.

"Let me assure you," Derek said, his voice quavering with righteousness. "You've got this all wrong." He glared indignantly at his older brother. "Ellen isn't that kind of woman. I resent the implication. You owe us both an apology."

From the stunned look on Reed's face, Ellen surmised that this could well be the first time Derek had stood up to his domineering brother. Her impulse was to clap her hands and shout: "Attaboy!" With immense effort she restrained herself.

Reed wiped a hand over his face and pinched the bridge of his nose. "Perhaps I do."

The front door opened and closed again. "Anyone here?" Monte's eager voice rang from the living room. The slam of his books hitting the stairs echoed through the hallway that led to the kitchen. "Something smells good." Skidding to an abrupt halt just inside the room, the tall student looked around at the somber faces. "What's up? You three look like you're about to attend a funeral."

"Are you Pat?" Reed asked.

"No, Monte."

Reed closed his eyes and wearily rubbed the back of his neck. "Just how many bedrooms have you rented out?"

Derek lowered his gaze to his hands. "Three."

"My room?" Reed asked.

"Yes, well, Ellen needed a place and it seemed logical to give her that one. You were supposed to be gone for a year. What happened?"

"I came home early."

Stepping forward, her fingers nervously laced together, Ellen broke into the tense interchange. "I'll move up a floor. I don't mind." No one was using the third floor of the house, which had at one time been reserved for the servants. The rooms were small and airless, but sleeping there was preferable to suffering the wrath of Derek's brother. Or worse, having to find somewhere else to live.

Reed responded with a dismissive gesture of his hand. "Don't worry about it. Until things are straightened out, I'll sleep up there. Once I've taken a long, hot shower and gotten some rest I might be able to make sense out of this mess."

"No, please," Ellen persisted. "If I'm in your room, then I should move."

"No," Reed grumbled on his way out the door, waving aside her offer. "It's only my house. I'll sleep in the servants' quarters."

Before Ellen could argue further, Reed was out of the kitchen and halfway up the stairs.

"Is there a problem?" Monte asked, opening the refrigerator. He didn't seem very concerned, but then he rarely worried about anything unless it directly affected his stomach. Ellen didn't know how any one person could eat so much. He never seemed to gain weight, but if it were up to him he'd feed himself exclusively on pizza and french fries.

"Do you want to tell me what's going on?" Ellen

pressed Derek, feeling guilty but not quite knowing why. "I assumed your family owned the house."

"Well...sort of." He sank slowly into one of the kitchen chairs.

"It's the *sort of* that worries me." She pulled out the chair across from Derek and looked at him sternly.

"Reed *is* family."

"But he didn't know you were renting out the bedrooms?"

"He told me this job would last nine months to a year. I couldn't see any harm in it. Everywhere I looked there were ads for students wanting rooms to rent. It didn't seem right to live alone in this house with all these bedrooms."

"Maybe I should try to find someplace else to live," Ellen said reluctantly. The more she thought about it, the harder it was to see any other solution now that Reed had returned.

"Not before dinner," Monte protested, bringing a loaf of bread and assorted sandwich makings to the table.

"There's no need for anyone to leave," Derek said with defiant bravado. "Reed will probably only be around for a couple of weeks before he goes away on another assignment."

"Assignment?" Ellen asked, her curiosity piqued.

"Yeah. He travels all over the place—we hardly ever see him. And from what I hear, I don't think Danielle likes him being gone so much, either."

"Danielle?"

"They've been practically engaged for ages and... I

don't know the whole story, but apparently Reed's put off tying the knot because he does so much traveling."

"Danielle must really love him if she's willing to wait." Ellen watched as Monte spread several layers of smoked ham over the inch-thick slice of Swiss cheese. She knew better than to warn her housemate that he'd ruin his dinner. After his triple-decker sandwich, Monte could sit down to a five-course meal—and then ask about dessert.

"I guess," Derek answered nonchalantly. "Reed's perfect for her. You'd have to meet Danielle to understand." Reaching into the teddy-bear-shaped cookie jar and helping himself to a handful, Derek continued. "Reed didn't mean to snap at everyone. Usually, he's a great brother. And Danielle's all right," he added without enthusiasm.

"It takes a special kind of woman to stick by a man that long without a commitment."

Derek shrugged. "I suppose. Danielle's got her own reasons, if you know what I mean."

Ellen didn't, but she let it go. "What does Reed do?"

"He's an aeronautical engineer for Boeing. He travels around the world working on different projects. This last one was somewhere in Saudi Arabia."

"What about the house?"

"Well, that's his, an inheritance from his mother's family, but he's gone so much of the time that he asked me if I'd live here and look after the place."

"What about us?" Monte asked. "Will big brother want us to move out?"

"I don't think so. Tomorrow morning I'll ask him.

I can't see me all alone in this huge old place. It's not like I'm trying to make a fortune by collecting a lot of rent."

"If Reed wants us to leave, I'm sure something can be arranged." Already Ellen was considering different options. She didn't want her fate to be determined by a whim of Derek's brother.

"Let's not do anything drastic. I doubt he'll mind once he has a chance to think it through," Derek murmured with a thoughtful frown. "At least, I hope he won't."

Later that night as Ellen slipped between the crisply laundered sheets, she wondered about the man whose bed she occupied. Tucking the thick quilt around her shoulders, she fought back a wave of anxiety. Everything had worked out so perfectly that she should've expected *something* to go wrong. If anyone voiced objections to her being in Reed's house, it would probably be his almost-fiancée. Ellen sighed apprehensively. She had to admit that if the positions were reversed, she wouldn't want the man she loved sharing his house with another woman. Tomorrow she'd check around to see if she could find a new place to live.

Ellen was scrambling eggs the next morning when Reed appeared, coming down the narrow stairs that led from the third floor to the kitchen. He'd shaved, which emphasized the chiseled look of his jaw. His handsome face was weathered and everything about him spoke of health and vitality. Ellen paused, her fork suspended with raw egg dripping from the tines. She wouldn't call Reed Morgan handsome so much as striking. He had an unmistakable masculine appeal. Apparently the duties of an aeronautical engineer were more physically demanding than she'd suspected. Strength showed in the wide muscular shoulders and lean, hard build. He looked even more formidable this morning.

"Good morning," she greeted him cheerfully, as she continued to beat the eggs. "I hope you slept well."

Reed poured coffee into the same mug he'd used the day before. A creature of habit, Ellen mused. "Morning," he responded somewhat gruffly.

"Can I fix you some eggs?"

"Derek and I have already talked. You can all stay."

"Is that a yes or a no to the eggs?"

"I'm trying to tell you that you don't need to worry about impressing me with your cooking."

With a grunt of impatience, Ellen set the bowl aside and leaned forward, slapping her open palms on the countertop. "I'm scrambling eggs here. Whether you want some or not is entirely up to you. Believe me, if I was concerned about impressing you, I wouldn't do it with eggs."

For the first time, Ellen saw a hint of amusement touch those brilliant green eyes. "No, I don't suppose you would."

"Now that we've got that settled, would you like breakfast or not?"

"All right."

His eyes boldly searched hers and for an instant Ellen found herself regretting that there was a Danielle. With an effort, she turned away and brought her concentration back to preparing breakfast.

"Do you do all the cooking?" Just the way he asked made it sound as though he was already criticizing their household arrangements. Ellen bit back a sarcastic reply and busied herself melting butter and putting bread in the toaster. She'd bide her time. If Derek was right, his brother would soon be away on another assignment.

"Most of it," Ellen answered, pouring the eggs into the hot skillet.

"Who pays for the groceries?"

Ellen shrugged, hoping to give the appearance of nonchalance. "We all chip in." She did the shopping and most of the cooking. In return, the boys did their share of the housework—now that she'd taught them how.

The bread popped up from the toaster and Ellen reached for the butter knife, doing her best to ignore the overpowering presence of Reed Morgan.

"What about the shopping?"

"I enjoy it," she said simply, putting two more slices of bread in the toaster.

"I thought women all over America were fighting to get out of the kitchen."

"When a replacement is found, I'll be happy to step aside." She wasn't comfortable with the direction this conversation seemed to be taking. Reed was looking at her as though she was some kind of 1950s throwback.

Ellen liked to cook and as it turned out, the boys needed someone who knew her way around a kitchen, and she needed an inexpensive place to live. Everything had worked out perfectly....

She spooned the cooked eggs onto one plate and piled the toast on another, then carried it to the table, which gave her enough time to control her indignation. She was temporarily playing the role of surrogate mother to a bunch of college-age boys. All right, maybe that made her a little unusual these days, but she enjoyed living with Derek and the others. It helped her feel at home, and for now she needed that.

"Aren't you going to eat?" Reed stopped her on her way out of the kitchen.

"I'll have something later. The only time I can count on the bathroom being free in the mornings is when the boys are having breakfast. That is, unless you were planning to use it?"

Reed's eyes narrowed fractionally. "No."

"What's the matter? You've got that look on your face again."

"What look?"

"The one where you pinch your lips together as if you aren't pleased about something and you're wondering just how much you should say."

His tight expression relaxed into a slow, sensual grin. "Do you always read people this well?"

Ellen shook her head. "Not always. I just want to know what I've done this time."

"Aren't you concerned about living with three men?"

"No. Should I be?" She crossed her arms and leaned against the doorjamb, almost enjoying their conversation. The earlier antagonism had disappeared. She'd agree that her living arrangements were a bit unconventional, but they suited her. The situation was advantageous for her *and* the boys.

"Any one of them could fall in love with you."

With difficulty, Ellen restrained her laughter. "That's unlikely. They see me as their mother."

The corners of his mouth formed deep grooves as he tried—and failed—to suppress a grin. Raising one brow, he did a thorough inspection of her curves.

Hot color flooded her pale cheeks. "All right—a sister. I'm too old for them."

Monte sauntered into the kitchen, followed closely by Pat who muttered, "I thought I smelled breakfast."

"I was just about to call you," she told them and hurried from the room, wanting to avoid a head-on collision with Reed. And that was where this conversation was going.

Fifteen minutes later, Ellen returned to the kitchen. She was dressed in cords and an Irish cable-knit sweater; soft dark curls framed her small oval face. Ellen had no illusions about her looks. Men on the street weren't going to stop and stare, but she knew she was reasonably attractive. With her short, dark hair and deep brown eyes, she considered herself average. Ordinary. Far too ordinary for a man like Reed Morgan. One look at Ellen, and Danielle would feel completely reassured. Angry at the self-pitying thought, she grabbed a pen and tore out a sheet of notebook paper.

Intent on making the shopping list, Ellen was halfway into the kitchen before she noticed Reed standing at the sink, wiping the frying pan dry. The table had been cleared and the dishes were stacked on the counter, ready for the dishwasher.

"Oh," she said, a little startled. "I would've done that."

"While I'm here, I'll do my share." He said it without looking at her, his eyes avoiding hers.

"But this is your home. I certainly don't mind—"

"I wouldn't be comfortable otherwise. Haven't you got a class this morning?" He sounded anxious to be rid of her.

"Not until eleven."

"What's your major?" He'd turned around, leaning against the sink and crossing his arms. He was the picture of nonchalance, but Ellen wasn't fooled. She knew very well that he wasn't pleased about her living in his home, and she felt he'd given his permission reluctantly. She suspected he was even looking for ways to dislike her. Ellen understood that. Reed was bound to face some awkward questions once Danielle discovered there was a woman living in his house. Especially a woman who slept in his bed and took charge of his kitchen. But that would change this afternoon—at least the sleeping in his bed part.

"I'm majoring in education."

"That's the mother in you coming out again."

Ellen hadn't thought of it that way. Reed simply felt more comfortable seeing her in that light—as a maternal, even matronly figure—she decided. She'd let him, if it meant he'd be willing to accept her arrangement with Derek and the others.

"I suppose you're right," she murmured as she began

opening and closing cupboard doors, checking the contents on each shelf, and scribbling down several items she'd need the following week.

"What are you doing now?"

Mentally, Ellen counted to ten before answering. She resented his overbearing tone, and despite her earlier resolve to humor him, she snapped, "I'm making a grocery list. Do you have a problem with that?"

"No," he answered gruffly.

"I'll be out of here in just a minute," she said, trying hard to maintain her patience.

"You aren't in my way."

"And while we're on the subject of being in someone's way, I want you to know I plan to move my things out of your room this afternoon."

"Don't. I won't be here long enough to make it worth your while."

Two

So Reed was leaving. Ellen felt guilty and relieved at the same time. Derek had told her Reed would probably be sent on another job soon, but she hadn't expected it to be quite *this* soon.

"There's a project Boeing is sending me on. California this time—the Monterey area."

Resuming her task, Ellen added several more items to the grocery list. "I've heard that's a lovely part of the state."

"It is beautiful." But his voice held no enthusiasm.

Ellen couldn't help feeling a twinge of disappointment for Reed. One look convinced her that he didn't want to leave again. After all, he'd just returned from several months in the Middle East and already he had another assignment in California. If he was dreading this latest job, Ellen could well imagine how Danielle must feel.

"Nonetheless, I think it's important to give you back your room. I'll move my things this afternoon." She'd ask the boys to help and it wouldn't take long.

With his arms crossed, Reed lounged against the doorjamb, watching her.

"And if you feel that my being here is a problem," she went on, thinking of Danielle, "I'll look for another place. The only thing I ask is that you give me a couple of weeks to find something."

He hesitated as though he was considering the offer, then shook his head, grinning slightly. "I don't think that'll be necessary."

"I don't mind telling you I'm relieved to hear it, but I'm prepared to move if necessary."

His left brow rose a fraction of an inch as the grin spread across his face. "Having you here does have certain advantages."

"Such as?"

"You're an excellent cook, the house hasn't been this clean in months and Derek's mother says you're a good influence on these boys."

Ellen had briefly met Mary Morgan, Derek's mother, a few weeks before. "Thank you."

He sauntered over to the coffeepot and poured himself a cup. "And for that matter, Derek's right. This house is too big to sit empty. I'm often out of town, but there's no reason others shouldn't use it. Especially with someone as…domestically inclined as you around to keep things running smoothly."

So he viewed her as little more than a live-in house-keeper and cook! Ellen felt a flush of anger. Before she could say something she'd regret, she turned quickly and fled out the back door on her way to the local grocery store. Actually, Reed Morgan had interpreted the situation correctly, but it somehow bothered her that he saw her in such an unflattering light.

Ellen didn't see Reed again until late that night. Friday evenings were lazy ones for her. She'd dated Charlie Hanson, a fellow student, a couple of times but usually preferred the company of a good book. With her heavy class schedule, most of Ellen's free time was devoted to her studies. Particularly algebra. This one class was getting her down. It didn't matter how hard she hit the books, she couldn't seem to grasp the theory.

Dressed in her housecoat and a pair of bright purple knee socks, she sat at the kitchen table, her legs propped on the chair across from her. Holding a paperback novel open with one hand, she dipped chocolate-chip cookies in a tall glass of milk with the other. At the unexpected sound of the back door opening, she looked curiously up from her book.

Reed seemed surprised to see her. He frowned as his eyes darted past her to the clock above the stove. "You're up late."

"On weekends my mommy doesn't make me go to bed until midnight," she said sarcastically, doing her best to ignore him. Reed managed to look fantastic without even trying. He didn't need her gawking at him to tell him that. If his expensive sports jacket was anything to judge by, he'd spent the evening with Danielle.

"You've got that look," he grumbled.

"What look?"

"The same one you said I have—wanting to say something and unsure if you should."

"Oh." She couldn't very well deny it.

"And what did you want to tell me?"

"Only that you look good." She paused, wondering how much she should say. "You even smell expensive."

His gaze slid over her. "From the way you're dressed, you look to me as though you'd smell of cotton candy."

"Thank you, but actually it's chocolate chip." She pushed the package of cookies in his direction. "Here. Save me from myself."

"No, thanks," Reed murmured and headed toward the living room.

"Don't go in there," Ellen cried, swinging her legs off the chair and coming abruptly to her feet.

Reed's hand was on the kitchen door, ready to open it. "Don't go into the living room?"

"Derek's got a girl in there."

Reed continued to stare at her blankly. "So?"

"So. He's with Michelle Tanner. *The* Michelle Tanner. The girl he's been crazy about for the last six weeks. She finally agreed to a date with him. They rented a movie."

"That doesn't explain why I can't go in there."

"Yes, it does," Ellen whispered. "The last time I peeked, Derek was getting ready to make his move. You'll ruin everything if you barge in there now."

"His move?" Reed didn't seem to like the sound of this. "What do you mean, 'his move'? The kid's barely nineteen."

Ellen smiled. "Honestly, Reed, you must've been

young once. Don't you remember what it's like to have a crush on a girl? All Derek's doing is plotting that first kiss."

Reed dropped his hand as he stared at Ellen. He seemed to focus on her mouth. Then the glittering green eyes skimmed hers, and Ellen's breath caught somewhere between her throat and her lungs as she struggled to pull her gaze away from his. Reed had no business giving her that kind of look. Not when he'd so recently left Danielle's arms. And not when Ellen reacted so profoundly to a mere glance.

"I haven't forgotten," he said. "And as for that remark about being young *once,* I'm not exactly over the hill."

This was ridiculous! With a sigh of annoyance, Ellen sat down again, swinging her feet onto the opposite chair. She picked up her book and forced her eyes—if not her attention—back to the page in front of her. "I'm glad to hear that." If she could get a grip on herself for the next few days everything would be fine. Reed would leave and her life with the boys would settle back into its routine.

She heard the refrigerator opening and watched Reed pour himself a glass of milk, then reach for a handful of chocolate-chip cookies. When he pulled out the chair across from her, Ellen reluctantly lowered her legs.

"What are you reading?"

Feeling irritable and angry for allowing him to affect her, she deliberately waited until she'd finished the page before answering. "A book," she muttered.

"My, my, you're a regular Mary Sunshine. What's wrong—did your boyfriend stand you up tonight?"

With exaggerated patience she slowly lowered the paperback to the table and marked her place. "Listen. I'm twenty-five years old and well beyond the age of *boyfriends*."

Reed shrugged. "All right. Your lover."

She hadn't meant to imply that at all! And Reed knew it. He'd wanted to fluster her and he'd succeeded.

"Women these days have this habit of letting their mouths hang open," he said pointedly. "I suppose they think it looks sexy, but actually, they resemble beached trout." With that, he deposited his empty glass in the sink and marched briskly up the back stairs.

Ellen closed her eyes and groaned in embarrassment. He must think she was an idiot, and with good reason. She'd done a remarkable job of imitating one. She groaned again, infuriated by the fact that she found Reed Morgan so attractive.

Ellen didn't climb the stairs to her new bedroom on the third floor for another hour. And then it was only after Derek had paid her a quick visit in the kitchen and given her a thumbs-up. At least his night had gone well.

Twenty minutes after she'd turned off her reading light, Ellen lay staring into the silent, shadow-filled room. She wasn't sleepy, and the mystery novel no longer held her interest. Her thoughts were troubled by that brief incident in the kitchen with Reed. Burying her head in her pillow, Ellen yawned and closed her eyes. But sleep still wouldn't come. A half-hour later, she threw back the covers and grabbed her housecoat from the end of the bed. Perhaps another glass of milk would help.

Not bothering to turn on any lights, she took a clean glass from the dishwasher and pulled the carton of milk from the refrigerator. Drink in hand, she stood at the kitchen window, looking out at the huge oak tree in the backyard. Its bare limbs stretched upward like skeletal hands, silhouetted against the full moon.

"I've heard that a woman's work is never done, but this is ridiculous."

She nearly spilled her milk at the sudden sound of Reed's voice behind her. She whirled around and glared at him. "I see there's a full moon tonight. I wonder if it's safe to be alone with you. And wouldn't you know it, I left my silver bullet upstairs."

"No woman's ever accused me of being a werewolf. A number of other things," he murmured, "but never that."

"Maybe that's because you hadn't frightened them half out of their wits."

"I couldn't resist. Sorry," he said, reaching for the milk carton.

"You know, if we'd stop snapping at each other, it might make life a lot easier around here."

"Perhaps," he agreed. "I will admit it's a whole lot easier to talk to you when you're dressed."

Ellen slammed down her empty glass. "I'm getting a little tired of hearing about that."

But Reed went on, clearly unperturbed. "Unfortunately, ever since that first time when I found you in your bra, you've insisted on overdressing. From one extreme to another—too few clothes to too many." He paused. "Do you always wear socks to bed?"

"Usually."

"I pity the man you sleep with."

"Well, you needn't worry—" She expelled a lungful of oxygen. "We're doing it again."

"So, you're suggesting we stop trading insults for the sake of the children."

"I hadn't thought of it that way," she said with an involuntary smile, "but you're right. No one's going to be comfortable if the two of us are constantly sniping at each other. I'm willing to try if you are. Okay?"

"Okay." A smile softened Reed's features, angular and shadowed in the moonlight.

"And I'm not a threat to your relationship with Danielle, am I? In fact, if you'd rather, she need never even know I'm here," Ellen said casually.

"Maybe that would've been best," he conceded, setting aside his empty glass. "But I doubt it. Besides, she already knows. I told her tonight." He muttered something else she didn't catch.

"And?"

"And," he went on, "she says she doesn't mind, but she'd like to meet you."

This was one encounter Ellen wasn't going to enjoy.

The next morning, Ellen brought down her laundry and was using the washing machine and the dryer before Reed and the others were even awake.

She sighed as she tested the iron with the wet tip of her index finger and found that it still wasn't hot, although she'd turned it on at least five minutes earlier. This house was owned by a wealthy engineer, so why were there only two electrical outlets in the kitchen? It meant that she couldn't use the washer, the dryer and the iron at the same time without causing a blow-out.

"Darn it," she groaned, setting the iron upright on the padded board.

"What's the matter?" Reed asked from the doorway leading into the kitchen. He got himself a cup of coffee.

"This iron."

"Hey, Ellen, if you're doing some ironing, would you press a few things for me?" Monte asked, walking barefoot into the kitchen. He peered into the refrigerator and took out a slice of cold pizza.

"I was afraid this would happen," she grumbled, still upset by the house's electrical problems.

"Ellen's not your personal maid," Reed said sharply. "If you've got something you want pressed, do it yourself."

A hand on her hip, Ellen turned to Reed, defiantly meeting his glare. "If you don't mind, I can answer for myself."

"Fine," he snorted and took a sip of his coffee.

She directed her next words to Monte, who stood looking at her expectantly. "I am not your personal maid. If you want something pressed, do it yourself."

Monte glanced from Reed to Ellen and back to Reed again. "Sorry I asked," he mumbled on his way out of the kitchen. The door was left swinging in his wake.

"You said that well," Reed commented with a soft chuckle.

"Believe me, I was conned into enough schemes by my sister and brother to know how to handle Monte and the others."

Reed's gaze was admiring. "If your brother's anything like mine, I don't doubt it."

"All brothers are alike," she said. Unable to hold back a grin, Ellen tested the iron a second time and noticed that it was only slightly warmer. "Have you ever thought about putting another outlet in this kitchen?"

Reed looked at her in surprise. "No. Do you need one?"

"Need one?" she echoed. "There are only two in here. It's ridiculous."

Reed scanned the kitchen. "I hadn't thought about it." Setting his coffee mug aside, he shook his head. "Your mood's not much better today than it was last night." With that remark, he hurried out of the room, following in Monte's footsteps.

Frustrated, Ellen tightened her grip on the iron. Reed was right. She was being unreasonable and she really didn't understand why. But she was honest enough to admit, at least to herself, that she was attracted to this man whose house she occupied. She realized she'd have to erect a wall of reserve between them to protect them both from embarrassment.

"Morning, Ellen," Derek said as he entered the kitchen and threw himself into a chair. As he emptied a box of cornflakes into a huge bowl, he said, "I've got some shirts that need pressing."

"If you want anything pressed, do it yourself," she almost shouted.

Stunned, Derek blinked. "Okay."

Setting the iron upright again, Ellen released a lengthy sigh. "I didn't mean to scream at you."

"That's all right."

Turning off the iron, she joined Derek at the table and reached for the cornflakes.

"Are you still worried about that math paper you're supposed to do?" he asked.

"I'm working my way to an early grave over it."

"I would've thought you'd do well in math."

Ellen snickered. "Hardly."

"Have you come up with a topic?"

"Not yet. I'm going to the library later, where I pray some form of inspiration will strike me."

"Have you asked the other people in your class what they're writing about?" Derek asked as he refilled his bowl, this time with rice puffs.

Ellen nodded. "That's what worries me most. The brain who sits beside me is doing hers on the probability of solving Goldbach's conjecture in our lifetime."

Derek's eyes widened. "That's a tough act to follow."

"Let me tell you about the guy who sits behind me. He's doing his paper on mathematics during World War II."

"You're in the big leagues now," Derek said with a sympathetic shake of his head.

"I know," Ellen lamented. She was taking this course only because it was compulsory; all she wanted out of it was a passing grade. The quadratic formula certainly wasn't going to have any lasting influence on *her* life.

"Good luck," Derek said.

"Thanks. I'm going to need it."

After straightening up the kitchen, Ellen changed into old jeans and a faded sweatshirt. The jeans had been washed so many times they were nearly white. They fit her hips so snugly she could hardly slide her fingers into the pockets, but she hated the idea of throwing them out.

She tied an old red scarf around her hair and headed for the garage. While rooting around for a ladder a few days earlier, she'd discovered some pruning shears. She'd noticed several overgrown bushes in the backyard and decided to tackle those first, before cleaning the drainpipes.

After an hour, she had a pile of underbrush large enough to be worth a haul to the dump. She'd have one of the boys do that later. For now, the drainpipes demanded her attention.

"Derek!" she called as she pushed open the back door. She knew her face was flushed and damp from exertion.

"Yeah?" His voice drifted toward her from the living room.

Ellen wandered in to discover him on the phone. "I'm ready for you now."

"Now?" His eyes pleaded with her as his palm covered the mouthpiece. "It's Michelle."

"All right, I'll ask Monte."

"Thanks." He gave her a smile of appreciation.

But Monte was nowhere to be found, and Pat was at the Y shooting baskets with some friends. When she stuck her head into the living room again, she saw

Derek still draped over the sofa, deep in conversation. Unwilling to interfere with the course of young love, she decided she could probably manage to climb onto the roof unaided.

Dragging the aluminum ladder from the garage, she thought she might not need Derek's help anyway. She'd mentioned her plan earlier in the week, and he hadn't looked particularly enthusiastic.

With the extension ladder braced against the side of the house, she climbed onto the roof of the back porch. Very carefully, she reached for the ladder and extended it to the very top of the house.

She maneuvered herself back onto the ladder and climbed slowly and cautiously up.

Once she'd managed to position herself on the slanting roof, she was fine. She even took a moment to enjoy the spectacular view. She could see Lake Washington, with its deep-green water, and the spacious grounds of the university campus.

Using the brush she'd tucked—with some struggle—into her back pocket, Ellen began clearing away the leaves and other debris that clogged the gutters and drainpipes.

She was about half finished when she heard raised voices below. Pausing, she sat down, drawing her knees against her chest, and watched the scene unfolding on the front lawn. Reed and his brother were embroiled in a heated discussion—with Reed doing most of the talking. Derek was raking leaves and didn't seem at all pleased about devoting his Saturday morning to chores.

Ellen guessed that Reed had summarily interrupted the telephone conversation between Derek and Michelle.

With a lackadaisical swish of the rake, Derek flung the multicolored leaves skyward. Ellen restrained a laugh. Reed had obviously pulled rank and felt no hesitation about giving him orders.

To her further amusement, Reed then motioned toward his black Porsche, apparently suggesting that his brother wash the car when he'd finished with the leaves. Still chuckling, Ellen grabbed for the brush, but she missed and accidentally sent it tumbling down the side of the roof. It hit the green shingles over the front porch with a loud thump before flying onto the grass only a few feet from where Derek and Reed were standing.

Two pairs of astonished eyes turned swiftly in her direction. "Hi," she called down and waved. "I don't suppose I could talk one of you into bringing that up to me?" She braced her feet and pulled herself into a standing position as she waited for a reply.

Reed pointed his finger at her and yelled, "What do you think you're doing up there?"

"Playing tiddlywinks," she shouted back. "What do *you* think I'm doing?"

"I don't know, but I want you down."

"In a minute."

"Now."

"Yes, *sir*." She gave him a mocking salute and would have bowed if she hadn't been afraid she might lose her footing.

Derek burst out laughing but was quickly silenced by a scathing glance from his older brother.

"Tell Derek to bring me the broom," Ellen called, moving closer to the edge.

Ellen couldn't decipher Reed's response, but from the way he stormed around the back of the house, she figured it was best to come down before he had a heart attack. She had the ladder lowered to the back-porch roof before she saw him.

"You idiot!" he shouted. He was standing in the driveway, hands on his hips, glaring at her in fury. "I can't believe anyone would do anything so stupid."

"What do you mean?" The calmness of her words belied the way the blood pulsed through her veins. Alarm rang in his voice and that surprised her. She certainly hadn't expected Reed, of all people, to be concerned about her safety. He held the ladder steady until she'd climbed down and was standing squarely in front of him. Then he started pacing. For a minute Ellen didn't know what to think.

"What's wrong?" she asked. "You look as pale as a sheet."

"What's wrong?" he sputtered. "You were on the *roof* and—"

"I wasn't in any danger."

He shook his head, clearly upset. "There are people who specialize in that sort of thing. I don't want you up there again. Understand?"

"Yes, but—"

"No buts. You do anything that stupid again and you're out of here. Have you got that?"

"Yes," she said with forced calm. "I understand."

"Good."

Before she could think of anything else to say, Reed was gone.

"You all right?" Derek asked a minute later. Shocked by Reed's outburst, Ellen hadn't moved. Rarely had anyone been that angry with her. Heavens, she'd cleaned out drainpipes lots of times. Her father had died when Ellen was fourteen, and over the years she'd assumed most of the maintenance duties around the house. She'd learned that, with the help of a good book and a well-stocked hardware store, there wasn't anything she couldn't fix. She'd repaired the plumbing, built bookshelves and done a multitude of household projects. It was just part of her life. Reed had acted as though she'd done something hazardous, as though she'd taken some extraordinary risk, and that seemed totally ridiculous to her. She knew what she was doing. Besides, heights didn't frighten her; they never had.

"Ellen?" Derek prompted.

"I'm fine."

"I've never seen Reed act like that. He didn't mean anything."

"I know," she whispered, brushing the dirt from her knees. Derek drifted off, leaving her to return the ladder to the garage single-handed.

Reed found her an hour later folding laundry in her bedroom. He knocked on the open door.

"Yes?" She looked up expectantly.

"I owe you an apology."

She continued folding towels at the foot of her bed. "Oh?"

"I didn't mean to come at you like Attila the Hun."

Hugging a University of Washington T-shirt to her stomach, she lowered her gaze to the bedspread and nodded. "Apology accepted and I'll offer one of my own. I didn't mean to come back at you like a spoiled brat."

"Accepted." They smiled at each other and she caught her breath as those incredible green eyes gazed into hers. It was a repeat of the scene in the kitchen the night before. For a long, silent moment they did nothing but stare, and she realized that a welter of conflicting emotions must have registered on her face. A similar turmoil raged on his.

"If it'll make you feel any better, I won't go up on the roof again," she said at last.

"I'd appreciate it." His lips barely moved. The words were more of a sigh than a sentence.

She managed a slight nod in response.

At the sound of footsteps, they guiltily looked away.

"Say, Ellen." Pat stopped in the doorway, a basketball under his left arm. "Got time to shoot a few baskets with me?"

"Sure," she whispered, stepping around Reed. At that moment, she would've agreed to just about anything to escape his company. There was something happening between them and she felt frightened and confused and excited, all at the same time.

The basketball hoop was positioned above the garage door at the end of the long driveway. Pat was attending the University of Washington with the express hope of making the Husky basketball team. His whole life revolved around the game. He was rarely seen without a ball tucked under his arm and sometimes Ellen wondered if he showered with it. She was well aware that the invitation to practice a few free throws with him was not meant to be taken literally. The only slam dunk Ellen had ever accomplished was with a doughnut in her hot chocolate. Her main job was to stand on the sidelines and be awed by Pat's talent.

They hadn't been in the driveway fifteen minutes when the back door opened and Derek strolled out. "Say, Ellen, have you got a minute?" he asked, frowning.

"What's the problem?"

"It's Michelle."

Sitting on the concrete porch step, Derek looked at Ellen with those wide pleading eyes of his.

Ellen sat beside him and wrapped her arms around her bent knees. "What's wrong with Michelle?"

"Nothing. She's beautiful and I think she might even fall in love with me, given the chance." He paused to sigh expressively. "I asked her out to dinner tonight."

"She agreed. Right?" If Michelle was anywhere near as taken with Derek as he was with her, she wasn't likely to refuse.

The boyishly thin shoulders heaved in a gesture of despair. "She can't."

"Why not?" Ellen watched as Pat bounced the basketball across the driveway, pivoted, jumped high in the air and sent the ball through the net.

"Michelle promised her older sister that she'd babysit tonight."

"That's too bad." Ellen gave him a sympathetic look.

"The thing is, she'd probably go out with me if there was someone who could watch her niece and nephew for her."

"Uh-huh." Pat made another skillful play and Ellen applauded vigorously. He rewarded her with a triumphant smile.

"Then you will?"

Ellen switched her attention from Pat's antics at the basketball hoop back to Derek. "Will I what?"

"Babysit Michelle's niece and nephew?"

"What?" she exploded. "Not me. I've got to do research for a term paper."

"Ellen, please, please, please."

"No. No. No." She sliced the air forcefully with her hand and got to her feet.

Derek rose with her. "I sense some resistance to this idea."

"The boy's a genius," she mumbled under her breath as she hurried into the kitchen. "I've got to write my term paper. You know that."

Derek followed her inside. "Ellen, please? I promise I'll never ask anything of you again."

"I've heard that before." She tried to ignore him as he trailed her to the refrigerator and watched her take out sandwich makings for lunch.

"It's a matter of the utmost importance," Derek pleaded anew.

"What is?" Reed spoke from behind the paper he was reading at the kitchen table.

"My date with Michelle. Listen, Ellen, I bet Reed would help you. You're not doing anything tonight, are you?"

Reed lowered the newspaper. "Help Ellen with what?"

"Babysitting."

Reed glanced from the intent expression on his younger brother's face to the stubborn look on Ellen's. "You two leave me out of this."

"Ellen. Dear, *sweet* Ellen, you've got to understand that it could be weeks—weeks," he repeated dramatically, "before Michelle will be able to go out with me again."

Ellen put down an armload of cheese, ham and assorted jars of mustard and pickles. "*No!* Can I make it any plainer than that? I'm sorry, Derek, honest. But I can't."

"Reed," Derek pleaded with his brother. "Say something that'll convince her."

"Like I said, I'm out of this one."

He raised the paper again, but Ellen could sense a smile hidden behind it. Still, she doubted that Reed would be foolish enough to involve himself in this situation.

"Ellen, puleease."

"No." Ellen realized that if she wanted any peace, she'd have to forget about lunch and make an immediate escape. She whirled around and headed out of the kitchen, the door swinging in her wake.

"I think she's weakening," she heard Derek say as he followed her.

She was on her way up the stairs when she caught sight of Derek in the dining room, coming toward her on his knees, hands folded in supplication. "Won't you please reconsider?"

Ellen groaned. "What do I need to say to convince you? I've got to get to the library. That paper is due Monday morning."

"I'll write it for you."

"No, thanks."

At just that moment Reed came through the door. "It shouldn't be too difficult to find a reliable sitter. There are a few families with teenagers in the neighbourhood, as I recall."

"I...don't know," Derek hedged.

"If we can't find anyone, then Danielle and I'll manage. It'll be good practice for us. Besides, just how much trouble can two kids be?"

When she heard that, Ellen had to swallow a burst of laughter. Reed obviously hadn't spent much time around children, she thought with a mischievous grin.

"How old did you say these kids are?" She couldn't resist asking.

"Nine and four." Derek's dark eyes brightened as he leaped to his feet and gave his brother a grateful smile. "So I can tell Michelle everything's taken care of?"

"I suppose." Reed turned to Ellen. "I was young once myself," he said pointedly, reminding her of the comment she'd made the night before.

"I really appreciate this, Reed," Derek was saying.

"I'll be your slave for life. I'd even lend you money if I had some. By the way, can I borrow your car tonight?"

"Don't press your luck."

"Right." Derek chuckled, bounding up the stairs. He paused for a moment. "Oh, I forgot to tell you. Michelle's bringing the kids over here, okay?"

He didn't wait for a response.

The doorbell chimed close to six o'clock, just as Ellen was gathering up her books and preparing to leave for the library.

"That'll be Michelle," Derek called excitedly. "Can you get it, Ellen?"

"No problem."

Coloring books and crayons were arranged on the coffee table, along with some building blocks Reed must have purchased that afternoon. From bits and pieces of information she'd picked up, she concluded that Reed had discovered it wasn't quite as easy to find a baby-sitter as he'd assumed. And with no other recourse, he and Danielle were apparently taking over the task. Ellen wished him luck, but she really did need to concentrate on this stupid term paper. Reed hadn't suggested that Ellen wait around to meet Danielle. But she had to admit she'd been wondering about the woman from the time Derek had first mentioned her.

"Hello, Ellen." Blonde Michelle greeted Ellen with a warm, eager smile. They'd met briefly the other night, when she'd come over to watch the movie. "This sure is great of Derek's brother and his girlfriend, isn't it?"

"It sure is."

The four-year-old boy was clinging to Michelle's trouser leg so that her gait was stiff-kneed as she limped into the house with the child attached.

"Jimmy, this is Ellen. You'll be staying in her house tonight while Auntie Michelle goes out to dinner with Derek."

"I want my mommy."

"He won't be a problem," Michelle told Ellen confidently.

"I thought there were two children."

"Yeah, the baby's in the car. I'll be right back."

"Baby?" Ellen swallowed down a laugh. "What baby?"

"Jenny's nine months."

"Nine *months?*" A small uncontrollable giggle slid from her throat. This would be marvelous. Reed with a nine-month-old was almost too good to miss.

"Jimmy, you stay here." Somehow Michelle was able to pry the four-year-old's fingers from her leg and pass the struggling child to Ellen.

Kicking and thrashing, Jimmy broke into loud sobs as Ellen carried him into the living room. "Here's a coloring book. Do you like to color, Jimmy?"

But he refused to talk to Ellen or even look at her as he buried his face in the sofa cushions. "I want my mommy," he wailed again.

By the time Michelle had returned with a baby carrier and a fussing nine-month-old, Derek sauntered out from the kitchen. "Hey, Michelle, you're lookin' good."

Reed, who was following closely behind, came to

a shocked standstill when he saw the baby. "I thought you said they were nine and four."

"I did," Derek explained patiently, his eyes devouring the blonde at his side.

"They won't be any trouble," Michelle cooed as Derek placed an arm around her shoulders and led her toward the open door.

"Derek, we need to talk," Reed insisted.

"Haven't got time now. Our reservations are for seven." His hand slid from Michelle's shoulders to her waist. "I'm taking my lady out for a night on the town."

"Derek," Reed demanded.

"Oh." Michelle tore her gaze from Derek's. "The diaper bag is in the entry. Jenny should be dry, but you might want to check her later. She'll probably cry for a few minutes once she sees I'm gone, but that'll stop almost immediately."

Reed's face was grim as he cast a speculative glance at Jimmy, who was still howling for his mother. The happily gurgling Jenny stared up at the unfamiliar dark-haired man and noticed for the first time that she was at the mercy of a stranger. She immediately burst into heart-wrenching tears.

"I want my mommy," Jimmy wailed yet again.

"I can see you've got everything under control," Ellen said, reaching for her coat. "I'm sure Danielle will be here any minute."

"Ellen…"

"Don't expect me back soon. I've got hours of research ahead of me."

"You aren't really going to leave, are you?" Reed gave her a horrified look.

"I wish I could stay," she lied breezily. "Another time." With that, she was out the door, smiling as she bounded down the steps.

Three

An uneasy feeling struck Ellen as she stood waiting at the bus stop. But she resolutely hardened herself against the impulse to rush back to Reed and his disconsolate charges. Danielle would show up any minute and Ellen really was obliged to do the research for her yet-to-be-determined math paper. Besides, she reminded herself, Reed had volunteered to babysit and she wasn't responsible for rescuing him. But his eyes had pleaded with her so earnestly. Ellen felt herself beginning to weaken. *No!* she mumbled under her breath. Reed had Danielle, and as far as Ellen was concerned, they were on their own.

However, by the time she arrived at the undergraduate library, Ellen discovered that she couldn't get Reed's pleading look out of her mind. From everything she'd heard about Danielle, Ellen figured the woman probably didn't know the first thing about babies. As for the term paper, she supposed she could put it off until Sunday. After all, she'd found excuses all day to avoid working on it. She'd done the laundry, trimmed the shrubs, cleaned the drainpipes and washed the upstairs walls in an effort to escape that paper. One more night wasn't going to make much difference.

Hurriedly, she signed out some books and journals that looked as though they might be helpful and headed for the bus stop. Ellen had to admit that she was curious enough to want to meet Danielle. Reed's girlfriend had to be someone very special to put up with his frequent absences—or else a schemer, as Derek had implied. But Ellen couldn't see Reed being duped by a woman, no matter how clever or sophisticated she might be.

Her speculations came to an end as the bus arrived, and she quickly jumped on for the short ride home.

Reed was kneeling on the carpet changing the still-tearful Jenny's diaper when Ellen walked in the front door. He seemed to have aged ten years in the past hour. The long sleeves of his wool shirt were rolled up to the elbows as he struggled with the tape on Jenny's disposable diaper.

Reed shook his head and sagged with relief. "Good thing you're here. She hasn't stopped crying from the minute you left."

"You look like you're doing a good job without me. Where's Danielle?" She glanced around, smiling at Jimmy; the little boy hadn't moved from the sofa, his face still hidden in the cushions.

Reed muttered a few words under his breath. "She couldn't stay." He finally finished with the diaper. "That wasn't so difficult after all," he said, glancing proudly at Ellen as he stood Jenny up on the floor, holding the baby upright by her small arms.

Ellen swallowed a laugh. The diaper hung crookedly, bunched up in front. She was trying to think of a tactful way of pointing it out to Reed when the whole thing began to slide down Jenny's pudgy legs, settling at her ankles.

"Maybe you should try," Reed conceded, handing her the baby. Within minutes, Ellen had successfully secured the diaper. Unfortunately, she didn't manage to soothe the baby any more than Reed had.

Cradling Jenny in her arms, Ellen paced the area in front of the fireplace, at a loss to comfort the sobbing child. "I doubt I'll do any better. It's been a long while since my brother was this size."

"Women are always better at this kind of stuff," Reed argued, rubbing a hand over his face. "Most women," he amended, with such a look of frustration that Ellen smiled.

"I'll bet Jimmy knows what to do," she suggested next, pleased with her inspiration. The little boy might actually come up with something helpful, and involving him in their attempts to comfort Jenny might distract him from his own unhappiness. Or so Ellen hoped. "Jimmy's a good big brother. Isn't that right, honey?"

The child lifted his face from the cushion. "I want my mommy."

"Let's pretend Ellen is your mommy," Reed coaxed.

"No! She's like that other lady who said bad words."

Meanwhile, Jenny wailed all the louder. Digging around in the bag, Reed found a stuffed teddy bear and pressed it into her arms. But Jenny angrily tossed the toy aside, the tears flowing unabated down her face.

"Come on, Jimmy," Reed said desperately. "We need a little help here. Your sister's crying."

Holding his hands over his eyes, Jimmy straightened and peeked through two fingers. The distraught Jenny continued to cry at full volume in spite of Ellen's best efforts.

"Mommy bounces her."

Ellen had been gently doing that from the beginning. "What else?" she asked.

"She likes her boo-loo."

"What's that?"

"Her teddy bear."

"I've already tried that," Reed said. "What else does your mommy do when she cries like this?"

Jimmy was thoughtful for a moment. "Oh." The four-year-old's eyes sparkled. "Mommy nurses her."

Reed and Ellen glanced at each other and dissolved into giggles. The laughter faded from his eyes and was replaced with a roguish grin. "That could be interesting."

Hiding a smile, Ellen decided to ignore Reed's comment. "Sorry, Jenny," she said softly to the baby girl.

"But maybe he's got an idea," Reed suggested. "Could she be hungry?"

"It's worth a try. At this point, anything is."

Jenny's bellowing had finally dwindled into a few hiccuping sobs. And for some reason, Jimmy suddenly straightened and stared at Reed's craggy face, at his deep auburn hair and brilliant green eyes. Then he pointed to the plaid wool shirt, its long sleeves rolled up to the elbow. "Are you a lumberjack?"

"A lumberjack?" Reed repeated, looking puzzled. He broke into a full laugh. "No, but I imagine I must look like one to you."

Rummaging through the diaper bag, Ellen found a plastic bottle filled with what was presumably formula. Jenny eyed it skeptically, but no sooner had Ellen removed the cap than Jenny grabbed it from her hands and began sucking eagerly at the nipple.

Sighing, Ellen sank into the rocking chair and swayed back and forth with the baby tucked in her arms. "I guess that settles that."

The silence was so blissful that she wanted to wrap it around herself. She felt the tension drain from her muscles as she relaxed in the rocking chair. From what Jimmy had dropped, she surmised that Danielle hadn't been much help. Everything she'd learned about the other woman told Ellen that Danielle would probably find young children frustrating—and apparently she had.

Jimmy had crawled into Reed's lap with a book and demanded the lumberjack read to him. Together the two leafed through the storybook. Several times during the peaceful interlude, Ellen's eyes met Reed's across the room and they exchanged a contented smile.

Jenny sucked tranquilly at the bottle, and her eyes slowly drooped shut. At peace with her world, the baby was satisfied to be held and rocked to sleep. Ellen gazed down at the angelic face and brushed fine wisps of hair from the untroubled forehead. Releasing her breath in a slow, drawn-out sigh, she glanced up to discover Reed watching her, the little boy still sitting quietly on his lap.

"Ellen?" Reed spoke in a low voice. "Did you finish your math paper?"

"Finish it?" She groaned. "Are you kidding? I haven't even started it."

"What's a math paper?" Jimmy asked.

Rocking the baby, Ellen looked solemnly over at the boy. "Well, it's something I have to write for a math class. And if I don't write a paper, I haven't got a hope of passing the course." She didn't think he'd understand any algebraic terms. For that matter, neither did she.

"What's math?"

"Numbers," Reed told the boy.

"And, in this case, sometimes letters—like *x* and *y*."

"I like numbers," Jimmy declared. "I like three and nine and seven."

"Well, Jimmy, my boy, how would you like to write my paper for me?"

"Can I?"

Ellen grinned at him. "You bet."

Reed got out pencil and paper and set the four-year-old to work.

Glancing up, she gave Reed a smile. "See how easy this is? You're good with kids." Reed smiled in answer as he carefully drew numbers for Jimmy to copy.

After several minutes of this activity, Jimmy decided it was time to put on his pajamas. Seeing him yawn, Reed brought down a pillow and blanket and tucked him into a hastily made bed on the sofa. Then he read a bedtime story until the four-year-old again yawned loudly and fell almost instantly asleep.

Ellen still hadn't moved, fearing that the slightest jolt would rouse the baby.

"Why don't we set her down in the baby seat?" Reed said.

"I'm afraid she'll wake up."

"If she does, you can rock her again."

His suggestion made sense and besides, her arms were beginning to ache. "Okay." He moved to her side and took the sleeping child. Ellen held her breath momentarily when Jenny stirred. But the little girl simply rolled her head against the cushion and returned to sleep.

Ellen rose to her feet and turned the lamp down to its dimmest setting, surrounding them with a warm circle of light.

"I couldn't have done it without you," Reed whispered, coming to stand beside her. He rested his hand at the back of her neck.

An unfamiliar warmth seeped through Ellen, and she began to talk quickly, hoping to conceal her sudden nervousness. "Sure you could have. It looked to me as if you had everything under control."

Reed snorted. "I was ten minutes away from calling the crisis clinic. Thanks for coming to the rescue." He casually withdrew his hand, and Ellen felt both relieved and disappointed.

"You're welcome." She was dying to know what had happened with Danielle, but she didn't want to ask. Apparently, the other woman hadn't stayed around for long.

"Have you eaten?"

Ellen had been so busy that she'd forgotten about dinner, but once Reed mentioned it, she realized how hungry she was. "No, and I'm starved."

"Do you like Chinese food?"

"Love it."

"Good. There's enough for an army out in the kitchen. I ordered it earlier."

Ellen didn't need to be told that he'd made dinner plans with Danielle in mind. He'd expected to share an intimate evening with her. "Listen," she began awkwardly, clasping her hands. "I really have to get going on this term paper. Why don't you call Danielle and invite her back? Now that the kids are asleep, I'm sure everything will be better. I—"

"Children make Danielle nervous. She warned me about it, but I refused to listen. She's home now and has probably taken some aspirin and gone to sleep. I can't see letting good food go to waste. Besides, this gives me an opportunity to thank you."

"Oh." It was the longest speech that Reed had made. "All right," she agreed with a slight nod.

While Reed warmed the food in the microwave, Ellen set out plates and forks and prepared a large pot of green tea, placing it in the middle of the table. The swinging door that connected the kitchen with the living room was left open in case either child woke.

"What do we need plates for?" Reed asked with a questioning arch of his brow.

"Plates are the customary eating device."

"Not tonight."

"Not tonight?" Something amusing glinted in Reed's

eyes as he set out several white boxes and brandished two pairs of chopsticks. "Since it's only the two of us, we can eat right out of the boxes."

"I'm not very adept with chopsticks." The smell drifting from the open boxes was tangy and enticing.

"You'll learn if you're hungry."

"I'm famished."

"Good." Deftly he took the first pair of chopsticks and showed her how to work them with her thumb and index finger.

Imitating his movements Ellen discovered that her fingers weren't nearly as agile as his. Two or three tries at picking up small pieces of spicy diced chicken succeeded only in frustrating her.

"Here." Reed fed her a bite from the end of his chopsticks. "Be a little more patient with yourself."

"That's easy for you to say while you're eating your fill and I'm starving to death."

"It'll come."

Ellen grumbled under her breath, but a few tries later she managed to deliver a portion of the hot food to her eager mouth.

"See, I told you you'd pick this up fast enough."

"Do you always tell someone 'I told you so'?" she asked with pretended annoyance. The mood was too congenial for any real discontent. Ellen felt that they'd shared a special time together looking after the two small children. More than special—astonishing. They hadn't clashed once or found a single thing to squabble over.

"I enjoy teasing you. Your eyes have an irresistible way of lighting up when you're angry."

"If you continue to insist that I eat with these absurd pieces of wood, you'll see my eyes brighten the entire room."

"I'm looking forward to that," he murmured with a laugh. "No forks. You can't properly enjoy Chinese food unless you use chopsticks."

"I can't properly *taste* it without a fork."

"Here, I'll feed you." Again he brought a spicy morsel to her mouth.

A drop of the sauce fell onto her chin and Ellen wiped it off. "You aren't any better at this than me." She dipped the chopsticks into the chicken mixture and attempted to transport a tidbit to Reed's mouth. It balanced precariously on the end of her chopsticks, and Reed lowered his mouth to catch it before it could land in his lap.

"You're improving," he told her, his voice low and slightly husky.

Their eyes met. Unable to face the caressing look in his warm gaze, Ellen bent her head and pretended to be engrossed in her dinner. But her appetite was instantly gone—vanished.

A tense silence filled the room. The air between them was so charged that she felt breathless and weak, as though she'd lost the energy to move or speak. Ellen didn't dare raise her eyes for fear of what she'd see in his.

"Ellen."

She took a deep breath and scrambled to her feet. "I think I hear Jimmy," she whispered.

"Maybe it was Jenny," Reed added hurriedly.

Ellen paused in the doorway between the two rooms. They were both overwhelmingly aware that neither child had made a sound. "I guess they're still asleep."

"That's good." The scraping sound of his chair against the floor told her that Reed, too, had risen from the table. When she turned, she found him depositing the leftovers in the refrigerator. His preoccupation with the task gave her a moment to reflect on what had just happened. There were too many problems involved in pursuing this attraction; the best thing was to ignore it and hope the craziness passed. They were mature adults, not adolescents, and besides, this would complicate her life, which was something she didn't need right now. Neither, she was sure, did he. Especially with Danielle in the picture...

"If you don't mind, I'm going to head upstairs," she began awkwardly, taking a step in retreat.

"Okay, then. And thanks. I appreciated the help."

"I appreciated the dinner," she returned.

"See you in the morning."

"Right." Neither seemed eager to bring the evening to an end.

"Good night, Ellen."

"Night, Reed. Call if you need me."

"I will."

Turning decisively, she took the stairs and was panting by the time she'd climbed up the second narrow flight. Since the third floor had originally been built to accommodate servants, the five bedrooms were small and opened onto a large central room, which was where

Ellen had placed her bed. She'd chosen the largest of the bedrooms as her study.

She sat resolutely down at her desk and leafed through several books, hoping to come across an idea she could use for her term paper. But her thoughts were dominated by the man two floors below. Clutching a study on the origins of algebra to her chest, she sighed deeply and wondered whether Danielle truly valued Reed. She must, Ellen decided, or she wouldn't be so willing to sit at home waiting, while her fiancé traipsed around the world directing a variety of projects.

Reed had been so patient and good-natured with Jimmy and Jenny. When the little boy had climbed into his lap, Reed had read to him and held him with a tenderness that stirred her heart. And Reed was generous to a fault. Another man might have told Pat, Monte and Ellen to pack their bags. This was his home, after all, and Derek had been wrong to rent out the rooms without Reed's knowledge. But Reed had let them stay.

Disgruntled with the trend her thoughts were taking, Ellen forced her mind back to the books in front of her. But it wasn't long before her concentration started to drift again. Reed had Danielle, and she had…Charlie Hanson. First thing in the morning, she'd call dependable old Charlie and suggest they get together; he'd probably be as surprised as he was pleased to hear from her. Feeling relieved and a little light-headed, Ellen turned off the light and went to bed.

"What are you doing?" Reed arrived in the kitchen early the next afternoon, looking as though he'd just finished eighteen holes of golf or a vigorous game of tennis. He'd already left by the time she'd wandered down to the kitchen that morning.

"Ellen?" he repeated impatiently.

She'd taken the wall plates off the electrical outlets and pulled the receptacle out of its box, from which two thin colored wires now protruded. "I'm trying to figure out why this outlet won't heat the iron," she answered without looking in his direction.

"You're what!" he bellowed.

She wiped her face to remove a layer of dust before she straightened. "Don't yell at me."

"Good grief, woman. You run around on the roof like a trapeze artist, cook like a dream and do electrical work on the side. Is there anything you *can't* do?"

"Algebra," she muttered.

Reed closed the instruction manual Ellen had propped against the sugar bowl in the middle of the table. He took her by the shoulders and pushed her gently aside, then reattached the electrical wires and fastened the whole thing back in place.

As he finished securing the wall plate, Ellen burst out, "What did you do that for? I've almost got the problem traced."

"No doubt, but if you don't mind, I'd rather have a real electrician look at this."

"What can I say? It's your house."

"Right. Now sit down." He nudged her into a chair. "How much longer are you going to delay writing that term paper?"

"It's written," she snapped. She wasn't particularly

pleased with it, but at least the assignment was done. Her subject matter might impress four-year-old Jimmy, but she wasn't too confident that her professor would feel the same way.

"Do you want me to look it over?"

The offer surprised her. "No, thanks." She stuck the screwdriver in the pocket of her gray-striped coveralls.

"Well, that wasn't so hard, was it?"

"I just don't think I've got a snowball's chance of getting a decent grade on it. Anyway, I have to go and iron a dress. I've got a date."

A dark brow lifted over inscrutable green eyes and he seemed about to say something.

"Reed." Unexpectedly, the kitchen door swung open and a soft, feminine voice purred his name. "What's taking you so long?"

"Danielle, I'd like you to meet Ellen."

"Hello." Ellen resisted the urge to kick Reed. If he was going to introduce her to his friend, the least he could have done was waited until she looked a little more presentable. Just as she'd figured, Danielle was beautiful. No, the word was *gorgeous*. She wore a cute pale blue tennis outfit with a short, pleated skirt. A dark blue silk scarf held back the curly cascade of long blond hair—Ellen should have known the other woman would be blonde. Naturally, Danielle possessed a trim waist, perfect legs and blue eyes to match the heavens. She'd apparently just finished playing golf or tennis with Reed, but she still looked cool and elegant.

"I feel as though I already know you," Danielle was

saying with a pleasant smile. "Reed told me how much help you were with the children."

"It was nothing, really." Embarrassed by her ridiculous outfit, Ellen tried to conceal as much of it as possible by grabbing the electrical repair book and clasping it to her stomach.

"Not according to Reed." Danielle slipped her arm around his and smiled adoringly up at him. "Unfortunately, I came down with a terrible headache."

"Danielle doesn't have your knack with young children," Reed said.

"If we decide to have our own, things will be different," Danielle continued sweetly. "But I'm not convinced I'm the maternal type."

Ellen sent the couple a wan smile. "If you'll excuse me, I've got to go change my clothes."

"Of course. It was nice meeting you, Elaine."

"Ellen," Reed and Ellen corrected simultaneously.

"You, too." Gallantly, Ellen stifled the childish impulse to call the other woman Diane. As she turned and hurried up the stairs leading from the kitchen, she heard Danielle whisper that she didn't mind at all if Ellen lived in Reed's home. Of course not, Ellen muttered to herself. How could Danielle possibly be jealous?

Winded by the time she'd marched up both flights, Ellen walked into the tiny bedroom where she stored her clothes. She threw down the electrical manual and slammed the door shut. Then she sighed with despair as she saw her reflection in the full-length mirror on the back of the door; it revealed baggy coveralls, a faded white T-shirt and smudges of dirt across her cheekbone.

She struck a seductive pose with her hand on her hip and vampishly puffed up her hair. "Of course, I don't mind if sweet little Elaine lives here, darling," she mimicked in a high-pitched falsely sweet voice.

Dropping her coveralls to the ground, Ellen gruffly kicked them aside. Hands on her hips, she glared at her reflection. Her figure was no less attractive than Danielle's, and her face was pretty enough—even if she did say so herself. But Danielle had barely looked at Ellen and certainly hadn't seen her as a potential rival.

As she brushed her hair away from her face, Ellen's shoulders suddenly dropped. She was losing her mind! She liked living with the boys. Their arrangement was ideal, yet here she was, complaining bitterly because her presence hadn't been challenged.

Carefully choosing a light pink blouse and denim skirt, Ellen told herself that Charlie, at least, would appreciate her. And for now, Ellen needed that. Her self-confidence had been shaken by Danielle's casual acceptance of her role in Reed's house. She didn't like Danielle. But then, she hadn't expected to.

"Ellen." Her name was followed by a loud pounding on the bedroom door. "Wake up! There's a phone call for you."

"Okay," she mumbled into her pillow, still caught in the dregs of sleep. It felt so warm and cozy under the blankets that she didn't want to stir. Charlie had taken her to dinner and a movie and they'd returned a little after ten. The boys had stayed in that evening, but Reed was out and Ellen didn't need to ask with whom. She hadn't heard him come home.

"Ellen!"

"I'm awake, I'm awake," she grumbled, slipping one leg free of the covers and dangling it over the edge of the bed. The sudden cold that assailed her bare foot made her eyes flutter open in momentary shock.

"It's long distance."

Her eyes did open then. She knew only one person who could be calling. Her mother!

Hurriedly tossing the covers aside, she grabbed her housecoat and scurried out of the room. "Why didn't you tell me it was long distance?"

"I tried," Pat said. "But you were more interested in sleeping."

A glance at her clock radio told her it was barely seven.

Taking a deep, calming breath, Ellen walked quickly down one flight of stairs and picked up the phone at the end of the hallway.

"Good morning, Mom."

"How'd you know it was me?"

Although they emailed each other regularly, this was the first time her mother had actually phoned since she'd left home. "Lucky guess."

"Who was that young man who answered the phone?"

"Patrick."

"The basketball kid."

Her mother had read every word of her emails. "That's him."

"Has Monte eaten you out of house and home yet?"

"Just about."

"And has this Derek kid finally summoned up enough nerve to ask out…what was her name again?"

"Michelle."

"Right. That's the one."

"They saw each other twice this weekend," Ellen told her, feeling a sharp pang of homesickness.

"And what about you, Ellen? Are you dating?" It wasn't an idle question. Through the years, Ellen's mother had often fretted that her oldest child was giving up her youth in order to care for the family. Ellen didn't deny that she'd made sacrifices, but they'd been willing ones.

Her emails had been chatty, but she hadn't mentioned Charlie, and Ellen wasn't sure she wanted her mother to know about him. Her relationship with him was based on friendship and nothing more, although Ellen suspected that Charlie would've liked it to develop into something romantic.

"Mom, you didn't phone me long distance on a Monday morning to discuss my social life."

"You're right. I called to discuss mine."

"And?" Ellen's heart hammered against her ribs. She already knew what was coming. She'd known it months ago, even before she'd moved to Seattle. Her mother was going to remarry. After ten years of widowhood, Barbara Cunningham had found another man to love.

"And—" her mother faltered "—James has asked me to be his wife."

"And?" It seemed to Ellen that her vocabulary had suddenly been reduced to one word.

"And I've said yes."

Ellen closed her eyes, expecting to feel a rush of bittersweet nostalgia for the father she remembered so well and had loved so much. Instead, she felt only gladness that her mother had discovered this new happiness.

"Congratulations, Mom."

"Do you mean that?"

"With all my heart. When's the wedding?"

"Well, actually…" Her mother hedged again. "Honey, don't be angry."

"Angry?"

"We're already married. I'm calling from Reno."

"Oh."

"Are you mad?"

"Of course not."

"James has a winter home in Arizona and we're going to stay there until April."

"April," Ellen repeated, feeling a little dazed.

"If you object, honey, I'll come back to Yakima for Christmas."

"No…I don't object. It's just kind of sudden."

"Dad's been gone ten years."

"I know, Mom. Don't worry, okay?"

"I'll email you soon."

"Do that. And much happiness, Mom. You and James deserve it."

"Thank you, love."

They spoke for a few more minutes before saying goodbye. Ellen walked down the stairs in a state of stunned disbelief, absentmindedly tightening the belt of her housecoat. In a matter of months, her entire family had disintegrated. Her sister and mother had married and Bud had joined the military.

"Good morning," she cautiously greeted Reed, who was sitting at the kitchen table dressed and reading the paper.

"Morning," he responded dryly, as he lowered his paper.

Her hands trembling, Ellen reached for a mug, but it slipped out of her fingers and hit the counter, luckily without breaking.

Reed carefully folded the newspaper and studied her face. "What's wrong? You look like you've just seen a ghost."

"My mom's married," she murmured in a subdued voice. Tears burned in her eyes. She was no longer sure just what she was feeling. Happiness for her mother, yes, but also sadness as she remembered her father and his untimely death.

"Remarried?" he asked.

"Yes." She sat down across from him, holding the mug in both hands and staring into its depths. "It's not like this is sudden. Dad's been gone a lot of years. What surprises me is all the emotion I'm feeling."

"That's only natural. I remember how I felt when my dad remarried. I'd known about Mary and Dad for months. But the day of the wedding I couldn't help feeling, somehow, that my father had betrayed my mother's memory. Those were heavy thoughts for a ten-year-old boy." His hand reached for hers. "As I recall, that was the last time I cried."

Ellen nodded. It was the only way she could thank him, because speaking was impossible just then. She knew instinctively that Reed didn't often share the hurts of his youth.

Just when her throat had relaxed and she felt she could speak, Derek threw open the back door and dashed in, tossing his older brother a set of keys.

"I had them add a quart of oil," Derek said. "Are you sure you can't stay longer?"

The sip of coffee sank to the pit of Ellen's stomach and sat there. "You're leaving?" It seemed as though someone had jerked her chair out from under her.

He released her hand and gave it a gentle pat. "You'll be fine."

Ellen forced her concentration back to her coffee. For days she'd been telling herself that she'd be relieved and delighted when Reed left. Now she dreaded it. More than anything, she wanted him to stay.

Four

"Ellen," Derek shouted as he burst in the front door, his hands full of mail. "Can I invite Michelle to dinner on Friday night?"

Casually, Ellen looked up from the textbook she was studying. By mutual agreement, they all went their separate ways on Friday evenings and Ellen didn't cook. If one of the boys happened to be in the house, he heated up soup or put together a sandwich or made do with leftovers. In Monte's case, he did all three.

"What are you planning to fix?" Ellen responded cagily.

"Cook? Me?" Derek slapped his hand against his chest and looked utterly shocked. "I can't cook. You know that."

"But you're inviting company."

His gaze dropped and he restlessly shuffled his feet. "I was hoping that maybe this one Friday you could…" He paused and his head jerked up. "You don't have a date, do you?" He sounded as if that was the worst possible thing that could happen.

"Not this Friday."

"Oh, good. For a minute there, I thought we might have a problem."

"We?" She rolled her eyes. "I don't have a problem, but it sounds like you do." She wasn't going to let him con her into his schemes quite so easily.

"But you'll be here."

"I was planning on soaking in the tub, giving my hair a hot-oil treatment and hibernating with a good book."

"But you could still make dinner, couldn't you? Something simple like seafood jambalaya with shrimp, stuffed eggplant and pecan pie for dessert."

"Are you planning to rob a bank, as well?" At his blank stare, she elaborated. "Honestly, Derek, have you checked out the price of seafood lately?"

"No, but you cooked that Cajun meal not long ago and—"

"Shrimp was on sale," she broke in.

He continued undaunted. "And it was probably the most delicious meal I've ever tasted in my whole life. I was kicking myself because Reed wasn't here and he would have loved it as much as everyone else."

At the mention of Reed's name, Ellen's lashes fell, hiding the confusion and longing in her eyes. The house had been full of college boys, yet it had seemed astonishingly empty without Reed. He'd been with them barely a week and Ellen couldn't believe how much his presence had affected her. The morning he'd left, she'd walked him out to his truck, trying to think of a way to say goodbye and to thank him for understanding the emotions that raged through her at the news of her mother's remarriage. But nothing had turned out quite as she'd expected. Reed had seemed just as reluctant to say goodbye as she was, and before climbing into the truck, he'd leaned forward and lightly brushed his lips over hers. The kiss had been so spontaneous that Ellen wasn't sure if he'd really meant to do it. But intentional or not, he *had,* and the memory of that kiss stayed with her. Now hardly a day passed that he didn't enter her thoughts.

A couple of times when she was on the second floor she'd wandered into her old bedroom, forgetting that it now belonged to Reed. Both times, she'd lingered there, enjoying the sensation of remembering Reed and their verbal battles.

Repeatedly Ellen told herself that it was because Derek's brother was over twenty-one and she could therefore carry on an adult conversation with him. Although she was genuinely fond of the boys, she'd discovered that a constant diet of their antics and their adolescent preoccupations—Pat's basketball, Monte's appetite and Derek's Michelle—didn't exactly make for stimulating conversation.

"You really are a fantastic cook," Derek went on. "Even better than my mother. You know, only the other day Monte was saying—"

"Don't you think you're putting it on a little thick, Derek?"

He blinked. "I just wanted to tell you how much I'd appreciate it if you decided to do me this tiny favor."

"You'll buy the ingredients yourself?"

"The grocery budget couldn't manage it?"

"Not unless everyone else is willing to eat oatmeal three times a week for the remainder of the month."

"I don't suppose they would be," he muttered. "All right, make me a list and I'll buy what you need."

Ellen was half hoping that once he saw the price of fresh shrimp, he'd realize it might be cheaper to take Michelle to a seafood restaurant.

"Oh, by the way," Derek said, examining one of the envelopes in his hand. "You got a letter. Looks like it's from Reed."

"Reed?" Her lungs slowly contracted as she said his name, and it was all she could do not to snatch the envelope out of Derek's hand. The instant he gave it to her, she tore it open.

"What does he say?" Derek asked, sorting through the rest of the mail. "He didn't write me."

Ellen quickly scanned the contents. "He's asking if the electrician has showed up yet. That's all."

"Oh? Then why didn't he just call? Or send an email?"

She didn't respond, but made a show of putting the letter back inside the envelope. "I'll go into the kitchen and make that grocery list before I forget."

"I'm really grateful, Ellen, honest."

"Sure," she grumbled.

As soon as the kitchen door swung shut, Ellen took out Reed's letter again, intent on savoring every word.

Dear Ellen,
I realized I don't have your email address, so I thought I'd do this the old-fashioned way—by

mail. There's something so leisurely and personal about writing a letter, isn't there?

You're right, the Monterey area is beautiful. I wish I could say that everything else is as peaceful as the scenery here. Unfortunately it's not. Things have been hectic. But if all goes well, I should be back at the house by Saturday, which is earlier than I expected.

Have you become accustomed to the idea that your mother's remarried? I know it was a shock. Like I said, I remember how I felt, and that was many years ago. I've been thinking about it all—and wondering about you. If I'd known what was happening, I might have been able to postpone this trip. You looked like you needed someone. And knowing you, it isn't often that you're willing to lean on anyone. Not the independent, self-sufficient woman I discovered walking around my kitchen half-naked. I can almost see your face getting red when you read that. I shouldn't tease you, but I can't help it.

By the way, I contacted a friend of mine who owns an electrical business and told him about the problem with the kitchen outlet. He said he'd try to stop by soon. He'll call first.

I wanted you to know that I was thinking about you—and the boys, but mostly you. Actually, I'm pleased you're there to keep those kids in line.

Take care and I'll see you late Saturday.

Say hi to the boys for me. I'm trusting that they aren't giving you any problems.

Reed

Ellen folded the letter and slipped it into her pocket. She crossed her arms, smiling to herself, feeling incredibly good. So Reed had been thinking about her. And she sensed that it was more than the troublesome kitchen outlet that had prompted his letter. Although she knew it would be dangerous for her to read too much into Reed's message, Ellen couldn't help feeling encouraged.

She propped open her cookbook, compiling the list of items Derek would need for his fancy dinner with Michelle. A few minutes later, her spirits soared still higher when the electrical contractor phoned and arranged a date and a time to check the faulty outlet. Somehow, that seemed like a good omen to her—a kind of proof that she really was in Reed's thoughts.

"Was the phone for me?" Derek called from halfway down the stairs.

Ellen finished writing the information on the pad by the phone before answering. "It was the electrician."

"Oh. I'm expecting a call from Michelle."

"Speaking of your true love, here's your grocery list."

Derek took it and slowly ran his finger down the items she'd need for his dinner with Michelle. "Is this going to cost more than twenty-five dollars?" He glanced up, his face doubtful.

"The pecans alone will be that much," she exaggerated.

With only a hint of disappointment, Derek shook his head. "I think maybe Michelle and I should find a nice, cozy, *inexpensive* restaurant."

Satisfied that her plan had worked so well, Ellen hid

a smile. "Good idea. By the way," she added, "Reed says he'll be home Saturday."

"So soon? He's just been gone two weeks."

"Apparently it's a short job."

"Apparently," Derek grumbled. "I don't have to be here, do I? Michelle wanted me to help her and her sister paint."

"Derek," Ellen said. "I didn't even know you could wield a brush. The upstairs hallway—"

"Forget it," he told her sharply. "I'm only doing this to help Michelle."

"Right, but I'm sure Michelle would be willing to help you in exchange."

"Hey, we're students, not slaves."

The following afternoon, the electrician arrived and was in and out of the house within thirty minutes. Ellen felt proud that she'd correctly traced the problem. She could probably have fixed it if Reed hadn't become so frantic at the thought of her fumbling around with the wiring. Still, recalling his reaction made her smile.

That evening, Ellen had finished loading the dishwasher and had just settled down at the kitchen table to study when the phone rang. Pat, who happened to be walking past it, answered.

"It's Reed," he told Ellen. "He wants to talk to you."

With reflexes that surprised even her, Ellen bounded out of her chair.

"Reed," she said into the receiver, holding it tightly against her ear. "Hello, how are you?"

"Fine. Did the electrician come?"

"He was here this afternoon."

"Any problems?"

"No," she breathed. He sounded wonderfully close, his voice warm and vibrant. "In fact, I was on the right track. I probably could've handled it myself."

"I don't want you to even think about fixing anything like that. You could end up killing yourself or someone else. I absolutely forbid it."

"Aye, aye, sir." His words had the immediate effect of igniting her temper, sending the hot blood roaring through her veins. She hadn't been able to stop thinking about Reed since he'd left, but two minutes after picking up the phone, she was ready to argue with him again.

There was a long, awkward silence. Reed was the first to speak, expelling his breath sharply. "I didn't mean to snap your head off," he said. "I'm sorry."

"Thank you," she responded, instantly soothed.

"How's everything else going?"

"Fine."

"Have the boys talked you into any more of their schemes?"

"They keep trying."

"They wouldn't be college kids if they didn't."

"I know." It piqued her a little that Reed assumed she could be manipulated by three teenagers. "Don't worry about me. I can hold my own with these guys."

His low sensuous chuckle did funny things to her pulse. "It's not you I'm concerned about."

"Just what are you implying?" she asked with mock seriousness.

"I'm going to play this one smart and leave that last comment open-ended."

"Clever of you, my friend, very clever."

"I thought as much."

After a short pause, Ellen quickly asked, "How's everything with you?" She knew there really wasn't anything more to say, but she didn't want the conversation to end. Talking to Reed was almost as good as having him there.

"Much better, thanks. I shouldn't have any problem getting home by Saturday."

"Good."

Another short silence followed.

"Well, I guess that's all I've got to say. If I'm going to be any later than Saturday, I'll give you a call."

"Drive carefully."

"I will. Bye, Ellen."

"Goodbye, Reed." Smiling, she replaced the receiver. When she glanced up, all three boys were staring at her, their arms crossed dramatically over their chests.

"I think something's going on here." Pat spoke first. "I answered the phone and Reed asked for Ellen. He didn't even ask for Derek—his own brother."

"Right." Derek nodded vigorously.

"I'm wondering," Monte said, rubbing his chin. "Could we have the makings of a romance on our hands?"

"I think we do," Pat concurred.

"Stop it." Ellen did her best to join in the banter, although she felt the color flooding her cheeks. "It makes sense that Reed would want to talk to me. I'm the oldest."

"But I'm his brother," Derek countered.

"I refuse to listen to any of this," she said with a small laugh and turned back to the kitchen. "You three are being ridiculous. Reed's dating Danielle."

All three followed her. "He could have married Danielle months ago if he was really interested," Derek informed the small gathering.

"Be still, my beating heart," Monte joked, melodramatically folding both hands over his chest and pretending to swoon.

Not to be outdone, Pat rested the back of his hand against his forehead and rolled his eyes. "Ah, love."

"I'm out of here." Before anyone could argue, Ellen ran up the back stairs to her room, laughing as she went. She had to admit she'd found the boys' little performances quite funny. But if they pulled any of their pranks around Reed, it would be extremely embarrassing. Ellen resolved to say something to them when the time seemed appropriate.

Friday afternoon, Ellen walked into the kitchen, her book bag clutched tightly to her chest.

"What's the matter? You're as pale as a ghost," Monte remarked, cramming a chocolate-chip cookie in his mouth.

Derek and Pat turned toward her, their faces revealing concern.

"I got my algebra paper back today."

"And?" Derek prompted.

"I don't know. I haven't looked."

"Why not?"

"Because I know how tough Engstrom was on the others. The girl who wrote about solving that oddball conjecture got a C-minus and the guy who was so enthusiastic about Mathematics in World War II got a D. With impressive subjects like that getting low grades, I'm doomed."

"But you worked hard on that paper." Loyally, Derek defended her and placed a consoling arm around her shoulders. "You found out a whole bunch of interesting facts about the number nine."

"You did your paper on that?" Pat asked, his smooth brow wrinkling with amusement.

"Don't laugh." She already felt enough of a fool.

"It isn't going to do any good to worry," Monte insisted, pulling the folded assignment from between her fingers.

Ellen watched his expression intently as he looked at the paper, then handed it to Derek who raised his brows and gave it to Pat.

"Well?"

"You got a B-minus," Pat said in obvious surprise. "I don't believe it."

"Me neither." Ellen reveled in the delicious feeling of relief. She sank luxuriously into a chair. "I'm calling Charlie." Almost immediately she jumped up again and dashed to the phone. "This is too exciting! I'm celebrating."

The other three had drifted into the living room and two minutes later, she joined them there. "Charlie's out, but his roommate said he'd give him the message." Too happy to contain her excitement, she added, "But I'm not sitting home alone. How about if we go out for pizza tonight? My treat."

"Sorry, Ellen." Derek looked up with a frown. "I've already made plans with Michelle."

"I'm getting together with a bunch of guys at the gym," Pat informed her. "Throw a few baskets."

"And I told my mom I'd be home for dinner."

Some of the excitement drained from her, but she put on a brave front. "No problem. We'll do it another night."

"I'll go."

The small group whirled around, shocked to discover Reed standing there, framed in the living-room doorway.

Five

"Reed," Ellen burst out, astonished. "When did you get here?" The instant she'd finished speaking, she realized how stupid the question was. He'd just walked in the back door.

With a grin, he checked his wristwatch. "About fifteen seconds ago."

"How was the trip?" Derek asked.

"Did you drive straight through?" Pat asked, then said, "I don't suppose you had a chance to see the Lakers play, did you?"

"You must be exhausted," Ellen murmured, noting how tired his eyes looked.

As his smiling gaze met hers, the fine laugh lines that fanned out from his eyes became more pronounced. "I'm hungry *and* tired. Didn't I just hear you offer to buy me pizza?"

"Ellen got a B-minus on her crazy algebra paper," Monte said with pride.

Rolling her eyes playfully toward the ceiling, Ellen

laughed. "Who would have guessed it—I'm a mathematical genius!"

"So that's the reason for this dinner. I thought you might have won the lottery."

He was more deeply tanned than Ellen remembered. Handsome. Vital. And incredibly male. He seemed glad to be home, she thought. Not a hint of hostility showed in the eyes that smiled back at her.

"No such luck."

Derek made a show of glancing at his watch. "I gotta go or I'll be late picking up Michelle. It's good to see you, Reed."

"Yeah, welcome home," Pat said, reaching for his basketball. "I'll see you later."

Reed raised his right hand in salute and picked up his suitcase, then headed up the wide stairs. "Give me fifteen minutes to shower and I'll meet you down here."

The minute Reed's back was turned, Monte placed his hand over his heart and batted his lashes wildly as he mouthed something about love, true love. Ellen practically threw him out of the house, slamming the door after him.

At the top of the stairs, Reed turned and glanced down at her. "What was that all about?"

Ellen leaned against the closed door, one hand covering her mouth to smother her giggles. But the laughter drained from her as she looked at his puzzled face, and she slowly straightened. She cleared her throat. "Nothing. Did you want me to order pizza? Or do you want to go out?"

"Whatever you prefer."

"If you leave it up to me, my choice would be to get away from these four walls."

"I'll be ready in a few minutes."

Ellen suppressed a shudder at the thought of what would've happened had Reed caught a glimpse of Monte's antics. She herself handled the boys' teasing with good-natured indulgence, but she was fairly sure that Reed would take offense at their nonsense. And heaven forbid that Danielle should ever catch a hint of what was going on—not that anything *was* going on.

With her thoughts becoming more muddled every minute, Ellen made her way to the third floor to change into a pair of gray tailored pants and a frilly pale blue silk blouse. One glance in the mirror and she sadly shook her head. They were only going out for pizza—there was no need to wear anything so elaborate. Hurriedly, she changed into dark brown cords and a turtleneck sweater the color of summer wheat. Then she ran a brush through her short curls and freshened her lipstick.

When Ellen returned to the living room, Reed was already waiting for her. "You're sure you don't mind going out?" she asked again.

"Are you dodging your pizza offer?"

He was so serious that Ellen couldn't help laughing. "Not at all."

"Good. I hope you like spicy sausage with lots of olives."

"Love it."

His hand rested on her shoulder. "And a cold beer."

"This is sounding better all the time." Ellen would

have guessed that Reed was the type of man who drank martinis or expensive cocktails. In some ways, he was completely down-to-earth and in others, surprisingly complex. Perceptive, unpretentious and unpredictable— she knew that much about him, but she didn't expect to understand him anytime soon.

Reed helped her into his pickup, which was parked in the driveway. The evening sky was already dark and Ellen regretted not having brought her coat.

"Cold?" Reed asked her when they stopped at a red light.

"Only a little."

He adjusted the switches for the heater and soon a rush of warm air filled the cab. Reed chatted easily, telling her about his project in California and explaining why his work demanded so much travel. "That's changing now."

"Oh?" She couldn't restrain a little shiver of gladness at his announcement. "Will you be coming home more often?"

"Not for another three or four months. I'm up for promotion and then I'll be able to pick and choose my assignments more carefully. Over the past four years, I've traveled enough to last me a lifetime."

"Then it's true that there's no place like home."

"Be it ever so humble," he added with a chuckle.

"I don't exactly consider a three-storey, twenty-room turn-of-the-century mansion all that humble."

"Throw in four college students and you'll quickly discover how unassuming it can become."

"Oh?"

"You like that word, don't you?"

"Yes," she agreed, her mouth curving into a lazy smile. "It's amazing how much you can say with that one little sound."

Reed exited the freeway close to the Seattle Center and continued north. At her questioning glance, he explained, "The best pizza in Seattle is made at a small place near the Center. You don't mind coming this far, do you?"

"Of course not. I'll travel a whole lot farther than this for a good pizza." Suddenly slouching forward, she dropped her forehead into her hand. "Oh, no. It's happening."

"What is?"

"I'm beginning to sound like Monte."

They both laughed. It felt so good to be sitting there with Reed, sharing an easy, relaxed companionship, that Ellen could almost forget about Danielle. Almost, but not quite.

Although Ellen had said she'd pay for the pizza, Reed insisted on picking up the tab. They sat across from each other at a narrow booth in the corner of the semidarkened room. A lighted red candle in a glass bowl flickered on the table between them and Ellen decided this was the perfect atmosphere. The old-fashioned jukebox blared out the latest country hits, drowning out the possibility of any audible conversation, but that seemed just as well since she was feeling strangely tongue-tied.

When their number was called, Reed slid from the booth and returned a minute later with two frothy beers in ice-cold mugs and a huge steaming pizza.

"I hope you don't expect us to eat all this?" Ellen said, shouting above the music. The pizza certainly smelled enticing, but Ellen doubted she'd manage to eat more than two or three pieces.

"We'll put a dent in it, anyway," Reed said, resuming his seat. "I bought the largest, figuring the boys would enjoy the leftovers."

"You're a terrific older brother."

The song on the jukebox was fading into silence at last.

"There are times I'd like to shake some sense into Derek, though," Reed said.

Ellen looked down at the spicy pizza and put a small slice on her plate. Strings of melted cheese still linked the piece to the rest of the pie. She pulled them loose and licked her fingers. "I can imagine how you felt when you discovered that Derek had accidentally-on-purpose forgotten to tell you about renting out rooms."

Reed shrugged noncommittally. "I was thinking more about the time he let you climb on top of the roof," he muttered.

"He didn't *let* me, I went all by myself."

"But you won't do it again. Right?"

"Right." Ellen nodded reluctantly. Behind Reed's slow smiles and easy banter, she recognized his unrelenting male pride. "You still haven't forgiven me for that, have you?"

"Not you. Derek."

"I think this is one of those subjects on which we should agree to disagree."

"Have you heard from your mother?" Reed asked, apparently just as willing to change the subject.

"Yes. She's emailed me several times. She seems very happy and after a day or two, I discovered I couldn't be more pleased for her. She deserves a lot of contentment."

"I knew you'd realize that." Warmth briefly showed in his green eyes.

"I felt a lot better after talking to you. I was surprised when Mom announced her marriage, but I shouldn't have been. The signs were there all along. I suppose once the three of us kids were gone, she felt free to remarry. And I suppose she thought that presenting it to the family as a fait accompli would make it easier for all of us."

There was a comfortable silence as they finished eating. The pizza was thick with sausage and cheese, and Ellen placed her hands on her stomach after leisurely eating two narrow pieces. "I'm stuffed," she declared, leaning back. "But you're right, this has got to be the best pizza in town."

"I thought you'd like it."

Reed brought over a carry-out box and Ellen carefully put the leftovers inside.

"How about a movie?" he asked once they were in the car park.

Astounded, Ellen darted him a sideways glance, but his features were unreadable. "You're kidding, aren't you?"

"I wouldn't have asked you if I was."

"But you must be exhausted." Ellen guessed he'd probably spent most of the day driving.

"A little," he admitted.

Her frown deepened. Suddenly, it no longer seemed right for them to be together—because of Danielle. The problem was that Ellen had been so pleased to see him that she hadn't stopped to think about the consequences of their going out together. "Thanks anyway, but it's been a long week. I think I'll call it a night."

When they reached the house, Reed parked on the street rather than the driveway. The light from the stars and the silvery moon penetrated the branches that hung overhead and created shadows on his face. Neither of them seemed eager to leave the warm cab of the pickup truck. The mood was intimate and Ellen didn't want to disturb this moment of tranquillity. Lowering her gaze, she admitted to herself how attracted she was to Reed and how much she liked him. She admitted, too, that it was wrong for her to feel this way about him.

"You're quiet all of a sudden."

Ellen's smile was decidedly forced. She turned toward him to apologise for putting a damper on their evening, but the words never left her lips. Instead, her eyes met his. Paralyzed, she stared at Reed, fighting to disguise the intense attraction she felt for him. It seemed the most natural thing in the world to lean toward him and brush her lips against his. She could smell the woodsy scent of his aftershave and could almost taste his mouth on hers. With determination, she pulled her gaze away and reached for the door, like a drowning person grasping a life preserver.

She was on the front porch by the time Reed joined her. Her fingers shook as she inserted the key in the lock.

"Ellen." He spoke her name softly and placed his hand on her shoulder.

"I don't know why we went out tonight." Her voice was high and strained as she drew free of his touch. "We shouldn't have been together."

In response, Reed mockingly lifted one eyebrow. "I believe it was you who asked me."

"Be serious, will you," she snapped irritably and shoved open the door.

Reed slammed it shut behind him and followed her into the kitchen. He set the pizza on the counter, then turned to face her. "What the hell do you mean? I *was* being serious."

"You shouldn't have been with me tonight."

"Why not?"

"Where's Danielle? I'm not the one who's been patiently waiting around for you. *She* is. You had no business taking me out to dinner and then suggesting a movie. You're my landlord, not my boyfriend."

"Let's get two things straight here. First, what's between Danielle and me is none of *your* business. And second, you invited *me* out. Remember?"

"But...it wasn't like that and you know it."

"Besides, I thought you said you were far too old for *boyfriends.*" She detected an undertone of amusement in his voice.

Confused, Ellen marched into the living room and immediately busied herself straightening magazines. Reed charged in after her, leaving the kitchen door swinging in his wake. Clutching a sofa pillow, she searched for some witty retort. Naturally, whenever she needed a clever comeback, her mind was a total blank.

"You're making a joke out of everything," she told him, angry that her voice was shaking. "And I don't like that. If you want to play games, do it with someone other than me."

"Ellen, listen—"

The phone rang and she jerked her attention to the hallway.

"I didn't mean—" Reed paused and raked his fingers through his hair. The phone pealed a second time. "Go ahead and answer that."

She hurried away, relieved to interrupt this disturbing conversation. "Hello." Her voice sounded breathless, as though she'd raced down the stairs.

"Ellen? This is Charlie. I got a message that you phoned."

For one crazy instant, Ellen forgot why she'd wanted to talk to Charlie. "I phoned? Oh, right. Remember that algebra paper I was struggling with? Well, I got it back today."

"How'd you do?"

A little of the surprised pleasure returned. "I still can't believe it. I got a B-minus. My simple paper about the wonders of the number nine received one of the highest marks in the class. I'm still in shock."

Charlie's delighted chuckle came over the wire. "This calls for a celebration. How about if we go out tomorrow night? Dinner, drinks, the works."

Ellen almost regretted the impulse to contact Charlie. She sincerely liked him, and she hated the thought of stringing him along or taking advantage of his attraction to her. "Nothing so elaborate. Chinese food and a movie would be great."

"You let me worry about that. Just be ready by seven."

"Charlie"

"No arguing. I'll see you at seven."

By the time Ellen got off the phone, Reed was nowhere to be seen. Nor was he around the following afternoon. The boys didn't comment and she couldn't very well ask about him without arousing their suspicions. As it was, the less she mentioned Reed around them, the better. The boys had obviously read more into the letter, phone call and dinner than Reed had intended. But she couldn't blame them; she'd read enough into it herself to be frightened by what was happening between them. He'd almost kissed her when he'd parked in front of the house. And she'd wanted him to—that was what disturbed her most. But if she allowed her emotions to get involved, she knew that someone would probably end up being hurt. And the most likely *someone* was Ellen herself.

Besides, if Reed was attracted to Danielle's sleek elegance, then he would hardly be interested in her own more homespun qualities.

A few minutes before seven, Ellen was ready for her evening with Charlie. She stood before the downstairs hallway mirror to put the finishing touches on her appearance, fastening her gold earrings and straightening the single chain necklace.

"Where's Reed been today?" Pat inquired of no one in particular.

"His sports car is gone," Monte said, munching on a chocolate bar. "I noticed it wasn't in the garage when I took out the garbage."

Slowly Ellen sauntered into the living room. She didn't want to appear too curious, but at the same time, she was definitely interested in the conversation.

She had flopped into a chair and picked up a two-month-old magazine before she noticed all three boys staring at her.

"What are you looking at me for?"

"We thought you might know something."

"About what?" she asked, playing dumb.

"Reed," all three said simultaneously.

"Why should I know anything?" Her gaze flittered from them to the magazine and back again.

"You went out with him last night."

"We didn't *go out* the way you're implying."

Pat pointed an accusing finger at her. "The two of you were alone together, and both of you have been acting weird ever since."

"And I say the three of you have overactive imaginations."

"All I know is that Reed was like a wounded bear this morning," Derek volunteered.

"Everyone's entitled to an off day." Hoping to give a casual impression, she leafed through the magazine, idly fanning the pages with her thumb.

"That might explain Reed. But what about you?"

"Me?"

"For the first time since you moved in, you weren't downstairs until after ten."

"I slept in. Is that a crime?"

"It just might be. You and Reed are both acting really strange. It's like the two of you are avoiding each other and we want to know why."

"It's your imagination. Believe me, if there was anything to tell you, I would."

"Sure, you would," Derek mocked.

From the corner of her eye, Ellen saw Charlie's car pull up in front of the house. Releasing a sigh of relief, she quickly stood and gave the boys a falsely bright smile. "If you'll excuse me, my date has arrived."

"Should we tell Reed you're out with Charlie if he wants to know where you are?" Monte looked uncomfortable asking the question.

"Of course. Besides, he probably already knows. He's free to see anyone he wants and so am I. For that matter, so are you." She whirled around and made her way to the front door, pulling it open before Charlie even got a chance to ring the doorbell.

The evening didn't go well. Charlie took her out for a steak dinner and spent more money than Ellen knew he could afford. She regretted having phoned him. Charlie had obviously interpreted her call as a sign that she was interested in becoming romantically involved. She wasn't, and didn't know how to make it clear without offending him.

"Did you have a good time?" he asked as they drove back toward Capitol Hill.

"Lovely, thank you, Charlie."

His hand reached for hers and squeezed it reassuringly. "We don't go out enough."

"Neither of us can afford it too often."

"We don't need to go to a fancy restaurant to be together," he said lightly. "Just being with you is a joy."

"Thank you." If only Charlie weren't so nice. She hated the idea of hurting him. But she couldn't allow him to go on hoping that she would ever return his feelings. As much as she dreaded it, she knew she had to disillusion him. Anything else would be cruel and dishonest.

"I don't think I've made a secret of how I feel about you, Ellen. You're wonderful."

"Come on, Charlie, I'm not that different from a thousand other girls on campus." She tried to swallow the tightness in her throat. "In fact, I saw the way that girl in our sociology class—what's her name—Lisa, has been looking at you lately."

"I hadn't noticed."

"I believe you've got yourself an admirer."

"But I'm only interested in you."

"Charlie, listen. I think you're a very special person. I—"

"Shh," he demanded softly as he parked in front of Ellen's house and turned off the engine. He slid his arm along the back of the seat and caressed her shoulder. "I don't want you to say anything."

"But I feel I may have—"

"Ellen," he whispered seductively. "Be quiet and just let me kiss you."

Before she could utter another word, Charlie claimed her mouth in a short but surprisingly ardent kiss. Charlie had kissed her on several occasions, but that was as far as things had ever gone.

When his arms tightened around her, Ellen resisted.

"Invite me in for coffee," he whispered urgently in her ear.

She pressed her forehead against his shirt collar. "Not tonight."

He tensed. "Can I see you again soon?"

"I don't know. We see each other every day. Why don't we just meet after class for coffee one day next week?"

"But I want more than that," he protested.

"I know," she answered, dropping her eyes. She felt confused and miserable.

Ellen could tell he was disappointed from the way he climbed out of the car and trudged around to her side. There was tense silence between them as he walked her up to the front door and kissed her a second time. Again, Ellen had to break away from him by pushing her hands against his chest.

"Thank you for everything," she whispered.

"Right. Thanks, but no thanks."

"Oh, Charlie, don't start that. Not now."

Eyes downcast, he wearily rubbed a hand along the side of his face. "I guess I'll see you Monday," he said with a sigh.

"Thanks for the lovely evening." She didn't let herself inside until Charlie had climbed into his car and driven away.

Releasing a jagged breath, Ellen had just started to

unbutton her coat when she glanced up to find Reed standing in the living room, glowering at her.

"Is something wrong?" The undisguised anger that twisted his mouth and hardened his gaze was a shock.

"Do you always linger outside with your boy-friends?"

"We didn't linger."

"Right." He dragged one hand roughly through his hair and marched a few paces toward her, only to do an abrupt about-face. "I saw the two of you necking."

"Necking?" Ellen was so startled by his unreason-able anger that she didn't know whether to laugh or argue. "Be serious, will you? Two chaste kisses hardly constitute necking."

"What kind of influence are you on Derek and the others?" He couldn't seem to stand still and paced back and forth in agitation.

He was obviously furious, but Ellen didn't under-stand why. He couldn't possibly believe these absurd insinuations. Perhaps he was upset about something else and merely taking it out on her. "Reed, what's wrong?" she finally asked.

"I saw you out there."

"You were spying on me?"

"I wasn't spying," he snapped.

"Charlie and I were in his car. You must've been staring out the window to have seen us."

He didn't answer her, but instead hurled another ac-cusation in her direction. "You're corrupting the boys."

"I'm *what?*" She couldn't believe what she was hear-ing. "What year do you think this is?" She shook her head, bewildered. "They're nineteen. Trust me, they've kissed girls before."

"You can kiss anyone you like. Just don't do it in front of the boys."

From the way this conversation was going, Ellen could see that Reed was in no mood to listen to reason. "I think we should discuss this some other time," she said quietly.

"We'll talk about it right now."

Ignoring his domineering tone as much as possible, Ellen forced a smile. "Good night, Reed. I'll see you in the morning."

She was halfway to the stairs when he called her, his voice calm. "Ellen."

She turned around, holding herself tense, watching him stride quickly across the short distance that separated them. With his thumb and forefinger, he caught her chin, tilting it slightly so he could study her face. He rubbed his thumb across her lips. "Funny, you don't look kissed."

In one breath he was accusing her of necking and in the next, claiming she was unkissed. Not knowing how to respond, Ellen didn't. She merely gazed at him, her eyes wide and questioning.

"If you're going to engage in that sort of activity, the least you can do—" He paused. With each word his mouth drew closer and closer to hers until his lips hovered over her own and their breath mingled. "The least you can do is look kissed." His hand located the vein pounding wildly in her throat as his mouth settled over hers.

Slowly, patiently, his mouth moved over hers with an exquisite tenderness that left her quivering with anticipation and delight. Timidly, her hands crept across his chest to link behind his neck. Again his lips descended on hers, more hungrily now, as he groaned and pulled her even closer.

Ellen felt her face grow hot as she surrendered to the sensations that stole through her. Yet all the while, her mind was telling her she had no right to feel this contentment, this warmth. Reed belonged to another woman. Not to her…to someone else.

Color seeped into her face. When she'd understood that he intended to kiss her, her first thought had been to resist. But once she'd felt his mouth on hers, all her resolve had drained away. Embarrassed now, she realized she'd pliantly wrapped her arms around his neck. And worse, she'd responded with enough enthusiasm for him to know exactly what she was feeling.

He pressed his mouth to her forehead as though he couldn't bear to release her.

Ellen struggled to breathe normally. She let her arms slip from his neck to his chest and through the palm of her hand she could feel the rapid beating of his heart. She closed her eyes, knowing that her own pulse was pounding no less wildly.

She could feel his mouth move against her temple. "I've been wanting to do that for days." The grudging admission came in a voice that was low and taut.

The words to tell him that she'd wanted it just as much were quickly silenced by the sound of someone walking into the room.

Guiltily Reed and Ellen jerked apart. Her face turned a deep shade of red as Derek stopped in his tracks, staring at them.

"Hi."

"Hi," Reed and Ellen said together.

"Hey, I'm not interrupting anything, am I? If you like, I could turn around and pretend I didn't see a thing."

"Do it," Reed ordered.

"No," Ellen said in the same moment.

Derek's eyes sparkled with boyish delight. "You know," he said, "I had a feeling about the two of you." While he spoke, he was taking small steps backward until he stood pressed against the polished kitchen door. He gave his brother a thumbs-up as he nudged open the door with one foot and hurriedly backed out of the room.

"Now look what you've done," Ellen wailed.

"Me? As I recall you were just as eager for this as I was."

"It was a mistake," she blurted out. A ridiculous, illogical mistake. He'd accused her of being a bad influence on the boys and then proceeded to kiss her senseless.

"You're telling me." A distinct coolness entered his eyes. "It's probably a good thing I'm leaving."

There was no hiding her stricken look. "Again? So soon?"

"After what's just happened, I'd say it wasn't soon enough."

"But…where to this time?"

"Denver. I'll be back before Thanksgiving."

Mentally, Ellen calculated that he'd be away another two weeks.

When he spoke again, his voice was gentle. "It's just as well, don't you think?"

Six

"Looks like rain." Pat stood in front of the window above the kitchen sink and frowned at the thick black clouds that darkened the late afternoon sky. "Why does it have to rain?"

Ellen glanced up at him. "Are you seeking a scientific response or will a simple 'I don't know' suffice?"

The kitchen door swung open and Derek sauntered in. "Has anyone seen Reed?"

Instantly, Ellen's gaze dropped to her textbook. Reed had returned to Seattle two days earlier and so far, they'd done an admirable job of avoiding each other. Both mornings, he'd left for his office before she was up. Each evening, he'd come home, showered, changed and then gone off again. It didn't require much detective work to figure out that he was with Danielle. Ellen had attempted—unsuccessfully—not to think of Reed at all. And especially not of him and Danielle together.

She secretly wished she'd had the nerve to arrange an opportunity to talk to Reed. So much remained unclear in her mind. Reed had kissed her and it had been wonderful, yet that was something neither seemed willing to admit. It was as if they'd tacitly agreed that the kiss had been a terrible mistake and should be forgotten. The problem was, Ellen *couldn't* forget it.

"Reed hasn't been around the house much," Pat answered.

"I know." Derek sounded slightly disgruntled and cast an accusing look in Ellen's direction. "It's almost like he doesn't live here anymore."

"He doesn't. Not really." Pat stepped away from the window and gently set his basketball on a chair. "It's sort of like he's a guest who stops in now and then."

Ellen preferred not to be drawn into this conversation. She hastily closed her book and stood up to leave.

"Hey, Ellen." Pat stopped her.

She sighed and met his questioning gaze with a nervous smile. "Yes?"

"I'll be leaving in a few minutes. Have a nice Thanksgiving."

Relieved that the subject of Reed had been dropped, she threw him a brilliant smile. "You, too."

"Where are you having dinner tomorrow?" Derek asked, as if the thought had unexpectedly occurred to him.

Her mother was still in Arizona, her sister had gone to visit her in-laws and Bud couldn't get leave, so Ellen had decided to stay in Seattle. "Here."

"In this house?" Derek's eyes widened with concern. "But why? Shouldn't you be with your family?"

"My family is going in different directions this year.

It's no problem. In fact, I'm looking forward to having the whole house to myself."

"There's no reason to spend the day alone," Derek argued. "My parents wouldn't mind putting out an extra plate. There's always plenty of food."

Her heart was touched by the sincerity of his invitation. "Thank you, but honestly, I prefer it this way."

"It's because of Reed, isn't it?" Both boys studied her with inquisitive eyes.

"Nonsense."

"But, Ellen, he isn't going to be there."

"Reed isn't the reason," she assured him. Undoubtedly, Reed would be spending the holiday with Danielle. She made an effort to ignore the flash of pain that accompanied the thought; she knew she had no right to feel hurt if Reed chose to spend Thanksgiving with his "almost" fiancée.

"You're sure?" Derek didn't look convinced.

"You could come and spend the day with my family," Pat offered next.

"Will you two quit acting like it's such a terrible tragedy? I'm going to *enjoy* an entire day alone. Look at these nails." She fanned her fingers and held them up for their inspection. "For once, I'll have an uninterrupted block of time to do all the things I've delayed for weeks."

"All right, but if you change your mind, give me a call."

"I asked her first," Derek argued. "You'll call me. Right?"

"Right to you both."

* * *

Thanksgiving morning, Ellen woke to a torrential downpour. Rain pelted against the window and the day seemed destined to be a melancholy one. She lounged in her room and read, enjoying the luxury of not having to rush around, preparing breakfast for the whole household.

She wandered down to the kitchen, where she was greeted by a heavy silence. The house was definitely empty. Apparently, Reed, too, had started his day early. Ellen couldn't decide whether she was pleased or annoyed that she had seen so little of him since his return from Denver. He'd been the one to avoid her, and she'd concluded that two could play his silly game. So she'd purposely stayed out of his way. She smiled sadly as she reflected on the past few days. She and Reed had been acting like a couple of adolescents.

She ate a bowl of cornflakes and spent the next hour wiping down the cupboards, with the radio tuned to the soft-rock music station. Whenever a particularly romantic ballad aired, she danced around the kitchen with an imaginary partner. Not so imaginary, really. In her mind, she was in Reed's arms.

The silence became more oppressive during the afternoon, while Ellen busied herself fussing over her nails. When the final layer of polish had dried, she decided to turn on the television to drown out the quiet. An hour into the football game, Ellen noticed that it was nearly dinnertime, and she suddenly felt hungry.

She made popcorn in the microwave and splurged by dripping melted butter over the top. She carried the bowl into the living room and got back on the sofa, tucking her legs beneath her. She'd just found a comfortable position when she heard a noise in the kitchen.

Frowning, she twisted around, wondering who it could be.

The door into the living room swung open and Ellen's heart rate soared into double time.

"Reed?" She blinked to make sure he wasn't an apparition.

"Hello."

He didn't vanish. Instead he took several steps in her direction. "That popcorn smells great."

Without considering the wisdom of her offer, she held out the bowl to him. "Help yourself."

"Thanks." He took off his jacket and tossed it over the back of a chair before joining her on the sofa. He leaned forward, studying the TV. "Who's winning?"

Ellen was momentarily confused, until she realized he was asking about the football game. "I don't know. I haven't paid that much attention."

Reed reached for another handful of popcorn and Ellen set the bowl on the coffee table. Her emotions were muddled. She couldn't imagine what Reed was doing here when he was supposed to be at Danielle's. Although the question burned in her mind, she couldn't bring herself to ask. She glanced at him covertly, but Reed was staring at the TV as though he was alone in the room.

"I'll get us something to drink," she volunteered.

"Great."

Even while she was speaking, Reed hadn't looked

in her direction. Slightly piqued by his attitude, she stalked into the kitchen and took two Pepsis out of the refrigerator.

When she returned with the soft drinks and two glasses filled with ice, Reed took one set from her. "Thanks," he murmured, popping open the can. He carefully poured his soda over the ice and set the can aside before taking a sip.

"You're welcome." She flopped down again, pretending to watch television. But her mind was spinning in a hundred different directions. When she couldn't tolerate it any longer, she blurted out the question that dominated her thoughts.

"Reed, what are you doing here?"

He took a long swallow before answering her. "I happen to live here."

"You know what I mean. You should be with Danielle."

"I was earlier, but I decided I preferred your company."

"I don't need your sympathy," she snapped, then swallowed painfully and averted her gaze. Her fingers tightened around the cold glass until the chill extended up her arm. "I'm perfectly content to spend the day alone. I just wish everyone would quit saving me from myself."

His low chuckle was unexpected. "That wasn't my intention."

"Then why are you here?"

"I already told you."

"I can't accept that," she said shakily. He was toying

with her emotions, and the thought made her all the more furious.

"All right." Determinedly, he set down his drink and turned toward her. "I felt this was the perfect opportunity for us to talk."

"You haven't said more than ten words to me in three days. What makes this one day so special?"

"We're alone, aren't we, and that's more than we can usually say." His voice was strained. He hesitated a moment, his lips pressed together in a thin, hard line. "I don't know what's happening with us."

"Nothing's happening," she said wildly. "You kissed me, and we both admitted it was a mistake. Can't we leave it at that?"

"No," he answered dryly. "I don't believe it was such a major tragedy, and neither do you."

If it had really been a mistake, Ellen wouldn't have remembered it with such vivid clarity. Nor would she yearn for the taste of him again and again, or hurt so much when she knew he was with Danielle.

Swiftly she turned her eyes away from the disturbing intensity of his, unwilling to reveal the depth of her feelings.

"It wasn't a mistake, was it, Ellen?" he prompted in a husky voice.

She squeezed her eyes shut and shook her head. "No," she whispered, but the word was barely audible.

He gathered her close and she felt his deep shudder of satisfaction as he buried his face in her hair. Long moments passed before he spoke. "Nothing that felt so right could have been a mistake."

Tenderly he kissed her, his lips touching hers with a gentleness she hadn't expected. As if he feared she was somehow fragile; as if he found her highly precious. Without conscious decision, she slipped her arms around him.

"The whole time Danielle and I were together this afternoon, I was wishing it was you. Today, of all days, it seemed important to be with you."

Ellen gazed up into his eyes and saw not only his gentleness, but his confusion. Her fingers slid into the thick hair around his lean, rugged face. "Danielle couldn't have been pleased when you left."

"She wasn't. I didn't even know how to explain it to her. I don't know how to explain it to myself."

Ellen swallowed the dryness that constricted her throat. "Do you want me to move out of the house?"

"No," he said forcefully, then added more quietly, "I think I'd go crazy if you did. Are you a witch who's cast some spell over me?"

She tried unsuccessfully to answer him, but no words of denial came. The knowledge that he was experiencing these strange whirling emotions was enough to overwhelm her.

"If so, the spell is working," he murmured, although he didn't sound particularly happy about the idea.

"I'm confused, too," she admitted and leaned her forehead against his chest. She could feel his heart pounding beneath her open hand.

His long fingers stroked her hair. "I know." He leaned down and kissed the top of her head. "The night you went out with Charlie, I was completely unreasonable. I need to apologize for the things I said. To put it simply, I was jealous. I've acknowledged that, these last weeks in Denver." Some of the tightness left his voice, as though the events of that night had weighed heavily on his mind. "I didn't like the idea of another man holding you, and when I saw the two of you kissing, I think I went a little berserk."

"I...we don't date often."

"I won't ask you not to see him again," he said reluctantly. "I can't ask anything of you."

"Nor can I ask anything of you."

His grip around her tightened. "Let's give this time."

"It's the only thing we can do."

Reed straightened and draped his arm around Ellen's shoulders, drawing her close to his side. Her head nestled against his chest. "I'd like us to start going out together," he said, his chin resting on the crown of her head. "Will that cause a problem for you?"

"Cause a problem?" she repeated uncertainly.

"I'm thinking about the boys."

Remembering their earlier buffoonery and the way they'd taken such delight in teasing her, Ellen shrugged. If those three had any evidence of a romance between her and Reed, they could make everyone's lives miserable. "I don't know."

"Then let's play it cool for a while. We'll move into this gradually until they become accustomed to seeing us together. That way it won't be any big deal."

"I think you might be right." She didn't like pretence or deceit, but she'd be the one subjected to their heckling. They wouldn't dare try it with Reed.

"Can I take you to dinner tomorrow night?"

"I'd like that."

"Not as much as I will. But how are we going to do this? It'll be obvious that we're going out," he mused aloud.

"Not if we leave the house at different times," she said.

She could feel his frown. "Is that really necessary?"

"I'm afraid so…."

Ellen and Reed spent the rest of the evening doing nothing more exciting than watching television. His arm remained securely around her shoulders and she felt a sense of deep contentment that was new to her. It was a peaceful interlude during a time that had become increasingly wrought with stress.

Derek got back to the house close to nine-thirty. They both heard him lope in through the kitchen and Reed gave Ellen a quick kiss before withdrawing his arm.

"Hi." Derek entered the room and stood beside the sofa, shuffling his feet. "Dad wondered where you were." His gaze flitted from Ellen to his brother.

"I told them I wouldn't be there for dinner."

"I know. But Danielle called looking for you."

"She knew where I was."

"Apparently not." Reed's younger brother gestured with one hand. "Are you two friends again?"

Reed's eyes found Ellen's and he smiled. "You could say that."

"Good. You haven't been the easiest people to be around lately." Without giving them a chance to respond, he whirled around and marched upstairs.

Ellen placed a hand over her mouth to smother her giggles. "Well, he certainly told us."

Amusement flared in Reed's eyes, and he chuckled softly. "I guess he did, at that." His arm slid around Ellen's shoulders once again. "Have you been difficult lately?"

"I'm never difficult," she said.

"Me neither."

They exchanged smiles and went back to watching their movie.

As much as Ellen tried to concentrate on the television, her mind unwillingly returned to Derek's announcement. "Do you think you should call Danielle?" She cast her eyes down, disguising her discomfort. Spending these past few hours with Reed had been like an unexpected Christmas gift, granted early. But she felt guilty that it had been at the other woman's expense.

Impatience tightened Reed's mouth. "Maybe I'd better. I didn't mean to offend her or her family by leaving early." He paused a moment, then added, "Danielle's kind of high-strung."

Ellen had noticed that, but she had no intention of mentioning it. And she had no intention of listening in on their conversation, either. "While you're doing that, I'll wash up the popcorn dishes, then go to bed."

Reed's eyes widened slightly in a mock reprimand. "It's a little early, isn't it?"

"Perhaps," she said, faking a yawn, "but I've got this hot date tomorrow night and I want to be well rested for it."

The front door opened and Pat sauntered in, carrying his duffle bag. "Hi." He stopped and studied them curiously. "Hi," he repeated.

"I thought you were staying at your parents' for the weekend." Ellen remembered that he'd said something about being gone for the entire four-day holiday.

"Mom gave my bedroom to one of my aunts. I can't see any reason to sleep on the floor when I've got a bed here."

"Makes sense," Reed said with a grin.

"Are you two getting along again?"

"We never fought."

"Yeah, sure," Pat mumbled sarcastically. "And a basket isn't worth two points."

Ellen had been unaware how much her disagreement with Reed had affected the boys. Apparently, Reed's reaction was the same as hers; their eyes met briefly in silent communication.

"I'll go up with you," she told Pat. "See you in the morning, Reed."

"Sure thing."

She left Pat on the second floor to trudge up to the third.

It shouldn't have been a surprise that she slept so well. Her mind was at ease and she awoke feeling contented and hopeful. Neither she nor Reed had made any commitments yet. They didn't know if what they felt would last a day or a lifetime. They were explorers, discovering the uncharted territory of a new relationship.

She hurried down the stairs early the next morning. Reed was already up, sitting at the kitchen table drinking coffee and reading the paper.

"Morning," she said, pouring water into the tea kettle and setting it on the burner.

"Morning." His eyes didn't leave the paper.

Ellen got a mug from the cupboard and walked past Reed on her way to get the canister of tea. His hand reached out and clasped her around the waist, pulling her down into his lap.

Before she could protest, his mouth firmly covered hers. When the kiss was over, Ellen straightened, resting her hands on his shoulders. "What was that for?" she asked to disguise how flustered he made her feel.

"Just to say good morning," he said in a warm, husky voice. "I don't imagine I'll have too many opportunities to do it in such a pleasant manner."

"No," she said and cleared her throat. "Probably not."

Ellen was sitting at the table, with a section of the paper propped up in front of her, when the boys came into the kitchen.

"Morning," Monte murmured vaguely as he opened the refrigerator. He was barefoot, his hair was uncombed and his shirt was still unbuttoned. "What's for breakfast?"

"Whatever your little heart desires," she told him, neatly folding over a page of the paper.

"Does this mean you're not cooking?"

"That's right."

"But—"

Reed lowered the sports page and glared openly at Monte.

"Cold cereal will be fine," Monte grumbled and took

down a large serving bowl, emptying half the contents
of a box of rice crisps inside.

"Hey, save some for me," Pat hollered from the doorway. "That's my favorite."

"I was here first."

Derek strolled into the kitchen. "Does everyone have
to argue?"

"Everyone?" Reed cocked a brow in his brother's
direction.

"First it was you and Ellen, and now it's Pat and
Monte."

"Hey, that's right," Monte cried. "You two aren't
fighting. That's great." He set his serving bowl of rice
crisps on the table. "Does this mean…you're…you
know."

Lowering the paper, Ellen eyed him sardonically.
"No, I don't know."

"Are you…seeing each other?" A deep flush darkened Monte's face.

"We see each other every day."

"That's not what I'm asking."

"But that's all I'm answering." From the corner of
her eye, she caught sight of Pat pantomiming a fiddler,
and she groaned inwardly. The boys were going to make
it difficult to maintain any kind of romantic relationship with Reed. She cast him a speculative glance. But
if Reed had noticed the activity around him, he wasn't
letting on, and Ellen was grateful.

"I've got a practice game tonight," Pat told Ellen as
he buttered a piece of toast. "Do you want to come?"

Flustered, she automatically sought out Reed. "Sorry…I'd like to come, but I've got a date."

"Bring him along."

"I…don't know if he likes basketball."

"Yeah, he does," Derek supplied. "Charlie and I were talking about it recently and he said it's one of his favorite games."

She didn't want to tell an outright lie. But she would save herself a lot of aggravation if she simply let Derek and the others assume it was Charlie she'd be seeing.

"What about you, Reed?" Derek asked.

His gaze didn't flicker from the paper and Ellen marveled at his ability to appear so dispassionate. "Not tonight. Thanks anyway."

"Have you got a date, too?" Derek pressed.

It seemed as though everyone in the kitchen was watching Reed, waiting for his response. "I generally go out on Friday nights."

"Well," Ellen said, coming to her feet. "I think I'll get moving. I want to take advantage of the holiday to do some errands. Does anybody need anything picked up at the cleaners?"

"I do," Monte said, raising his hand. "If you'll wait a minute, I'll get the slip."

"Sure."

By some miracle, Ellen was able to avoid any more questions for the remainder of the day. She went about her errands and didn't see Reed until late in the afternoon, when their paths happened to cross in the kitchen. He quickly whispered a time and meeting place and explained that he'd leave first. Ellen didn't have a chance to do more than agree before the boys were upon them.

At precisely seven, Ellen met Reed at the grocery store parking lot two blocks from the house. He'd left ten minutes earlier to wait for her there. As soon as he spotted her, he leaned across the cab of the pickup and opened the door on her side. Ellen found it slightly amusing that when he was with her he drove the pickup, and when he was with Danielle he took the sports car. She wondered whether or not this was a conscious decision. In any event, it told her quite a bit about the way Reed viewed the two women in his life.

"Did you get away unscathed?" he asked, chuckling softly.

She slid into the seat beside him in the cab and shook her head. "Not entirely. All three of them were curious about why Charlie wasn't coming to the house to pick me up. I didn't want to lie, so I told them they'd have to ask him."

"Will they?"

"I certainly hope not."

Reed's hand reached for hers and his eyes grew serious. "I'm not convinced that keeping this a secret is the right thing to do."

"I don't like it, either, but it's better than their constant teasing."

"I'll put a stop to that." His voice dropped ominously and Ellen didn't doubt that he'd quickly handle the situation.

"But, Reed, they don't mean any harm. I was hoping we could lead them gradually into accepting us as a couple. Let them get used to seeing us together before we spring it on them that we're...dating."

"Ellen, I don't know."

"Trust me on this," she pleaded, her eyes imploring him. This arrangement, with its furtiveness and deception, was far from ideal, but for now it seemed necessary. She hoped the secrecy could end soon.

His kiss was brief and ardent. "I don't think I could deny you anything." But he didn't sound happy about it.

The restaurant he took her to was located in the south end of Seattle, thirty minutes from Capitol Hill. At first, Ellen was surprised that he'd chosen one so far from home but the food was fantastic and the view from the Des Moines Marina alone would have been worth the drive.

Reed ordered a bottle of an award-winning wine, a sauvignon blanc from a local winery. It was satisfyingly clear and crisp.

"I spoke to Danielle," Reed began.

"Reed." She stopped him, placing her hand over his. "What goes on between you and Danielle has nothing to do with me. We've made no promises and no commitments." In fact, of course, she was dying to know about the other woman Reed had dated for so long. She hoped that if she pretended no interest in his relationship with Danielle, she'd seem more mature and sophisticated than she really was. She didn't want Reid to think she was threatened by Danielle or that she expected anything from him. Hoped, yes. Expected, no.

He looked a little stunned. "But—"

Swiftly she lowered her gaze. "I don't want to know." Naturally, she was longing to hear every detail. As it was, she felt guilty about the other woman. Danielle might have had her faults, but she loved Reed. She must love him to be so patient with his traveling all these months. And when Derek had first mentioned her, he'd spoken as though Reed and Danielle's relationship was a permanent one.

Danielle and Ellen couldn't have been more different. Ellen was practical and down-to-earth. She'd had to be. After her father's death, she'd become the cornerstone that held the family together.

Danielle, on the other hand, had obviously been pampered and indulged all her life. Ellen guessed that she'd been destined from birth to be a wealthy socialite, someone who might, in time, turn to charitable works to occupy herself. They were obviously women with completely dissimilar backgrounds, she and Danielle.

"I'll be in Atlanta the latter part of next week," Reed was saying.

"You're full of good news, aren't you?"

"It's my work, Ellen."

"I wasn't complaining. It just seems that five minutes after you get home, you're off again."

"I won't be long this time. A couple of days. I'll fly in for the meeting and be back soon afterward."

"You'll be here for Christmas?" Her thoughts flew to her family and how much she wished they could meet Reed. Bud, especially. He'd be in Yakima over the holidays and Ellen was planning to take the bus home to spend some time with him. But first she had to get through her exams.

"I'll be here."

"Good." But it was too soon to ask Reed to join her for the trip. He might misinterpret her invitation, see something that wasn't there. She had no desire to pressure him into the sort of commitment that meeting her family might imply.

After their meal, they walked along the pier, holding hands. The evening air was chilly and when Ellen shivered, Reed wrapped his arm around her shoulders.

"I enjoyed tonight," he murmured.

"I did, too." She bent her arm so that her fingers linked with his.

"Tomorrow night—"

"No." She stopped him, turning so that her arm slid around his middle. Tilting her head back, she stared into the troubled green eyes. "Let's not talk about tomorrow. For right now, let's take one day at a time."

His mouth met hers before she could finish speaking. A gentle brushing of lips. Then he deepened the kiss, and his arms tightened around her, and her whole body hummed with joy.

Ellen was lost, irretrievably lost, in the taste and scent of this man. She felt frightened by her response to him—it would be so easy to fall in love with Reed. *Completely* in love. But she couldn't allow that to happen. Not yet. It was too soon.

Her words about taking each day as it came were forcefully brought to Ellen's mind the following evening. She'd gone to the store and noticed Reed's Porsche parked in the driveway. When she returned, both Reed and the sports car had disappeared.

He was with Danielle.

Seven

"Why couldn't I see that?" Ellen moaned, looking over the algebraic equation Reed had worked out. "If I can fix a stopped-up sink, tune a car engine and manage a budget, why can't I understand something this simple?" She was quickly losing a grip on the more advanced theories they were now studying.

"Here, let me show it to you again."

Her hand lifted the curls off her forehead. "Do you think it'll do any good?"

"Yes, I do." Reed obviously had more faith in her powers of comprehension than she did. Step by step, he led her through another problem. When he explained the textbook examples, the whole process seemed so logical. Yet when she set out to solve a similar equation on her own, nothing went right.

"I give up." Throwing her hands over her head, she leaned back in the kitchen chair and groaned. "I should've realized that algebra would be too much for me. I had difficulty memorizing the multiplication tables, for heaven's sake."

"What you need is a break."

"I couldn't agree more. Twenty years?" She stood up and brought the cookie jar to the table. "Here, this will help ease the suffering." She offered him a chocolate-chip cookie and took one herself.

"Be more patient with yourself," Reed urged.

"There's only two weeks left in this term—and then exams. I need to understand this stuff and I need to understand it now."

He laid his hands on her shoulders, massaging gently. "No, you don't. Come on, I'm taking you to a movie."

"I've got to study," she protested, but not too strenuously. Escaping for an hour or two sounded infinitely more appealing than struggling with these impossible equations.

"There's a wonderful foreign film showing at the Moore Egyptian Theatre and we're going. We can worry about that assignment once we get back."

"But, Reed—"

"No buts. We're going." He took her firmly by the hand and led her into the front hall. Derek and Monte were watching TV and the staccato sounds of machine guns firing could be heard in the background. Neither boy noticed them until Reed opened the hall closet.

"Where are you two headed?" Derek asked, peering around the living-room door as Reed handed Ellen her jacket.

"A movie."

Instantly Derek muted the television. "The two of you alone? Together?"

"I imagine there'll be one or two others at the cinema," Reed responded dryly.

"Can I come?" Monte had joined Derek in the doorway.

Instantly Derek's elbow shoved the other boy in the ribs. "On second thought, just bring me back some popcorn, okay?"

"Sure."

Ellen pulled a knit cap over her ears. "Do either of you want anything else? I'd buy out the concession stand if one of you felt inclined to do my algebra assignment."

"No way."

"Bribing them won't help," Reed commented.

"I know, but I was hoping…."

It was a cold, blustery night. An icy north wind whipped against them as they hurried to Reed's truck. He opened the door for her before running around to the driver's side.

"Brr." Ellen shoved her hands inside her pockets. "If I doubted it was winter before, now I know."

"Come here and I'll warm you." He patted the seat beside him, indicating that she should slide closer.

Willingly she complied, until she sat so near him that her thigh pressed against his. Neither of them moved. It had been several days since they'd been completely alone together and longer still since he'd held or kissed her without interruption. The past week had been filled with frustration. Often she'd noticed Reed's gaze on her, studying her face and her movements, but it seemed that every time he touched her one of the boys would unexpectedly appear.

Reed turned to her. Their thoughts seemed to echo each other's; their eyes locked hungrily. Ellen required no invitation. She'd been longing for his touch. With a tiny cry she reached for him just as his arms came out to encircle her, drawing her even closer.

"This is crazy," he whispered fervently into her hair.

"I know."

As though he couldn't deny himself any longer, he cradled her face with both hands and he slowly lowered his mouth to hers.

Their lips clung and Reed's hand went around her ribs as he held her tight. The kiss was long and thoroughly satisfying.

Panting, he tore his mouth from hers and buried his face in her neck. "We'd better get to that movie."

It was all Ellen could do to nod her head in agreement.

They moved apart and fastened their seat belts, both of them silent.

When Reed started the truck, she saw that his hand was trembling. She was shaking too, but no longer from the cold. Reed had promised to warm her and he had, but not quite in the way she'd expected.

They were silent as Reed pulled onto the street. After days of carefully avoiding any kind of touch, any lingering glances, they'd sat in the driveway kissing in direct view of curious eyes. She realized the boys could easily have been watching them.

Ellen felt caught up in a tide that tossed her closer and closer to a long stretch of rocky beach. Powerless to alter the course of her emotions, she feared for her heart, afraid of being caught in the undertow.

"The engineering department is having a Christmas party this weekend at the Space Needle," Reed murmured.

Ellen nodded. Twice in the past week he'd left the house wearing formal evening clothes. He hadn't told her where he was going, but she knew. He'd driven the Porsche and he'd come back smelling of expensive perfume. For a Christmas party with his peers, Reed would escort Danielle. She understood that and tried to accept it.

"I want you to come with me."

"Reed," she breathed, uncertain. "Are you sure?"

"Yes." His hand reached for hers. "I want you with me."

"The boys—"

"Forget the boys. I'm tired of playing games with them."

Her smile came from her heart. "I am, too," she whispered.

"I'm going to have a talk with them."

"Don't," she pleaded. "It's not necessary to say anything."

"They'll start in with their teasing," he warned. "I thought you hated that."

"I don't care as much anymore. And if they do, we can say something then."

He frowned briefly. "All right."

The Moore Egyptian was located in the heart of downtown Seattle, so parking was limited. They finally found a spot on the street three blocks away. They left the truck and hurried through the cold, arm in arm, not talking. The French film was a popular one; by the time they got to the cinema, a long line had already formed outside.

A blast of wind sliced through Ellen's jacket and she buried her hands in her pockets. Reed leaned close to ask her something, then paused, slowly straightening.

"Morgan." A tall, brusque-looking man approached Reed.

"Dailey," Reed said, quickly stepping away from Ellen.

"I wouldn't have expected to see you out on a night like this," the man Reed had called Dailey was saying.

"I'm surprised to see you, too."

"This film is supposed to be good," Dailey said.

"Yeah. It's got great reviews."

Dailey's eyes returned to the line and rested on Ellen, seeking an introduction. Reed didn't give him one. Reed was obviously pretending he wasn't with Ellen.

She offered the man a feeble smile, wondering why Reed would move away from her, why he wouldn't introduce her to his acquaintance. The line moved slowly toward the ticket booth and Ellen went with it, leaving Reed talking to Dailey on the pavement. She felt a flare of resentment when he rejoined her a few minutes later.

"That was a friend of a friend."

Ellen didn't respond. Somehow she didn't believe him. And she resented the fact that he'd ignored the most basic of courtesies and left her standing on the sidewalk alone, while he spoke with a friend. The way he'd acted, anyone would assume Reed didn't want the man to know Ellen was with him. That hurt. Fifteen minutes earlier she'd been soaring with happiness at his unexpected invitation to the Christmas party, and now she was consumed with doubt and bitterness. Perhaps this Dailey was a friend of Danielle's and Reed didn't want the other woman to know he was out with Ellen. But that didn't really sound like Reed.

Once inside the cinema, Reed bought a huge bucket of buttered popcorn. They located good seats, despite the crowd, and sat down, neither of them speaking. As the lights went down, Reed placed his hand on the back of her neck.

Ellen stiffened. "Are you sure you want to do that?"

"What?"

"Touch me. Someone you know might recognize you."

"Ellen, listen…"

The credits started to roll on the huge screen and she shook her head, not wanting to hear any of his excuses.

But maintaining her bad mood was impossible with the comedy that played out before them. Unable to stop herself, Ellen laughed until tears formed in her eyes; she was clutching her stomach because it hurt from laughing. Reed seemed just as amused as she was, and a couple of times during the film, their smiling gazes met. Before she knew it, Reed was holding her hand and she didn't resist when he draped his arm over her shoulders.

Afterward, as they strolled outside, he tucked her

hand in the crook of his elbow. "I told you a movie would make you feel better."

It had and it hadn't. Yes, she'd needed the break, but Reed's behavior outside the cinema earlier had revived the insecurities she was trying so hard to suppress. She knew she wasn't nearly as beautiful or sophisticated as Danielle.

"You *do* feel better?" His finger lifted her chin to study her eyes.

There was no denying that the film had been wonderful. "I haven't laughed so hard in ages," she told him, smiling.

"Good."

Friday night, Ellen wore her most elaborate outfit— slim black velvet pants and a silver lamé top. She'd spent hours debating whether an evening gown would have been more appropriate, but had finally decided on the pants. Examining herself from every direction in the full-length mirror that hung from her closet door, Ellen released a pent-up breath and closed her eyes. This one night, she wanted everything to be perfect. Her heels felt a little uncomfortable, but she'd get used to them. She rarely had any reason to wear heels. She'd chosen them now because Reed had said there'd be dancing and she wanted to adjust her height to his.

By the time she reached the foot of the stairs, Reed was waiting for her. His eyes softened as he looked at her. "You're lovely."

"Oh, Reed, are you sure? I don't mind changing if you'd rather I wear something else."

His eyes held hers for a long moment. "I don't want you to change a thing."

"Hey, Ellen." Derek burst out of the kitchen, and stopped abruptly. "Wow." For an instant he looked as though he'd lost his breath. "Hey, guys," he called eagerly. "Come and see Ellen."

The other two joined Derek. "You look like a movie star," Pat breathed.

Monte closed his mouth and opened it again. "You're *pretty*."

"Don't sound so shocked."

"It's just that we've never seen you dressed…like this," Pat mumbled.

"Are you going out with Charlie?"

Ellen glanced at Reed, suddenly unsure. She hadn't dated Charlie in weeks. She hadn't wanted to.

"She's going out with me," Reed explained in an even voice that didn't invite comment.

"With you? Where?" Derek's eyes got that mischievous twinkle Ellen recognized immediately.

"A party."

"What about—" He stopped suddenly, swallowing several times.

"You had a comment?" Reed lifted his eyebrows.

"I thought I was going to say something," Derek muttered, clearly embarrassed, "but then I realized I wasn't."

Hiding a smile, Reed held Ellen's coat for her.

She slipped her arms into the satin-lined sleeves and reached for her beaded bag. "Good night, guys, and don't wait up."

"Right." Monte raised his index finger. "We won't wait up."

Derek took a step forward. "Should I say anything to someone…anyone…in case either of you gets a phone call?"

"Try *hello*," Reed answered, shaking his head.

"Right." Derek stuck his hand in his jeans pocket. "Have a good time."

"We intend to."

Ellen managed to hold back her laughter until they were on the front porch. But when the door clicked shut the giggles escaped and she pressed a hand to her mouth. "Derek *thought* he was going to say something."

"Then he realized he wasn't," Reed finished for her, chuckling. His hand at her elbow guided her down the steps. "They're right about one thing. You do look gorgeous."

"Thank you, but I hadn't expected it to be such a shock."

"The problem is, the boys are used to seeing you as a substitute mother. It's suddenly dawned on them what an attractive woman you are."

"And how was it *you* noticed?"

"The day I arrived and found you in my kitchen wearing only a bra, I knew."

"I was wearing more than that," she argued.

"Maybe, but at the time that was all I saw." He stroked her cheek with the tip of his finger, then tucked her arm in his.

Ellen felt a warm contentment as Reed led her to the sports car. This was the first time she'd been inside, and the significance of that seemed unmistakable. She sensed that somewhere in the past two weeks Reed had made an unconscious decision about their relationship. Maybe she was being silly in judging the strength of their bond by what car he chose to drive. And maybe not. Reed was escorting her to this party in his Porsche because he viewed her in a new light. He saw her now as a beautiful, alluring woman—no longer as the college student who seemed capable of mastering everything but algebra.

The Space Needle came into view as Reed pulled onto Denny Street. The world-famous Needle, which had been built for the 1962 World's Fair, rose 605 feet above the Seattle skyline. Ellen had taken the trip up to the observation deck only once and she'd been thrilled at the unobstructed view of the Olympic and Cascade mountain ranges. Looking out at the unspoiled beauty of Puget Sound, she'd understood immediately why Seattle was described as one of the world's most livable cities.

For this evening, Reed explained, his office had booked the convention rooms on the hundred-foot level of the Needle. The banquet facilities had been an addition, and Ellen wondered what sort of view would be available.

As Reed stopped in front of the Needle, a valet appeared, opening Ellen's door and offering her his gloved hand. She climbed as gracefully as she could from the low-built vehicle. Her smile felt a little strained, and she took a deep breath to dispel the gathering tension. She wanted everything about the evening to be perfect;

she longed for Reed to be proud of her, to feel that she belonged in his life—and in his world.

Her curiosity about the view was answered as soon as they stepped from the elevator into the large room. She glanced at the darkened sky that resembled folds of black velvet, sprinkled with glittering gems. When she had a chance she'd walk over toward the windows. For now, she was more concerned with fitting into Reed's circle and being accepted by his friends and colleagues.

Bracing herself for the inevitable round of introductions, she scanned the crowd for the man she'd seen outside the cinema. He didn't seem to be at the party and Ellen breathed easier. If Dailey was there, he would surely make a comment about seeing her with Reed that night, and she wouldn't know how to respond.

As they made their way through the large room, several people called out to Reed. When he introduced Ellen, two or three of them appeared to have trouble concealing their surprise that he wasn't with Danielle. But no one mentioned Danielle and they all seemed to accept Ellen freely, although a couple of people gave her curious looks. Eventually, Ellen relaxed and smiled up at Reed.

"That wasn't so bad, was it?" he asked, his voice tender.

"Not at all."

"Would you like something to drink?"

"Please."

"Wine okay?"

"Of course."

"I'll be right back."

Ellen watched Reed cross the room toward the bar. She was absurdly proud of him and made no attempt to disguise her feelings when he returned to her, carrying two glasses of white wine.

"You shouldn't look at me like that," he murmured, handing her a glass.

"Why?" she teased, her eyes sparkling. "Does it embarrass you?"

"No. It makes me wish I could ignore everyone in this room and kiss you right this minute." A slow, almost boyish grin spread across his features.

"That would certainly cause quite a commotion."

"But not half the commotion it would cause if they knew what else I was thinking."

"Oh?" She hid a smile by taking another sip of wine.

"Are we back to that word again?"

"Just what do you have in mind?"

He dipped his head so that he appeared to be whispering something in her ear, although actually his lips brushed her face. "I'll show you later."

"I'll be waiting."

They stood together, listening to the music and the laughter. Ellen found it curious that he'd introduced her to so few people and then only to those who'd approached him. But she dismissed her qualms as petty and, worse, paranoid. After all, she told herself, she was here to be with Reed, not to make small talk with his friends.

He finished his drink and suggested another. While he returned to the bar for refills, Ellen wandered through the crowd, walking over to the windows for a glimpse of the magnificent view. But as she moved, she kept her gaze trained on Reed.

A group of men stopped him before he could reach the bar. His head was inclined toward them, and he seemed to be giving them his rapt attention. Yet periodically his eyes would flicker through the crowd, searching for her. When he located her by the huge floor-to-ceiling windows, he smiled as though he felt relieved. With an abruptness that bordered on rudeness, he excused himself from the group and strolled in her direction.

"I didn't see where you'd gone."

"I wasn't about to leave you," she told him. Turning, she faced the window, watching the lights of the ferry boats gliding across the dark green waters of Puget Sound.

His hands rested on her shoulders and Ellen leaned back against him, warmed by his nearness. "It's lovely from up here."

"Exquisite," he agreed, his mouth close to her ear. "But I'm not talking about the view." His hands slid lazily down her arms. "Dance with me," he said, taking her hand and leading her to the dance floor.

Ellen walked obediently into his arms, loving the feel of being close to Reed. She pressed her cheek against the smooth fabric of his jacket as they swayed gently to the slow, dreamy music.

"I don't normally do a lot of dancing," he whispered.

Ellen wouldn't have guessed that. He moved with confident grace, and she assumed he'd escorted Danielle around a dance floor more than once. At the thought of the other woman, Ellen grew uneasy, but she forced her tense body to relax. Reed had chosen to bring *her,* and not Danielle, to this party. That had to mean something—something exciting.

"Dancing was just an excuse to hold you."

"You don't need an excuse," she whispered.

"In a room full of people, I do."

"Shall we wish them away?" She closed her eyes, savoring the feel of his hard, lithe body against her own.

He maneuvered them into the darkest corner of the dance floor and immediately claimed her mouth in a kiss that sent her world spinning into orbit.

Mindless of where they were, Ellen arched upward, Reed responded by sliding his hands down her back, down to her hips, drawing her even closer.

He dragged his mouth across her cheek. "I'm sorry we came."

"Why?"

"I don't want to waste time with all these people around. We're hardly ever alone. I want you, Ellen."

His honest, straightforward statement sent the fire roaring through her veins. "I know. I want you, too." Her voice was unsteady. "But it's a good thing we aren't alone very often." At the rate things were progressing between them, Ellen felt relieved that the boys were at the house. Otherwise—

"Hey, Reed." A friendly voice boomed out a few feet away. "Aren't you going to introduce me to your friend?"

Reed stiffened and for a moment Ellen wondered if he was going to pretend he hadn't heard. He looked at her through half-closed eyes, and she grinned up at him, mutely telling him she didn't mind. Their private world couldn't last forever. She knew that. They were at a party, an office party, and Reed was expected to mingle with his colleagues.

"Hello, Ralph." Reed's arm slid around Ellen's waist, keeping her close.

"Hello there." But Ralph wasn't watching Reed. "Well, aren't you going to introduce me?"

"Ellen Cunningham, Ralph Forester."

Ralph extended his hand and held Ellen's in both of his for a long moment. His eyes were frankly admiring.

"I don't suppose you'd let me steal this beauty away for a dance, would you?" Although the question was directed at Reed, Ralph didn't take his eyes from Ellen. "Leave it to you to be with the most beautiful woman here," the other man teased. "You sure do attract them."

Reed's hand tightened around Ellen. "Ellen?" He left the choice to her.

"I don't mind." She glanced at Reed and noted that his expression was carefully blank. But she knew him too well to be fooled. She could see that his jaw was rigid with tension and that his eyes showed annoyance at the other man's intrusion. Gradually he lowered his arm, releasing her.

Ralph stepped forward and claimed Ellen's hand, leading her onto the dance floor.

She swallowed as she placed her left hand on his shoulder and her right hand in his. Wordlessly they moved to the soft music. But when Ralph tried to bring her closer, Ellen resisted.

"Have you known Reed long?" Ralph asked, his hand trailing sensuously up and down her back.

She tensed. "Several months now." Despite her efforts to keep her voice even and controlled, she sounded slightly breathless.

"How'd you meet?"

"Through his brother." The less said about their living arrangements, the better. Ellen could just guess what Ralph would say if he knew they were living in the same house. "Do you two work together?"

"For the last six years."

They whirled around, and Ellen caught a glimpse of Reed standing against the opposite wall, studying them like a hawk zeroing in on its prey. Ralph apparently noticed him, as well.

"I don't think Reed was all that anxious to have you dance with me."

Ellen merely shrugged.

Ralph chortled gleefully, obviously enjoying Reed's reaction. "Not if the looks he's giving me are any indication. I can't believe it. Reed Morgan is jealous," he said with another chuckle, leading her out of Reed's sight and into the dimly lit center of the floor.

"I'm sure you're mistaken."

"Well, look at him."

All Ellen could see was Reed peering suspiciously at them across the crowded dance floor.

"This is too good to be true," Ralph murmured.

"What do you mean?"

"There isn't a woman in our department who wouldn't give her eyeteeth to go out with Reed."

Ellen was shocked, yet somehow unsurprised. "Oh?"

"Half the women are in love with him and he ignores them. He's friendly, don't get me wrong. But it's all business. Every time a single woman gets transferred into our area it takes her a week, maybe two, to fall for Reed. The rest of us guys just stand back and shake our heads. But with Reed otherwise occupied, we might have a chance."

"He *is* wonderful," Ellen admitted, managing to keep a courteous smile on her face. What Ralph was describing sounded so much like her own feelings that she couldn't doubt the truth of what he said.

Ralph arched his brows and studied her. "You too?"

"I'm afraid so."

"What's this guy got?" He sighed expressively, shaking his head. "Can we bottle it?"

"Unfortunately, I don't think so," Ellen responded lightly, liking Ralph more. His approach might have been a bit overpowering at first, but he was honest and compelling in his own right. "I don't imagine you have much trouble attracting women."

"As long as I don't bring them around Reed, I'm fine." A smile swept his face. "The best thing that could happen would be if he got married. I don't suppose that's in the offing between you two?"

He was so blithely serious that Ellen laughed. "Sorry."

"You're sure?"

Ralph was probably thinking of some rumor he'd heard about Danielle. "There's another woman he's seeing. They've known each other for a long time and apparently, they're quite serious," she explained, keeping her voice calmly detached.

"I don't believe it," Ralph countered, frowning. "Reed wouldn't be tossing daggers at my back if he was involved with someone else. One thing I suspect about this guy, he's a one-woman man."

Ellen closed her eyes, trying to shut out the pain. She didn't know what to believe about Reed anymore. All she could do was hold on to the moment. Wasn't that what she'd told him earlier—that they'd have to take things day by day? She was the one who hadn't wanted to talk about Danielle. In any case, she didn't want to read too much into his actions. She couldn't. She was on the brink of falling in love with him…if she hadn't already. To allow herself to think he might feel the same way was asking for trouble. For heartbreak.

The music ended and Ralph gently let her go. "I'd better return you to Reed or he's likely to come after me."

"Thank you for…everything."

"You're welcome, Ellen." With one hand at her waist, he steered her toward Reed.

They were within a few feet of him when Danielle suddenly appeared. She seemed to have come out of nowhere. "Reed!" She was laughing delightedly, flinging herself into his arms and kissing him intimately. "Oh, darling, you're so right. Being together is more important than any ski trip. I'm so sorry. Will you forgive me?"

Eight

"Ellen," Ralph asked. "Are you all right?"

"I'm fine," she lied.

"Sure you are," he mocked, sliding his arm around her waist and guiding her back to the dance floor. "I take it the blonde is Woman Number One?"

"You got it." The anger was beginning to build inside her. "Beautiful, too, you'll notice."

"Well, you aren't exactly chopped liver."

She gave a small, mirthless laugh. "Nice of you to say so, but by comparison, I come in a poor second."

"I wouldn't say that."

"Then why can't you take your eyes off Danielle?"

"Danielle. Hmm." He looked away from the other woman and stared blankly into Ellen's face. "Sorry." For her part, Ellen instinctively turned her back on Reed, unable to bear the sight of him holding and kissing another woman.

"Someone must have got their wires crossed."

"Like me," Ellen muttered. She'd been an idiot to

assume that Reed had meant anything by his invitation. He'd just needed someone to take to this party, and his first choice hadn't been available. She was a substitute, and a second-rate one at that.

"What do you want to do?"

Ellen frowned, her thoughts fragmented. "I don't know yet. Give me a minute to think."

"You two could always fight for him."

"The stronger woman takes the spoils? No, thanks." Despite herself she laughed. It certainly would've created a diversion at this formal, rather staid party.

Craning his neck, Ralph peered over at the other couple. "Reed doesn't seem too pleased to see her."

"I can imagine. The situation's put him in a bit of a bind."

"I admit it's unpleasant for you, but, otherwise, I'm enjoying this immensely."

Who wouldn't? The scene was just short of comical. "I thought you said Reed was a one-woman man."

"I guess I stand corrected."

Ellen was making a few corrections herself, revising some cherished ideas about Reed Morgan.

"I don't suppose you'd consider staying with me for the rest of the evening?" Ralph suggested hopefully.

"Consider it? I'd say it's the best offer I've had in weeks." She might feel like a fool, but she didn't plan to hang around looking like one.

Ralph nudged her and bent his head to whisper in her ear. "Reed's staring at us. And like I said, he doesn't seem pleased."

With a determination born of anger and pride, she

forced a smile to her lips and gazed adoringly up at Ralph. "How am I doing?" she asked, batting her lashes at him.

"Wonderful, wonderful." He swung her energetically around to the beat of the music. "Uh-oh, here he comes."

Reed weaved his way through the dancing couples and tapped Ralph on the shoulder. "I'm cutting in."

Ellen tightened her grip on Reed's colleague, silently pleading with him to stay. "Sorry, buddy, but Ellen's with me now that your lady friend has arrived."

"Ellen?" Reed's eyes narrowed as he stared at her intently. The other couples were dancing around them and curiously watching the party of three that had formed in the center of the room.

She couldn't remember ever seeing anyone look more furious than Reed did at this moment. "Maybe I'd better leave," she said in a low, faltering voice.

"I'll take you home," Ralph offered, dropping his hand to her waist.

"You came with me. You'll leave with me." Reed grasped her hand, pulling her toward him.

"Obviously you were making provisions," Ellen said, "on the off-chance Danielle showed up. How else did she get in here?"

"How am I supposed to know? She probably told the manager she was with me."

"And apparently she is," Ellen hissed.

"Maybe Reed and I should wrestle to decide the winner," Ralph suggested, glancing at Ellen and sharing a comical grin.

"Maybe."

Obviously, Reed saw no humor in the situation. Anger darkened his handsome face, and a muscle twitched in his jaw as the tight rein on his patience slipped.

Ralph withdrew his hand. "Go ahead and dance. It's obvious you two have a lot to talk about."

Reed took Ellen in his arms. "I suppose you're furious," he muttered.

"Have I got anything to be angry about?" she asked calmly. Now that the initial shock had worn off, she felt somewhat distanced from the whole predicament.

"Of course you do. But I want a chance to explain."

"Don't bother. I've got the picture."

"I'm sure you don't."

Ellen stubbornly refused to look up at him, resisting for as long as she could, but eventually she gave in. "It doesn't matter. Ralph said he'd take me home and—"

"I've already made my feelings on that subject quite clear."

"Listen, Reed. Your Porsche seats two. Is Danielle supposed to sit on my lap?"

"She came uninvited. Let her find her own way home."

"You don't mean that."

"I certainly do."

"You can't humiliate Danielle like that." Ellen didn't mention how *she* felt. What was the point? "Don't—"

"She deserves it," he broke in.

"Reed, no." Her hold on his forearm tightened. "This is unpleasant enough for all of us. Don't compound it."

The song ended and the music faded from the room. Reed fastened his hand on Ellen's elbow, guiding her across the floor to where Danielle was standing with Ralph. The two of them were sipping champagne.

"Hello again," Ellen began amicably, doing her utmost to appear friendly, trying to smooth over an already awkward situation.

"Hello." Danielle stared at Ellen curiously, apparently not recognizing her.

"You remember Ellen Cunningham, don't you?" Reed said.

"Not that college girl your brother's renting a room to—" Danielle stopped abruptly, shock etched on her perfect features. "*You're* Ellen Cunningham?"

"In the flesh." Still trying to keep things light, she cocked her head toward Ralph and spoke stagily out of the side of her mouth, turning the remark into a farcical aside. "I wasn't at my best when we met the first time."

"You were fiddling around with that electrical outlet and Reed was horrified," Danielle inserted, her voice completely humorless, her eyes narrowed assessingly. "You didn't even look like a girl."

"She does now." Ralph beamed her a brilliant smile.

"Yes." Danielle swallowed, her face puckered with concern. "She looks very…nice."

"Thank you." Ellen bowed her head.

"I've made a terrible mess of things," Danielle continued, casually handing her half-empty glass to a passing waiter. "Reed mentioned the party weeks ago, and Mom and I had this ski party planned. I told him I couldn't attend and then I felt guilty because Reed's been so sweet, escorting me to all the charity balls."

Ellen didn't hear a word of explanation beyond the fact that Reed had originally asked Danielle to the party. The other woman had just confirmed Ellen's suspicions, and the hurt went through her like a thousand needles. He'd invited her only because Danielle couldn't attend.

"There's no problem," Ellen said in a bland voice. "I understand how these things happen. He asked you first, so you stay and I'll leave."

"I couldn't do that," Danielle murmured.

Reed's eyes were saying the same thing. Ellen ignored him, and she ignored Danielle. Slipping her hand around Ralph's arm, she looked up at him and smiled, silently thanking him for being her friend. "As I said, it's not a problem. Ralph's already offered to take me home."

Reed's expression was impassive, almost aloof, as she turned toward him. "I'm sure you won't mind."

"How understanding of you," Danielle simpered, locking her arm around Reed's.

"It's better than hand-to-hand combat. I don't really care for fighting."

Danielle looked puzzled, while Ralph choked on a swallow of his drink, his face turning several shades of red as he struggled to hide his amusement. The only one who revealed no sense of humor was Reed, whose face grew more and more shadowed.

The band struck up a lively song and the dance floor quickly filled. "Come on, Reed," Danielle said, her blue eyes eager. "Let's dance." She tugged at Reed's hand

and gave a little wriggle of her hips. "You know how much I love to dance."

So Reed *had* done his share of dancing with Danielle—probably at all those charity balls she'd mentioned. Ellen had guessed as much and yet he'd tried to give her the impression that he rarely danced.

But noticing the stiff way Reed held himself now, Ellen could almost believe him.

Ralph placed a gentle hand on her shoulder. "I don't know about you, but I'm ready to get out of here."

Watching Reed with Danielle in his arms was absurdly painful; her throat muscles constricted in an effort to hold back tears and she simply nodded.

"Since we'll be skipping the banquet, shall we go have dinner somewhere?"

Ellen blinked. Dinner. "I'm not really hungry," she said.

"Sure you're hungry," Ralph insisted. "We'll stop at a nice restaurant before I drive you home. I know where Reed's place is, so I know where you live. Don't look so shocked. I figured it out from what you and Danielle were saying. But don't worry, I understand—impoverished students sharing a house and all that. So, what do you say? We'll have a leisurely dinner and get home two hours after Reed. That should set him thinking."

Ellen didn't feel in any mood to play games at Reed's expense. "I'd rather not."

Ralph's jovial expression sobered. "You've got it bad."

"I'll be fine."

He smiled. "I know you will. Come on, let's go."

The night that had begun with such promise had evaporated so quickly, leaving a residue of uncertainty and suspicion. As they neared the house, her composure gradually crumbled until she was nervously twisting the delicate strap of her evening bag over and over between her fingers. To his credit, Ralph attempted to carry the conversation, but her responses became less and less animated. She just wanted to get home and bury her head in her pillow.

By the time Ralph pulled up in front of the Capitol Hill house, they were both silent.

"Would you like to come in for coffee?" she asked. The illusion she'd created earlier of flippant humor was gone now. She hurt, and every time she blinked, a picture of Danielle dancing with Reed came to mind. How easy it was to visualize the other woman's arms around his neck, her voluptuous body pressed against his. The image tormented Ellen with every breath she took.

"No, I think I'll make it an early night."

"Thank you," she said affectionately. "I couldn't have handled this without you."

"I was happy to help. And, Ellen, if you want a shoulder to cry on, I'm available."

She dropped her gaze to the tightly coiled strap of her bag. "I'm fine. Really."

He patted her hand. "Somehow I don't quite believe that." Opening the car door, he came around to her side and handed her out.

On the top step of the porch, Ellen kissed his cheek. "Thanks again."

"Good night, Ellen."

"Night." She took out her keys and unlocked the front door. Pushing it open, she discovered that the house was oddly dark and oddly deserted. It was still relatively early and she would've expected the boys to be around. But not having to make excuses to them was a blessing she wasn't about to question.

As she removed her coat and headed for the stairs, she noticed the shadows bouncing around the darkened living room. She walked over to investigate and, two steps into the room, heard soft violin music.

Ellen stood there paralyzed, taking in the romantic scene before her. A bottle of wine and two glasses were set out on the coffee table. A fire blazed in the brick fireplace. And the music seemed to assault her from all sides.

"Derek," she called out.

Silence.

"All right, Pat and Monte. I know you're here some-where."

Silence.

"I'd suggest the three of you get rid of this...stuff before Reed comes home. He's with Danielle." With that, she marched up the stairs, uncaring if they heard her.

"With Danielle?" she heard a male voice shout after her.

"What happened?"

Ellen pretended not to hear.

The morning sun sneaked into her window, splash-ing the pillow where Ellen lay awake staring sightlessly at the ceiling. Sooner or later she'd have to get out of bed, but she couldn't see any reason to rush the process. Besides, the longer she stayed up here, the greater her chances of missing Reed. The unpleasantness of facing him wasn't going to vanish, but she might be able to postpone it for a morning. Although she had to wonder whether Reed was any more keen on seeing her than she was on seeing him. She could always kill time by dragging out her algebra books and studying for the exam— but that was almost as distasteful as facing Reed.

No, she decided suddenly, she'd stay in her room until she was weak with hunger. Checking her wristwatch, she figured that would be about another five minutes.

Someone knocked on her bedroom door. Sitting up, Ellen pulled the sheet to her neck. "Who is it?" she shouted, not particularly eager to talk to anyone.

Reed threw open the door and stalked inside. He stood in the middle of the room with his hands on his hips. "Are you planning to stay up here for the rest of your life?"

"The idea has distinct possibilities." She glared back at him, her eyes flashing with outrage and ill humor. "By the way, you'll note that I asked who was at the door. I didn't say, 'come in.'" Her voice rose to a mockingly high pitch. "You might have walked in on me when I was dressing."

A smile crossed his mouth. "Is that an invitation?"

"Absolutely not." She rose to a kneeling position, taking the sheets and blankets with her, and pointed a finger in the direction of the door. "Would you kindly leave? I'd like to get dressed."

"Don't let me stop you."

"Reed, please," she said irritably. "I'm not in any mood to talk to you."

"I'm not leaving until we do."

"Unfair. I haven't had my cup of tea and my mouth feels like the bottom of Puget Sound."

"All right," he agreed reluctantly. "I'll give you ten minutes."

"How generous of you."

"Considering my frame of mind since you walked out on me last night, I consider it pretty generous."

"Walked out on you!" She flew off the bed. "That's a bit much!"

"Ten minutes," he repeated, his voice low.

The whole time Ellen was dressing, she fumed. Reed had some nerve accusing her of walking out on him. He obviously didn't have any idea what it had cost her to leave him at that party with Danielle. He was thinking only of his own feelings, showing no regard for hers. He hadn't even acknowledged that she'd swallowed her pride to save them all from an extremely embarrassing situation.

Four male faces met hers when she appeared in the kitchen. "Good morning," she said with false enthusiasm.

The three boys looked sheepishly away. "Morning," they droned. Each found something at the table to occupy his hands. Pat, who was holding his basketball, carefully examined its grooves. Monte read the back of the cereal box and Derek folded the front page of the paper, pretending to read it.

"Ellen and I would like a few minutes of privacy," Reed announced, frowning at the three boys.

Derek, Monte and Pat stood up simultaneously.

"I don't think there's anything we have to say that the boys can't hear," she said.

The three boys reclaimed their chairs, looking with interest first at Reed and then at Ellen.

Reed's scowl deepened. "Can't you see that Ellen and I need to talk?"

"There's nothing to discuss," Ellen insisted, pouring boiling water into her mug and dipping a tea bag in the water.

"Yes, there is," Reed countered.

"Maybe it would be best if we did leave," Derek hedged, noticeably uneasy with his brother's anger and Ellen's feigned composure.

"You walk out of this room and there will be no packed lunches next week," Ellen said, leaning against the counter. She threw out the bag and began sipping her tea.

"I'm staying." Monte crossed his arms over his chest as though preparing for a long standoff.

Ellen knew she could count on Monte; his stomach would always take precedence. Childishly, she flashed Reed a saucy grin. He wasn't going to bulldoze her into any confrontation.

"Either you're out of here *now*, or you won't have a place to *live* next week," Reed flared back. At Derek's smug expression, Reed added, "And that includes you, little brother."

The boys exchanged shocked glances. "Sorry, Ellen,"

Derek mumbled on his way out of the kitchen. "I told Michelle I'd be over in a few minutes anyway." Without another moment's hesitation, Reed's brother was out the door.

"Well?" Reed stared at Monte and Pat.

"Yeah, well…I guess I should probably…" Pat looked to Ellen for guidance, his resolve wavering.

"Go ahead." She dismissed them both with a wave of her hand.

"Are you sure you want us to go?" Monte asked anxiously.

Ellen smiled her appreciation at this small display of mettle. "Thanks, but I'll be okay."

The sound of the door swinging back and forth echoed through the kitchen. Ellen drew a deep, calming breath and turned to Reed, who didn't look all that pleased to have her alone, although he'd gone to some lengths to arrange it. His face was pinched, and fine lines fanned out from his eyes and mouth. Either he'd had a late night or he hadn't slept at all. Ellen decided it must have been the former.

"Well, I'm here within ten minutes, just as you decreed. If you've got something to say, then say it."

"Don't rush me," he snapped.

Ellen released an exaggerated sigh. "First you want to talk to me—and then you're not sure. This sounds like someone who asked me to a party once. First he wanted me with him—and then he didn't."

"I wanted you there last night."

"Oh, was I talking about you?" she asked in fake innocence.

"You're not making this easy." He ploughed his fingers through his hair, the abrupt movement at odds with the self-control he usually exhibited.

"Listen," she breathed, casting her eyes down. "You don't need to explain anything. I have a fairly accurate picture of what happened."

"I doubt that." But he didn't elaborate.

"I can understand why you'd prefer Danielle's company."

"I didn't. That had to be one of the most awkward moments of my life. I wanted you—not Danielle."

Sure, she mused sarcastically. That was why he'd introduced her to so few people. She'd had plenty of time in the past twelve hours to think. If she hadn't been so blinded by the stars in her eyes, she would have figured it out sooner. Reed had taken her to his company party and kept her shielded from the other guests; he hadn't wanted her talking to his friends and colleagues. At the time, she'd assumed he wanted her all to himself. Now she understood the reason. The others knew he'd invited Danielle; they knew that Danielle usually accompanied him to these functions. The other woman had an official status in Reed's life. Ellen didn't.

"It wasn't your fault," she told him. "Unfortunately, under the circumstances, this was unavoidable."

"I'd rather Danielle had left instead of you." He walked to her side, deliberately taking the mug of tea from her hand and setting it on the counter. Slowly his arms came around her.

Ellen lacked the will to resist. She closed her eyes

as her arms reached around him, almost of their own accord. He felt so warm and vital.

"I want us to spend the day together."

Her earlier intention of studying for her algebra exam went out the window. Despite all her hesitations, all her doubts and fears, she couldn't refuse this chance to be with him. Alone, the two of them. "All right," she answered softly.

"Ellen." His breath stirred her hair. "There's something you should know."

"Hmm?"

"I'm flying out tomorrow morning for two days."

Her eyes flew open. "How long?"

"Two days, but after that, I won't be leaving again until the Christmas holidays are over."

She nodded. Traveling was part of his job, and any woman in his life would have to accept that. She was touched that he felt so concerned for her. "That's fine," she whispered. "I understand."

Ellen couldn't fault Reed's behavior for the remainder of the weekend. Saturday afternoon, they went Christmas shopping at the Tacoma Mall. His choice of shopping area surprised her, since there were several in the immediate area, much closer than Tacoma, which was a forty-five-minute drive away. But they had a good time, wandering from store to store. Before she knew it, Christmas would be upon them and this was the first opportunity she'd had to do any real shopping. With Reed's help, she picked out gifts for the boys and her brother.

"You'll like Bud," she told him, licking a chocolate

ice-cream cone. They found a place to sit, with their packages gathered around them, and took a fifteen-minute break.

"I imagine I will." A flash of amusement lit his eyes, then he abruptly looked away.

Ellen lowered her ice-cream cone. "What's so funny? Have I got chocolate on my nose?"

"No."

"What, then?"

"You must have forgiven me for what happened at the party."

"What do you mean?"

"The way you looked into the future and said I'd like your brother, as though you and I are going to have a long relationship."

The ice cream suddenly became very important and Ellen licked away at it with an all-consuming energy. "I told you before that I feel things have to be one day at a time with us. There are too many variables in our... relationship." She waved the ice cream in his direction. "And I use that term loosely."

"There *is* a future for us."

"You seem sure of yourself."

"I'm more sure of you." He said it so smoothly that Ellen wondered if she heard him right. She would have challenged his arrogant assumption, but just then, he glanced at his wristwatch and suggested a movie.

By the time they returned to the house it was close to midnight. He kissed her with a tenderness that somehow reminded her of an early-summer dawn, but his touch was as potent as a sultry August afternoon.

"Ellen?" he murmured into her hair.

"Hmm?"

"I think you'd better go upstairs now."

The warmth of his touch had melted away the last traces of icy reserve. She didn't want to leave him. "Why?"

His hands gripped her shoulders, pushing her away from him, putting an arm's length between them. "Because if you don't leave now, I may climb those stairs with you."

At his straightforward, honest statement, Ellen swallowed hard. "I enjoyed today. Thank you, Reed." He dropped his arms and she placed a trembling hand on the railing. "Have a safe trip."

"I will." He took a step toward her. "I wish I didn't have to go." His hand cupped her chin and he drew her face toward his, kissing her with a hunger that shook Ellen to the core. She needed all her strength not to throw her arms around him again.

Monday afternoon, when Ellen walked into the house after her classes, the three boys were waiting for her. They looked up at her with peculiar expressions on their faces, as though they'd never seen her before and they couldn't understand how she'd wandered into their kitchen.

"All right, what's up?"

"Up?" Derek asked.

"You've got that guilty look."

"*We're* not the guilty party," Pat said.

She sighed. "You'd better let me know what's going on so I can deal with it before Reed gets back."

Monte swung open the kitchen door so that the dining-room table came into view. In the center of the table stood the largest bouquet of red roses Ellen had ever seen.

A shocked gasp slid from the back of her throat. "Who...who sent those?"

"We thought you'd ask so we took the liberty of reading the card."

Their prying barely registered in her numbed brain as she walked slowly into the room and removed the small card pinned to the bright red ribbon. It could have been Bud—but he didn't have the kind of money to buy roses. And if he did, Ellen suspected he wouldn't get them for his sister.

"Reed did it," Pat inserted eagerly.

"Reed?"

"We were as surprised as you."

Her gaze fell to the tiny envelope. She removed the card, biting her lip when she read the message. *I miss you. Reed.*

"He said he misses you," Derek added.

"I see that."

"Good grief, he'll be back tomorrow. How can he possibly miss you in such a short time?"

"I don't know." Her finger lovingly caressed the petals of a dewy rosebud. They were so beautiful, but their message was even more so.

"I'll bet this is his way of telling you he's sorry about the party," Derek murmured.

"Not that any of us actually knows what happened. We'd like to, but it'd be considered bad manners to ask," Pat explained. "That is, unless you'd like to tell us why he'd take you to the party and then come back alone."

"He didn't get in until three that morning," Monte said accusingly. "You aren't going to let him off so easy are you, Ellen?"

Bowing her head to smell the sweet fragrance, she closed her eyes. "Roses cover a multitude of sins."

"Reed's feeling guilty, I think," Derek said with authority. "But he cares, or else he wouldn't have gone to this much trouble."

"Maybe he just wants to keep the peace," Monte suggested. "My dad bought my mom flowers once for no reason."

"We all live together. Reed's probably figured out that he had to do something if he wanted to maintain the status quo."

"Right," Ellen agreed tartly, scooping up the flowers to take to her room. Maybe it was selfish to deprive the boys of their beauty, but she didn't care. They'd been meant for her, as a private message from Reed, and she wanted them close.

The following day, Ellen cut her last morning class, knowing that Reed's flight was getting in around noon. She could ill afford to skip algebra, but it wouldn't have done her any good to stay. She would've spent the entire time thinking about Reed—so it made more sense to hurry home.

She stepped off the bus a block from the house and

even from that distance she could see his truck parked in the driveway. It was the first—and only—thing she noticed. She sprinted toward the house and dashed up the front steps.

Flinging open the door, she called breathlessly, "Anyone here?"

Both Reed and Derek came out of the kitchen.

Her eyes met Reed's from across the room. "Hi," she said in a low, husky voice. "Welcome home."

He advanced toward her, his gaze holding hers.

Neither spoke as Ellen threw her bag of books on the sofa and moved just as quickly toward him.

He caught her around the waist as though he'd been away for months instead of days, hugging her fiercely.

Ellen savored the warmth of his embrace, closing her eyes to the overwhelming emotion she suddenly felt. Reed was becoming far too important in her life. But she no longer had the power to resist him. If she ever had…

"His plane was right on time," Derek was saying. "And the airport was hardly busy. And—"

Irritably, Reed tossed a look over his shoulder. "Little brother, get lost."

Nine

"I've got a game today," Pat said, his fork cutting into the syrup-laden pancakes. "Can you come?"

Ellen's eyes met Reed's in mute communication. No longer did they bother to hide their attraction to each other from the boys. They couldn't. "What time?"

"Six."

"I can be there."

"What about you, Reed?"

Reed wiped the corners of his mouth with the paper napkin. "Sorry, I've got a meeting. But I should be home in time for the victory celebration."

Ellen thrilled at the way the boys automatically linked her name and Reed's. It had been like that from the time he'd returned from his most recent trip. But then, they'd given the boys plenty of reason to think of her and Reed as a couple. He and Ellen were with each other every free moment; the time they spent together was exclusively theirs. And Ellen loved it. She loved Reed, she loved being with him…and she loved every single thing about him. Almost. His reticence on the subject of Danielle had her a little worried, but she pushed it to the back of her mind. She couldn't bring herself to question him, especially after her own insistence that they not discuss Danielle. She no longer felt that way—she wanted reassurance—but she'd decided she'd just assume that the relationship was over. As far as she knew, Reed hadn't spoken to Danielle since the night of the Christmas party. Even stronger evidence was the fact that he drove his truck every day. The Porsche sat in the garage, gathering dust.

Reed stood up and delivered his breakfast plate to the sink. "Ellen, walk me to the door?"

"Sure."

"For Pete's sake, the door's only two feet away," Derek scoffed. "You travel all over the world and all of a sudden you need someone to show you where the back door is?"

Ellen didn't see the look the two brothers exchanged, but Derek's mouth curved upward in a knowing grin. "Oh, I get it. Hey, guys, they want to be alone."

"Just a minute." Monte wolfed down the last of his breakfast, still chewing as he carried his plate to the counter.

Ellen was mildly surprised that Reed didn't comment on Derek's needling, but she supposed they were both accustomed to it.

One by one, the boys left the kitchen. Silently, Reed stood by the back door, waiting. When the last one had departed, he slipped his arms around Ellen.

"You're getting mighty brave," she whispered, smiling into his intense green eyes. Lately, Reed almost seemed to invite the boys' comments. And when they responded, the teasing rolled off his back like rain off a well-waxed car.

"It's torture being around you every day and not touching you," he said just before his mouth descended on hers in an excruciatingly slow kiss that seemed to melt Ellen's very bones.

Reality seemed light-years away as she clung to him, and she struggled to recover her equilibrium. "Reed," she whispered, "you have to get to work."

"Right." But he didn't stop kissing her.

"And I've got classes." If he didn't end this soon, they'd both reach the point of no return. Each time he held and kissed her, it became more difficult to break away.

"I know. I know." His voice echoed through the fog that held her captive. "Now isn't the time or place."

Her arms tightened around his middle as she burrowed her face into his chest. One second, she was telling Reed they had to stop and in the next, she refused to let him go.

"I'll be late tonight," he murmured into her hair.

She remembered that he'd told Pat something about a meeting. "Me, too," she said. "I'm going to the basketball game."

"Right. Want to go out to dinner afterward?" His breath fanned her temple. "Just the two of us. I love being alone with you."

Ellen wanted to cry with frustration. "I can't. I promised the boys dinner. Plus exams start next week and I've got to study."

"Need any help?"

"Only with one subject." She looked up at him and sadly shook her head. "I don't suppose you can guess which one."

"Aren't you glad you've got me?"

"Eternally grateful." Ellen would never have believed that algebra could be both her downfall and her greatest ally. If it weren't for that one subject, she wouldn't have had the excuse to sit down with Reed every night to work through her assignments. But then, she didn't really need an excuse anymore….

"We'll see how grateful you are when grades come out."

"I hate to disappoint you, but it's going to take a lot more than your excellent tutoring to rescue me from my fate this time." The exam was crucial. If she didn't do well, she'd probably end up repeating the class. The thought filled her with dread. It would be a waste of her time and, even worse, a waste of precious funds.

Reed kissed her lightly before releasing her. "Have a good day."

"You, too." She stood at the door until he'd climbed inside the pickup and waved when he backed out of the driveway.

Ellen loaded the dirty dishes into the dishwasher and cleaned off the counter, humming a Christmas carol as she worked.

One of the boys knocked on the door. "Is it safe to come in yet?"

"Sure. Come on in."

All three innocently strolled into the kitchen. "You and Reed are getting kind of friendly, aren't you?"

Running hot tap water into the sink, Ellen nodded. "I suppose."

"Reed hasn't seen Danielle in a while."

Ellen didn't comment, but she did feel encouraged that Derek's conclusion was the same as hers.

"You know what I think?" he asked, hopping onto the counter so she was forced to look at him.

"I can only guess."

"I think Reed's getting serious about you."

"That's nice."

"*Nice*—is that all you can say?" He gave her a look of disgust. "That's my brother you're talking about. He could have any woman he wanted."

"I know." She poured soap into the dishwasher, then closed the door and turned the dial. The sound of rushing water drowned out Derek's next comment.

"Sorry, I have to get to class. I'll talk to you later." She sauntered past Pat and Monte, offering them a cheerful smile.

"She's got it bad." Ellen heard Monte comment. That was the same thing Ralph had said the night of the party. "She hardly even bakes anymore. Remember how she used to make cookies every week?"

"I didn't know love did that to a person," Pat grumbled.

"I'm not sure I like Ellen in love," Monte flung after her as she stepped out the door.

"I just hope she doesn't get hurt."

The boy's remarks echoed in her mind as the day wore on. Ellen didn't need to hear their doubts; she had more than enough of her own. Qualms assailed her when she least expected it—like during the morning's algebra class, or during the long afternoon that followed.

But one look at Reed that evening and all her anxieties evaporated. As soon as she entered the house, she walked straight into the living room, hoping to find him there, and she did.

He put some papers back in a file when she walked in. "How was the game?"

"Pat scored seventeen points and is a hero. Unfortunately, the Huskies lost." Sometimes, that was just the way life went—winning small victories yet losing the war.

She hurried into the kitchen to begin dinner preparations.

"Something smells good." Monte bounded in half an hour later, sniffing appreciatively.

"There's a roast in the oven and an apple pie on the counter," she answered him. She'd bought the pie in hopes of celebrating the Huskies' victory. Now it would soothe their loss. "I imagine everyone's starved."

"I am," Monte announced.

"That goes without saying," Reed called from the living room.

Gradually, the other boys trailed in, and it was time to eat.

After dinner, the evening was spent at the kitchen table, poring over her textbooks. Reed came in twice to make her a fresh cup of tea. Standing behind her chair, he glanced over her shoulder at the psychology book.

"Do you want me to get you anything?" she asked. She was studying in the kitchen, rather than in her room, just to be close to Reed. Admittedly, her room offered more seclusion, but she preferred being around people—one person, actually.

"I don't need a thing." He kissed the top of her head. "And if I did, I'd get it myself. You study."

"Thanks."

"When's the first exam?"

"Monday."

He nodded. "You'll do fine."

"I don't want fine," she countered nervously. "I want fantastic."

"Then you'll do fantastic."

"Where are the boys?" The house was uncommonly silent for a weekday evening.

"Studying. I'm pleased to see they're taking exams as seriously as you are."

"We have to," she mumbled, her gaze dropping to her notebook.

"All right. I get the message. I'll quit pestering you."

"You're not pestering me."

"Right." He bent to kiss the side of her neck as his fingers stroked her arms.

Shivers raced down her spine and Ellen closed her eyes, unconsciously swaying toward him. "Now...now you're pestering me."

He chuckled, leaving her alone at the kitchen table

when she would much rather have had him with her every minute of every day.

The next morning, Ellen stood by the door, watching Reed pull out of the driveway.

"Why do you do that?" Pat asked, giving her a glance that said she looked foolish standing there.

"Do what?" She decided the best reaction was to pretend she didn't have any idea what he was talking about.

"Watch Reed leave every morning. He's not likely to have an accident pulling out of the driveway."

Ellen didn't have the courage to confess that she watched so she could see whether Reed drove the pickup or the Porsche. It would sound ridiculous to admit that she gauged their relationship by which vehicle he chose to drive that day.

"She watches because she can't bear to see him go," Derek answered when she didn't. "From what I hear, Michelle does the same thing. What can I say? The woman's crazy about me."

"Oh, yeah?" Monte snickered. "And that's the reason she was with Rick Bloomfield the other day?"

"She was?" Derek sounded completely shocked. "There's an explanation for that. Michelle and I have an understanding."

"Sure you do," Monte teased. "She can date whoever she wants and you can date whoever you want. Some *understanding.*"

To prove to the boys that she wasn't as infatuated as they assumed—and maybe to prove the same thing to herself—Ellen didn't watch Reed leave for work the next two mornings. It was pointless, anyway. So what if he drove his Porsche? He had the car, and she could see no reason for him to not drive it. Except for her unspoken insecurities. And there seemed to be plenty of those. As Derek had said earlier in the week, Reed could have any woman he wanted.

She was the first one home that afternoon. Derek was probably sorting things out with Michelle, Pat had basketball practice and no doubt Monte was in someone's kitchen.

Gathering the ingredients for spaghetti sauce, she arranged them neatly on the counter. She was busy reading over her recipe when the phone rang.

"Hello," she said absently.

"This is Capitol Hill Cleaners. Mr. Morgan's evening suit is ready."

"Pardon?" Reed hadn't told her he was having anything cleaned. Ellen usually picked up his dry cleaning because it was no inconvenience to stop there on her way home from school. And she hadn't minded at all. As silly as it seemed, she'd felt very wifely doing that for him.

"Is it for Reed or Derek?" It was just like Derek to forget something like that.

"The slip says it's for Mr. Reed Morgan."

"Oh?"

"Is there a problem with picking it up? He brought it in yesterday and told us he had to have it this evening."

This evening? Reed was going out tonight?

"From what he said, this is for some special event."

Well, he wouldn't wear a suit to a barbecue. "I'll let him know."

"Thank you. Oh, and be sure to mention that we close at six tonight."

"Yes, I will."

A strange numbness overpowered Ellen as she hung up. Something was wrong. Something was very, very wrong. Without even realizing it, she moved rapidly through the kitchen and then outside.

Reed had often told her the importance of reading a problem in algebra. Read it carefully, he always said, and don't make any quick assumptions. It seemed crazy to remember that now. But he was right. She couldn't jump to conclusions just because he was going out for the evening. He had every right to do so. She was suddenly furious with herself. All those times he'd offered information about Danielle and she'd refused to listen, trying to play it so cool, trying to appear so unconcerned when on the inside she was dying to know.

By the time she reached the garage she was trembling, but it wasn't from the cold December air. She knew without looking that Reed had driven his sports car to work. The door creaked as she pushed it open to discover the pickup, sitting there in all its glory.

"Okay, he drove his Porsche. That doesn't have to mean anything. He isn't necessarily seeing Danielle. There's a logical explanation for this." Even if he *was* seeing Danielle, she had no right to say anything. They'd made no promises to each other.

Rubbing the chill from her arms, Ellen returned to the house. But the kitchen's warmth did little to chase away the bitter cold that cut her to the heart. Ellen moved numbly toward the phone and ran her finger down the long list of numbers that hung on the wall beside it. When she located the one for Reed's office, she punched out the seven numbers, then waited, her mind in turmoil.

"Mr. Morgan's office," came the efficient voice.

"Hello…this is Ellen Cunningham. I live, that is, I'm a friend of Mr. Morgan's."

"Yes, I remember seeing you the night of the Christmas party," the voice responded warmly. "We didn't have a chance to meet. Would you like me to put you through to Mr. Morgan?"

"No," she said hastily. "Could you give him a message?" Not waiting for a reply, she continued, "Tell him his suit is ready at the cleaners for that…party tonight."

"Oh, good, he wanted me to call. Thanks for saving me the trouble. Was there anything else?"

Tears welled in Ellen's eyes. "No, that's it."

Being reminded by Reed's assistant that they hadn't met the night of the Christmas party forcefully brought to Ellen's attention how few of his friends she did know. None, really. He'd gone out of his way *not* to introduce her to people.

"Just a minute," Ellen cried, her hand clenching the receiver. "There *is* something else you can tell Mr. Morgan. Tell him goodbye." With that, she severed the connection.

A tear rolled down her cheek, searing a path as it made its way to her chin. She'd been a fool not to have seen the situation more clearly. Reed had a good thing going, with her living at the house. She was close to falling in love with him. In fact, she was already there and anyone looking at her could tell. It certainly wasn't any secret from the boys. She cooked his meals, ran his errands, vacuumed his rugs. How convenient she'd become. How useful she'd been to the smooth running of his household.

But Reed had never said a word about his feelings. Sure, they'd gone out, but always to places where no one was likely to recognize him. And the one time Reed did see someone he knew, he'd pretended he wasn't with her. When he *had* included her in a social event, he'd only introduced her to a handful of people, as though… as though he didn't really want others to know her. As it turned out, that evening had been a disaster, and this time he'd apparently decided to take Danielle. The other woman was far more familiar with the social graces.

Fine. She'd let Reed escort Danielle tonight. But she was going to quit making life so pleasant for him. How appropriate that she now used the old servants' quarters, she thought bitterly. Because that was all she was to him—a servant. Well, no more. She would never be content to live a backstairs life. If Reed didn't want to be seen with her, or include her in his life, that was his decision. But she couldn't…she *wouldn't* continue to live this way.

Without analyzing her actions, Ellen punched out a second set of numbers.

"Charlie, it's Ellen," she said quickly, trying to swallow back tears.

"Ellen? It doesn't sound like you."

"I know." The tightness in her chest extended all the way to her throat, choking off her breath until it escaped in a sob.

"Ellen, are you all right?"

"Yes...no." The fact that she'd called Charlie was a sign of her desperation. He was so sweet and she didn't want to do anything to hurt him. "Charlie, I hate to ask, but I need a friend."

"I'm here."

He said it without the least hesitation, and his un-questioning loyalty made her weep all the louder. "Oh, Charlie, I've got to find a new place to live and I need to do it today."

"My sister's got a friend looking for a roommate. Do you want me to call her?"

"Please." Straightening, she wiped the tears from her face. Charlie might have had his faults, but he'd recog-nized the panic in her voice and immediately assumed control. Just now, that was what she needed—a friend to temporarily take charge of things. "How soon can you talk to her?"

"Now. I'll call her and get right back to you. On second thought, I'll come directly to your place. If you can't move in with Patty's friend, my parents will put you up."

"Oh, Charlie, how can I ever thank you?"

The sound of his chuckle was like a clean, fresh breeze. "I'll come up with a way later." His voice soft-ened. "You know how I feel about you, Ellen. If you only want me for a friend, I understand. But I'm deter-mined to be a good friend."

The back door closed with a bang. "Anyone home?"

Guiltily, Ellen turned around, coming face to face with Monte. She replaced the receiver, took a deep breath and squared her shoulders. She'd hoped to get away without having to talk to anyone.

"Ellen?" Concern clouded his face. "What's wrong? You look like you've been crying." He narrowed his eyes. "You *have* been crying. What happened?"

"Nothing." She took a minute to wipe her eyes with a tissue. "Listen, I'll be up in my room, but I'd appreciate some time alone, so don't get me unless it's important."

"Sure. Anything you say. Are you sick? Should I call Reed?"

"No!" she almost shouted at him, then instantly re-gretted reacting so harshly. "Please don't contact him…. He's busy tonight anyway." She rubbed a hand over her face. "And listen, about dinner—"

"Hey, don't worry. I can cook."

"You?" This wasn't the time to get into an argument. How messy he made the kitchen was no longer her problem. "There's a recipe on the counter if you want to tackle spaghetti sauce."

"Sure. I can do that. How long am I supposed to boil the noodles?"

One of her lesser concerns at the moment was boil-ing noodles. "Just read the back of the package."

Already he was rolling up his sleeves. "I'll take care of everything. You go lie down and do whatever women do when they're crying and pretending they're not."

"Thanks," she returned evenly. "I'll do that." Only in this case, she wasn't going to lie on her bed, hiding her face in her pillow. She was going to pack up everything she owned and cart it away before Reed even had a hint that she was leaving.

Sniffling as she worked, Ellen dumped the contents of her drawers into open suitcases. A couple of times she stopped to blow her nose. She detested tears. At the age of fifteen, she'd broken her leg and gritted her teeth against the agony. But she hadn't shed a tear. Now she wept as though it were the end of the world. Why, oh why, did her emotions have to be so unpredictable?

Carrying her suitcases down the first flight of stairs, she paused on the boys' floor to shift the weight. Because she was concentrating on her task and not watching where she was going, she walked headlong into Derek. "Sorry," she muttered.

"Ellen." He glanced at her suitcases and said her name as though he'd unexpectedly stumbled into the Queen of Sheba. "What…what are you doing?"

"Moving."

"Moving? But…why?"

"It's a long story."

"You're crying." He sounded even more shocked by her tears than by the fact that she was moving out of the house.

"It's Reed, isn't it? What did he do?"

"He didn't do a thing. Stay out of it, Derek. I mean that."

He looked stunned. "Sure." He stepped aside and stuck his hand in his pocket. "Anything you say."

She made a second trip downstairs, this time bringing a couple of tote bags and the clothes from her closet, which she draped over the top of the two suitcases. There wasn't room in her luggage for everything. She realized she'd have to put the rest of her belongings in boxes.

Assuming she'd find a few empty boxes in the garage, she stormed through the kitchen and out the back door. Muttering between themselves, Monte and Derek followed her. Soon her movements resembled a small parade.

"Will you two stop it," she shouted, whirling around and confronting them. The tears had dried now and her face burned with the heat of anger and regret.

"We just want to know what happened," Monte interjected.

"Or is this going to be another one of your 'stay tuned' responses?" Derek asked.

"I'm moving out. I don't think I can make it any plainer than that."

"Why?"

"That's none of your business." She left them standing with mouths open as she trooped up the back stairs to her rooms.

Heedlessly she tossed her things into the two boxes, more intent on escaping than on taking care to ensure that nothing was broken. When she got to the vase that had held the roses Reed had sent her, Ellen picked it up and hugged it. She managed to forestall further tears by taking deep breaths and blinking rapidly. Setting the vase down, she decided not to bring it with her. As much as possible, she wanted to leave Reed in this house and not carry the memories of him around with her like a constant, throbbing ache. That would be hard enough without taking the vase along as a constant reminder of what she'd once felt.

The scene that met her at the foot of the stairs made her stop in her tracks. The three boys were involved in a shouting match, each blaming the others for Ellen's unexpected decision to move out.

"It's your fault," Derek accused Monte. "If you weren't so concerned about your stomach, she'd stay."

"My stomach? *You're* the one who's always asking her for favors. Like babysitting and cooking for you and your girlfriend and—"

"If you want my opinion…" Pat began.

"We don't," Monte and Derek shouted.

"Stop it! All of you," Ellen cried. "Now, if you're the least bit interested in helping me, you can take my things outside. Charlie will be here anytime."

"Charlie?" the three echoed in shock.

"Are you moving in with him?"

She didn't bother to respond. Once the suitcases, the bags, two boxes and her clothes had been lugged onto the porch, Ellen sat on the top step and waited.

She could hear the boys pacing back and forth behind her, still bickering quietly. When the black sports car squealed around the corner, Ellen covered her face with both hands and groaned. The last person she wanted to see now was Reed. Her throat was already swollen with the effort of not giving way to tears.

He parked in front of the house and threw open the car door.

She straightened, determined to appear cool and calm.

Seconds later, Reed stood on the bottom step. "What's going on here?"

"Hello, Reed," she said with a breathlessness she couldn't control. "How was your day?"

He jerked his fingers through his hair as he stared back at her in utter confusion. "How am I supposed to know? I get a frantic phone call from Derek telling me to come home right away. As I'm running out the door, my assistant hands me a message. Some absurd thing about you saying goodbye. What is going on? I thought you'd hurt yourself!"

"Sorry to disappoint you."

"Ellen, I don't know what's happening in that overworked mind of yours, but I want some answers and I want them now."

"I'm leaving." Her hands were clenched so tight that her fingers ached.

"I'm not blind," he shouted, quickly losing control of his obviously limited patience. "I can see that. I'm asking you *why*."

Pride demanded that she raise her chin and meet his probing gaze. "I've decided I'm an unstable person," she told him, her voice low and quavering. "I broke my leg once and didn't shed a tear, but when I learn that you're going to a party tonight, I start to cry."

"Ellen." He said her name gently, then shook his

head as if clearing his thoughts. "You're not making any sense."

"I know. That's the worst part."

"In the simplest terms possible, tell me why you're leaving."

"I'm trying to." Furious with herself, she wiped a tear from her cheek. How could she explain it to him when everything was still so muddled in her own mind? "I'm leaving because you're driving the Porsche."

"What!" he exploded.

"You tell me," she burst out. "Why did you drive the Porsche today?"

"Would you believe that my truck was low on fuel?"

"I may be confused," she said, "but I'm not stupid. You're going out with Danielle. Not that I care."

"I can tell." His mocking gaze lingered on her suitcases. "I hate to disillusion you, but Danielle won't be with me."

She didn't know whether to believe him or not. "It doesn't matter."

"None of this is making sense."

"I don't imagine it would. I apologize for acting so unreasonable, but that's exactly how I feel. So, I'm getting out of here with my pride intact."

"Is your pride worth so much?"

"It's the only thing I have left," she said. She'd already given him her heart.

"She's moving in with Charlie," Derek said in a worried voice. "You aren't going to let her, are you, Reed?"

"You can't," Monte added.

"He won't," Pat stated confidently.

For a moment, the three of them stared intently at Reed. Ellen noticed the way his green eyes hardened. "Yes, I can," he said at last. "If this is what you want, then so be it. Goodbye, Ellen." With that, he marched into the house.

Ten

"I'm swearing off men for good," Ellen vowed, taking another long swallow of wine.

"Me, too," Darlene, her new roommate, echoed. To toast the promise, Darlene bent forward to touch the rim of her wineglass against Ellen's and missed. A shocked moment passed before they broke into hysterical laughter.

"Here." Ellen replenished their half-full glasses as tears of mirth rolled down her face. The world seemed to spin off its axis for a moment as she straightened. "You know what? I think we're drunk."

"Maybe you are," Darlene declared, slurring her words, "but not me. I can hold my wine as well as any man."

"I thought we weren't going to talk about men anymore."

"Right, I forgot."

"Do you think they're talking about us?" Ellen asked, putting a hand to her head in an effort to keep the walls from going around and around.

"Nah, we're just a fading memory."

"Right." Ellen pointed her index finger toward the ceiling in emphatic agreement.

The doorbell chimed and both women stared accusingly at the door. "If it's a man, don't answer it," Darlene said.

"Right again." Ellen staggered across the beige carpet. The floor seemed to pitch under her feet and she placed a hand on the back of the sofa to steady herself. Facing the door, she turned around. "How do I know if it's a man or not?"

The doorbell sounded again.

Darlene motioned languidly with her hand to show that she no longer cared who was at the door. "Just open it."

Holding the knob in a death grip, Ellen pulled open the door and found herself glaring at solid male chest. "It's a man," she announced to Darlene.

"Who?"

Squinting, Ellen studied the blurred male figure until she recognized Monte. "Monte," she cried, instantly sobering. "What are you doing here?"

"I…I was in the neighborhood and thought I'd stop by and see how you're doing."

"Come in." She stepped aside to let him enter. "What brings you to this neck of the woods?" She hiccuped despite her frenzied effort to look and act sober. "It's a school night. You shouldn't be out this late."

"It's only ten-thirty. You've been drinking."

"Me?" She slammed her hand against her chest. "Have we been drinking, Darlene?"

Her roommate grabbed the wine bottle—their second—from the table and hid it behind her back. "Not us."

Monte cast them a look of disbelief. "How'd your exams go?" he asked Ellen politely.

"Fine," she answered and hiccuped again. Embarrassed, she covered her mouth with her hand. "I think."

"What about algebra?"

"I'm making it by the skin of my nose."

"Teeth," both Darlene and Monte corrected.

"Right."

Looking uncomfortable, Monte said, "Maybe I should come back another time."

"Okay." Ellen wasn't about to argue. If she was going to run into her former housemates, she'd prefer to do it when she looked and felt her best. Definitely not when she was feeling...tipsy and the walls kept spinning. But on second thought, she couldn't resist asking about the others. "How's...everyone?"

"Fine." But he lowered his gaze to the carpet. "Not really, if you want the truth."

A shaft of fear went through her, tempering the effects of several glasses of wine. "It's not Reed, is it? Is he ill?"

"No, Reed's fine. I guess. He hasn't been around much lately."

No doubt he was spending a lot of his time at parties and social events with Danielle. Or with any number of other women, all of them far more sophisticated than Ellen.

"Things haven't been the same since you left," Monte added sheepishly.

"Who's doing the cooking?"

He shrugged his shoulders. "We've been taking turns."

"That sounds fair." She hoped that in the months she'd lived with them the three boys had at least learned their way around the kitchen.

"Derek started a fire yesterday."

Ellen couldn't conceal her dismay. "Was there any damage?" As much as she tried to persuade herself that she didn't need to feel guilty over leaving the boys, this news was her undoing. "Was anyone hurt?" she gasped out.

"Not really, and Reed said the insurance would take care of everything."

"What happened?" Ellen was almost afraid to ask.

"Nothing much. Derek forgot to turn off the burner and the fat caught fire. Then he tried to beat it out with a dish towel, but that burst into flames, too. The real mistake was throwing the burning towel into the sink because when he did, it set the curtains on fire."

"Oh, good grief." Ellen dropped her head into her hands.

"It's not too bad, though. Reed said he wanted new kitchen walls, anyway."

"The walls too?"

"Well, the curtains started burning the wallpaper."

Ellen wished she hadn't asked. "Was anyone hurt?"

Monte moved a bandaged hand from behind his back. "Just me, but only a little."

"Oh, Monte," she cried, fighting back her guilt. "What did you do—try and pound out the fire with your fist?"

Leave it to Monte. He'd probably tried to rescue whatever it was Derek had been cooking.

"No, I grabbed a hot biscuit from the oven and blistered one finger."

"Then why did you wrap up your whole hand?" From the size of the bandage, it looked as though he'd been lucky not to lose his arm.

"I thought you might feel sorry for me and come back."

"Oh, Monte." She reached up to brush the hair from his temple.

"I didn't realize what a good cook you were until you left. I kept thinking maybe it was something I'd done that caused you to leave."

"Of course not."

"Then you'll come back and make dinners again?"

Good ol' Monte never forgot about his stomach. "The four of you will do fine without me."

"You mean you won't come back?"

"I can't." She felt like crying, but she struggled to hold back the tears stinging her eyes. "I'm really sorry, but I can't."

Hanging his head, Monte nodded. "Well, have a merry Christmas anyway."

"Right. You, too."

"Bye, Ellen." He turned back to the door, his large hand gripping the knob. "You know about Pat making varsity, don't you?"

She'd read it in the *Daily*. "I'm really proud of him. You tell him for me. Okay?"

"Sure."

She closed the door after him and leaned against it while the regrets washed over her like a torrent of rain. Holding back her tears was difficult, but somehow she managed. She'd shed enough tears. It was time to put her grief behind her and to start facing life again.

"I take it Monte is one of the guys," Darlene remarked. She set the wine back on the table, but neither seemed interested in another glass.

Ellen nodded. "The one with the stomach."

"He's so skinny!"

"I know. There's no justice in this world." But she wasn't talking about Monte's appetite in relation to his weight. She was talking about Reed. If she'd had any hope that he really did care for her, that had vanished in the past week. He hadn't even tried to get in touch with her. She knew he wouldn't have had any problem locating her. The obvious conclusion was that he didn't *want* to see her. At first she thought he might have believed the boys' ridiculous claim that she was moving in with Charlie. But if he'd loved her half as much as she loved him, even that shouldn't have stopped him from coming after her.

Apparently, presuming that Reed cared for her was a mistake on her part. She hadn't heard a word from him all week. Exam week, at that. Well, fine. She'd wipe him out of her memory—just as effectively as she'd forgotten every algebraic formula she'd ever learned. A giggle escaped and Darlene sent her a curious look. Ellen carried their wineglasses to the sink, ignoring her new roommate, as she considered her dilemma. The trouble was, she wanted to remember the algebra, which seemed to slip out of her mind as soon as it entered, and she wanted to forget Reed, who never left her thoughts for an instant.

"I think I'll go to bed," Darlene said, holding her hand to her stomach. "I'm not feeling so great."

"Me neither." But Ellen's churning stomach had little to do with the wine. "Night."

"See you in the morning."

Ellen nodded. She was fortunate to have found Darlene. The other woman, who had recently broken up with her fiancé after a two-year engagement, understood how Ellen felt. It seemed natural to drown their sorrows together. But…she missed the boys and—Reed.

One thing she'd learned from this experience was that men and school didn't mix. Darlene might not have been serious about swearing off men, but Ellen was. She was through with them for good—or at least until she obtained her degree. For now, she was determined to bury herself in her books, get her teaching credentials and then become the best first-grade teacher around.

Only she couldn't close her eyes without remembering Reed's touch or how he'd slip up behind her and hold her in his arms. Something as simple as a passing glance from him had been enough to thrill her. Well, that relationship was over. And just in the nick of time. She could have been hurt. Really hurt. She could be feeling terrible. Really terrible.

Just like she did right now.

Signs of Christmas were everywhere. Huge decorations adorned the streetlights down University Way.

Store windows displayed a variety of Christmas themes, and the streets were jammed with holiday traffic. Ellen tried to absorb some of the good cheer that surrounded her, with little success.

She'd gone to the university library to return some books and was headed back to Darlene's place. Her place, too, even though it didn't feel that way.

She planned to leave for Yakima the next morning. But instead of feeling the pull toward home and family, Ellen's thoughts drifted to Reed and the boys. They'd been her surrogate family since September and she couldn't erase them from her mind as easily as she'd hoped.

As she walked across campus, sharp gusts of wind tousled her hair. Her face felt numb with cold. All day she'd been debating what to do with the Christmas gifts she'd bought for the boys. Her first inclination had been to bring them over herself—when Reed wasn't home, of course. But just the idea of returning to the lovely old house had proved so painful that Ellen abandoned it. Instead, Darlene had promised to deliver them the next day, after Ellen had left for Yakima.

Hugging her purse, Ellen trudged toward the bus stop. According to her watch, she had about ten minutes to wait. Now her feet felt as numb as her face. She frowned at her pumps, cursing the decrees of fashion and her insane willingness to wear elegant shoes at this time of year. It wasn't as though a handsome prince was likely to come galloping by only to be overwhelmed by her attractive shoes. Even if one did swoop Ellen and her frozen toes onto his silver steed, she'd be highly suspicious of his character.

Smiling, she took a shortcut across the lawn in the Quad.

"Is something funny?"

A pair of men's leather loafers had joined her fashionable gray pumps, matching her stride. Stunned, Ellen glanced up. Reed.

"Well?" he asked again in an achingly gentle voice. "Something seems to amuse you."

"My…shoes. I was thinking about attracting a prince…a man." Oh heavens, why had she said that? "I mean," she mumbled on, trying to cover her embarrassment, "my feet are numb."

"You need to get out of the cold." His hands were thrust into his pockets and he was so compellingly handsome that Ellen forced her eyes away. She was afraid that if she stared at him long enough, she'd give him whatever he asked. She remembered the way his face had looked the last time she'd seen him, how cold and steely his eyes had been the day she'd announced she was moving out. One word from him and she would've stayed. But the "might-have-beens" didn't matter anymore. He hadn't asked her to stay, so she'd gone. Pure and simple. Or so it had seemed at the time.

Determination strengthened her trembling voice as she finally spoke. "The bus will be at the corner in seven minutes."

Her statement was met with silence. Together they reached the pavement and strolled toward the sheltered bus area.

Much as she wished to appear cool and composed, Ellen's gaze was riveted on the man at her side. She noticed how straight and dark Reed's brows were and how his chin jutted out with stubborn pride. Every line of his beloved face emanated strength and unflinching resolve.

Abruptly, she looked away. Pride was no stranger to her, either. Her methods might have been wrong, she told herself, but she'd been right to let Reed know he'd hurt her. She wasn't willing to be a victim of her love for him.

"Ellen," he said softly, "I was hoping we could talk."

She made a show of glancing at her watch. "Go ahead. You've got six and a half minutes."

"Here?"

"As you so recently said, I need to get out of the cold."

"I'll take you to lunch."

"I'm not hungry." To further her embarrassment, her stomach growled and she pressed a firm hand over it, commanding it to be quiet.

"When was the last time you ate a decent meal!?"

"Yesterday. No," she corrected, "today."

"Come on, we're getting out of here."

"No way."

"I'm not arguing with you, Ellen. I've given you a week to come to your senses. I still haven't figured out what went wrong. And I'm not waiting any longer for the answers. Got that?"

She ignored him, looking instead in the direction of the traffic. She could see the bus approaching, though it was still several blocks away. "I believe everything that needed to be said—" she motioned dramatically with her hand "—was already said."

"And what's this I hear about you succumbing to the demon rum?"

"I was only a little drunk," she spat out, furious at Monte's loose tongue. "Darlene and I were celebrating. We've sworn off men for life." Or at least until Reed freely admitted he loved her and needed her. At the moment that didn't appear likely.

"I see." His eyes seemed to be looking all the way into her soul. "If that's how you want it, fine. Just answer a couple of questions and I'll leave you alone. Agreed?"

"All right."

"First, what were you talking about when you flew off the handle about me driving the Porsche?"

"Oh, that." Now it just seemed silly.

"Yes, that."

"Well, you only drove the Porsche when you were seeing Danielle."

"But I wasn't! It's been completely over between us since the night of the Christmas party."

"It has?" The words came out in a squeak.

Reed dragged his fingers through his hair. "I haven't seen Danielle in weeks."

Ellen stared at the sidewalk. "But the cleaners phoned about your suit. You were attending some fancy party."

"So? I wasn't taking another woman."

"It doesn't matter," she insisted. "You weren't taking me, either."

"Of course not!" he shouted, his raised voice attracting the attention of several passersby. "You were studying for your exams. I couldn't very well ask you to attend an extremely boring business dinner with me. Not when you were spending every available minute hitting the books." He lowered his voice to a calm, even pitch.

The least he could do was be more unreasonable, Ellen thought irritably. She simply wasn't in the mood for logic.

"Did you hear what I said?"

She nodded.

"There is only one woman in my life. You. To be honest, Ellen, I can't understand any of this. You may be many things, but I know you're not the jealous type. I wanted to talk about Danielle with you. Any other woman would've loved hearing all the details. But not you." His voice was slightly raised. "Then you make these ridiculous accusations about the truck and the Porsche, and I'm at a loss to understand."

Now she felt even more foolish. "Then why were you driving the Porsche?" Her arms tightened around her purse. "Forget I asked that."

"You really have a thing for that sports car, don't you?"

"It's not the car."

"I'm glad to hear that."

Squaring her shoulders, Ellen decided it was time to be forthright, time to face things squarely rather than skirt around them. "My feelings are that you would rather not be seen with me," she said bluntly.

"What?" he exploded.

"You kept taking me to these out-of-the-way restaurants."

"I did it for privacy."

"You didn't want to be seen with me," she countered.

"I can't believe this." He took three steps away from her, then turned around sharply.

"Don't you think the Des Moines Marina is a bit far to go for a meal?"

"I was afraid we'd run into one of the boys."

More logic, and she was in no mood for it. "You didn't introduce me to your friend the night we went to that French film."

His eyes narrowed. "You can bet I wasn't going to introduce you to Tom Dailey. He's a lecher. I was protecting you."

"What about the night of the Christmas party? You only introduced me to a handful of people."

"Of course. Every man in the place was looking for an excuse to take you away from me. If you'd wanted to flirt with them, you should've said something."

"I only wanted to be with you."

"Then why bring up that evening now?"

"I was offended."

"I apologize," he shouted.

"Fine. But I didn't even meet your assistant…."

"You left so fast, I didn't exactly have a chance to introduce you, did I?"

He was being logical again, and she couldn't really argue.

The bus arrived then, its doors parting with a swish. But Ellen didn't move. Reed's gaze commanded her to stay with him, and she was torn. Her strongest impulse, though, was not to board the bus. It didn't matter that she was cold and the wind was cutting through her thin coat or that she could barely feel her toes. Her heart was telling her one thing and her head another.

"You coming or not?" the driver called out to her.

"She won't be taking the bus," Reed answered, slipping his hand under her elbow. "She's coming with me."

"Whatever." The doors swished shut and the bus roared away, leaving a trail of black diesel smoke in its wake.

"You *are* coming with me, aren't you?" he coaxed.

"I suppose."

His hand was at the small of her back, directing her across the busy street to a coffee shop, festooned with tinsel and tired-looking decorations. "I wasn't kidding about lunch."

"When was the last time *you* had a decent meal?" she couldn't resist asking.

"About a week ago," he grumbled. "Derek's cooking is a poor substitute for real food."

They found a table at the back of the café. The waitress handed them each a menu and filled their water glasses.

"I heard about the fire."

Reed groaned. "That was a comedy of errors."

"Is there much damage?"

"Enough." The look he gave her was mildly accusing. The guilt returned. Trying to disguise it, Ellen made a show of glancing through the menu. The last thing on her mind at the moment was food. When the waitress returned, Ellen ordered the daily special without knowing what it was. The day was destined to be full of surprises.

"Ellen," Reed began, then cleared his throat. "Come back."

Her heart melted at the hint of anguish in his low voice. Her gaze was magnetically drawn to his. She wanted to tell him how much she longed to be…home. She wanted to say that the house on Capitol Hill was the only real home she had now, that she longed to walk through its front door again. With him.

"Nothing's been the same since you left."

The knot in her stomach pushed its way up to her throat, choking her.

"The boys are miserable."

Resolutely she shook her head. If she went back, it had to be for Reed.

"Why not?"

Tears blurred her vision. "Because."

"That makes about as much sense as you being angry because I drove the Porsche."

Taking several deep, measured breaths, Ellen said, "If all you need is a cook, I can suggest several who—"

"I couldn't care less about the cooking."

The café went silent as every head turned curiously in their direction. "I wasn't talking about the cooking *here,*" Reed explained to the roomful of shocked faces.

The normal noise of the café resumed.

"Good grief, Ellen, you've got me so tied up in knots I'm about to get kicked out of here."

"Me, tie *you* in knots?" She was astonished that Reed felt she had so much power over him.

"If you won't come back for the boys, will you consider doing it for me?" The intense green eyes demanded a response.

"I want to know why you want me back. So I can cook your meals and—"

"I told you I don't care about that. I don't care if you never do another thing around the house. I want you there because I love you, damn it."

Her eyes widened. "You love me, damn it?"

"You're not making this any easier." He ripped the napkin from around the silverware and slammed it down on his lap. "You must have known. I didn't bother keeping it secret."

"You didn't bother keeping it secret…from anyone but me," she repeated hotly.

"Come on. Don't tell me you didn't know."

"I didn't know."

"Well, you do now," he yelled back.

The waitress cautiously approached their table, standing back until Reed glanced in her direction. Hurriedly the girl set their plates in front of them and promptly moved away.

"You frightened her," Ellen accused him.

"I'm the one in a panic here. Do you or do you not love me?"

Again, it seemed as though every customer there had fallen silent, awaiting her reply.

"You'd better answer him, miss," the elderly gentleman sitting at the table next to theirs suggested. "Fact is, we're all curious."

"Yes, I love him."

Reed cast her a look of utter disbelief. "You'll tell a stranger but not me?"

"I love you, Reed Morgan. There, are you happy?"

"Overjoyed."

"I can tell." Ellen had thought that when she admitted her feelings, Reed would jump up from the table and throw his arms around her. Instead, he looked as angry as she'd ever seen him.

"I think you'd better ask her to marry you while she's in a friendly mood," the older man suggested next.

"Well?" Reed looked at her. "What do you think?"

"You want to get married?"

"It's the time of year to be generous," the waitress said shyly. "He's handsome enough."

"He is, isn't he?" Ellen agreed, her sense of humor restored by this unexpected turn of events. "But he can be a little hard to understand."

"All men are, believe me," a woman across the room shouted. "But he looks like a decent guy. Go ahead and give him another chance."

The anger washed from Reed's dark eyes as he reached for Ellen's hand. "I love you. I want to marry you. Won't you put me out of my misery?"

Tears dampened her eyes as she nodded wildly.

"Let's go home." Standing, Reed took out his wallet and threw a couple of twenties on the table.

Ellen quickly buttoned her jacket and picked up her

purse. "Goodbye, everyone," she called with a cheerful wave. "Thank you—and Merry Christmas!"

The amused customers broke into a round of applause as Reed took Ellen's hand and pulled her outside.

She was no sooner out the door when Reed hauled her into his arms. "Oh, Ellen, I've missed you."

Reveling in the warmth of his arms, she nuzzled closer. "I've missed you, too. I've even missed the boys."

"As far as I'm concerned, they're on their own. I want you back for myself. That house was full of people, yet it's never felt so empty." Suddenly he looked around, as though he'd only now realized that their private moment was taking place in the middle of a busy street. "Let's get out of here." He slipped an arm about her waist, steering her toward the campus car park. "But I think I'd better tell you something important."

"What?"

"I didn't bring the truck."

"Oh?" She swallowed her disappointment. She could try, but she doubted she'd ever be the Porsche type.

"I traded in the truck last week."

"For what?"

"Maybe it was presumptuous of me, but I was hoping you'd accept my marriage proposal."

"What's the truck got to do with whether I marry you or not?"

"*You're* asking me that? The woman who left me—"

"All right, all right, I get the picture."

"Okay, I don't have the truck *or* the Porsche. I gave it to Derek."

"I'm sure he's thrilled."

"He is. And…"

"And?"

"I traded the truck for an SUV. More of a family-friendly vehicle, wouldn't you say?"

"Oh, Reed." With a small cry of joy, she flung her arms around this man she knew she'd love for a lifetime. No matter what kind of car he drove.

* * * * *

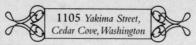

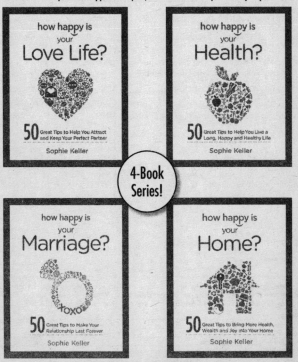

DEBBIE MACOMBER

32988	OUT OF THE RAIN	___ $7.99 U.S.	___ $9.99 CAN.
32971	92 PACIFIC BOULEVARD	___ $7.99 U.S.	___ $9.99 CAN.
32970	8 SANDPIPER WAY	___ $7.99 U.S.	___ $9.99 CAN.
32969	74 SEASIDE AVENUE	___ $7.99 U.S.	___ $9.99 CAN.
32968	6 RAINIER DRIVE	___ $7.99 U.S.	___ $9.99 CAN.
32967	44 CRANBERRY POINT	___ $7.99 U.S.	___ $9.99 CAN.
32962	50 HARBOR STREET	___ $7.99 U.S.	___ $9.99 CAN.
32946	311 PELICAN ROAD	___ $7.99 U.S.	___ $9.99 CAN.
32929	HANNAH'S LIST	___ $7.99 U.S.	___ $9.99 CAN.
32918	AN ENGAGEMENT IN SEATTLE	___ $7.99 U.S.	___ $9.99 CAN.
32911	THE MANNING SISTERS	___ $7.99 U.S.	___ $9.99 CAN.
32884	SUSANNAH'S GARDEN	___ $7.99 U.S.	___ $9.99 CAN.
32883	TWENTY WISHES	___ $7.99 U.S.	___ $9.99 CAN.
32861	204 ROSEWOOD LANE	___ $7.99 U.S.	___ $9.99 CAN.
32860	16 LIGHTHOUSE ROAD	___ $7.99 U.S.	___ $9.99 CAN.
32858	HOME FOR THE HOLIDAYS	___ $7.99 U.S.	___ $9.99 CAN.
32828	ORCHARD VALLEY BRIDES	___ $7.99 U.S.	___ $9.99 CAN.
32822	CHRISTMAS IN CEDAR COVE	___ $7.99 U.S.	___ $9.99 CAN.
32806	1022 EVERGREEN PLACE	___ $7.99 U.S.	___ $9.99 CAN.
32798	ORCHARD VALLEY GROOMS	___ $7.99 U.S.	___ $9.99 CAN.
32783	THE MAN YOU'LL MARRY	___ $7.99 U.S.	___ $9.99 CAN.
32743	THE SOONER THE BETTER	___ $7.99 U.S.	___ $9.99 CAN.
32702	FAIRY TALE WEDDINGS	___ $7.99 U.S.	___ $9.99 CAN.
32701	WYOMING BRIDES	___ $7.99 U.S.	___ $8.99 CAN.
32602	THE MANNING GROOMS	___ $7.99 U.S.	___ $7.99 CAN.
32569	ALWAYS DAKOTA	___ $7.99 U.S.	___ $7.99 CAN.
32506	CHRISTMAS WISHES	___ $7.99 U.S.	___ $9.50 CAN.
32474	THE MANNING BRIDES	___ $7.99 U.S.	___ $7.99 CAN.
32362	COUNTRY BRIDES	___ $7.99 U.S.	___ $9.50 CAN.
31251	1105 YAKIMA STREET	___ $7.99 U.S.	___ $9.99 CAN.
20000	THE MATCHMAKERS	___ $4.99 U.S.	___ $5.99 CAN.

(limited quantities available)

TOTAL AMOUNT	$	_____
POSTAGE & HANDLING	$	_____
($1.00 for 1 book, 50¢ for each additional)		
APPLICABLE TAXES*	$	_____
TOTAL PAYABLE	$	_____

(check or money order—please do not send cash)

To order, complete this form and send it, along with a check or money order for the total above, payable to MIRA Books, to: **In the U.S.:** 3010 Walden Avenue, P.O. Box 9077, Buffalo, NY 14269-9077; **In Canada:** P.O. Box 636, Fort Erie, Ontario, L2A 5X3.

Name: _____
Address: _____ City: _____
State/Prov.: _____ Zip/Postal Code: _____
Account Number (if applicable): _____
075 CSAS

*New York residents remit applicable sales taxes.
*Canadian residents remit applicable GST and provincial taxes.

H HARLEQUIN®
www.Harlequin.com

MDM1111BL